RUSTLER'S CHOICE

The bunch-cutters had herded the seven cows into a little box cove, and were still looking at them when a rider appeared, ambling up the draw like a fellow without a care in the world.

"Howdy," Mouse said. "Found yourself some cows, huh?"

One of the men nodded. "Blamedest thing, they must have strayed up from Texas. That's a Texas brand, ain't it?"

Mouse rested an elbow on his saddle horn. "Sure is. Problem is those cows didn't stray up here. They was drove just like the others that was with them when y'all cut those out back yonder."

The nearest man had his gun half-drawn before he noticed that Mouse's .45 was looking at him like a big, dark eyeball.

"I wouldn't," Mouse suggested.

A voice behind them agreed. "Same goes for all of you."

The rustlers looked around and went pale. There were men all around them with drawn guns.

A sturdy young fellow with a Peacemaker the size of a shoat's leg glared down at them. "You gents are in a mess of trouble," he said. "Your choice what kind. And that means if them guns of yours aren't on the ground before I blink my eyes, ever' one of y'all is dead and just don't know it yet!"

DAN PARKINSON

THE GUNS OF
NO MAN'S LAND

ZEBRA BOOKS
KENSINGTON PUBLISHING CORP.

Dedicated, with love, to a blue-eyed lady

Special thanks to Frederick Bohme, Chief, Census History Staff, United States Bureau of the Census, and to those several others with the Census Bureau, Department of Commerce and the Fort Worth and Washington National Archives who were so helpful in providing information . . . no matter what I intended to do with it.

ZEBRA BOOKS

are published by

Kensington Publishing Corp.
475 Park Avenue South
New York, NY 10016

First Printing: November, 1992

Printed in the United States of America

I

In the spring of 1890, when Robert E. Lee Smith turned 25, he started a run of luck. Some folks wouldn't have considered it luck, but it was Bobby Lee's view— Robert E. Lee Smith being such a mouthful of words, everybody had taken to calling the boy Bobby Lee right early on—that luck is what you make of it. Many's the time he had occasion to say that very thing. And that being Bobby Lee's view of the matter, there was just no other way about it. Everybody who ever knew him agreed that Bobby Lee Smith was nothing if not stubborn.

There were generally a few young bucks around, like there always are, who would argue about most anything. Some of them would debate whether it was Thursday or not, just for the fun of it, and if debate came to knuckle-dusting, which it did as often as not, well, a good knock-down-drag-out now and again was any young man's fitten right as they saw it.

Bobby Lee ran into some argument once in a while when he got boneheaded about some issue, but that didn't happen often once he had his size. Despite being an easy-going type—most of the time—Bobby Lee Smith was a big old boy who could butt heads with the best of them when he took a notion to. And though he rarely toted iron, it was generally known that when he did strap on a hogleg it wasn't for show. That was one of the things old Doc Holt taught the boy, was bulk metal delivery from a .45.

The run of luck started on his birthday—or as near to his birthday as he could reckon, not having any blood kin, or none that would admit to it, to keep track of things like that for him. But Doc Holt was certain that Bobby Lee was born about the middle of March, because of when Doc's wife Nanny found the child on their doorstep. She just went to the door and there he was, a suckling infant that didn't have a thing to his name but an old quilt.

There was a lot of that going around in those days— the spring of '64 it would have been—babies being left here and yonder and the like. That was wartime, and folks can get right forgetful when wars are going on.

Being good, God-fearing folk, Doc and Nanny took the boy in and cared for him. It came clear after a time that nobody was fixing to come back and retrieve the infant, so Doc held that he ought to have a name. Nanny wouldn't stand for him having the name Holt, because of what folks might think—Doc's occasional habits being what they were and the Holts having no natural offspring of their own—so Doc named him Smith. Come christening time, and Doc feeling particularly patriotic right about then, the tad was christened Robert Edward Lee Smith.

It wasn't any time at all before he was just plain Bobby Lee.

Doc and Nanny did him right, all things considered. They raised him about as decent as most, and saw after his reading education, and Doc saw to it that the boy learned some skills of several kinds. Skills that might see him into some trade or other once he grew up and got some sense, and some other skills to help him live long enough to do that. Just the sort of general know-hows that any good Texas boy ought to have. And boys being like they are, as the years went by, just about

6

everybody around got to know Bobby Lee.

Not a bad boy, most would agree. Not ornery mean or given to cussedness, no more than any other boy. Not one given to double-dealing, and hardly ever rude when there were ladies present. Not bad at all, really. Just maybe the most mule-headed, stubbornest human being that God ever saw fit to wrap hide around.

At any rate, twenty-five years after he was found on the doorstep, Bobby Lee Smith picked himself a day—the fifteenth of March, it was—and decided that was his birthday. Middle of March, Doc had told him, and in most months, the fifteenth is about as middle as it gets. Naturally, once Bobby Lee decided on the fifteenth, then that was in fact his birthday and no two ways about it.

It was the way he was about things. He'd always been that way, and being twenty-five years old didn't change that at all. Once Bobby Lee Smith made up his mind about a thing, that was just plain how it would be, even if it harelipped half of Texas.

On that day, the fifteenth of March, 1890, Bobby Lee hung up his farrier's apron and kick-strap at Jack Priddy's livery, collected his pay and walked on over to the Shades of Paradise to make his announcement.

Since it was Friday, and the late train never ran between Thursday and Sunday, he'd picked himself a good time to be heard by a lot of folks. There were drummers in town, caught between Big Spring and Waco or between Fort Worth and Lardeo, or between Palestine and El Paso—wherever drummers got caught between, seemed like they always wound up stopping over at Abilene. There were some who suspected that the Shades of Paradise and several other unwinding emporiums that the town boasted might have had something to do with that.

Then there were the hands in from the spreads all around—Friday was always a prime night to howl for cowhands just wintered out and not yet started on the

7

spring cutting. They could raise hell Friday night, sleep it off on Saturday and have all day Sunday to get back on the good side of their maker. In addition, there was the usual crowd of drifters fresh off the winter grubline and thinking about maybe looking for work. All of which drew cardsharps and medicine shows and every sort of immigrant entrepreneur, so there were plenty of that kind around, too.

The Shades of Paradise was packed pretty full when Bobby Lee walked in that evening, banged on the bar with Alf Tide's mind-y'all's-manners stick to get folks' attention, and pulled two dollars out of his pocket.

"I have an announcement to make, to one and all," he said, "Today I have put in twenty-five years on this earth, and never had any luck to speak of—neither good nor bad. I've just been here, is all. For one-fourth of a century. Well, as of now, I intend to have me a run of luck."

Windy Mullins was helping Alf tend bar at the time, and he asked, "Which kind, Bobby Lee? Good or bad?"

Bobby Lee just got one of those looks of his—the one like there was flies in the buttermilk, but he'd try not to notice. "Luck is what a man makes of it," he said. "I have here two dollars. Who'll play me some cards?"

For the next hour or two, seemed like Bobby Lee had hit it square on the head. Pretty soon he had better than fifteen dollars in his pile, and had cleaned out Slim Hanks and Joe Dell McGuire, and the cardsharps were starting to gather around like barn cats at rendering time.

But Bobby Lee picked up his money, poked it away and said, "Now that was just to show y'all that I'm serious about a run of luck. I don't aim to do it all with cards, though."

"You want to try dominoes, Bobby Lee?" Windy Mullins asked. "I got a set of planks here someplace."

"No," Bobby Lee said, slow and deliberate, like a man trying to talk a ground squirrel out of his boot.

"No, Windy, I don't want to play dominoes." He pushed back his chair. "What would y'all say is the luckiest thing a man can do?"

There was some head-scratching, then Jimbo Riley said, "Face down the house on a busted flush?"

"I'd say more like get elected governor," Clinton Sears suggested.

"Or *not* get elected governor," Pappy Jameson snapped. Pappy had been over to Austin once, and swore he'd never go back.

"Dig a posthole and strike gold," Sam Nabors offered.

"Not have to sleep in the same bunkhouse with Charlie Bliss," somebody said, and that brought a round of chuckles because most everybody knew about Charlie's bathing habits. He didn't have any.

"Marry a bow-legged woman?" Windy suggested.

"How 'bout a rich one?" Newt Waverly tossed in. Newt Waverly was a church-going man from time to time, and had a more reverent view of some matters than Windy did.

"Stay on top of one of old man Jackson's rough string," a cowboy at the bar decided. "That'd be blessed lucky."

Another cowboy suggested, "Get a herd through the deadline up to Dodge, without spendin' more'n they're worth on dippin'." Bobby Lee glanced across at the waddy and lifted one eyebrow, but the chatterers went right on.

"Maybe marry a dumb woman," somebody allowed.

Somebody else asked, "Dumb which way, Charlie? Can't talk, or ain't got the sense God gave a jackrabbit?"

"Y'all are not being properly serious about this," Bobby Lee said. "I'm talkin' about real, honest-to-Pete luck."

"All right, Bobby Lee," Pappy got himself a fresh beer and set it on the table. "We don't know the answer.

9

What is it?"

"That's easy," Bobby Lee told them. "The luckiest thing a man can do is to start with ten dollars and parlay it into a workin' spread of land that's his very own."

"Is that all?" somebody huffed. "Lordy, I can think of other . . ."

And somebody else put in, "There's luckier things than that, Bobby Lee. Far as I'm concerned, a man'd be lucky to . . ."

"Luck," Bobby Lee said, cutting them off, "is what a man makes of it." He raised his eyes to look again toward the bar, and picked out that one dusty cowboy that had remarked about herding critters to Dodge. "That deadline still holdin' up yonder, Willie?" he asked.

Willie Sutter nodded, looking like the whole matter was painful to discuss. "Tighter'n ever, Bobby Lee. Them Kansas farmers get downright wormy about Texas cows. You didn't hear about what happened to Shad Ames?"

Bobby Lee shook his head. "Not a word, Willie. Ain't laid eyes on Shad in near a year now. What happened?"

"He's been stayin' shy 'cause he's embarrassed," Willie said. "He got some ol' boys to help him push a herd of mosshorns up through the Territory—what, last spring, was it? Yeah. Well, they set off with near five thousand head, an' made it all the way to the Cimarron with no more'n twenty lost, then they hit the Kansas line an' that was all she wrote."

Everybody in the place was listening, because none of them had heard about all this before. Windy Mullins leaned his elbows on the bar and asked, "What was it, Willie? Injuns?"

Willie sighed, getting a look on his face like a man fetching up a carbuncle on his downside. "No, Windy, it wasn't Injuns. It was sodbusters an' Kansas law.

They'd got word a Texas herd was comin', an' they met 'em at the line. Onliest way they was about to let Shad through with his cows was if they was dipped first."

"I reckon that's when the shootin' commenced?" Pappy wondered.

"No, Shad's got better sense than that. Man takes to shootin' at Kansas sodbusters these days, has got a problem. They've got so they shoot right back." Willie stood silent for a moment, looking puzzled and kind of sad. "Times sure have changed," he muttered. Then he shrugged and went on, "Shad didn't have any choice about it. He was already out a year's hard wages, just gettin' them mosshorns that far. So they dug their-selves a trench an' spent three days haulin' water to fill it cow-deep, an' the Kansans sent out a wagonload of barrels of carbo . . . car . . ."

"Carbolic acid?" Pappy Jameson asked with a shudder.

"Yeah," Willie nodded, "carbolic acid—Shad had to pay for that, too, includin' delivery—an' all them Kansans stood around and laughed while Shad an' his boys baptized ever' last cow in that herd, right out there in front of God an' ever'body. It was a pitiful sight, sure enough."

"Lord," somebody whispered.

Pappy set down his empty mug and belched. "Clean 'em of ticks, did it, Willie?"

"I reckon," the puncher nodded. "They let 'em pass after that. But that was such a sorry-lookin' herd, from bein' carbolicized and downright humiliated . . ."

"Can't humiliate cows," Windy pointed out.

Willie looked like a man that has just ate frog eggs. "Windy, do you want to tell this story, or let me do it?"

"I don't know what it's about," Windy admitted. "So you go ahead on."

"Obliged," Willie said. "Anyways, ol' Shad made it up to Dodge with that pitiful herd of *humiliated* Texas critters, but they was so poor by then that he didn't get

11

four bits on the dollar for 'em. He didn't even break even. It was just pathetic."

There was silence in the Shades of Paradise for a minute or two, except for the sound of Windy Mullins whistling *Cotton-Eye Joe* through his teeth.

Then Bobby Lee thumped the table top with his fist and said, "Well, Willie, you've hit on how I intend to start my run of luck. I intend to put together a herd and take it north, and sell it direct to the railroad, an' I don't intend to dip a single critter doin' it, either."

They all looked at him. "The railhead up yonder is in Kansas, Bobby Lee, because that's where the railroad is."

Bobby Lee got a smug look on his face, like the grin a catch-wolf gets when the chase-wolf has a rabbit headed its way. "Not all of it," he said. "They're 'way on west of Dodge now, with those rails. An' that railhead won't be in Kansas much longer. I aim to be there with beef on the hoof when they cross the border."

Now that brought some more silence to the Shades of Paradise, because most everybody couldn't believe their ears.

Pappy Jameson was the first one to speak up. "Bobby Lee, you can't chouse cows up yonder where you're talkin' about. Not without a army, you can't. You'd have to cross No Man's Land."

Bobby Lee grinned like a possum. "That's the whole idea, don't y'all see? Everybody an' his uncle just naturally thinks No Man's Land can't be crossed with valuables. Well, I say everybody an' his uncle is wrong. It can be done, and I aim to do it."

12

II

Now, up yonder in what folks had taken to calling the Southwest Cattle Range, it was thirty-five miles from Texas to Kansas. Just thirty-five miles—an easy day's ride with time out to let your horse graze, or two-three days of trailing a herd. Thirty-five miles of high plains, with the Beaver River behind you and the Cimarron ahead.

Thirty-five miles. But that thirty-five miles lay across a place that wasn't like any other place anywhere. No Man's Land, it was called. The Neutral Strip. Most folks who had been there and made it out again, had other names for it, though. "The Devil's Playground," was a name you'd hear, though there were those that reckoned the only reason No Man's Land was still there was that Hell wouldn't have it.

A big old piece of ground shaped kind of like one of Windy Mullins' dominoes laid on edge. No Man's Land was thirty-five miles across, north to south, and maybe a hundred and sixty-five east to west. On its north side it bordered Kansas and a piece of Colorado Territory. On its south side was Texas. To the west, where Black Mesa stood above the Cimarron Breaks, was New Mexico Territory, and at the east end of it where Kiowa Creek met the Beaver, was the Oklahoma Territory—that part known as the Cherokee Strip.

The thing about No Man's Land was, there wasn't any law there. The government of the United States of America, in its infinite wisdom, had created the Neutral Strip after the War Between the States, so that there would be some space between Kansas and Texas. Probably seemed like a good idea at the time.

Nobody lived in the Neutral Strip. Back in Washington, D.C., they knew that to be true because they said it was so. The Neutral Strip was empty. It was No Man's Land. And there not being anybody there, the place had no use for laws. So no laws extended to No Man's Land. It wasn't in any legal jurisdiction. No court, no judicial district and no policing authority had any say about what went on in No Man's Land.

Law can be like that, especially when the law comes from someplace far away like Washington, D.C. If the Congress of the United States declares that there are no razorback hogs in Arkansas, and the President of the United States climbs up on the White House roof, looks westward toward Arkansas and agrees that he doesn't see any razorbacks yonder, and the courts of the land uphold all the best intentions of all those worthy gentlemen, well, then, by thunder, there just ain't any razorbacks in Arkansas, and that's just the way it is.

Some ways, Bobby Lee Smith might have fit right in at Washington, D.C. His reasoning now and again could be just as faultless as those gentlemen's.

So the government declared that there weren't any residents in No Man's Land, and that being the case there wasn't any legal jurisdiction, all of which resulted in those several thousand folks who didn't exist there just doing whatever came naturally. Which usually meant whatever they were man enough to get away with.

Basically, there were three classes of folks who had a notion that No Man's Land was not uninhabited. There were those who actually lived there, who figured they knew better. And there was most everybody in the two states and three territories surrounding the Strip, who knew who had been chased into the Strip a step ahead of a hanging posse or a gun and hadn't come out yet. And there was the United States Census Office, that had been ordered to count every nose between Mexico and Canada. The Census Office tended to be full of literal-minded people, who took it that counting everybody meant *count everybody*. So, about that time, arrangements were being made to count noses in No Man's Land, right along with the noses back East and the noses out West.

There wasn't even a lot of concern over whether people who weren't legally where they were might want to be counted. The question probably never even came up, and that was understandable. Next to figuring how to count wild Comanches in Texas, and Shoshones in the Colorado Territory, and old Red Cloud's friends and neighbors up north, a little thing like No Man's Land wouldn't have seemed much of a bronc to straddle. Not to people all that way off there at Washington, D.C., it wouldn't. They had maps, and they knew the Neutral Strip was only thirty-five miles wide.

But that spring of '90, not Bobby Lee Smith nor anybody else around Abilene was giving much thought to matters like a United States Census that hadn't quite commenced yet and nobody cared about, anyway.

A lot more folks around there were paying attention to Bobby Lee's new horse then what was hatching up in Washington, D.C.

Once Bobby Lee had decided that he aimed to trail cattle across No Man's Land to meet the railhead where it busted loose from that dippy bunch in Kansas, he went about getting ready to do that, in his own methodical Bobby Lee Smith way.

To even think about trailing cows, a man needed a good horse. Bobby Lee had selected his horse, and

15

somehow it wasn't much of a surprise to most folks which particular horse he had selected. Folks knew how Bobby Lee was, and most folks in those parts knew about Tarnation. It seemed truly natural that those two should come together.

Not that Tarnation was a bad-looking horse. Right handsome piece of horseflesh, as a matter of fact. Sixteen hands high he stood—a big, tough, blaze-face sorrel with three white stockings and the lineage of kings in his blood. He wasn't a knothead or a stargazer, or any of the ordinary bad types that a horse can be. He was a fine-looking, bright-eyed stud that for the five years since his foaling had been the property of Milo Hastings, who owned the Lazy Eight.

There were just a couple of problems about Tarnation. One was that he couldn't seem to sire any offspring—though nobody ever accused him of being shy about trying. The other thing was, nobody had stayed on top of that big horse for more than about five seconds. Folks who tried to ride Tarnation learned right off how he came to be named what he was. Many a man had tried to ride him. Cactus Jack Priestley had even tried it twice, but then Cactus Jack never did have the sense God gave a sourdough biscuit.

The second time Cactus Jack climbed up on that horse, he wound up with a separated shoulder and three days' picking of cactus spines in him from being tossed into a prickly pear patch.

Everybody around knew about Tarnation, and most felt real sympathy for Milo Hastings. There he was, stuck with an unridable saddle critter that couldn't sire a foal, but was still too good-looking to shoot.

That was why Milo Hastings—and everybody else who'd followed Bobby Lee out to the Lazy Eight to see what he'd do next—was amazed at that day's events.

Bobby Lee knew what he wanted, all right. He climbed down from behind Willie Sutter, howdied

16

Milo and said, "Mr. Hastings, I have come to buy a horse."

Milo nodded at the boy, and said, "All right, Bobby Lee. How much money do you have?"

"Fifteen dollars, but I don't intend to spend it all," Bobby Lee told him.

Milo blinked, then laughed like he just knew he was being joked. "Why, Bobby Lee, I couldn't let go of any critter on the Lazy Eight for that. Even Old Sway yonder would go for twenty."

"I don't want Old Sway," Bobby Lee said. He walked over to the pasture fence and pointed. "There's the horse I aim to have, right out there."

"Tarnation?" Milo couldn't believe his ears, and most of the rest couldn't, either.

"That's right," Bobby Lee said. "I stand ready to give you ten dollars for that horse. Cash money. And you know as well as I do that's a sight more than he's worth."

It took a while for Milo to come around to the fact that Bobby Lee was serious, but when he did, he said, "I'll tell you what I'll do, Bobby Lee. I'll go fifteen dollars or nothing. You catch up that bronc and ride him, I'll let you have him for a handshake, and I'll throw in a saddle for ten dollars. But if you can't ride him, the price is fifteen dollars as he stands."

You know, Bobby Lee didn't even hesitate. He just said, "Done," shook Milo's hand on the matter, and went to fetch a catch-rope.

No telling how the word got back to Abilene, but by the time Bobby Lee was ready to make his ride, there was a good three dozen more visitors out at Lazy Eight, waiting to see the show.

Tarnation was always a peculiar horse. He'd been saddle-broke for years. He'd never minded a bit when folks plopped a forty-pound rocking chair up on his back and hauled the cinches tight under his belly, and he'd stand still for the halter, and take the bit as easy as

17

a hound dog takes a stew bone. He'd never been one to mind wearing a saddle.

But he drew the line at having anybody sit on it.

There were wagers being made all around the fenced corral when Bobby Lee suited up that horse and led him out for a try. And there were sighs of sympathy when Bobby Lee put his boot in Tarnation's stirrup, swung aboard and flew head over heels across the corral.

Everybody wondered what the young fool aimed to do with fifteen dollars worth of useless horse.

But Bobby Lee picked himself up, dusted himself off and got that look on his face—like a balky mule that's just been pushed too far—and said, "All right, horse, I know that trick now. Let's just see if you got any others."

Nobody had expected him to get back on and try it again. Generally, one tangle with Tarnation was enough for anybody. But Milo Hastings just shrugged and said, "A bet's a bet, and nothin' was said about extra tries. I reckon it's up to Bobby Lee, how many times he can stand to be throwed."

And that set up a whole new round of side bets, because that made it a different kind of contest. Just which of those two critters was the stubbornest, the horse or Bobby Lee? When Bobby Lee picked himself up and went and took Tarnation's reins, and those two looked each other right in the eye—Bobby Lee with his jaw set so the muscles stood out in front of his ears, and Tarnation with his ears perked up and a look in his eyes like a cardsharp palming aces—well, the odds jumped around all over the board. There just wasn't a soul present that could honestly say which way it would go.

That big horse stood still as you please, while Bobby Lee tidied his rig, and got his stance alongside. The critter even looked around at him, like to make sure he was comfortable. Bobby Lee put his boot in the stirrup and got a good hold on the saddle horn, with the reins in his left hand. Tarnation braced himself, and the muscles in his haunches began to ripple. His ears went back, and he bared his teeth like a boarding house drummer grinning at Sunday dinner.

"Okay, horse," Bobby Lee hissed, "let's see what you can really do."

He swung astraddle, his right toe found the stirrup, and all hell broke loose.

Tarnation opened the ball with a double crow-hop, just to hear Bobby Lee's tailbone smack the saddle, then he swapped ends like a badger at bay, got the bit in his teeth and reared tall, swatting the wind with both front hooves. That horse stood so tall it looked like he was going over backward, then he did a half-spin, hit the ground stiff-legged as fence posts, put his head between his front legs and kicked his rear end skyward.

Bobby Lee parted company with the saddle right then, and took three or four watchers down with him when he flew over the top rail. Dust hung in the air, and for a minute nobody could see who in that pile was still in one piece—or if anybody was. For a time, there was hardly a sound around that corral.

Then somebody moved in the dust, and Bobby Lee stood up, untangling himself from Shorty Mars and Jimbo Riley and some others. He was bleeding from a cut lip, one eye was swelling shut and he limped like a cripple, but he dusted himself off again, hitched up his britches and climbed right back into that corral.

"I believe that scutter is a crazy man," Milo Hastings remarked. "Nobody ever went up a third time on Tarnation. Not even Cactus Jack Priestley, and he ain't got the sense God have a horny toad."

There was a good bit of commotion, what with wagers being adjusted all around, then everybody went quiet when Bobby Lee walked up to that horse, growled at it like a mountain lion, ducking under its head, grabbed it around the front legs and heaved backward. Tarnation's eyes went wide, his head went up and he went down, sprawling in the dust as Bobby Lee backed away.

"You see there?" Bobby Lee explained. "That's how it is, gettin' throwed."

Tarnation went mean-eyed and scrambled to his feet, then just stood there looking bewildered until he noticed that Bobby Lee was on top of him. Bobby Lee had slapped saddle and rode him up, and there he was, right up there in the saddle, taking a short hold on the reins.

Just as Tarnation realized he was there, Bobby Lee spread his legs and kicked the horse hard in both flanks. "Let's us try that again, one more time," he yelled.

If ever a bucking horse went hog wild, Tarnation did then. That bronc had a whole deck of tricks for separating a rider from his saddle, and he used them everyone and sometimes all at once, and maybe made up some new ones. He skywalked and tumbled, he swapped ends and spun, he stump-jumped, angel-danced, bolted and shied. He swivelled and skidded, backtracked and crow-hopped, and high-ended so hard that he went right on over in a rolling somersault. But when he came up again, Bobby Lee was still up there, yelling at him in good Texas horse talk and pummeling his flanks with hard heels.

It was just more than Tarnation was fixing to tolerate. His eyes went white-rimmed, and his ears were laid right back on his neck. He pawed the hard ground, snorted up clouds of dust and shrilled a whinny like a war cry, then he switched ends, bunched his haunches and took off straight across the corral while spectators there scattered in all directions. That horse never even slowed down. He just took off and flew, and his rear hooves knocked the top rail right out of its socket as he went over. He lit and bounded, and took off in a belly-down run past Milo's pole barn and out across the prairie, and Bobby Lee clung to him like a tick on a cow's rump.

Up the rise they went, then over the low ridge and there wasn't anything to see out there but wind-feathered dust where they had gone.

Most everybody piled out of Milo's headquarters lot, some afoot and some on horseback, and ran to see what was going on. At the top of the ridge, they pulled up, shading their eyes, looking around. Then somebody pointed off to the left and hollered, "By thunder, just look-ee yonder!"

Sure enough, out there a quarter mile or so, Tarnation was just turning around, responding to the reins in Bobby Lee's hand just like that was all he'd ever intended to do. They started back, and Bobby Lee let the horse walk a piece, then kicked him to a trot. Passing the crowd on the ridge, Bobby Lee waved to Milo Hastings. "Owe you ten dollars, Mr. Hastings," he said, "That's for the saddle."

Several of them looked at one another, and Clinton Sears hauled off his hat and scratched his head. "I never seen the like of that," he said. "Land, I wonder what that Bobby Lee is like to do next?"

Pappy Jameson stuck his old pipe in his mouth and shook his head. "Well, he's got hisself a horse now, like he said he would. I wouldn't be surprised if he's aimin' to get hisself a herd of cows."

III

There were a lot of interesting folks up yonder in No Man's Land in those days. Some said Frank James was there, and word was the Wild Bunch from up in Utah—or some of them anyway—might have been seen there, and Pearly Gates and Scalp Harrison and maybe Blue Duck . . . though others said they'd hung Blue Duck some time back.

Around Abilene, the figuring was that Pete Thayer and Slap Jackson and that bunch of no-good rustling varmints that had caused all the trouble on the Tuttle Trail, had all headed up to No Man's Land and likely was still there. Some said Whitey Ford—that every sheriff and ranger west of Dimebox had been trying to catch for eight-nine years—might be there, too.

But one gent who most definitely was up there by then was a sharper by the name of George Scrannon, who saw fortunes to be made in a place that didn't exist in any legal sense. He saw opportunity just laying out there like gold on the ground, and he was well on his way to raking up all of it.

Scrannon's game was land grabbing. And outside of Washington, D.C.—and maybe Texas—George Scrannon may have been the sharpest general-purpose land grabber that the Lord ever saw fit to let stand on hind legs. He was a specialist at taking what wasn't his, and at hanging on to it and selling it so he could take it back again and sell it again. And he was a specialist at making the illegal sound legal enough to fool most folks, and at making anybody that got in his way disappear.

Like any true specialist, Scrannon was single-minded and let nothing distract him from his goals. It served him considerably that he was—or could seem to be—just a harmless, serious-looking gentleman with a sort of baggy-eyed, honest seeming face. At a glance, you wouldn't know he didn't have a scruple to his name.

George Scrannon had come to the Neutral Strip and just naturally decided that it was his for the taking. He had mostly taken over a town named Beaver City, and filled it up with citizens of his choosing who didn't any more legally live there than he did, but were there all the same. He had a Vigilance Committee to keep law and order—which meant to keep things going his way—and a judge whose warrant came straight from Scrannon.

He had given the whole mess an aura of respectability by filing a proposal with the United States Government to have the Neutral Strip recognized as a territory—the Cimarron Territory. In some circles, No Man's Land was already thought of as the Cimarron Proposal, and to advance the notion a little farther, Scrannon had named a "governor" and a "territorial secretary."

The proposal did all that could have been expected of it. It confused the issue of what the Strip was or wasn't, to where it might take years to sort it all out back in Washington, D.C. And in the meantime, Scrannon and his faction were booming towns and grabbing land up and down the Strip. They had folks out all over, armed with legal-looking papers, selling whatever they could sell, as many times as they could sell it, to whoever would buy it.

23

Most of which was not common knowledge around Abilene, Texas, because it was all a long ways away. News of a bank robbery or a train holdup, or about the untimely death by suspended strangulation of some notorious bad man, news like that travels far and fast. But land swindles don't seem to get reported that easy, and the bigger they are, the less anybody any distance away is likely to know.

It is a good piece from No Man's Land to Abilene, Texas, about as far as it is from No Man's Land to the Big Muddy—the Missouri River—back East yonder where it lights out of Kansas City and Independence, and heads for St. Louis.

Certainly the last thing that Annabel Susanna Finch would have thought, when she closed the deal to buy a section of "the highest quality of unspoiled land in the Cimarron Proposal, bonded and deed certified, ready for the plow or the choicest of chattel," was that anything might be even slightly odorous about the deal.

The gentlemen who sold the property to her, aboard a brass-bound riverboat cruising up the Muddy, were obviously above reproach. One of them was Col. Chadwick Booth-Sykes, and his manners and dress were as impeccable as his name sounded. He even spoke English with a funny accent, like Englishmen and folks from Massachusetts do. He was traveling in the company of a retired United States Congressman, a wise and kindly silver-haired lawyer, a notary public with a silk vest, and a minister of the gospel. All of them vouched for the quality of the land the colonel had put up for sale, and attested to the quality of the colonel.

Annie Sue—folks tended to call her that because of how she looked, until they learned that appearances could be deceiving—was nobody's fool. If there had been even the slightest hint of impropriety about the whole thing, she would have had second thoughts right away.

24

She might have held off closing the deal until she got to Kansas City, anyway, but she didn't want to take the chance. The money from her Aunt Claudine's estate was in a bank in Kansas City, and there was a middling fair chance that her brother Jason might have people watching the docks.

Annie Sue knew very well that if her brother, or his lawyers, caught her and served her with papers, they could tie up the estate for years. But not if the money was already spent. And she knew what she wanted to spend it on, so she made two transactions on that riverboat the day before it reached Kansas City. She bought herself a section of land out in the new territory, the Cimarron Proposal, and she cashed a draft with the ship's purser for ten dollars short of the remainder of Aunt Claudine's account. She went to her stateroom, then, and had Milicent stand by the door while she stuck the currency away in her garter.

Annie Sue knew that just as soon as that steamboat landed at the Kansas City docks, those two banks drafts would be on their way to the bank. Folks being folks—and the colonel and the ship's purser no exceptions—she knew that the quicker a bank draft was cashed, the easier everybody would breathe.

So she had a plan for making sure the drafts were cashed and done before Jason and his lawyers could stop payment.

"We'll get all packed before we dock," she told Milicent. "And when the gangplank rolls out, I want us to be the first two off the boat. You turn left and I'll turn right. The thing I need to do is dodge process servers for as long as I can. That should leave you free to make the arrangements we discussed."

"I can do that," Milicent agreed. "But are you sure you'll be all right, Miss Annie Sue?"

"I'll be perfectly all right, Milicent." Annie Sue's chin went up, and her big blue eyes darkened like thunderclouds. "My brother is a twit, not a hoodlum. I

25

know how to handle him. You make our arrangements, and meet me in the evening at the hotel. I expect then we can get on with our business."

Then she went up to the Texas deck and looked out over the river and thought, There now, by heaven, Jason can serve all the papers he wants to. Aunt Claudine said the money was mine, and I should do what I want with it. Now I've done it, and Jason can just go hang.

There wasn't a man on the Texas deck that didn't notice her standing there looking smug. With her honey-blonde hair and big blue eyes, and her pert little nose and determined small chin, Annie Sue was always noticed. Had it not been for certain unmistakable contours that never failed to catch the masculine eye, Annie Sue might have been taken for a child of fourteen or fifteen. A face like that, on a person barely more than five feet tall and not weighing a hundred pounds, might have seemed childlike and angelic at certain angles, until a body noted that she didn't have any angles—just curves.

There wasn't a man on the Texas deck that wouldn't have been mighty proud to defend that pretty little thing's honor, either, nor would have guessed that Annie Sue's honor had all the defense it required, thank you. Just looking at her, not a one of them would ever have guessed that yonder stood the stubbornest, most certifiably mule-headed female that God ever saw fit to set loose on unsuspecting mankind.

That sweet little thing may have looked like an angel, but she never took kindly to being crossed. Even a highbinder like Chad Sykes—or Colonel Chadwick Booth-Sykes as he called himself then—might have had second thoughts about his dealings had he known just what kind of forces he was fiddling with in Annie Sue Finch.

All of that, though, was taking place a far piece from Abilene, Texas, where there were other events afoot.

*   *   *

Bobby Lee Smith rode his new horse into town and left it off at Jack Priddy's livery barn. Old Jack, he took one look at that big blaze sorrel and said, "Tarnation, by dang. Heard you rode that devil, Bobby Lee. You gone back to wranglin'?"

"Nope," Bobby Lee told him. "I'm on a streak of luck, Jack."

"Well, I'd say a man's damn lucky to have stayed on top of that horse," Priddy pointed out. "But I can't say as how offerin' good money for him qualifies. What you aim to do, hire out to a Wild West show back East?"

"I aim to use him to drive cows. It's all part of my plan."

"Whose cows? You don't have any cows, Bobby Lee."

"Well, I aim to have some. I done told you, Jack, I'm on a streak of luck. You get out to see Shad Ames now and again, don't you?"

"Sometimes," Jack nodded. "Poor soul hardly ever comes to town these days, you know."

"I heard," Bobby Lee said, sympathetically. "He tried to go to Kansas and got dipped. He's still got a good herd, I reckon?"

"Yeah, Shad's got cows. Shad always has cows. He just ain't got anything to do with 'em is all." He squinted up at Bobby Lee. "That where you aim to get cows? From Shad Ames?"

"Might as well," Bobby Lee shrugged. "I want cows to drive, and he's got cows. Only thing is, the last I heard, the critters on Shad's range wears ever' brand you can think of, and I'll need a herd marked for travel. And a bill of sale."

"You want *legal* cows, then." Jack wrinkled his face in thought. "That kind comes high, Bobby Lee. You got some money?"

27

"I still got five dollars."

"Well, that ought to buy you four-five regular cows, or about two legal ones. How many cows was you thinking about?"

Bobby Lee didn't even hesitate. "Five hundred head, at least. Tell you what, Jack, why don't you tell ol' Shad I'd like to talk some business with him. Tell him I'm willin' to dicker." He turned away and headed across the street.

Jack Priddy stared after the boy, his eyes as wide as dollars. "You want five . . . five hundred head of legal cows?" he muttered. "For five dollars?" Jack went to saddle up his old dun, still talking to himself. "I got to see this," he said. "Land, I'd never forgive myself if I didn't go ahead on and see how this all comes out. Five dollars? For five hundred head of *legal* stock? Lordy, that's gonna be some kind of a dicker."

By the time Jack Priddy was headed out to Shad Ames' Aces Over spread, half the folks in town had heard about what Bobby Lee intended to do, and there was just a lot of learned conversation among those dusty denizens of the Shades of Paradise who had no more than got back from the festivities out at Lazy Eight and begun wetting their whistles when this latest revelation came to light.

Jack Priddy's swamper, Shiloh Murdock, brought the news and parlayed it into some free drinks. What he said was, "What y'all reckon that Bobby Lee Smith aims to do now?"

"I don't know," Clinton Sears admitted. "Run for governor?"

"Rob a bank?" Jimbo Riley suggested, hopefully.

"Hire out for wages?" Newt Waverly asked. Newt always was a plain-minded man.

"Marry a bow-legged woman?" Windy Mullins reckoned.

Old Shiloh got a look on his face like a man that had his mouth set for beefsteak and bit into fish. "No,

28

Windy," he said, slowly, "He ain't aiming to marry a bow-legged woman. Leastways, not right now."

Pappy Jameson fired up his old pipe. "We give up, Shiloh. Just what is it the boy's got in mind?"

"I'm plumb dry," Shiloh allowed. "Ain't had me a beer all day."

Alf Tide set him up a beer and leaned his elbows on the bar. "All right, Shiloh. What does Bobby Lee Smith aim to do now?"

"Cows." Shiloh wiped suds off his whiskers and grinned. "He aims to get hisself some cows."

"I ain't surprised," Pappy Jameson muttered.

"We already figured that out," Willie Sutter told Shiloh.

"Yeah, but I bet you didn't know where he aims to get them."

"No, I don't believe I heard that part," Sam Nabors admitted. "Where?"

"That was fine beer," Shiloh set down his empty mug. With a frown, Alf Tide filled it up, then pointedly laid his mind-y'all's-manners stick on the bar and said, "All right, Shiloh. Where does Bobby Lee aim to get cows?"

"From Shad Ames," Shiloh told them. "Five hundred head, he says, an' all legal critters."

There were looks exchanged all around the room. "Five hundred head?" somebody said. "And him with not but five dollars to his name?"

"Well, Shad's got a lot of cows," somebody else said. "Where his spread is, yonder in the gap, he can't hardly help but have cows. But has he got *legal* ones?"

"That's what Bobby Lee aims to have," Shiloh emphasized. "Legal cows."

"How does he aim to get five hundred legal cows off Shad Ames?" Clinton Sears wondered.

Shiloh looked like he was about to answer, but just couldn't get the words out because of dryness in the gullet. Alf Tide shrugged, filled the swamper's mug one

29

more time, and put his hand on his mind-y-all's-manners stick. "You're fixin' to aggravate me, Shiloh," he growled.

Shiloh eased his throat with a long gulp, and told them the rest of it. "He aims to dicker. That's what he said."

"I don't believe a word of it," Jimbo Riley shook his head. "Shad Ames? Willie, you know Shad Ames. Does he strike you as a man to dicker, come cows?"

"Nope." Willie looked thoughtful. "I've knowed him to dip, but never to dicker. Wonder what Bobby Lee thinks he's got to dicker with?"

Pappy Jameson puffed on his pipe, thinking so hard you could almost hear the wheels turn. Then he fished in his pocket and hauled out a gold piece. "I got twenty dollars here that says Bobby Lee will get five hundred head of legal cows from Shad Ames."

"I'll take that," Alf Tide said.

Willie Sutter looked at Pappy with slitted eyes. "You know somethin' the rest of us don't, Pappy?"

"Naw, not really. All I heard is what you heard."

"But you think Bobby Lee is gonna get them cows from Shad Ames?"

"Got me a notion," Pappy said. "Y'all heard the boy. He said he was fixin' to have a run of luck."

IV

It was ten minutes shy of noon when the *Queen of Springfield* laid alongside the Kansas City docks. Men hustled to tie her off and set fenders, and the gangway was hauled out and set in place.

Annie Sue had already spotted Jason. For a mile, approaching the docks, she had been up in the wheelhouse, looking through the captain's spyglass while the captain looked at her and left it to the pilot to bring in his vessel safe and sound.

They were there, in the crowd at the docks—Jason and three other men, all bunched together at first, then spreading to different points on the dock as the riverboat approached. Waiting for Annie Sue. She had seen them, though. She saw their faces, and saw where they went.

So the instant the gangway was secured, Milicent marched down it carrying a pair of large valises, with Annie Sue right behind her. Milicent Moriarty was a strapping big woman with a red Irish temper, and folks tended to step aside and make way for her, so all Annie Sue had to do was follow in her wake, and within seconds they were off the boat, off the gangway and well into the dockside crowds.

Annie Sue nudged Milicent then, and said, "All right. Go!"

Milicent made an abrupt left turn, almost bowling over a porter, and waded into the crowd, heading for the upriver promenade. Half-hidden by a stack of bales, Annie Sue watched her go, and saw two of Jason's hired men scurrying to follow.

"Good," she muttered. With a quick look around, she hoisted her satchel and headed right, toward the downriver promenade. She was beyond the docks, up the ramps and on the fronting street when she heard a shout somewhere behind her. Without looking back, she strode to a waiting hansom, tossed her satchel aboard and climbed up after it. "I am in a hurry," she told the surprised driver. "Get going!"

"Yes, ma'am," he said, and snapped his whip above the ears of his horse. They took off at a good clip, up the angling road that led to the city atop the bluff.

Annie Sue looked back, then. Jason and one of his men were just stepping into the street back there, and Jason pointed toward her. Then they ran to another hansom and climbed in. And in the crowd beyond them, separately, she glimpsed Colonel Booth-Sykes and his companions, and the ship's purser, all starting up the hill.

"Good," she told herself. "Driver, turn right at the first intersection, then pull over and let me off."

"Yes, ma'am."

By the time Jason's cab arrived at the intersection, she would be gone from sight. They would find her eventually, and serve her with court orders, then go straight to the bank and seal Aunt Claudine's account. It wouldn't matter, though. She smiled angelically. Jason was welcome to what would be in the account by the time he got his hands on it. Ten dollars for his troubles. Jason was probably worth ten dollars, just for nuisance value.

Knowing that she had succeeded with her plan, she turned her thoughts to her next plan—the one Milicent

32

was attending to. Two railroad tickets, westward to Dodge City.

As the hansom trundled up the slope toward the intersection, Annie Sue got out her map and glanced at it. Three hundred miles to Dodge City. Then seventy miles southwest of there, by passable road, was the southern boundary of Kansas, and beyond it the new territory, the Cimarron Proposal. South of Kansas just a few miles—due west of something called Beaver City—was her land. Her own land. The land she had bought, fee, simple deed and title.

She could hardly wait to get there, to start living her own life, her own way, in the style to which she intended to become accustomed. Improved property, they had assured her. That meant the buildings were already in place. They hadn't said much about the house—what were men likely to know about houses?— but she was sure it would do just fine, with maybe a bit of redecorating.

It was Pappy Jameson himself who said, one time, "Things don't just happen, y'all know. Anytime anything ever happened, there sure enough was a reason why it did." Of course, Pappy was drunk at the time. Man like Pappy Jameson, he'd no more spout philosophy than he'd bark at the moon, unless he had himself a dang good reason. But then, being drunk is reason enough, in most cases.

Anyway, Pappy was holding forth one time at the Shades of Paradise, and he said that. Everybody heard him, "Y'all just think about it," he said. He squinched up his face and added, "There is a season for each event, and each thing has its reason . . . or somethin' like that. It's somethin' that somebody wrote. Anyhow, that's how things work. Ever' last thing that has ever happened on this earth, turns out there was a reason

33

why it did."

"What was the reason that Pete Thayer and Slap Jackson rustled the church herd?" somebody asked, sourly.

"I know that one!" Windy Mullins chimed in. "They taken it because it was there."

Pappy got a kind of nose-wrinkle look on his face, like his pickle had come from the bottom of the vat. "That ain't much of a reason," he said. "I'm talkin' complic . . . comp . . . *dang,* that's good whiskey! I'm talkin' a serious subject here, boys."

"Yeah," Clinton Sears nodded. "We can tell you are. We just don't know what it is."

Pappy never did get much farther with that line of reasoning, and by the time he sobered up he probably forget all about it. But he might have been right. Things that happen, that seem to just drift together and occur, maybe it isn't like that at all. Maybe there is a reason. It's just that you never know until afterward what it was that happened beforehand, that led to what came later, you see. So if what happened was because of all those other circumstances, and wouldn't have happened except for them, then those things are the reason why that thing happened. Of course, it doesn't make any difference, because in that case it always was going to happen anyway, and since nobody knew about those other things beforehand, then there never was any way to change that.

That pretty well explains it.

It's like when Bobby Lee Smith was waiting for Shad Ames to come and dicker about cows. Bobby Lee didn't have any way of knowing that 'way off up yonder in the Neutral Strip, right about then, a jasper named George Scrannon was booming towns and grabbing land, or that a blonde-haired little darling 'way off yonder at Kansas City was stepping aboard a passenger coach with her woman companion, to go and take pos-

34

session of some land she had bought. And if he knew that No Man's Land had a new name in some circles— the Cimarron Proposal—well, that wouldn't have had a thing to do with him as far as he could see.

And, of course he didn't any more know about the United States Census Office's orders from the Congress than he knew Victor Hugo's middle name. Bobby Lee was just going his own way—which was the only way Bobby Lee generally saw fit to go—and all those other things going on weren't even mysteries to him, because to be mysteries he'd have had to wonder about them. And to wonder about them, he'd have had to know about them. And he didn't.

Most likely, Pappy Jameson was right now and again, when he got drunk enough.

There was a small wager or two as to whether Shad Ames would come into town to see Bobby Lee. Old Shad hadn't been off Aces Over in maybe a year, as far as anybody knew. That whole business of having to herd humiliated cows across seventy miles of Kansas prairie had nigh broke his spirit, it seemed like. He was ashamed to show his face around Abilene.

But Jack Priddy brought him in, sure enough. Old Shad had listened to all that about Bobby Lee Smith aiming to buy five hundred head of legal livestock for five dollars, and it amazed him so much that he just had to hear it for himself.

So he came, and Bobby Lee was waiting for him at the Shades of Paradise.

Some of the boys cleared a table right in the middle of Alf's place, and Bobby Lee sat down at one side and Shad at the other. Bobby Lee nodded at the older man and said, "I'm obliged to you for comin' in to dicker, Mr. Ames. Saved me an' all these other fellas from havin' to ride out to Aces Over."

Old Shad, he just frowned at the boy and said, "Well, I'm here, Bobby Lee. So what do you have in mind?"

35

"Well, sir, first I aim to buy you a beer." He turned, and waved at the bar. "Need a mug of beer for Mr. Ames, here!"

Windy Mullins came toting two mugs, and Bobby Lee looked at him like there was plugs in his ears. "Just one beer is enough, Windy. I ain't rich, you know." He took one of the mugs and set in in front of Shad Ames. Not having anything better to do with the other beer, Windy went off to drink it himself.

Bobby Lee just sat and watched while Shad Ames drained his mug, set it down and thumbed the foam off his whiskers. Then he said, "Well?"

"Obliged for the beer," Shad said.

"Don't mention it. Now let's dicker."

"From what I hear," Shad said, "you ain't got much to dicker with. I understand you want five dollars' worth of cows."

"Four dollars and ninety-five cents," Bobby Lee corrected him. "That beer cost me a nickel. What I'm in the market for is cows, all right. *Legal* cows. About five hundred head, to drive to the rails for sale at the end of the track."

Shad sat there for a time, just looking at Bobby Lee, then he shook his head. "I swear," he said. "It's just like Jack Priddy said. I couldn't hardly believe my ears when I heard what you had in mind, but now I reckon you're serious."

"Yes, sir, I am."

"Five hundred head, you say? Son, do you know what a pit full of carbolic acid does to five hundred cows? Not to mention what it does to them that has to dip 'em."

"I don't aim to get dipped, Mr. Ames. I intend to push a herd up to where the Chicago, Rock Island and Pacific Railroad comes out of Kansas, and sell 'em on this side of the line."

"Where the . . . where it comes out of Kansas? But,

boy, the Rock Island ain't come out of Kansas."

"It's about to, though. I read about it in the *New York Times*. The railroad has bought all its Kansas rights-of-way, and they're shippin' iron from Chicago. They'll . . ."

"The what?"

"What?"

"You read about it in the what?"

"The *New York Times*. It's a newspaper. When I was shoein' stock for Mr. Priddy, he got a span of cleats in for Mr. Harrison's prize mule. Shipped all the way from a foundry at Pittsburgh, Pennsylvania. You know how Mr. Harrison is about that mule. Land, them shoes was the prettiest things! Foundry cast, special alloy, buffed to a fare-thee-well and all crated up in a wood box for shippin' . . ."

"I heard all about Cecil Harrison's mule's new shoes," Shad cut in. "Ain't ever'body? But what does that have to do with the Chicago, Rock Island and Pacific Railroad and my cows?"

"Well, sir, that's what I'm tryin' to tell you. Them mule shoes was all individually packaged inside that crate, so they wouldn't rub together and get scratched. Lordy, a man coulda used any one of 'em for a mirror to shave hisself. They was that shiny . . ."

Shad sort of sighed and waved at the bar. "Alf, we gonna need some more beer here. An' a bottle of that Kentucky mash you keep hid, too."

"That nickel was all I allowed for hospitality," Bobby Lee pointed out. "The rest of my money is for buyin' your cows. I sure wouldn't want to short-change you, Mr. Ames."

"It's on me," Shad shook his head. "I'm beginnin' to need me a drink."

"I can understand that," Bobby Lee nodded. "Anyhow, them mule shoes come all the way from Pittsburgh, Pennsylvania, an' there wasn't a scratch on

37

'em. I unpacked 'em myself. Just goes to show you what careful plannin' can accomplish."

"Careful . . . plannin'?"

"Yes, sir. You see, whoever crated up Mr. Harrison's mule shoes didn't take any chances. Every shoe in that box was wrapped up in the *New York Times*. That's how I come to know about the railroad, an' where to meet up with the railhead to keep from crossin' into Kansas and gettin' dipped. It was on my birthday I read about that, so there just wasn't any doubt what I was fixin' to do."

Shad had already put down two shots of Kentucky mash. Now he poured himself another one. He was looking a little bit glassy-eyed, but it was more from keeping up with Bobby Lee than from the whiskey. "What you was fixin' to do," he said, slowly, like he just almost had the drift of it.

"Yes, sir. I'm havin' myself a streak of luck, you see, an' what I aim to do is buy myself a spread of my own someplace and build up a brand an' get rich."

Shad Ames poured himself another one. He gulped it down, cooled it off with some beer, and rubbed his eyes. "Bobby Lee, where is it you think you can meet the Chicago, Rock Island an' Pac . . . Pa . . . whatever. The railroad?"

"What?"

"Where?"

"Oh. Right where it comes out of Kansas. In No Man's Land. Now I figure with five hundred head of good, unhumiliated an' legal-billed stock, I can sell for . . ."

"No Man's Land?"

"Yes, sir. It's a golden opportunity, an' a man'd be fool to miss out on it, an' I know that even though you wound up havin' to dip your last herd an' all, well, I know you ain't any fool, Mr. Ames. An' I said to myself, I said, Bobby Lee, here's a chance for Mr. Shad

38

Ames to get square for the misery he's been put to, an' it's the Christian thing to do, to make sure he doesn't miss out on this opportunity, you see. That's when I made up my mind that I wasn't just going to invest in just anybody's cows, Mr. Ames. I realized for a fact that *your* cows were the ones I ought to buy. So that's why I'm here to dicker with you."

Shad belched and said, "'Scuse me." Then he squinched up his face. "Five hundred head? Of legal stock? What's in it for me, Bobby Lee?"

"Four dollars and ninety-five cents on account, an' a third of the profit when I sell, not to mention that you are invited to come along as ramrod so you can have the satisfaction of standin' on the Kansas line an' sayin' anything you dang well please, just as loud as you want to. Matter of fact, if you'd feel inclined to step up to the border line and piss on that sovereign state, I expect every man with you would be honored to line up and second your motion."

"Well, I sure enough got a few sentiments I'd like to express to Kansas," Shad allowed. "Half."

"What?"

"Not a third. I want half."

"That's what I call dickerin'," Bobby Lee grinned. "Well, sir, I know when I've met my match. You got yourself a deal, Mr. Ames." He stood up and reached across the table, and they shook on it, with everybody in the Shades of Paradise as witnesses.

Shad Ames poured himself another drink, and Bobby Lee said, "I'll leave the arrangements up to my ramrod, sir. Whatever hands you want to sign on, an' whatever supplies you see fit to buy, I'll approve it. I expect your cook-wagon will do just fine, an' the remuda is up to you except that I got my own horse for special use. If you can have everything ready by Monday, we can cut out my herd an' be on the trail first thing Tuesday. Is that all right?"

"I reckon," Shad said, talking mostly to his whiskey glass.

"Good." Bobby Lee looked around the room. "Any of you boys want to sign on for a drive to the railroad, talk to my ramrod here. We'll need good men." He yawned, nodded and went out, leaving a silent room behind him.

Pappy Jameson put away his pipe and walked over to the bar. He stuck out his hand toward Alf Tide. "Pay me," he said.

It was maybe fifteen minutes later when Shad Ames came up out of his chair like a man that's sat on a bee. "No Man's Land?" he declared. *"No Man's Land?"*

V

By the time Shad Ames finally got his wits about him, it was way too late to unagree what he had done agreed. The deal was done dealt, and the deed was did and done. So Shad, he took it like a man. Like a man with a cowchip on his shoulder, and a pressing need to have everybody understand just what kind of a State of Denmark deal he was living up to. Oh, he'd go along with it, all right, but he just had to carry on some about what admirable qualities it required of a man to live up to such an agreement.

"I'm hirin' on to drive my own cows!" he explained, to everybody who would listen. "For four dollars and ninety-five cents, I'm a'turnin' over the best critters I got to Bobby Lee Smith! Six-seven hundred dollars worth of prime stock! And then I'm gonna work for him to ramrod *his* herd right into the middle of the devil's stompin' ground! And it's me that's payin' the wages an' puttin' up the gear an' th' possibles!"

"Seems a mite strange to me that a man'd do that," Pappy Jameson told him. "But I knew you'd come through, Shad. I had me twenty dollars ridin' on it, that you would."

"Mule shoes!" Shad went right along, not wanting any interruption when he was in mid-fuss. "Mule shoes and Kentucky mash whiskey an' the *New York Times* . . ."

"Not to mention pissin' on Kansas," Willie Sutter reminded him. "I thought that was kind of a nice touch, myself."

". . . I consider it abundantly evident that Bobby Lee Smith has whickered me," Shad said, "though I can't rightly say how he done it."

"Just lucky, I guess," Pappy Jameson said.

"Yeah, an' that's another thing!" Old Shad sounded like he was getting his second wind. "All that about havin' hisself a lucky streak! What kind of foolishness is that?"

"The boy had two dollars to his name when he declared his luck," Pappy reasoned. "And fifteen dollars by the time he said what it was about. Now, not two days later, he's got a ridin' horse with a saddle an' five hundred head of legal cows. I reckon a man might consider that lucky, Shad."

"Luck happens! You don't just declare it, and there it is!"

"Bobby Lee might," Willie Sutter shrugged. "You know how he is sometimes." He sat down across from Shad and peered out from beneath his hat. "Might be the best thing that's come along, you know, Shad. Seems to me like you didn't have much luck last time you went north. Maybe Bobby Lee's luck is just the thing for you."

"I'll believe that when I see it." Shad sighed, leaned back and said, "All right, then. Y'all think so much of that boy's lucky streak, which ones of y'all are aimin' to sign on for the drive? An' keep in mind where we're goin'. No Man's Land."

"I'll give it a tumble," Willie decided. "Got nothin' better to do. My long gun's .44-40, an' my hogleg's a .45."

Shad looked up at him. "I expect there's a reason why you're volunteerin' that information, Willie?"

"Dang right. It's up to the ramrod to stock ammunition for a drive, an' I suggest you take along a Lord's plenty, considerin' where we aim to go."

Shad hauled out a piece of paper sack and began keeping lists. "How about you, Pappy? You goin', too?"

"Might as well," Pappy Jameson decided. "I tote .32-20 an' a .45. An' I cotton to horehound candy on a drive."

". . . .32-20, 'nother .45 . . ." Shad muttered, writing it down. ". . . an' horehound candy. All right, who else?"

It didn't take all that much to line up a crew, as it turned out. There was plenty of good drovers temporarily unemployed about then, and just a passel of curiosity to see what Bobby Lee Smith might do next in the furtherance of his lucky streak. Shad Ames would have cut it off at a dozen hands, that being plenty to move five hundred head of cows a few hundred miles, but there were still takers lined up, and when he thought about No Man's Land, he taken the notion that a few more guns wouldn't hurt.

Altogether, the Bobby Lee Smith herd—yet to be assembled—had itself eighteen nursemaids lined up and signed on before the sun went down that night. Eighteen names—counting Shad and Bobby Lee—and a righteous good list of social requirements ranging from .32 rimfire to .45 Peacemaker rounds, from .32-20 to .45-70 to horehound candy and Bull Durham and Cuba Twist chaws. That, and a list of supplies and provisions that made Shad frown harder every time he looked at it because—somehow—it was him who was financing all this, and he just couldn't hang a rope on how that had come to pass.

Fact was, though, the men with their marks on the trail crew roster for the Smith herd—all things considered—were about as good a trail crew as a man could want. Not a man among them hadn't done his

43

share of chousing, and most would have been top hands on anybody's outfit. All except maybe Wesley Watkins, they were men fit to cross rivers with, and nobody taken exception to having Wesley Watkins along because there wasn't a better trail cook that side of Waco.

Joe Dell McGuire, no matter how a man might have judged him otherwise, was a top-notch wrangler, and Slim Hanks not much less. Willie Sutter was a top hand in any outfit, and had the advantage of having trailed with Shad Ames before, so he knew the ramrod's ways. And old Willie was greased lightning with a Colt .45. Jimbo Riley and Clinton Sears were both fine drovers with first-hand knowledge of the sheer cussedness of cows. Pappy Jameson had trailed all the way to Wyoming in his time, and knew the trails like he knew the knots on his knuckles. Sam Nabors and Shorty Mars were first-rate chousers with a knack for drag. Bo Sayers, L.W. Bottoms (most folks called him Rock) and Christy Walker were backwoods boys from the Piney Woods, but long enough out of East Texas to have got some civilization about them. John Jay Hastings wasn't even a Texan by rights, but wherever he was from—he never seemed to say—he could move cows with the next man.

The Burnett brothers—Jason and Joe Pete—were noticeable by their size and by the scars on their wrists and ankles. Shackle marks, most folks figured, though it would have been impolite to mention it. But whatever their background, they had been handy on many a drive. And Mouse Moore—well, what does a body say about Mouse Moore? You just had to know him.

By and large, as good a crew as any trailboss could want. And there was something else about them, that gave Shad Ames a sight of comfort, considering. Pound for pound, knuckle or gun, they were probably the toughest one bunch of yahoos ever to plant their backsides on saddle leather and aim for the railhead markets.

Nobody in his right mind, folks figured, would push a prime herd into No Man's Land with less than an army behind him. But 'til an army came along, the bunch that gathered in front of the Shades of Paradise that Sunday afternoon, ready to head on out to Aces Over, was a bunch that a man would sure enough rather have on his own side than on the other one.

Aces Over—Shad Ames' spread out west of Abilene—was on what they called the Sweetwater Gap. The gap is a rimmed valley that funnels up from the south, making a natural trail that gets narrower as it approaches the Clear Fork of the Brazos. The thing about having his place sprawled across the gap like it was, was that Shad Ames always had a lot of cows. Some of them were his, but a lot more were volunteers that carried the brands and jinglebobs of every spread from Lardeo to Brownsville, and from Big Spring to Beaumont, not to mention a nice assortment of Mexican brands, to boot.

Because of being on the gap, Aces Over was just a sort of catchall for every mosshorn and stray that got spilled from any herd pushing up from the coast spreads or the Rio Grande Valley. Anybody chousing critters up from down there—and moving fast like a lot of them did since the cows they were trailing might not rightly belong to them—tended to lose a sight of stock along the way. And a rustled herd northbound along there—naturally swinging far enough east to avoid the sheep-shearers and goat-ropers that had taken over the Concho ranges—generally wound up in the gap.

So Shad always had cows. He just couldn't help having cows, where he was located. But most of them weren't legal cows.

Shad generally did the honorable thing about that. Every year or two, he'd buy an advertisement in the *Abilene Gazette* or the *Big Spring Times*, to let it be known by one and all that he had extra cows on his land, and their owners were welcome to come and get them.

Hardly anybody ever did, though. So Shad would sell off some of the steers from time to time—just local sales, of course. And he took the calves that his visiting cows dropped, and put his own brand on them as fair exchange for storage of their mothers. In that way, Shad managed to keep a fair herd of legal-resident critters on his best graze, and it was these that Bobby Lee Smith was going after, to pick out his five hundred head.

Most everybody was in town and ready to go, when Bobby Lee hauled up in Doc Holt's old buckboard and turned the reins over to Jubal Joy, Doc's hired man. Bobby Lee had been out saying his goodbyes to Doc and Nanny, telling them how they needn't worry and take on, because he was on a lucky streak and everything was going to be just fine. Now he climbed down from the buckboard, lifted his bedroll and trap out of the back, and touched his hat—a brand-new Stetson—to old Jubal. "Look after 'em," he said. "Tell Nanny I'll write."

"Yes, suh," Jubal nodded, watching as Bobby Lee turned away and headed for Jack Priddy's barn to get Tarnation. "My," the old man told Pappy Jameson, "don't the boy look fine, a 'headin' out to get hisself rich an' all."

Pappy had to admit that Bobby Lee did look like a young man with great things in his future. He was wearing his best boots, and a new flannel shirt that Nanny had made for him, and his new hat—a present from Doc—didn't have so much as a speck of dust on it. He was wearing his shell-belt rig with a Colt Peacemaker riding comfortable in oiled leather, and he walked like a man with things going his way.

He disappeared into Priddy's, and came out a few minutes later leading that big, handsome blaze-face

46

sorrel, all saddled and packed and ready to put miles behind him.

He looked at the trail crew assembled there, counting noses—Bobby Lee Smith was a natural-born counter, and he counted everything. It was just his way.

"Everybody ready?" he asked. "Where's Shad?"

"He went on ahead with the trail supplies," Willie Sutter nodded. "He'll meet us out at his spread." He pulled a branding iron from his saddlebag and held it out. "Milo Hastings sent this in, Bobby Lee. Had his smith make it up special for your trail herd."

Bobby Lee looked at the brand. Its face and a half circle over a half circle, or like a letter "C" with another "C" reversed below it. "Mighty nice, Willie. Thoughty of ol' Milo. What's he call it?"

"Busted S. Said it's in honor of how you got yourself that horse."

"Busted S. Right nice ring to it." Bobby Lee handed back the iron and turned full around, taking a last look at Abilene. Then he put his foot in his stirrup and said, "All right, then. Let's get goin'."

He swung aboard, took his reins and raised his hat. "Far places, here we . . ."

Tarnation coiled himself like a rattler, haunches bunched tight, and went straight up into the air, and when he came down Bobby Lee was still up there, saying, ". . . come! Oh, for God's sake, horse . . . !"

He lit alongside Tarnation, sprawled flat-out in the street, and that horse just stepped daintily aside and looked down at him for all the world like it was saying, "Well, hello, there. Glad you could drop by."

There was murder in Bobby Lee's eyes when he got up, dusted himself off, retrieved his new hat from Alf Tide's horse trough, and climbed aboard again, tight-kneed this time, and short-reined. Tarnation immediately went into a tailspin, and Bobby Lee clung like a leech, even getting the horse pointed the right direction before it took off in a series of bone-jarring, stiff-leg

47

jumps down the street.

The rest of them watched in silence, then touched heels and followed along.

"Right spirited way to start off on a cow drive," Willie Sutter allowed. Then, "Woops! Yonder he goes!"

Ahead of them, Tarnation had quit bucking, got the bit in his teeth and taken off at a belly-down run on the outbound road. As one, the cowhands in the crew dug spurs in their mounts and set out in pursuit.

The thunder of departing hooves faded along the street, and dust settled in the sunset glow.

Old Jubal Joy still sat in the buckboard, out in front of the Shades of Paradise, his eyes bugged out and his mouth hanging open.

In the crowd along the walk, people stared into the distance where the Busted S crew had gone, and somebody said, "In a powerful hurry, ain't they? Where they off to?"

"That's Bobby Lee Smith's trail crew," somebody else explained. "They're gonna cut theirselves a herd out at Aces Over, an' drive it to the Chicago, Rock Island and Pacific railhead. That's up yonder about Kansas."

"What are they aimin' to do? Make it there an' back by Thursday?"

VI

There sure enough were some plans afoot, in that spring of 1890. There was the Chicago, Rock Island and Pacific Railroad, punching tracks on past a brand-new town called Liberal, going from there right on over into the Neutral Strip. Then there was Bobby Lee Smith, planning to take a herd of cows up into the Neutral Strip because the *New York Times* said there would be a railhead there, and Bobby Lee Smith was on a lucky streak.

There was the United States Census Office in Washington, D.C., planning to conduct a Decennial Census of Population and Social Characteristics of 1890, because the Congress of the United States wanted to know how many constituents it had to answer to and where they might best be avoided. There was George Scrannon and his Cimarron Proposal bunch, planning to get rich as robbers over the proposition that No Man's Land wasn't really No Man's Land, by making nobody's land everybody's land and putting the profits in their pockets.

There was old Shad Ames, planning to recover his investment in the Busted S cattle venture if he could, and to piss on the state of Kansas while he was about it. There was Jason Finch up in Kansas City, planning to get back Aunt Claudine's money that his sister Annie

49

Sue had somehow got away with.

Then there were Pete Thayer and Slap Jackson and their bunch—Texas boys gone sour and not inclined to come back to Texas because it was an unhealthy climate for them. So they were holed up on the Beaver River in the Neutral Strip, planning to get back to work at their chosen profession—stealing cows—just as soon as opportunity presented itself.

And there was a young hellion with a wild bunch of his own, who had his own notions about going into business. His name was Bart Sherrell, and he was a Kansan by birth. He had seen himself a vision, about how all those folks down in No Man's Land—none of whom existed according to some folk back East—had need of a stage line to ride around on. Bart was an enterprising young'un, and he was planning to see to that need, just as soon as he could make it out of Kansas with a big, new Concord coach that didn't rightly belong to him—but then, over in No Man's Land, it was rarely clear just what belonged to whom.

And on top of everything else, there were two traveling ladies with a plan of their own.

The plan had been, back in Kansas City, that Annie Sue Finch and Milicent Moriarty would purchase a wagon and suitable animal at Dodge City for the seventy-mile-or-so trip to the Cimarron Proposal. But like most plans made at one end of Kansas, it required considerable alteration to work out at the other end.

Anybody familiar with western Kansas could have told Annie Sue about that. It was the way Kansas was, and the main reason why western Kansans generally tended to ignore eastern Kansans—especially those serving in the state legislature at Topeka. Notions that seemed just fine east of the flint hills hardly ever made any sense at all west of Pratt.

Annie Sue and Milicent couldn't buy, beg, borrow or steal a wheeled contrivance anywhere around Dodge City. The reason was, there weren't any to spare. Every wagon, cart of carriage within a hundred miles—that wasn't in use or tied down—had been bought up by folks down in Seward County and Stevens County because they were moving towns around down yonder.

Word had it that Arkalon was already gone—every house, barn and privvy, everything but the three brick buildings that nobody could figure how to haul. Where Arkalon had been was nothing much more now than a ghost town, and not much of a one of those. Arkalon had moved to Liberal, which was where the Chicago, Rock Island and Pacific Railroad was heading.

The same went for Springfield and Fargo Springs, they said. Folks were tearing down, loading up and hauling out just as fast as they could, all wanting to get choice town lots in Liberal before the prices went up. That was how things went out in the high plains. Before the railroads had headed that way, there weren't all that many folks out there. But by the time the rails hit the flint hills in mid-state, the western Kansas lands were just full of folks establishing claims and building towns here and yonder—just anywhere that somebody was sure was where the tracks would go.

Now that everybody *knew* where the tracks were going, everybody and his cousin was just itching to be there to meet them.

It was one reason why Thomas Allen Fry had been sent out there from Topeka. The United States Census Office was fixing to count folks in all those little towns, and word kept coming back that some of those towns that everybody thought were there—that *had been* there the last time anybody looked—weren't there any more. And all the folks who were supposed to be in those towns were in some other town instead.

It made for an itchy situation for the Census Office, looking at congressional orders on the one hand and limited budgets on the other. A sight of manpower could go to waste, sending out enumerators to count noses if they didn't have some notion of where the

51

noses were that they were supposed to count. So Thomas Allen Fry had been sent out, to do a preliminary survey and see to the making of a plan.

He had ridden on the Atchison, Topeka and Santa Fe Railroad to Topeka, thinking he could work it all out from there—that being the state capital and all. But all he had learned in Topeka was that nobody knew whether Arkalon and Springfield and those other places were still there or not, and since they had already sent the army out yonder twice in the past year to resolve county seat disputes, they didn't have any interest in going to look.

So Thomas Allen Fry got back on the train, and went on west. Whether anybody in Topeka knew anything about Kansas or not, he had a job to do, and he intended to get it done. And somewhere along the way, a telegraph message from Washington, D.C. caught up with him.

Since he was going out there anyway, they had one more little chore for him. He was to perform a pre-census analysis of that area south of western Kansas—an area nobody was quite sure how to identify, since it was called everything from the Neutral Strip to No Man's Land to the Cimarron Proposal. At any rate, the Census Office had it on good authority that there were folks there, too, even though the Department of the Interior hotly denied it.

The Neutral Strip was uninhabited, legally, Interior said, so that meant there weren't any legal persons there.

The Congressional Order for the 1890 Census, however, didn't differentiate between legal persons and illegal persons. It just ordered the Census Office to employ enumerators to go where there were persons, and count those persons. Fry was to set out a system for counting noses there, too.

Arriving at Dodge City, though, he had the same problem that Annie Sue Finch had—how to get from Dodge City on down to the areas of confusion.

And that was when Bart Sherrell showed up, with a solution to the problem.

Thomas Allen Fry, Annie Sue Finch, Milicent Moriarty and several other weary travelers were just coming out of the Scofield and Landrum Feed and Wagon Barn—which had no wheeled conveyances to offer—when Bart Sherrell pulled up at the reins of a red and yellow Concord stagecoach. Two other fellows hurried around from the pasture out back with a change of team and several saddled horses.

"You taken your time, Bart," the biggest one—a man with two guns—snapped at him. "We been here since morning."

"Couldn't be helped," the driver said, hauling in, glancing around and then tipping his dusty hat at the pretty little blonde thing skittering back out of the way. Maybe he tipped his hat to the others there, too, but if he did it was an afterthought.

One of the men began switching out horses while the other—the big one—stepped over close to the Concord and raised his hand to hide a hoarse whisper, "I heard these folks askin' about transportation south, Bart. What do you think?"

Bart looked at the huddle of people beside the barn. Besides the pretty little blonde, there was a big, strong-looking woman, a portly gent in Eastern clothes, and three other men who might be drummers or boomers. There wasn't a one of them that looked like law.

"Little chancy, Mike," he whispered back, then looked at the pretty little blonde again and shrugged. He raised his voice. "My friend here tells me you folks are looking for transportation to the south, is that right?"

"That is correct," the blonde woman said. "Will you sell me your wagon?"

"Sell . . ." Bart stared at her, then grinned. "Darlin', this here is a Concord stagecoach built by Abbott, Downing and Company. It is the finest of its kind, and

53

it surely is not a 'wagon'."

"Whatever," she said. "How much do you want for it?"

"I'd like to submit a bid as well," the Easterner put in. "For some reasonable amount, of course."

"We was thinkin' more about a jump-seat buggy than a coach," one of the drummers said, "but we'd consider a fair price."

"Now, just hold on," Bart raised a hand to hush them. "This here Concord coach is fixin' to be my stock in trade, just as soon as we get it to where folks won't hang us for . . . but never mind about that. It isn't for sale, but I might consider taking passengers for a price."

"To where?" the little blonde asked, pointedly.

"Well, we're headed for the Neutral Strip, but I don't expect any of you good folks would want to go there, even if I was fool enough to take you . . ."

"My companion and I are en route to the Cimarron Proposal," the little blonde dumpling said.

Bart scratched his head. "I don't think I ever heard of that," he admitted. "But if you want a ride, we'll go by way of that new town, Liberal. That do?"

"Admirably," the Easterner nodded. "How much?"

Bart thought it over. "Twenty dollars apiece?"

"Not on your life!" the big, sturdy woman snapped. "That is outrageous. Try again."

"Ten?"

"Eight," the Easterner offered. "That's ten cents a mile. That's fair."

Bart shrugged. He had been wondering what kind of prices to charge, when he and the boys got into the stagecoach business. "Eight dollars apiece," he agreed. "Cash money."

"I shall need a receipt," the Easterner said. "For reimbursement by my office. Ah . . . what stage line is this?"

Bart frowned down at him. "Do you want to ask

questions, or ride?"

"Ride," the Easterner subsided.

With what seemed undue haste, the coach's team was changed, baggage thrown into the boot and the passengers were herded aboard along with the two rough-dressed men who seemed to be associated with the driver. Within minutes the tall coach was bouncing out of Dodge City, heading south.

"My name is Thomas Allen Fry," the portly passenger said. "It seems we all had need of the same transportation."

"David Jones," a drummer nodded. "These others are Lew Haley and Winston Overman. Winston's in ladies' ready-to-wear. Lew and me are in farm implements."

The other two men—the ones associated with the driver and the riders outside—looked away disinterestedly without introducing themselves.

After a moment, Annie Sue said, "My name is Annie Sue Finch. This is Milicent Moriarty."

All of the men tipped their hats, even the two who had not introduced themselves. "Ladies," some of them said.

The coach bounded out of a rut, and swayed like a living thing. "Mercy!" Milicent said. "It seems to me a bit strange, that a man who has invested in the price of a coach like this would treat it so roughly."

One of the unnamed men glanced across at her, and grinned. "You mean Bart, up there? He doesn't own it, ma'am. Not rightly, anyhow, though once past that Kansas line it won't matter."

"What do you mean by that?" Annie Sue frowned. "Who does own this vehicle, then?"

"The Grafton Overland Stage Company, ma'am. Out of Omaha, Nebraska. 'Leastways, they did own it before ol' Bart stole it from them just this side of Winburn. Said he would, an' sure enough, he did."

Annie Sue blinked at the man. "He stole it? Do you

55

mean to say that we are riding in an illegally acquired conveyance?"

"You might say that," the man nodded.

"I bet you couldn't say it, Sill," the big one—someone had called him Mike—grinned. To Annie Sue, he said, "Don't fret yourself about it, ma'am. This stagecoach is as secure as if it was legal, and you folks bein' our first passengers, we aim to take good care of you. Word of mouth is important to a new business enterprise."

"Word of mouth?" Milicent frowned.

"Yes, ma'am. We'd be obliged if you all would let folks know that the Beaver City Express is a good and reliable stage line. After you've satisfied yourselves about that, of course."

"Beaver City Express," Thomas Fry noted. "That's the name of your company, then?"

"We might call it that. How's it sound to you, Sill? I just made it up."

"Good as any," Sill nodded.

"Then since your enterprise has a name," the Easterner said, "you can give me a receipt for my eight dollars when we reach our destination. Fascinating," he added. "Stagecoach robbers running a stage line."

"We ain't no such a thing!" Sill snapped. "Ol' Bart, he wouldn't ever stand for robbin' stagecoaches. It's against his principles."

"But I understood that you gentlemen, or at least the one driving . . ."

"We *stole* this coach," Mile explained. "We didn't *rob* it. There's a difference."

"I suppose highway robbery would be a better choice of words," Annie Sue reasoned. "Ah, do you gentlemen steal all of your coaches?"

"We don't know yet," Sill told her, seriously. "This is our first one."

"Remarkable," Fry said.

"Yes, sir, it was Bart Sherrell's idea. His notion was,

we get ourselves a coach and go into business, and keep good books so as soon as we've made enough money we can pay back the outfit we stole the coach from. You can't get any fairer than that."

"But you plan to expand?"

"Oh, sure. If all this works out, we'll prob'ly steal us some more coaches and maybe set up runs all over No Man's Land. There's maybe two-three thousand folks yonder that could use regular transportation now and again. Bart thinks big, where business is concerned. You can count on it."

"Oh, I intend to do just that," the Easterner said.

A shadow appeared at the offside window, and Bart Sherrell leaned down from above, grinning upside-down at Annie Sue. "Surely glad to have you aboard, ma'am," he said. "Are you comfortable?"

Milicent grabbed a strap as the racing coach lurched and bounded across a wind-swept dune. "My goodness! Who is driving this thing?"

"I'll get back to that in a minute, ma'am," Bart said at the window. "I was just thinkin', though, I got a whole seat all to myself up here, an' you folks all crowded up in there . . ."

"You want one of us to ride shotgun, Bart?" Mike asked.

"Never you mind." Again Bart grinned at Annie Sue. "Be my pleasure to have you join me topside, miss. Real nice view from up yonder."

Annie Sue glanced at Milicent, then shrugged. "I don't suppose there would be any harm in . . ."

"Good!" Bart leaned further down the side of the bouncing coach, swung the offside door open, reached across the ladies' ready-to-wear drummer and took a firm grasp on Annie Sue's arm. "Up we go," he said.

Annie Sue gasped as he lifted her bodily out of the coach, swinging her toward the high seat on the front. "I thought you might stop," she complained as she clambered into the seat.

"No need for that, missy," Bart Sherrell clambered down beside her onto the right-hand side of the bench, and took up the reins that he had left tied off at the toe bar. Ahead of them six horses pounded happily along, unaware that they had ever been left unattended. "Thing about a stagecoach is time. Shame to waste it."

Inside, Mike glanced across at Sill and sighed. "I just knew he was gonna do that," he said. He turned, noticed the pale, pinched expression on Milicent's face, and assured her, "The missy will be all right up yonder, ma'am. Ol' Bart, he ain't got a mean bone in his body. It's just that he does so enjoy the company of nice-lookin' young ladies."

VII

It takes just a sight of work to cut out a trail herd from range stock. Even in the Gap, where Aces Over was, there is considerable chousing involved in pushing all those critters out of the thornies where cows prefer to congregate, gathering the herd down on the grass flats, then sorting them out, selecting which ones are fit to trail, and putting a road brand on each critter so honored.

All that requires a mess of tough, sweaty work. It would, even if the cows cooperated—which cows just naturally don't—and even if you haven't got Shad Ames on one side trying like blazes to cull out the poorest stock and Bobby Lee Smith on the other accepting no less than the best of the batch. And on top of everything else, there was this ongoing hollering match between them as to just how many head of livestock there was supposed to be.

As Shad Ames recollected the deal, he was to provide "more or less five hundred head." Bobby Lee's recollection was that it was to be "at least five hundred head." The difference between "more or less," and "at least," comes to about two hundred head. They finally agreed to resolve that difference by settling on *exactly* five hundred critters, and that meant a precise head-count at every branding fire, with at least half the men there keeping tally strings, and considerable time out for debates as to which side of the knot somebody had his thumb on when that last brand was slapped.

But Shad could have set his mind to rest, if he had thought about it. He knew Bobby Lee Smith, just like everybody else did. When Bobby Lee Smith set his mind on something, and got that tight-jawed look to his face—like a hound dog with a mouth full of rattlesnake and no time for learned argument—then that was how it was going to be.

When it was done, finally, the Busted S brand was sizzling on the rumps of five hundred bawling steers. Not five hundred and one, nor four hundred and ninety-nine. Five hundred. Bobby Lee had counted them personally.

And on Tuesday morning, Busted S hit the trail northward from the Gap—five hundred exact cow-critters, eighteen men, a cook-wagon with a trailer, and a remuda of fifty-five horses counting Wesley Watkins' draft animals. Shad and Bobby Lee had come to another famous agreement about the remuda. Shad had lined up forty or so cowponies, and Bobby Lee said they'd be fools to take less than fifty-four, which was three horses per man—counting two and a spare for the cook's wagon. They settled on exactly fifty-four horses. Not fifty-five, nor fifty-three. Fifty-four.

Then Bobby Lee sprung it that the remuda count didn't include Tarnation, because Tarnation was Bobby Lee's personal horse and no part of the contract they had shook on.

Old Shad, he was near fit to be tied, just on general principles, but there wasn't much he could do about it. When it came to stubborn, Bobby Lee Smith would beat any mule hands down, and about all a man could do about that was just go along with it because that was just how it was.

Many's the time Pappy Jameson said just that, and sometimes it was so profound an observation that he "amened" it as quick as he got it out.

At any rate, it was sunup of a Tuesday when Busted S hit the trail the first time, and for a rangy and un-trail-broke herd, those cows minded their manners right well.

For about a mile.

It didn't come as any great surprise, though, when the herd came unglued about the time the drags had got past the Gap and on the open slopes leading down toward the Brazos bottoms. Every man in Bobby Lee's crew had pushed cows, and every one of them knew what was coming. They just never knew when.

They say things about cows having a herd instinct, and how their natural inclinations that way make them driveable. Not cowboys, though. Cowboys don't say fool things like that. But folks back East, who maybe were out in God's country once upon a time and maybe saw a trail herd ambling along in fair order under a blue prairie sky, and were likely a safe distance upwind when they saw the sight, those folks might tend to remark on what a right satisfying sight that is—all those amiable cattle just plodding right along on their way to that great cow heaven where they will meet their maker for the ultimate good of all concerned.

Most likely, those folks who have seen such a vision of bovine splendor were sitting in a railroad dining car at the time, sipping their tea and waxing nostalgic about anything they didn't understand. Most likely, the ones that went back East and wrote poems about the heady glamour—poets are like Englishmen, if they're not sure of a spelling they throw in an extra letter or two—of the trail had never so much as traded howdies with any cowboy, for they would have been set straight on several points if they had.

Any cowboy knows that nostalgia is a thing of the past.

For example, if you see a well-behaved herd of cows on the trail, you can bet it is one of two situations.

61

Either it is a fresh herd just off the bed-ground and with its tails to water—in which case those critters might go an hour or so without making serious trouble—or it is a herd that has already expended all of its cussedness earlier in the day and is just resting up for the next breakout, spill, turn-back, mill, mass balk or stampede.

It's how cows are, and those Eastern poets that heap praise upon the bovine persuasion just generally seem to miss that point. "A trail-broke herd," they say, as though that meant easy to manage. There is no more such a thing as an easy-to-manage herd of cows than there is horns on a jackrabbit. Trail-broke means a herd that has learned to string itself out in a long line, with leaders in front and drags behind. A trail-broke herd is a herd that moves in line and generally all the same direction—at least as long as the cowboys can hold the cows' attention. An *unbroke* herd is something like a convention of Texas Democrats. Left to their own devices, there isn't a chance in the world that all those cows will take the notion to go the same direction at the same time.

On that Tuesday morning, in March of 1890, it was an unbroke herd that moseyed down toward the flats, and the Busted S crew had just begun to narrow it down. Willie Sutter was out ahead on point, three or four others were at the rear, pushing the drags, and everybody else was strung out along both sides to work swing and flank.

Things were just starting to shape out when a big old moss-horn near the head of the pack decided he had traveled as far as he aimed to go. He bawled, swung his head, rolled his eyes and stopped dead still, making those behind him pile up and swing aside to pass. When they were flowing past him, that steer turned around and headed back the way he had come.

Naturally, when those other critters all around him saw him going the other way, a lot of them decided that was the thing to do, and swung in to follow him. Within seconds, the whole herd looked like a formation of recruits on a parade ground, trying to execute a left-and-right-about. The cows on the outsides of the herd were still mostly going north, but those in the middle were going south, and every critter in between was deeply involved in the sort of decision-making process that only a cow can get the hang of.

Out on point, Willie Sutter saw it begin, and made himself a mental note to recollect that particular steer—the one that started it. The swing riders saw it next, and from each side it looked like a mill, so they swung their ponies around and headed into the herd to cut it off. The flank riders took their signal from the swings, and eased off from the herd to give them room so the mill-cutters wouldn't get packed and gored.

If it had been a regular mill, seven times out of ten that strategy would have stopped it. But a double mill to center, combined with a turnback, was something else. The swing riders from both sides met in the middle, with half the herd moving southward ahead of them and the other half spilling out both ways as the flanks eased back. The riders bringing up drag, just moseying along looking at cow rumps in the dust, suddenly found themselves face to face with an oncoming southbound herd led by a determined blue-brindle steer.

As the drag riders saw the cows, the cows saw them, and veered off both ways, taking a lot of the previously-uncommitted herd with them.

It was all over in a minute to two. Where there had been a herd of cows moving north, now there were several dozen little clumps of critters ambling off toward every point of the compass, and nobody to watch them go but the riders of Busted S, all grouped where their cows had been.

Willie Sutter came back at a trot and reined in raising his hat to scratch his head. "I believe I've found us a lead critter," he allowed. "Now all we need is a herd."

Bobby Lee shot a suspicious look across at Shad Ames. "You wouldn't have been educatin' them cows, would you, Mr. Ames?"

Shad just glared around in disgust. "Nobody educates cows," he pointed out. Then he sighed and spurred his mount. "All right," he said. "Let's start over."

The sun was standing high over the Brazos bottoms when they got their herd assembled again, with Willie Sutter paying personal attention to that brindle moss-horn. Then there was some more delay, because Bobby Lee Smith wanted to be sure they hadn't lost any. While sixteen riders held the bunch as still as cows can be held, he rode back and forth, through and through, muttering to himself, thumbing his tally-string and making scratches on his saddlehorn with his barlow knife.

"Five hundred, exactly," he said, when he finally had that done. "We can move on now. We still got some miles to make today."

"Yeah," Shad Ames muttered. "'Bout three, if we're lucky." He raised his hat, waved it and Willie Sutter, yonder at point, shouldered his mount toward his brindle steer and said, "Get to movin', Blue. You've just been elected president of this herd."

Wesley Watkins had watched the entire proceeding from his wagon rig, on a rise some ways from the herd. When he saw them moving again, he looked at the sun, looked out across the bottoms ahead where the Clear Fork of the Brazos meandered between downslopes on this side and upslopes on that, and slapped leather to his tandem team. Wesley had cooked for many a drive, and when the Busted S herd was bedded that evening—well within sight of where they had started that morning—the crew would find him right there with supper on the fire.

They would have the Clear Fork behind them then, and be on their way. As he drove northward, Wesley chanted to himself, "Clear Fork of the Brazos, just ahead. Double Mountain Fork is the next river bed. Rocky-bottom Salt Fork somewhere yonder, then across two Wichitas we got to wander. Pease River's next, then if we ain't dead, we'll cross the Prairie Dog Town Fork of the Red. Then the Salt Fork, an' North Fork, an' Clearwater's fall, but 'til you see the Canadian, boys, you ain't seen rivers at all."

It was the drover's litany of the Tuttle Trail—that beef route that skirted just east of the high canyon lands, up between the Llano Estacado and the Oklahoma Territory. Oklahoma Territory was what they had named the Cheyenne-Arapahoe leased lands and the Cherokee Strip, so folks wouldn't get it fussed up with the Indian Nations over east. Back yonder in Washington D.C., that made some kind of sense. About the same way the Neutral Strip made sense. If it wasn't for the Neutral Strip, there would be this big hole in the world.

Right. And nobody lived there, either.

Wesley's litany stopped short of where Busted S aimed to go, because the Tuttle Trail only went as far as Fort Supply over in the Territories. If Bobby Lee Smith had his way—and he generally did—the Busted S would be off on its own by then, pushing northward, aiming for parts where—in Wesley's opinion—only damn fools and outlaws would go.

Just fixing to fall into this big hole in the world.

"Canadian River," Wesley muttered, calling on his knowledge of the geography of the Southwest Rangers to try to extend the chant. "Wolf Creek an' the Kiowa, then No Man's Land. Outlaws and owlhoots and Beaver River sand." He brightened and grinned as words came to him. "Then yonder's the Cimarron, if we live to see it. For if God wants a bunch of goddamn fools, then by God this bunch'll be it."

Old Wesley might have sounded a little bit like Pappy Jameson then, when he took himself a deep breath and added. "Amen."

Two hundred and sixty miles of Texas lay ahead, and beyond that thirty-five miles of No Man's Land. If everything went just right—and Wesley had never seen a cattle drive where everything went just right—they might make it in a month or so.

Out on long point, Willie Sutter was working with his blue brindle steer, teaching it the fine points of leading a herd. Astraddle of one of the best cowponies in the remuda, he was using the time-honored method of educating a leader. Wear it out, run it ragged, frustrate it at every turn and show it beyond all doubt that there aren't any real choices in this world but one: either do what somebody bigger and smarter wants you to do, or don't and wish you had.

"You are the chosen critter, Blue," he explained as the steer tried to break to the left and found a cowpony there with a man atop it. The steer pawed ground, swung around and tried to bolt to the right, but there, somehow, was that same cowpony with the same man aboard.

"Just think of the honor of it all," Willie explained, clinging to his saddle as the cowpony danced here and there, out-thinking the steer like any good cowpony learns to do. "Out of all them cows back yonder, you alone have distinguished yourself with a display of sheer cussedness that has marked you as a critter among critters. You ought to feel humble an' a mite proud on that score."

The steer balked, swapped ends and tried to bolt back toward the herd. For an instant it seemed that the path was open, then there was the man and pony, looming over its right shoulder, crowding in. It veered, veered again and was going the way it had been going before it tried to turn back. It lowered its head, dipped a horn and tried to gore the horse, but met only air. The

66

pony had danced away, just out of reach. The steer bawled, went red-eyed and charged . . . and found no target ahead, only a crowding, irritating presence alongside, forcing it into its assigned direction.

"Just imagine," Willie told the steer. "If there's a hall of fame for cow critters somewhere past that great divide, why, Blue, you have done qualified for consideration, just by bein' chose as lead steer. Now all you got to do to get initiated is to aim ever' bit of cussedness you got in the direction I want you to go, and just keep on a'goin'."

By the time the leads came up to them, Willie had Blue about as near tame as any range critter could be. They had themselves an understanding, you might say. If ever that blue steer got the slightest chance to kill Willie Sutter—like catching him afoot or something— then he sure would give it his best shot. But until that happened, Blue would do what Willie wanted him to do.

Busted S bedded that night on good graze a mile north of the bottoms, and Bobby Lee Smith told Shad Ames, "I believe I'll ask eight dollars a head for these cows, when we get to railhead."

"Eight dollars?" Shad frowned over his plate of beans. "What kind of damn fool would pay eight dollars a head these days? You're crazy as a loon, Bobby Lee."

"Oh, I don't expect to *get* eight dollars a head," Bobby Lee shrugged. "I aim to settle for six an' a half. But I'll dicker with 'em about it. I figure with my half of three thousand, two hundred and fifty dollars . . ."

"How much?"

That's five hundred cows at six and a half a head. I figure with my share, I can . . ."

"Assumin' we get there with five hundred head . . ." Shad cut in.

"Which I aim for us to," Bobby Lee pointed out.

"Even assumin' that, you don't get half of the sale

price. What you get is half of the net."

Bobby Lee frowned around at him. "What net?"

"The net profit. That's what's left after expenses. You only get half of that."

"I know that, Shad," Bobby Lee got one of those looks of his, like a hound dog trying to gnaw a bridge spike. "All I'm sayin' is, my share will be enough to buy me a right nice piece of land, the way I figure it. Maybe a section." He got one of those other looks on his face, like he had just set his mind to something. "Yeah. At least a section . . . to start."

"A *section?* A whole section of land? For what you'll make on this drive—assumin' you make anything? Not around here, you won't."

"It don't have to be around here," Bobby Lee shrugged. "I don't intend to settle for less than a section of land, but I'm willin' to buy wherever I can get a good deal."

VIII

When enough coincidences commence to coincide, common consensus calls it fate, and that was what was shaping up back in the spring of '90. Coincidences, pure and simple, but a mighty lot of them, and a fateful lot of them commencing to point right at that piece of ground that most folks called No Man's Land.

It was plain coincidence that Bart Sherrell and his friends had decided to go into the stagecoach business without a monetary investment in rolling stock, and coincidence that there was one place where a thing like that might be pulled off. No Man's Land. It was coincidence that Annie Sue Finch had invested Aunt Claudine's leavings in a section of land in something called the Cimarron Proposal, and coincidence that the gentlemen she bought the section from was in the employ of the very man who had dreamed up the whole Cimarron Proposal notion—George Scrannon, of Beaver City, in No Man's Land.

Coincidence upon coincidence, the section that Annie Sue bought from Col. Chadwick Booth-Sykes was at a particular location a ways west of Beaver City, right where Jackson Creek trickles into the Beaver

River. It was one of the reasons why Annie Sue picked out that section on the colonel's plat map. With two lovely valleys converging there—the colonel assured her that they were both lovely—it should make for a good spread and a fine investment. The thing was, that Jackson Creek section was the very same one that George Scrannon had decided he would keep for himself, to headquarter the cattle operation he was planning.

It was coincidence that Thomas Fry was out that way at the time, fixing to commence the counting of noses for the United States Census Office, and it was sheer coincidence that Annie Sue Finch and Thomas Fry were passengers on Bart Sherrell's stolen stagecoach for its first paying run, from Dodge City, Kansas, to the new town of Liberal, Kansas, which was just exactly three miles from the north edge of No Man's Land.

Bart Sherrell might have carried them right on down to Beaver City, if they had wanted him to. A few hours on the driver's seat with Annie Sue, seeing how the wind blew her blonde hair and how the sunlight stroked her pretty cheeks, and Bart Sherrell would have walked off the south face of Black Mesa if she had wanted him to. Annie Sue had her head set on buying a wagon and team at Liberal, so the subject of going on to Beaver City just never came up.

It was coincidence that Bobby Lee Smith and the Busted S outfit were headed north from Abilene, Texas, with five hundred head of legal cows, bound for No Man's Land, at the same time that George Scrannon was hanging out a sign on a building in Beaver City—a sign that read: *Scrannon Land and Cattle Company, G. Scrannon Prop.* And it was coincidence that the old boys George Scrannon had contracted with, to provide him some cattle for the cattle end of his land and cattle company, were none

70

other than Pete Thayer and Slap Jackson, who had learned their trade around Abilene, Texas. Their trade—at least before things got too hot for them in Texas—was rustling herds of cattle along the Tuttle Trail.

They had been laying over in No Man's Land for a spell, waiting for things to cool off, and when George Scrannon said he would pay a price for cows, they figured maybe it was time to go back to work.

Thayer's plan was to round up a few good hands with outlaw experience—there wasn't any shortage of those around Beaver City those days—and mosey on down to Texas, as quiet as possible, to see what might be heading up to Fort Supply.

"Best thing to do," he told Jackson, "is spot us a herd, and cut it right yonder at Wolf Creek, where the trail crosses over into the Cherokee Strip. That way, if the federals over in the Territory get wind of us, we can scat back into Texas, and if the Rangers get wind of us, we can slip over into the Territory."

Slap was in a cantankerous mood, as usual, so he asked, "What happens if both of 'em get wind of us at the same time?"

"That," Thayer allowed, "is about as likely as gills on a goat. But either way, we won't be all that far from No Man's Land. We ought to be able to cut us a good herd and slip back here with it before anybody even knows what happened."

"Seems reasonable," Slap conceded. "'Less we happen onto some tough trail bunch like in the old days."

"Nothin' in life is certain, Slap," Thayer admitted. "But it ain't likely. Things has settled down a good bit, I hear. Trail crews nowadays ain't what they used to be. I don't reckon we'll have that much trouble."

Coincidence, that's all it was, that when Pete Thayer and Slap Jackson headed south with a double handful

71

of gun-toters, the herd coming up the Tuttle Trail toward them was Busted S. Five hundred legal cows, with Willie Sutter riding lead, and Joe Dell McGuire, Slim Hanks, Jimbo Riley, Clinton Sears, Shorty Mars and Pappy Jameson right behind him at swing, followed along by Sam Nabors, Bo Sayers, Rock Bottoms, Christy Walker, John Jay Hastings and Mouse Moore at flank. And if that wasn't enough, there was the Burnett brothers and the rest pushing drag, and Shad Ames straw-bossing, and the stubbornest young'un in six counties—Bobby Lee Smith—calling the shots.

Peter Thayer and Slap Jackson weren't the smartest pair that ever swung a wide loop—rustlers as a rule don't carry too much weight between their ears—but they did have some common sense between them. If they'd had any idea about the crew heading their way, they probably would have let George Scrannon go get his own cows. They might even have considered another line of work.

But that's how it is with coincidences. By the time a man hears the thunder, lightning has done already struck.

After that first bad start, Busted S made good time up through the brush country. Fourteen days out, by Wesley Watkins' count of chuckwagon meals and crossed rivers, they forded the north fork of the Red by evening light and bedded them on good graze with the wagon's tongue pointed at Clearwater Creek and the town of Mobeetie, just a day's push away.

The land was beginning to change now, from where they had started. Higher, rougher land than around Abilene. Short-grass country, with hundreds of little draws, gullies and mazes of breaks, and here and there, standing above it all like big, chopped-off anthills, were the high, lonesome flat-top mesas that signaled the beginnings of the Llano Estacado.

When they had the herd bedded and nighthawks assigned, and the day shift was gathering around Wesley Watkins' cookfires for supper, Pappy Jameson pointed off to the northeast where a line of gray shadow cut across the horizon, running off into the far yonders to the right and left. "That there is the Scarp," he told Bobby Lee. "Everything past that is high plains as far as the eye can see, and the eye can see almighty far up yonder. Nary a hill, tree nor fencepost to block a man's view of true monotony."

Bobby Lee winced, slipping his left arm out of its sling to flex the muscles and work out the stiffness in it. He had been wearing the sling the past few days—when he wasn't too busy—to ease a sprained shoulder. "Scarp, huh?" He peered into the blue distance. "Looks like it cuts us off yonder. How do we get over it?"

"Fools the eye, the Scarp does," Pappy explained. "Looks like a solid wall up yonder, and some places that's all it is. But other places there's breaks in it, an' trails that angles up that a body can follow. But where we're goin', up the Tuttle to the Territory bend, then northwest, it's mostly easy grade. Two-three days of good drive past Wolf Creek, an' we'll done be up yonder just like there wasn't no Scarp at all. Maybe a week from here, maybe two. But then comes No Man's Land, Bobby Lee, an' I surely hope you know what we're doing, goin' there."

"Don't give it a second thought," Bobby Lee said. "I know what we're doin'." He scanned the horizon northward, and pointed, wincing as his shoulder pained him. "That's Mobeetie yonder?"

"That's it," Pappy said. "We be there this time tomorrow, God willin'."

"Well, that's fine," Bobby Lee said. Gulping down the last of his beans, he walked to the wagon and dug around in the tack bin. Pappy followed along, and several others were already there, watching idly. There were various wagers among them, as to what Bobby Lee might do next. Rummaging in the wagon, he found his own possibles, got out his new shirt, and commenced to change. "I'll meet y'all in Mobeetie," he said. "I aim to listen around a while."

"Best not go alone," Pappy nodded. "That's a tough town yonder."

"I'll go," half a dozen of the others chimed out like a chorus.

"Y'all stay with the herd!" Shad Ames snapped. "Y'all hired on to tend cows, not to carouse."

"I'll go with the boy," Pappy Jameson announced. "I can watch his backside. Maybe me an' one other . . .?"

"I'll go," a dozen voices volunteered.

"Like hell y'all will!" Shad told them. "I can't spare any . . . well, maybe I can spare Mouse. He ain't much good here anyhow. Mouse, you go along with . . ." he stopped, turning around. "Where's Mouse?"

"He lit out a hour ago," Joe Dell McGuire shrugged. "You know how Mouse is."

Shad frowned and shook his head. He knew how Mouse Moore was. "Then maybe he'll be there waitin' for y'all," he said.

Bobby Lee had his fresh shirt on, and the dust slapped out of his britches. "Let's saddle up, Pappy. We got us a ways to go."

Some of the listeners straightened then, keenly interested. "What horse you fixin' to ride, Bobby Lee?" Willie Sutter wondered.

"My own horse, naturally," Bobby Lee told him. "I ain't workin' cows tonight. I'm goin' to town."

Willie turned to Shorty Mars and held out his hand. "That's a dollar you owe me, Shorty. He's gonna try it again."

"Double or nothin' on throws?" Shorty suggested.

Willie thought about it, and nodded. "No throw," he said.

74

"Even odds on one throw," Shorty stated his wager. "Double on each throw after that."

Unaware that he was the subject of another round of bets, Bobby Lee had picked up his saddle and catch-rope and was heading for the remuda. Pappy started to follow, then figured he had time for another cup of Wesley Watkins' coffee. Not everyone was partial to Wesley's coffee, but Pappy was. It was his belief that coffee that wouldn't patch a barn roof in a pinch wasn't worth the trouble to drink.

The best night horses were already out, but Bobby Lee wasn't making a selection from the remuda. He spotted Tarnation right off, strolled out to the big horse and dropped a catch-rope over his neck.

Tarnation twitched his ears and raised his head, looking at Bobby Lee with big, thoughtful eyes. But once that rope was on him he stood just as still and proud as a show horse, waiting for his saddle. Most of the crew had followed Bobby Lee out, and now they watched as he tossed a saddle blanket onto Tarnation and followed it with his saddle.

Many's the horse that will shy from a saddle, and many a one will expand its lungs when the cinches come tight. But such things were beneath Tarnation. He didn't any more than glance around, to make sure he approved of the saddle being tied to him, then stand and take it like the finest horse a man ever did see.

But all the time, his ears were high and his eyes were bright, and among the spectators they were laying odds. Even the best-broke cayuse will go finicky now and again, if it hasn't been ridden lately, and Tarnation hadn't had a saddle on him since the day he threw Bobby Lee into a stand of scrub oak, three days back. That was why Bobby Lee had been carrying his arm in a sling, and about half the crew allowed that devil horse knew about the young'un's sprained shoulder, and aimed to give him another one to match it.

75

That was why the betting got right spirited when Bobby Lee snugged his cinches, placed his headstall and put his boot into the left stirrup. He paused there, looked around, pulled his hat down tight on his head, and swung aboard.

Tarnation felt him there, and let him get settled in the saddle, then pawed ground with a forefoot. Bobby Lee grasped the reins, hauled around and tapped his heels against the big horse beneath him. "Let's go to town, horse," he said.

Tarnation hesitated, a shiver going up his neck. Then he turned, obeying the reins, pointed himself north and set off at an easy trot. Atop him, Bobby Lee glanced around and called, "Where's Pappy? I thought he was comin' along."

Willie Sutter turned to Shorty Mars. "That makes it two dollars," he grinned.

Yonder by the fire, Pappy Jameson saw Bobby Lee heading off and tossed back his coffee. "Wait for me!" he shouted. "I'll be right along."

Bobby Lee waved at him. "Follow when you're ready, Pappy! See you at Mobeetie!"

Joe Dell McGuire pushed back his hat to scratch his head. "Dang," he muttered. "I didn't think that horse would let him just . . ."

On the rise beyond the bed camp, Bobby Lee glanced back at them, then tapped heels to Tarnation. "I'm mighty proud of that send-off," he confided to the horse. "I didn't rightly know what you was fixin' to do this . . ."

His voice tailed off as Tarnation surged upward like a tidal wave, bowed in the middle and aimed for the sky. The stiff-legged landing almost knocked the wind out of Bobby Lee, and the immediate swap-ended spin that followed it had him clinging like a clothespin on a storm-day line. ". . . time," he got out, then, "Tarnation! Damn your hide . . . you blasted knothead . . . !"

His teeth clicked like gunhammers between the words, and he clung and bobbed as the big horse went into whole new spasms of enthusiasm.

Shorty Mars had been hauling money out of his breeches to pay Willie Sutter, but now he put it back and an angelic smile spread across his homely face as the show up on the rise went into its second act. Tarnation was pitching and spinning, turning every way a horse can turn except over, and giving serious thought to that, too. Shorty Mars smiled, shaking his head. "The night is young, Willie," he said. "How's about double or nothin' on whether Bobby Lee gets to Mobeetie at all?"

IX

Some things come just natural easy, and some things don't. Describing Mouse Moore so a body might recognize him was one of the latter. Most jaspers a man can look at and say, "He's a big'un, sort of slopey in the shoulders and anvil-headed, with a mop of dark hair and hardly any forehead at all," or "Well, he's a stringy little runt with bug eyes an' warts," or, "Him? Why, he's a beanpole that's been out in the sun too long." All of those are good, lucid descriptions that let a body know just how a man looks.

But not a one of them fit Mouse Moore. Trying to describe old Mouse was like trying to describe smoke. He wasn't long and he wasn't short. He wasn't light and he wasn't dark. He wasn't fat and he wasn't skinny. He had a face that—well—was a face. Pappy Jameson used to say that Mouse Moore came closer to looking just exactly like everybody else than anybody he ever saw.

Mouse was a good old boy, and everybody that knew him liked him—or liked *somebody,* and if they thought about it, it probably was him. He was always willing to lend a hand, if he was around—and maybe sometimes even if he wasn't. He was a fair hand with cows, and could mend a fence or fix a roof, and would put in a good day's work if a man kept track of him. One of those jaspers that got things done—or at least *somebody* got things done, and if there wasn't anybody else around to have done it, then it must have been Mouse.

But it was more than a body could do, to keep track of Mouse Moore. Old Mouse, he came and went pretty much as he pleased. It likely came of spending his whole life looking more like everybody than anybody. Mouse had just never got the hang of being where he was likely to be. Anybody that knew him could recollect just any number of times when it seemed like Mouse had been right yonder a minute ago, but wasn't now.

It wasn't any big thing, though. Folks get accustomed to the folks they know. Everybody knew that Mouse Moore was more likely to have just left than to still be here. It was just the way he was.

And he was just as much that way up at Mobeetie as he was yonder at Abilene.

He rode into that little cowtown about half past nine that spring evening. He looked the place over, picked out the likeliest looking unwinding emporiums and drop-looped his gray horse at the noisest hitch-rail. Then he dusted himself off with his hat, hoisted up his britches and went inside. It was a comfortable, down-homey place with iron screen in front of the mirrors, bullet holes in the rafters and furniture patched up from many a friendly Saturday night debate. To Mouse, it brought to mind the Shades of Paradise, back home. He drifted in, looked the place over and eased in between a couple of dusty fence-riders at the plank bar. The two sort of had their backs to one another, like pards just in from a hard day's work will when there's a rangy bunch of mustangers giving them the hard eye—which there was. Natural enough thing. If there's anything mustangers take to even less than goat-ropers, it's fencers.

Both of the fence-riders glanced around when

Mouse stepped in between them. He said "Howdy," and they said "Howdy" and went back to staring down the wild-horse wranglers on each side.

The barkeep stepped over and set down a mug of beer in front of each of the fence-riders, picked up their nickels and glanced at Mouse.

"Yeah," he said. He put down a nickel.

The bartender went off to draw another suds, and Mouse picked up the nearest fence-rider's beer and gulped it down. The jasper was too busy hard-eyeing mustangers right then to be paying mind to his beer, and Mouse was thirsty. He set down his empty mug and pushed his nickel over toward the man who didn't have a beer now.

He was still thirsty, though, and he could see that the other fence-rider wasn't using his beer either, so he picked it up. He was just reaching for another nickel when somebody across the room went to talking about the state of affairs up in No Man's Land, and that interested him so he turned away and moseyed over for a better listen.

Behind him, voices were suddenly raised, and a fight broke out. He looked back and frowned. He would have reckoned that those fence-riders would be swinging at mustangers pretty quick, but he hadn't expected them to be swinging at each other, or that the bartender would be right in the big middle of the fracas.

But then, there was just no accounting for taste. Mouse moved on across, to where he could listen to the latest news about No Man's Land. The jasper relating the news was a rumpled dude just down from Medicine Lodge by way of the Beaver City Road, and he was full of the latest happenings up yonder—right where the Busted S aimed to go. He presided over a table in one corner, where some leading citizens were getting brought up to date. There were a couple of gentlemen with cravats, a crusty rancher, a gent who might be a banker or a lawyer or something, and a federal

80

surveyor stopping over east-bound from Tucson.

The rumpled dude was putting away first-rate rotgut and laying out about the latest progress of the Chicago, Rock Island and Pacific Railroad. Everybody up yonder had expected that the railroad would go through Arkalon and Springfield, on the Cimarron River. Everybody, that is, except the railroad folks. They had bridged the Cimarron instead, and now were using good spring weather to lay a mile of track a day past that new town, Liberal. They aimed to be there at the line within a month, and to run line right on across the boundary of No Man's Land. The way the speaker had it, a section headquarters had already been built in the Neutral Strip, at a place called Tyrone Switch.

It had been built, but it wasn't there any more. Every board, stone, hinge and nail in the place was gone within two days after they finished it. Just gone, and hardly any trace that it had been there.

They knew where it was, though. East of Tyrone Switch and just south of Liberal, three miles away at the imaginary line where law ended and No Man's Land began, was a hustling little place of a whole different sort. They called it Beer City, and it offered every variety of sport and comfort that the law—places where there was law—didn't allow.

The dude was getting into that when the federal surveyor interrupted him. "Not to dispute your word, sir," he said, "but I don't see how there can be a place like that in the Neutral Strip. There isn't really anybody there, you know."

They all sort of gaped at him, and one of the locals said, "What do you mean, 'nobody there'? There's people all over the place up yonder."

"Not legally," the surveyor said. "Nobody lives in the Neutral Strip."

"Then who are all them folks?"

"Transients," the surveyor suggested.

"Transients?"

81

"Just passing through. The law doesn't say anything about people passing through."

A rancher squinted at him. "Well, I know for a fact that a lot of them jaspers passing through No Man's Land has been passing through for eight-ten years now, an' they're still there. And a good mess of my critters with 'em."

With the surveyor shushed, the rumpled dude got back to his story. Being in the lawless zone, Beer City had its own rules. A man could do anything he was man enough to do. There was just a mess of friction between Beer City and the righteous and pious among the Kansans across the line, because all the other Kansans there were Beer City's best customers.

The Chicago, Rock Island and Pacific Railroad people knew where their section headquarters was, all right. They knew because a delegation of Methodists from Liberal—spying out the ungodly—had reported two brand new buildings at Beer City. A saloon and a gambling hall with by-the-hour rooms upstairs. The saloon had a porch built on pilings made from brand new railroad trestle timbers, and the bawdy house had a sign over its door that said: *Chicago, Rock Island and Pacific Railroad Company.*

There were folks above the line who were some kind of upset about that, the rumpled dude said.

"Time was," he said sadly, "folks up in No Man's Land would take anything that wasn't nailed down. But times has changed. Now if it's nailed down they take the nails, too."

Beer City wasn't the worst of it, either. There were outright outlaw nests on Coldwater Creek and out around Black Mesa, and they had shooting wars twice a week at Blissful Valley.

Still, there was hope that the Neutral Strip might be aiming at civilization. There were some right enterprising souls at Beaver City, it seemed, who were parceling out choice land and town lots, and might just begin to attract a whole better crowd into No Man's Land. And they had themselves a vigilance committee to make sure Beaver City stayed peaceful.

Now, old Mouse, he knew that Bobby Lee Smith would want to know all about all that, so he just sidled himself into the crowd there at the corner table and took a listening.

It didn't last very long, because the knuckle-dusting at the bar had spread from those fence-riders to a rangy bunch of wranglers, and some of the other old boys commenced to get caught up in it, and before long there were chairs flying and bottles breaking, and it was hard to carry on a serious conversation.

Come to that point, the citizens at the corner table got up and took their talking to quieter quarters at another saloon down the street. But by then, everybody there had decided that somebody there knew who Mouse Moore was, so when they moved out they took him along.

It's just how Mouse was. You just had to know him. Everybody always thought he was somebody, but nobody ever quite pegged him as anybody, so he could just be nobody and fit right in. And he was a good listener, to boot.

By the time fighting broke out in the second saloon and the serious citizens moved along to a third one, Mouse was as much a part of the club as any of them, and none of them realized that not a one of them had the slightest notion of who he was. That's how Mouse Moore was.

It was near to midnight when Bobby Lee Smith and Pappy Jameson rode into Mobeetie, and things had quieted down a good bit. Most of the rowdy element was either in bed nursing bruises or in jail nursing grudges, and most of the upstanding citizens had gone staggering home to face whatever domestic reprisals they had coming. But there were some places still open, and they climbed down at one and went in to wet their whistles.

The place was kind of a mess. There were busted chairs all over, and broken glass on the floor, and one of the tables had been split right down the middle. Bobby Lee was admiring all that when a man stood up behind the bar, holding a shotgun. He glared at them and they stared at him and Pappy Jameson said, "Howdy. Have a fracas?"

"No, thanks," the man said. "Done had one." He lowered his shotgun. "Thought y'all might be some of them, comin' back to start over again."

"We just rode in," Bobby Lee assured him. "Thought we'd have us a beer. What was the commotion all about?"

"Don't rightly know," the man said, searching for some unbroken mugs. "It started over a nickel. But I know who commenced it an' if he shows up here again I aim to shoot him."

"Can't say I blame you," Pappy allowed.

They were drinking their beer when the broken batwings at the door creaked, and Mouse Moore walked in. "Howdy," he said. "Seen your horses out front."

The man behind the bar picked up his shotgun again and glared at Mouse. For a minute it seemed like he was going to open fire, then he hesitated. "You sure look familiar," he said.

"Yeah, I know," Mouse shrugged. "Everybody says that. You got another beer?" He leaned his elbows on the plank bar and said, "Only decent place to go in No Man's Land is Beaver City."

Bobby Lee glanced at him. "You been collectin' news, Mouse?"

"Some. The Camp Supply Road swings east at Wolf Creek, couple days up yonder. Straight north of that cutoff, there's good graze and it's about three day's push to Beaver City. They got a vigilance committee there. 'Cept one feller allows there ain't anybody

84

yonder at all."

"Nobody there?" Pappy Jameson frowned. "Don't hardly seem likely. Where'd they all go?"

"They never was anybody there, the feller said." Mouse shrugged and shook his head. "Feller's a gover'ment man."

"Oh."

The barman handed Mouse a beer and took his nickel. "You fellers pushin' cows?"

"We're Busted S," Bobby Lee told him. "Five hundred head of legal stock." To Mouse he said, "Beaver City, huh?"

"Beaver City's in No Man's Land," the bartender pointed out.

"Yeah, we know. That's where we're goin'."

"Railroad ought to be there soon," Mouse reported. "Dude that said so seemed to know what he's talkin' about. An' he wasn't gover'ment."

"No offense intended," the bartender said, "but anybody that would take legal cows to No Man's Land must be crazy."

"Amen to that," Pappy Jameson agreed, finishing his beer. "What you think, Bobby Lee? Want to get back to the herd, or do some sight-seein'?"

"Not much left to see around here," Mouse told them. "It's a lively town, but it rolls up real early. All the joints are busted up, an' everybody's went home."

"We'll head on back, I reckon," Bobby Lee decided.

Mouse followed them out, then snapped his fingers and turned back. At the doorway he called, "I almost forgot. I still owe you this for while ago." He tossed a nickel, the bartender caught it and Mouse stepped out.

They were just getting into their saddles when the bartender's voice barked from inside, "Him! By God, that was him!" A shotgun roared, and a charge of buckshot ripped through the broken batwings.

As one, the riders hauled rein and headed out of town at a run. Some ways out, Bobby Lee slowed

Tarnation and looked around. "What the blazes was that all about?"

"Danged if I know," Mouse said.

The next afternoon Busted S bypassed Mobeetie and bedded on high ground above the Canadian River. By evening light, they could see the rising lands beyond the river, and the double mesa that marked the Camp Supply turnoff. It was too far away to see details, but it was clear there was somebody over there. They could see cookfires in the twilight.

Bobby Lee had himself a hunch that whoever was yonder might not be friendly. But he figured they'd find out soon enough.

As he ladled out supper, Wesley Watkins crooned to himself, "The Brazos is behind us now, and so's the mighty Red. Yonder's the Canadian, with Tuttle turnoff just ahead. We're runnin' shy on Texas, but we must be long on sand, 'cause here's this bunch of bloody fools all bound for No Man's Land."

Some of the boys took their plates and went off somewhere else to eat.

X

Bart Sherrell's new stagecoach rolled into sight of the town of Springfield just about the time most of Springfield rolled out. Coming in from the north, down from the sandhills onto the broad prairie north of the Cimarron, Annie Sue Finch—"riding shotgun," as Bart put it, which meant sitting on the left side of the driver's seat—had a clear view of the town that billed itself the Star of the Plains, and she held her bonnet in place with one little hand and pointed with the other.

"What are all those people doing?" she asked.

Squinting, Bart shaded his eyes from the slanting sunlight. "Goin' some'eres," he decided.

"There certainly are a lot of them," she observed. "Hurry, and let's find out what is going on."

He turned to gaze at her. As usual, whatever expression he had intended to have on his face didn't last very long. As usual, it dissolved into a silly grin of admiration at sight of her face. And as usual, he forgot what he had been going to say and just sat there grinning.

It was not a new thing to Annie Sue. Healthy young men tended to behave that way in her presence. She was observant enough to realize that they did, and realistic enough to understand why. It was not her fault that she had such an effect, and she neither encouraged it nor knew of any way she might change it. It was just a fact of life. Somewhere in her ancestry, a large dose of small, blonde Scandinavian influence had met and mingled with a bit of the brand of Gaelic blood that folks call Black Irish. The blend, as perfected in the dainty features of Annie Sue Finch, had about the same impact on young men that fresh catnip does on a kitten . . . or of jimson weed on range critters.

She couldn't help it, and they couldn't, either.

In simple terms, looking at Annie Sue Finch could turn a young man's heart into a trip-hammer, and his brain to turnip greens.

The coach jolted across a runnel, both of them bounced, and someone below, inside the coach, said a word that Annie Sue was certain Milicent wouldn't appreciate. Frowning at Bart Sherrell, she snapped, "You really should watch the road, you know."

"Sorry," With a visible attempt to regain his equilibrium, Bart took charge of the team again.

"You were going to say something to me," Annie Sue reminded him. Then, quickly, "No, don't look. Just talk."

"Yes, ma'am. What I was going to ask was, you ain't from out here, are you?"

"Well, no, I'm not. Why?"

"What you said just then, about hurryin' up to see what's goin' on at that town yonder. How far do you reckon it is to that town?"

"I don't know," she admitted. "A mile or so?"

"That's what I thought," he grinned. "Well, missy, this here is the high plains an' that town yonder is at least twelve miles away, an' it could be twenty an' not look much different. It's how things look out here. Back-easters take time to get the hang of that."

Distinctly, in the eye-fooling distance, they could see two separate groups of people heading south out of Springfield. The further group, hazed by dust and shimmering with distortion, looked like at least fifty riders on horseback, and several wagons. The nearer group, which might have been in pursuit, was mostly horsemen with a surrey or light carriage here and there among them. And behind them all, in the town and just beyond, there were wagons rolling.

"I hope to Sam they didn't take all the horses in town," Bart said. "We planned to put on a fresh team at Springfield."

Annie Sue's eyes went wide. Far off out there, the furthest group of riders and wagons had parted company with the ground and seemed to be rising toward the sky. "They . . . they're flying!" she gasped.

"They're makin' time, right enough," Bart agreed. He turned, and again his expression melted into a foolish grin. "Must be in some kind of a hurry . . . Miss Annie Sue, I declare you are just about the prettiest little . . ."

"Mind your driving!" she snapped. "How are they doing that? How can they . . . fly?"

Bart concentrated again on the road ahead. "Oh, you mean that kind of flyin'. Well, they aren't, really. It just looks like they are because they're that far away. It's a mirage."

"I declare," she murmured.

Somewhere below, there was the sound of a slap and Milicent's voice drifted up, sharp with indignation. "You just mind your manners!"

Bart grinned. "That Sill! He does have an eye for sturdy ladies."

Annie Sue leaned down, turning. "Milicent? Are you all right?"

Milicent's flushed face appeared at the window. "Of course I'm all right. Is that a town we're coming to?"

"Yes, it is. It's called Springfield, but it still is several miles away."

"Why is it hanging in the air like that?"

Annie Sue looked. Now the entire town seemed to rest thirty or forty yards above ground level.

"Mirage," Bart said. "Tell your friend ol' Sill doesn't mean any harm. He just ain't exactly housebroke to company. If he pesters her, she can just swat him good an' he'll shape up."

"Milicent, Mr. Sherrell said if the gentleman bothers you, you should . . ."

"Heard him," Milicent said. "And I already did, but now he has a nosebleed."

Bart shook his head. "That Sill. Well, we'll be stoppin' directly."

Annie Sue looked into the distance ahead, fascinated by the scene out there—so near it seemed, and so bizarre, buildings clustered in air above the immensity of the prairie, riders in the sky beyond, heading away—and gasped again as the further group of riders and wagons began to disappear. In stately fashion, row by row, they vanished from the mirage sky as though they had dropped into a hole.

"Cimarron Valley," Bart explained, being careful to keep his eyes straight ahead. "It's a couple of miles across, but you can't see it from here because of the . . "

"Mirage," she said. "I know."

It was an hour later when the maiden run of the Beaver City Express rolled into Springfield. The town looked mostly deserted, but there were a few people here and there. Bart Sherrell stood tall in the driver's box as the big coach clattered along the main street. Squinting, he peered at the fenced corral of a livery outfit just ahead, then relaxed and sat down. "There's horses," he said.

"Do you intend to steal them?" Annie Sue wondered.

Bart got a pained look on his face, like a man who has been denounced for innocent bystanding. "We wouldn't steal horses," he said. "What do you think we are, outlaws?"

90

"You stole this stagecoach."

"Yes, ma'am, but not the horses on it. We bought them fair an' square, just like we'll buy replacements. We got our principles, after all. Horse stealin' is a reprehensible act."

"I see," Annie Sue shrugged. "But stealing a stage-coach isn't?"

"Never heard of anybody doin' that," Bart said proudly. "I expect the boys an' me is the very first."

Easing to the right, Sherrell tightened reins and slowed the horses. "Short layover here," he called. " 'Bout as long as it takes to change out a team." He reined in again and booted the brake, bringing the big coach to a clattering halt in front of the livery barn. "Passengers can stretch their . . ." he glanced around, and again there was that silly grin, ". . . their, uh, limbs for a few minutes. But don't go far. We sure don't want to waste any time this side of No Man's Land." He helped her down, again wearing a grin, and climbed down after her. The coach doors were open, and Milicent was just climbing out. Beyond her in the coach a man was helping her with one hand while he held a bloody kerchief over his nose with the other.

Directly across from the livery barn was a general store, and Annie Sue headed there with Milicent tagging along, towing the embarrassed and bleeding Sill. She had a grip on his free arm that brooked no argument.

In the store, a bespectacled clerk peered at them and past them at the bright new stagecoach in the street. "Didn't know we had a real stage line here," he said. "What can I do for you folks?"

"This man has a nosebleed," Milicent thrust Sill forward. "What do you have for it?"

"For a nosebleed?" the clerk shrugged. "I don't know. A clothespin? Maybe some putty?"

"Don't be ridiculous," Milicent snapped. "How

about oil of clove? Do you have any of that?"

"Oil of clove is for toothaches, Milicent," Annie Sue pointed out. And to the clerk, "We saw a great lot of people going south from here a while ago. What was that about?"

"County records, ma'am. We got some mustard poultice yonder. Would that work?"

"I don't think so. What do you mean, 'county records'?"

"County records. You know, like tax records and affidavits and deed records, and like that. Bunch of citizens came up from Liberal and took all the county records. Then a bunch from around here lit out after 'em to bring the records back. They do it all the time nowadays. Maybe bay rum?"

"What?"

"For the gentleman's nosebleed. We might bend him over and pour a little bay rum in his nose. It's a recommended antiseptic for . . . ."

Sill had gotten loose from Milicent's grip and was backing away. "Never mind!" he snapped. "It stopped by itself."

"That's too bad," the clerk said. "We might have made medical history, right here in this store. Where you folks bound for?"

"Liberal, to bargin for a wagon and supplies," Annie Sue said. "Then we shall go to Beaver City. I have bought land near there."

"Beaver City? You . . . bought land down yonder? I didn't know you could do that."

"Oh, yes. I bought a full section."

"Imagine that," he blinked. "A section . . . in No Man's Land."

"No, it's in the Cimarron Proposal."

"Where's that?"

"The Cimarron Proposal? It's where Beaver City is. I have a plat, explaining where my section is."

92

The man looked deeply concerned. "Your sec tion . . . did you pay for it?"

"In hard cash, yes. I own it outright."

He seemed even more distressed. "Miss, there's . . . well, there's folks around that'll sell anybody anything, for cash. Some of them are downright unscrupulous, as a matter of fact."

She stared at him, inadvertently fogging his glasses. Men with eyeglasses generally fogged over when Annie Sue looked at them with those eyes of hers. Not their fault, nor hers, either. It was just the way Annie Sue Finch was put together. "Are you suggesting that I might have been flim-flammed, then?"

"Oh, I surely hope not!" He took off his spectacles and wiped them with a pocket kerchief. "It's just that . . . .well . . . the last I heard there wasn't any legal land sales down there because there wasn't any law for legal sales to fit under, you see. Besides, nobody rightly lives there—in the Neutral Strip—for the same reason."

"That must have been before the Cimarron Proposal," she decided. "You have no need for concern, sir. I have purchased a piece of land, and I haven't the slightest doubt that my land belongs to me. Anything else is out of the question."

"Yes, ma'am," he said. "I hope you're right."

"I certainly am," Annie Sue assured him.

Bart Sherrell picked that moment to pull the front door open and lean through. "Sill? If you've stopped bleedin', we got a fresh team and miles to cover." Then he looked at Annie Sue and got that silly grin on his face again, like a full-moon coyote that's just discovered what wild life is all about.

"Ladies," he bowed and held the door wide. "Your carriage awaits."

The clerk stepped out to watch them go—the big stagecoach rolling high and handsome, bound for the

Cimarron Valley and beyond, to Liberal. When they were gone, he walked across to the Springfield City Marshal's office. Ben Wiggins was the only city law in Springfield, a job he'd taken to give two bullet holes time to heal. But he had a strong reputation as a lawman in Kansas and the territories, and everybody knew he liked to keep his hand in.

The store clerk entered, howdied and came straight to the point. "Ben, you heard of any land-sharkin' lately, down in No Man's Land?"

"Goes on all the time," Wiggins nodded. "Where, in particular?"

"Beaver City. I just talked to a lady that's bought herself a section down there. She called it the Cimarron Proposal."

Wiggins sat back in his battered chair, a look of revulsion on his square face. "Scrannon," he said. "George Scrannon. That's where he operates. I can't imagine why nobody's put a .45 slug through that polecat's head-bone yet. Nobody ever deserved it more."

"The lady's been slickered, then?"

"I'd say the odds are about a hundred to one that she has." He raised a brow, studying the younger man. "Nice-seemin' lady, was she, Sid?"

"Mighty nice-seemin'."

"Pretty, too, I reckon?"

"Like the sun comin' up of a morning."

"Shame."

"Sure is."

After the clerk had left, Ben Wiggins sat in thought for a time. The Springfield job wouldn't last much longer. Chances were, Springfield itself would be a ghost town before long. New railroads going other places tended to do that to towns.

George Scrannon. Wiggins rolled the name around in his mind. He had seen some varmints in his day, and

Scrannon was about as bad as they came. There was no law in the Neutral Strip, of course—except what each man carried on his hip—but the time was coming soon when Wiggins would be temporarily unemployed as a lawman. He had thought several times about taking himself a ride down toward Beaver City, just on general principles. But he had held off on doing that, because he just never had thought of a good reason to go.

Sometimes it did a man's soul good to mix up in something just because it needed mixing, and Ben Wiggins' heart was generally in the right place when it came down to it. Trouble was, he was also a practical man. He knew that the soul, fine as it is, is seldom the strong suit in any man's deck. A hand with only soul cards in it won't fade a bluff at the poker table of life.

On the other hand, that good soul hand—just like a busted flush—can take many a pot if there's a wild card in the spread. It's like having one sensible reason to raise the ante when all else says to fold. If a man is itching to play table stakes, all he needs to make up his mind sometimes is that extra one-eyed jack.

It was some time later that old Ben got around to reading the latest bulletins brought in from the wire over at Arkalon. A lot of the usual stuff. Somebody in Morton County had shot somebody else in Morton County over a strayed chicken. Somebody in Hays had shot somebody else in Hays over a strayed wife. Somebody in Stevens County had shot somebody else in Stevens County for no particular reason that anybody could think of. There was a fence-cutting at Iola, a penny-ante bank robbery at Woodrow, and somebody up past Pratt had reported a stolen stagecoach. . . .

Ben went back and read that one again. Not a *robbed* stagecoach. A *stolen* stagecoach. The coach was a brand-new Abbott, Downing & Company Concord, owned by a Nebraska line. A coach like the one he had seen go through Springfield earlier in the day. There was a reward for its return.

It was the first time Ben Wiggins had heard of anybody stealing a Concord coach.

That coach must have been where the pretty woman came from, who told Sid that she had bought land in No Man's Land.

Interesting, Ben Wiggins thought. Almighty interesting.

XI

Coincidences just kept on fixing to coincide, seemed like, in that spring of 1890—all kinds of folks doing all kinds of things, that one way or another would get done in No Man's Land, and mostly not knowing anything about what anybody else was doing.

It's how folks are. Everybody knows something about somebody—about as much as anybody knows about anybody if it's somebody they know anything about—but nobody knows everything about everybody, and anybody who knows anything about anybody knows there's somebody that he doesn't know about, if he thinks about it.

That's worth keeping in mind.

Marshal Ben Wiggins knew about George Scrannon and his land swindles down at Beaver City, and he knew there was a brand new Concord stagecoach headed that way, that might not just exactly belong to those who had possession of it.

Ben Wiggins knew about that, but there wasn't any way he could know about Bobby Lee Smith and the Busted S. And as if it happened, he didn't know anything about the United States Census Office and Mr. Thomas Allen Fry, either. Which wasn't to the discredit of Marshal Ben Wiggins. Hardly anybody generally pays much mind to the United States Census Office.

Thomas Allen Fry knew about the United States Census Office, because that was who he worked for. And he knew about how Miss Annie Sue Finch aimed to make her home in the Cimarron Proposal, which was what the people she had bought property from called the Neutral Strip. But Thomas Allen Fry didn't any more know about Bobby Lee Smith and the Busted S than Ben Wiggins did, and he didn't know about Ben Wiggins, either. He knew there were folks living where most everybody in Washington, D.C. was certain nobody lived, but he didn't know about George Scrannon, and there was just a whole lot he didn't know about No Man's Land.

George Scrannon, at Beaver City, knew that Slap Jackson and Pete Thayer were off someplace rustling up some cows which he figured to buy from them at no more than a dollar a head, and he knew that Jackson and Thayer had plenty of savvy about rustling cows. He also knew that Col. Chadwick Booth-Sykes was touring the Midwest selling parcels of land in the Cimarron Proposal, and that those transactions weren't worth the paper they were written down on. Which was all right with Scrannon, because he expected to get the land back, anyway—one way or another—before any legal ownerships were established.

What Scrannon didn't know about his cow rustlers was that the very place they had learned their trade was at Abilene, Texas, where the Busted S was trailing up from, and that there wasn't a man with Busted S who didn't know about Jackson and Thayer and them, nor a man who'd tolerate rustlers.

Also, George Scrannon didn't know that Colonel Booth-Sykes had got himself a bright idea and wasn't in the Midwest any more, but was over in Kansas and working his way west, selling land to a whole new crop of customers who were crowding one another in the high plains area.

98

Of course, by the time any of this got to rolling, Pete Thayer and Slap Jackson knew more about the Busted S than they had every wanted to know. They were resting in a jail cell in Mobeetie, Texas, waiting for Rangers out of Waco to come and take them away— them and all the surviving yayhoos that had ridden with them out of No Man's Land.

It hadn't been much of a show, there above the Canadian where the Tuttle Trail veered to the east. Before the rustlers ever got a good look at Bobby Lee Smith's five hundred legal cows, Mouse Moore had got a good look at *them*.

Those old boys riding Busted S just weren't the kind to abide rustlers. While Bobby Lee, Shad Ames and them pushed the herd across the Canadian at low water and commenced the climb to the rising plains beyond, Willie Sutter and Pappy Jameson took a few of the boys and headed off upstream to cross at the willow shoals. They circled back, then, and old Mouse pointed them at the outlaws.

Wasn't much of a shooting match, come right down to it. Four of those No Man's Land boys inherited a piece of Texas that morning—what they used to call "a cutter's spread" down around Abilene. It takes a sight of that dry land for a man to run cows, but it doesn't take much at all to be buried in. The prescribed dimensions are two by four by six. Two feet wide, six feet long and four feet deep. That's a cutter's spread in Texas. All the rest of the bunch they rounded up, like goat-roper sheepdogs bunching up the woolies. They lifted their guns, tied their feet to their cinch rings and backed off to howdy the herd as it passed. "We'll be along directly," Pappy told Bobby Lee.

As a matter of fact, it took the better part of a day to deliver those rustlers back to Mobeetie and turn them over to the law. Couple of them had a bad time of it, and couldn't hardly stay on top of their horses even with their feet tied like they were. Old memories die hard.

It would be a long time before Pete Thayer and Slap Jackson got the chance to duck out of Texas again, if ever. Texas Rangers being what they were, every old charge against those two was still a matter of record, and if one court didn't send them off to the grand slam at Huntsville for the next ten-fifteen years, there were a dozen more that would.

Meantime, just like nothing had happened, Busted S was making its way northward past Wolf Creek, with the Camp Supply Trail back yonder and No Man's Land straight ahead.

The route they had chosen would take them past Beaver City, with a stopover on Wolf Creek to graze and water and fatten the critters up, then right on up to the construction sites of the Chicago, Rock Island and Pacific Railroad Company.

Being on a streak of luck, like he was, Bobby Lee Smith was already counting his money and thinking about where to buy himself a section of land. In country as big as this, there was just bound to be somebody anxious to sell property, and a man might get a real good price if he knew what he wanted.

Now, Bobby Lee had been thinking on that some, and he had some notions about what he would be in the market for. Being from Abilene like he was, he just naturally saw land as something a man grazes cows on. But he figured it would be right nice if he had some trees, too, and a swimming hole—with a few catfish in it, should he take a mind to wet a hook now and again—and high ground where he could build himself a porch.

A porch with a rocking chair on it, he thought. Looking out on a slope with some big old cottonwoods for shade, and flowing water down below so a man could see the sunlight reflecting on it.

A good barn, of course. Man needed a good barn, and a stout privy, and a couple of pole sheds and a corral.

And a garden, he decided. Doc Holt and Nanny kept a garden, and Bobby Lee had a taste for fresh onions and greens and the like. So he'd need a garden, probably with a fence to keep the critters out.

Everything Bobby Lee could think of, that a man might want, he pictured there on that spread he aimed to buy. There would be a river and graze, and some cottonwood trees. He'd have him a barn, a privy, a corral and some sheds, maybe a flag pole and a cutting stump, a water well and a swimming hole, catfish and greens . . . and a porch with a rocking chair where he could sit and look at it all.

Now, if he had thought about it, he would have pictured a house, too. A porch with a rocking chair generally is connected to a house, and come to building it, he would have known that. But he had plenty to think on, and a house just never had crossed his mind. He did picture that porch, though.

And the more he thought about the view from that porch, the more he knew exactly what he was looking for. It wasn't long before he knew every rise, every rock and every cottonwood on the place, just like he had been seeing them all his life.

It wasn't any place he had ever set eyes on, but he was sure there was a place somewhere that looked like what he had in mind, and he'd know it when he saw it.

The second morning after the rustlers had been hauled away, all the boys were back and Busted S had a full crew again. The sun was shining, and those five hundred legal cows were in fine shape and fattening on day graze, and Bobby Lee just felt so fine about it all that he went and got his big horse and saddled him up for a ride.

Some of the boys gathered around to watch, and commenced to making their bets, like they generally did when Bobby Lee saddled Tarnation. But that morning they were disappointed. Bobby Lee swung aboard, and Tarnation bobbed his head and answered

101

the reins, and away they went, as handsome a couple as a man and his horse could be.

Pappy Jameson pushed back his hat, scratched his head and said, "I swear. If that don't beat all."

Willie Sutter made the rounds, collecting on his bets. "No accounting for horses," he allowed. "Just when a man knows for a fact they'll pitch, they don't."

Willie Sutter was right as rain about horses, but he might have said the same thing about cows.

Bobby Lee Smith hadn't gone a hundred yards when Willie's designated lead steer, old Blue, looked up and saw him and taken a notion to follow along. There is a school of thought that holds that cows can't tell one horse and rider from another, that a critter just figures if you've seen one, you've seen them all. That's pretty likely, considering that cow logic originates from twenty pounds of bone with horns on each side and sockets for eyeballs . . . and no other discernable attributes.

So probably old Blue saw a rider heading out of a morning, and just naturally did what he had been doing every morning since he became the chosen leader of the Busted S herd. He grabbed himself another mouthful of shortgrass, snorted and set out to follow. Nobody had told him that this was to be a day of rest.

By the time the rest of the crew set out after them, Bobby Lee Smith was out of sight past a rise, and the whole Busted S herd was headed due west at a high lope, following him.

"I'll want piped-in water." Annie Sue was telling Milicent as the stagecoach topped out south of the Cimarron and headed for the new town several miles away on the prairie. "And a tub with ball-and-claw legs, and a chain-tank commode, like the ones they have at the Regency."

Annie Sue had declined to ride shotgun any more,

102

when they boarded up at Springfield. The view was nice from the driver's seat, but Bart Sherrell just had a terrible time concentrating on his team when she was up there. So Sill was up there, now, and Annie Sue and Milicent had the center seats inside. They were the best seats in the coach, and the gentlemen didn't seem to mind, and it wouldn't have mattered if they had minded once Milicent Moriarty made up her mind about where to sit.

"But a three-story house?" Milicent wondered now. "Are you sure, Annie Sue? Did the colonel say definitely that your property has a three-story house?"

"I had that distinct impression," Annie Sue assured her. "I don't recall exactly what he said, but there was something about three levels, I'm sure."

"People can be misleading, sometimes, you know."

"Oh, certainly. But I'm sure Colonel Booth-Sykes wouldn't mislead anyone. Certainly not intentionally. He seemed such a gentleman."

"Perhaps it is two stories and a loft," Milicent suggested.

"Lofts are cramped," Annie Sue pointed out. "All those sloped ceilings, you know. A person feels hemmed in. I do hope it is a full three stories. There are distinct advantages in decorating a house with full floors and upright walls. And one doesn't have to worry about future expansion. Anyway, I want a lavatory room on each floor, with piped water and a drain field. The area may be somewhat sparsely developed, as the colonel was frank to tell me, but that is no reason not to have civilized amenities in one's home."

"I expect you are right, at that," Milicent agreed. "If Colonel Booth-Sykes left the impression of a three-story house, then that's what we shall find when we arrive. And a section of land fully as delightful as he told you. Ah, how much land is in a section?"

"Six hundred and forty acres," the large man with

two guns said. His name was Michael O'Riley, and he was one of Bart Sherrell's associates in the stolen stagecoach project. "It's a square mile of land. What do you aim to do with it?"

"Live there," Annie Sue said. She turned again to Milicent. "We will want a gracious parlor, of course. And a music room and a formal dining hall."

"With velvet drapes," Milicent nodded. "Lace curtains in the parlor, but in the dining hall one should have velvet tie-backs over sheers. It has a certain elegance about it, don't you think?"

"I meant, with six hundred and forty acres of land," Mike O'Riley butted in again. "What do you aim to do with the land?"

"It goes with the house," Anne Sue explained. "I expect we will need a fence. White picket might be nice."

"It might already have a fence," Milicent pointed out. "The finer houses generally do."

"Cows, maybe?" the ladies' ready-to-wear drummer, Winston Overman, suggested. "If you have water . . ."

"A river and a stream," Annie Sue assured him. "They are shown on the plat. But I hadn't thought of cows. The place is near enough to Beaver City that we should be able to have milk delivered."

Mike O'Riley glanced out the window, trying to keep a straight face. The three drummers glanced at one another and sort of shook their heads. The Easterner, Thomas Allen Fry, was asleep.

The stagecoach swayed and veered easily to the right, and a moment later there were riders and wagons thundering by, going the other way. The passengers stared out the windows in curiosity.

"County records," Annie Sue assumed, grateful that the speeding party had passed on the downwind side. They had stirred up a cloud of dust, but it was going the other way.

"I do hope the previous owners of your house left

dust covers on the furniture," Milicent said. "We'll have enough cleaning to do, without beating dust out of everything. And it leaves such a musty smell."

The stagecoach veered again, this time to the left, and a moment later a thick cloud of dust swept over and through the coach as a pack of armed riders swarmed past on the right, heading north.

"Goodness," Milicent muttered, covering her nose and mouth with a kerchief.

Thomas Allen Fry coughed, snorted and woke up. "What happened?" he asked.

"People arguing over county records," Annie Sue explained. "I understand it happens all the time out here."

As the dust cleared, Bart Sherrell's voice rang from above. "Liberal just ahead. Last passenger stop."

"I need to get my receipt," Thomas Allen Fry reminded himself. "Those accountants get testy when reimbursement claims are filed without documentary receipts."

Thomas Allen Fry hadn't been west of the Muddy for a month, but he was already beginning to talk like regular folks. There is one school of thought, that the reason Easterners talk so peculiar is that words are like britches. Both are cut and stitched back East, but they just don't wear comfortable until they've been hung out a few times under a prairie sun.

XII

The only post office in No Man's Land—at least that the Postmaster General of these United States knew about—was at Beaver City. Haygood Dobbs owned it and operated it, and had got himself legally designated as postmaster by riding up to Pratt, Kansas, and taking a civil service oath.

As official postmaster of Beaver City, Haygood Dobbs was kind of an enigma to folks in Washington, D.C.—especially those whose job it was to cipher out who got allocations of money to operate United States government facilities. Generally, as far as anybody knew, government bureaus didn't talk to each other about what they were doing, so the fact that one Haygood Dobbs was operating a post office at a place that didn't exist, forwarding sixty or eighty dollars' worth of mail every week from someplace where there wasn't anybody to write a letter—officially—and delivering bags of mail to people who didn't live where he officially didn't live either . . . and contracting for carriers and sending in a statement of accounts every month . . . didn't get noticed too often in Washington, D.C.

Except by the United States Accounting Office.

Every single month, the same thing happened when Haygood Dobbs' accounts—running about three months behind by the time it all got through the regional postal center at St. Louis and the Center for Districts at Philadelphia—arrived at Washington, D.C. Every single time, it was approved as part of overall operations by the postal accountants, then pulled out for review by the General Accounting Office.

It wasn't all that much money involved. It was just that the United States Postal System accounts allowed for 23,106 post offices operating in the west central sector, but the verifying documents from the Secretary of Interior's office—itemizing cities, towns and communitites where post offices could be—only allowed for 23,105.

So each month, there was a review of records to see why the numbers didn't match, and each time some clerk finally stumbled across Beaver City, which didn't exist in any state, territory or recognized holding of the United States of America. So how could there be a post office there? There wasn't anybody there to have a post office for. Every single month there was an inquiry to the Department of Interior, and a separate inquiry to the Postmaster General's office, about how come there was such a discrepancy.

The Department of Interior didn't care what the postal system did, but it knew blamed well that there wasn't any such thing as a resident in the Neutral Strip. Nobody resided there. And the Justice Department backed them up, because if anybody lived in the Neutral Strip—where there were no legal jurisdictions and no basis for congressional representation, then whoever was there didn't have a congressman to vote against, much less a senator to get upset about.

This was the United States of America, and people didn't live where such inalienable rights didn't. It wasn't allowed.

The Postmaster General, on the other hand, didn't give a gopher hole how the Department of Interior designated this or that piece of real estate. His job was to get the mail delivered, and by Sam, that was what he intended to do.

Same blame thing, every month:

Why is there a post office at Beaver City?

To handle Beaver City's United States mail.

Then where, exactly, is Beaver City?

It's in the Neutral Strip, between Kansas and Texas.

There are no cities in the Neutral Strip. No communities, towns, villages or even rural environs, either. There isn't anybody there.

Then who is generating and receiving all this mail?

Who says there is mail being generated and received?

The postmaster.

What postmaster?

The one at Beaver City.

How can there be a postmaster at Beaver City? There isn't any such place.

And like that. None of it made any difference to Haygood Dobbs, of course, because the United States Postal System went right ahead and paid its lawful accounts, so he got his money every month—three months late, but that was how things generally worked and he allowed for it.

He got a hundred dollars wages for himself, and sixty dollars for Calvin Gable, and reimbursement for the expenses of hauling mail back and forth between Beaver City and Pratt, which Haygood used as his district postal center.

What Calvin Gable was paid for was to help sort the mail, help deliver it and keep his double-barrel twelve gauge loaded at all times. In a place that doesn't have any laws, a man who stands six-feet-four and carries a Hopkins and Allen shotgun like it was a toothpick is good to have around. Folks in No Man's Land might steal the tailfeathers off a running rooster, but as long as Haygood Dobbs had Calvin Gable working for him, nobody was going to fool with the United States mail.

Some had tried, a time or two, but not lately.

The thing was, when the United States Census Office put out a broadside to all postmasters, introducing the notion of a 1890 Census of Population, they did it through the Department of State, and not the Postmaster General. Upshot was, those letters went to post offices—of which there were 23,105—instead of to postmasters. So, 23,105 postmasters got their marching orders about assisting with the Decennial Census, and one didn't. That one was Haygood Dobbs.

The first he heard about it was when a bright new Concord stagecoach rattled down the street at Beaver City and pulled up in front of his store.

Of course, it drew a crowd, because there never had been a stagecoach at Beaver City before. Stage lines avoided No Man's Land like it had ticks.

Folks came out all along the street to see the sight, and Haygood stepped out gawking just like everybody else. The big coach rattled to a stop, and the driver—a young fellow with dark eyes and a toothy grin—hollered, "Beaver City! Everybody get out!"

Haygood didn't know the driver, but he knew the fellow sitting up beside him. Lot of folks in No Man's Land knew Mike O'Riley. He was a good old boy, but nobody much wanted to mess with him. He was a big one, about like Calvin Gable, and he knew how to use the two big irons he wore.

As Haygood recognized him, O'Riley waved. "Howdy, Mr. Dobbs! This here is Bart Sherrell. Him and me an' Sill done went into business. What you're lookin' at is the Beaver City Express. Ain't it a beauty?"

Haygood had to admit that it was, and he was already thinking how it might be to have a regular stage run that he could contract to haul the mail for him.

Four passengers got down from the stage. Three carried drummers' cases, and the fourth was an Eastern-looking dude with a comfortable belly behind his vest. That one looked around, up and down the street, north—the way they had come—and south toward a hill that seemed to be pocked with fresh-turned earth. "Seventeen buildings?" he muttered, then corrected himself. "Eighteen. Nine commercial, the rest . . . whatever." He shrugged and glanced up at the sign on Haygood's store. *Dobbs General Merchandise,* it said, and right underneath, *United States Post Office, Beaver City.*

The man read the sign, then looked at Haygood. "You are the postmaster here, sir?"

"I am," Haygood assured him. "Dobbs is the name."

"Pleased to meet you, sir." The dude stepped forward and held out his hand. "I'm Fry. Thomas Allen Fry, United States Census Office. I believe you have plats to show me?"

Haygood shook his hand, just staring at him. Then he said, "What kind of flats? You mean packages?"

"Plats," Fry corrected. "Preliminary plats for the Decennial Census." When Haygood still looked blank, he added, "You know . . . the maps, showing places of residence?"

"What maps?"

"For the census."

"What census?"

Things had got noisy by then, what with folks coming to look at the stagecoach, and everybody talking at once like folks do.

Mike O'Riley was introducing Bart Sherrell and Sill—whose name seemed to be Andrew Sills—to Wade Meeker, who owned the livery barn, and to L.G. Stone, who kept a few spans of good draft horses and spent most of his time keeping folks from stealing them. The three arrived drummers were asking around for a hotel and talking about their wares all at the same time. Oliver Winshaw, who kept the Happy Times Saloon and was also the governor of the Cimarron Proposal, was haranguing Beauregard Jenkins, who headed up George Scrannon's Vigilance Committee

110

and also served as territorial secretary for the Cimarron Proposal, about the need for a licensing procedure for common carriers if there was going to be a stage line in the Strip, and Mrs. Polly Wentworth was trying to find out the price of eggs from Wilbur Cadwalder, who had left her standing in his produce emporium when he stepped out to look at the stagecoach.

"I knew we'd draw us a crowd," Bart Sherrell told Sill as they unloaded luggage. He turned to L.G. Stone, who was thumping him on the back. "No, Mr. Stone, I didn't suggest that we lease horses from you. I suggested you provide us with teams, and a station, for shares. We can all make us some money."

"What station?" Stone demanded. "I got horses, not a stagecoach station."

"We need a station, too," Sherrell pointed out.

Wade Meeker shouldered in. "What are you talkin' to him, for? I'm the one with the barn."

"Mr. Cadwalder!" Mrs. Polly Wentworth stamped her foot. "Do you have eggs to sell, or not?"

Thomas Allen Fry glanced around, frowning, then took Haygood Dobbs by the shoulder. "I think we should go inside and talk," he suggested.

Just then the crowd quieted down, and everybody turned to look down the street. A line of men was walking toward the stagecoach, spreading across the street as they came. A rough-looking, glowering bunch with guns plainly visible—on seven of them. The eighth, who was a step ahead of the rest, was a slender, baggy-eyed individual dressed in tailor-made clothes and polished boots. He carried a gun, too, but his coat covered it.

As they approached, this one eyeballed the tall stagecoach and yelled, "What is going on here?"

"Scrannon," Mike O'Riley muttered to Bart Sherrell. "He's the one I told you about."

"Whose coach is this?" George Scrannon demanded Bart Sherrell pushed through the crowd to face him.

"This here stagecoach is property of the Beaver City Express Stagecoach Company. Who wants to know?"

"And who are you, sir?"

"Barton W. Sherrell, president of the stagecoach company. That's me. And who are you?"

"George Scrannon," Scrannon snapped. "I haven't authorized any stage line for Beaver City."

"Doesn't matter whether you have or not, Mr. Scrannon. There is one now, and we're it."

Scrannon's seven thugs were edging forward, and folks were backing away. Things seemed a mite tense there on the street of Beaver City right then.

"You and who else, Mr. Sherrell?" Scrannon demanded.

"Me, for one," a deep voice said from one side. Scrannon and all his men looked that way, and there stood Mike O'Riley, with his guns in his hands—not pointed, exactly, but there wasn't any question that he was ready to shoot if it was needful.

"Me, too," a voice said from the other side. Sill stood there, with a handful of scattergun. The two of them had Scrannon's toughs pretty well flanked.

Scrannon looked from one to the other, his eyes flashing, then back at Bart Sherrell. "I think you should understand, Mr. Sherrell. I run things in Beaver City." He looked past Sherrell and snapped, "Jenkins! Get over here!"

Beauregard Jenkins stepped forward, kind of sheepish, and said, "Sir?"

"Where is the Vigilance Committee, Jenkins?"

"Why, they're all out . . . well, you know what they're doin', Mr. Scrannon. You said to . . ."

"Never mind! Jenkins, as territorial secretary of the Cimarron Proposal, it is your duty to license business ventures. Is there a license for a . . . a Beaver City Express Stage Line?"

"No, sir. There sure ain't."

"Isn't!"

"Isn't." Jenkins turned, spotted Scrannon's self-appointed "judge," Sylvester Magruder, and said, "Ain't that right, Judge?"

"I suppose so," Magruder nodded.

"Your stage line is in violation of territorial prerogative, Mr. Sherrell," Scrannon said, kind of purring. "Therefore your rolling stock and animals are subject to . . ."

"What's he doing?" Thomas Fry whispered to Haygood Dobbs. "Can he do that?"

"He's fixing to steal the stage line and run it on his own," Dobbs shrugged. "That's Scrannon. He takes what he wants. Unless . . ." Dobbs pushed through the crowd, frowning at Scrannon, and stepped to Sherrell. "Do you qualify for a mail contract, Mr. Sherrell?"

Scrannon said, "Stay out of this, Dobbs!"

Dobbs ignored him. "Do you?"

"I expect," Sherrell told him. "We got us a coach and some stock."

"Then I hereby officially award you a postal contract to carry the United States mail," Dobbs said. "I'll dispense with competitive bidding on the grounds that you have the only stagecoach around, and the jerk-line rigs are too slow. Do you accept?"

"Sure," Sherrell shrugged.

Dobbs turned to glare at Scrannon. "This stagecoach line has been granted a postal contract, Mr. Scrannon. Any interference with its operation is a federal offense and a felony." He glanced around at Magruder. "Under federal law, 'Judge,' not vigilante law."

George Scrannon looked at the postmaster like he was fixing to spit nails. "You're going to push this 'federal' business too far, Dobbs. You mark my words."

Dobbs stared right back at the town boss, holding his eyes. "Do you want a few federal marshals coming in here with range warrants, Scrannon? And taking a

113

look at your 'Cimarron Proposal' swindle while they're at it?" With a sneer, he turned his back on Scrannon. "I'd suggest you set up shop and schedules right away, Mr. Sherrell. I won't waste post office funds on a contractor who doesn't perform on schedule."

"Dobbs!" George Scrannon snapped. "There's still plenty of room up on that hill. You're pushing your luck!"

The postmaster turned slowly. "You're the one belongs on that hill, Scrannon, and I expect somebody will get around to putting you there."

With that, he strode back toward his store, glancing at Thomas Allen Fry as he passed. "What was it you said I was supposed to have for you?"

Fry fell in behind him, grinning. "Plats, Mr. Dobbs. Residential descriptions of the area you serve, so that a count of population may proceed. You know, I believe I shall enjoy planning a census with you, sir," he said.

XIII

"Vigilantes," Haygood Dobbs said. The look on his face was like a man trying to lime-out an overworked privy. "The Beaver City Vigilance Committee. Or Cimarron Proposal Vigilance Committee, or whatever. That Jenkins—Beauregard Jenkins, you saw him yonder—he's the 'chairman' of it, by name, but George Scrannon calls the shots, just like he tries to call all the shots around here. Jenkins hasn't got the sense God gave a cowchip."

They sat at a rickety table in *Dobbs General Merchandise,* along with several other men who had wandered in to join them. The place was a squat, pine-slab building with bullet holes in two walls and indications of a recent fire. The front three-quarters of the building was mostly hardware and dry goods. In the back, the "post office" was flanked by tiny cubicles where Dobbs and his assistant slept.

Fry had been introduced to Owen Lance, who had a sod house at the end of town called a "road ranch," because it was at the only good trail crossing of the Beaver River. He had also made the acquaintance of Mr. Cadwalder, who kept the produce store, a settler named Mason and to a very large, ugly individual named Gable, who seemed always to have a large shotgun in his hand. It didn't look large in his hand, though. Next to Calvin Gable, there wasn't much that looked large.

"Vigilante law," Haygood Dobbs went on, rattling a coffee pot on his little stove. "It isn't law at all . . . just a gang of toughs that Scrannon uses to take what he wants. But there isn't any real law here. Except that . . . ," he pointed at Calvin's shotgun. "And this." He pushed aside his stained apron and drew out a large pistol. Thomas Fry had not even been aware that it was there, though it occurred to him that he hadn't seen a man unarmed since the stagecoach entered what the locals called "No Man's Land."

He was beginning to understand why.

"Robbery, swindling, even outright murder," Dobbs told him. "Commonplace here. Nothing to stop it, except the fear of God and guns. Some of those thugs are skittish about being shot back at."

"And the threat of federal marshals," Fry pointed out.

"Oh, that. That's mostly bluff. I know it, and those ruffians know it. I don't know if I could get marshals here. Marshals work within court jurisdictions, and there aren't any court jurisdictions in the Neutral Strip."

"None?" Fry scowled.

"Why should there be? According to the government, there isn't anybody here."

"But there are people here!"

"Sure there are. Several hundred, right around Beaver City, and a lot more scattered around. I don't know, maybe a thousand, maybe two-three thousand folks, altogether. But according to the government, there's nobody here."

"That doesn't make any sense."

Dobbs looked at him the way a seasoned bird dog looks at a raw puppy. "You work for the government, Mr. Fry. Same as me. How much sense does it gener-

116

ally make?"

"Oh," Fry subsided. "Not all that much, I guess. But I have a job to do, anyway."

"So do I. Handling the mail. Now, this census business . . . what exactly is it that you are supposed to do?"

"Count the people," Fry shrugged.

"In No Man's Land?"

"There are people here. They're supposed to be counted. Everybody is."

"Everybody? *Here?*" Dobbs looked like he couldn't believe his ears. "They can't expect that. The people in the Neutral Strip—in No Man's Land—there's just a lot of them that aren't going to want to be counted. That's why a lot of them are here . . . to keep from being counted someplace else, and maybe hanged or jailed in the process."

"Well, I have it to do," Fry shrugged again. He leaned his elbows on the table, thoughtfully. "The 'federal marshals' thing works for you . . ."

"Maybe."

"Well, they leave the mail alone. And they backed off, out there."

"There isn't that much here to steal," Dobbs explained. "And I guess Scrannon is a little off guard about federal law, 'cause he isn't any surer about that than I am."

"I don't know, either," Fry admitted. "Oh, a census officer can summon a marshal if he needs one, but it takes a court order."

"Yeah," Dobbs nodded. "And a court order takes a court with jurisdiction."

"What's this 'Cimarron Proposal' business?"

"Nothing. Scrannon is a land shark, among other things. Cimarron Proposal is what he calls the strip. Makes it sound better to the ones he aims to swindle."

"Then he sells land to people, fraudulently?"

117

"You might say that." Dobbs raised a hand to tick off items on his fingers. "First, he doesn't own any land to sell. Nobody here owns the land. There's no procedure for claiming, buying and selling, proving up or holding. There's no law. Second, if he *had* a claim to any land, selling it wouldn't be a legal transaction because there's no jurisdiction here to transfer title . . . even if there were titles. Third, he sells the same tracts over and over again."

"How can he do that?"

"Who's to stop him? If somebody comes looking for his land and finds somebody else in possession, who does he complain to? Scrannon? Or the Vigilance Committee? Then there's item four," he tapped another finger, "a lot of what he sells—if it's any good—he takes back."

"How?"

"That's most of what the Vigilance Committee does. Probably why most of 'em aren't in town today. Prob'ly out running 'squatters' off their property. Most of them leave. The rest just disappear."

Fry thought of the enthusiastic, beautiful young woman he had met on the stage, and his cheeks went gray. "I see," he said. "God, what a pity."

"Latest twist," Owen Lance said, "is the cattle business. End of rail now is past Liberal, just across the line, and the railroad's ready to buy cattle. Scrannon's put up a sign, says he's in the cattle business. Shoot, he ain't got any cows."

"You sure?" Mason asked. "We had word of two separate herds headed up this way last season, but they never showed up here. Maybe the vigilantes have 'em on graze someplace."

"Naw," Lance shook his head. "Man's got cows on graze, word gets around. Wasn't Scrannon's bunch took those herds. Could have been most anybody else, though. I'll bet half the men in this strip are here

118

because folks someplace else got tired of them rustlin' cows." He looked sadly at the census officer. "You prob'ly fixin' to get yourself killed, you know . . . goin' around countin' noses. Lots of noses hereabouts got no intention of bein' counted."

"Oh, I won't actually be counting people," Fry assured him. "My job is to plan and supervise the census—both here and across the line, in the border counties. I'll have enumerators to do the counting."

Dobbs cocked his head. "Who are you going to get to go out and count fugitive cattle rustlers in a place where there's no law to back him up?"

"I'm sure I can find people," Fry said. "Can't do a census without enumerators."

"Enumerators? What is that, a fancy word for plain damn fools?"

"Actually, most anyone can qualify as an enumerator. It just has to be someone who can read, write and count."

Shad Ames was just lighting down after a shift at the drags when Bobby Lee came pounding up on a lathered remuda horse and skidded to a stop. "Saddle up, Shad!" he yelled. "We're missing some cows."

They had spent most of the day, trailing the Busted S herd through limestone breaks above Wolf Creek, every man of them working his tail off, and Shad was in no mood for foolishness. "You're crazy, Bobby Lee," he snapped. "We got ever' last critter we set out with. You think I wouldn't know if we'd spilled some?"

"I reckon not," Bobby Lee swung down from the tuckered mount and stooped to loosen his cinches. "Because I just circled this herd and counted 'em, and there ain't any five hundred head here. All we've got is four hundred and ninety three cows. We're missing seven." He hoisted his saddle and shouted, "Jimbo! Get

119

me a fresh horse and go spell Willie at point!"

Shad sighed. When Bobby Lee made up his mind about a thing, there just wasn't any changing it. Off a ways, Joe Dell McGuire and Pappy Jameson were heading for the remuda to remount, and he knew Bobby Lee had already told them. And Willie Sutter, who was heading back from point. "I swear," he husked. "Jimbo, bring me one, too!"

Within minutes the five were headed back toward the breaks. "There ain't no way we could have lost cows, comin' through there," Shad argued as they rode. "We had ever' bunch covered ever' minute. We'd a' seen strays."

"Then maybe they didn't stray," Bobby Lee said. "Maybe somebody took 'em."

"Out here? There ain't anybody out here but us. Maybe you miscounted."

Ahead of them, a lone rider appeared, coming up out of the breaks, coming their way.

"We're short seven cows," Bobby Lee repeated, getting one of those looks of his, like the expression on an ore wagon.

Evening sun slanted across the rolling lands, and for a moment the approaching rider was lost in shadows. Then he was there. It was Mouse Moore.

"Howdy," he said. "Y'all know we lost us some cows? Fellers was layin' up in the rocks yonder, waitin'. They cut out some when that gully bent around."

"How many?" Shad asked.

"Four ol' boys. Seven cows. They're just up yonder, layin' low 'til we get gone."

Shad glanced across at Bobby Lee. "I swear," he grunted. Then he dug heels into his mount. "Well, let's go get 'em back, then. Come on, we're burnin' daylight."

Back with the herd, upwind on a rise, Wesley Watkins watched them go, and started laying his cook-fire for supper. "Three miles out of Texas," he

120

crooned to himself. "Is three miles out of hand. There ain't no law around here, boys. We've come to No Man's Land."

The bunch-cutters hadn't gone more than a mile. They had their seven found cows in a little box cove, and were still looking them over when a rider appeared, ambling up the draw like a fellow without a care in God's world. The four pulled their guns at sight of him, but he just came on, riding right in among them.

"Howdy," he said. "Found yourselves some cows, huh?"

The four glanced at one another, then put away their guns. Every last one of them figured Mouse Moore was somebody that somebody else there knew. It's just how Mouse was.

The nearest one nodded at him. "I reckon," he said, "Blamedest thing, they must've strayed up from Texas." He pointed. "What do you make of that there brand? Like two horseshoes pointed different ways. Furley thinks it might be Backtrack, but it looks to me like C Jackleg."

Mouse rested his elbow on his saddle horn. "Could be either one, but it ain't. That brand is Busted S."

"Texas brand, is it?" Furley wondered.

"Sure is. Problem is, these Busted S cows didn't stray up here. They was drove, just like the other four hundred and ninety-three that was with 'em when y'all cut these out back yonder."

The first man had his gun half-drawn before he noticed that Mouse's .45 was looking at him like a big, dark eyeball.

"I wouldn't," Mouse suggested.

A voice behind them agreed, "Same goes for all of you."

They looked around, and went pale. There were men all around them, with drawn guns.

A sturdy young fellow with a Peacemaker the size of

121

a shoat's hind leg walked his horse down the rock slope and glared at them. "Don't you boys know it's considered impolite to steal folks' critters?"

A slit-eyed hardcase with a gun that looked like it could talk most any language eased down beside him. On the rim were a couple of older men—a frost-haired gent with a face about as easy as flint rock and a wide-shouldered old range bull with a slouch hat—and an itchy-looking jasper with a grin on his face that had all the warmth of pond ice.

"You gents are in just a mess of trouble," the young fellow with the Peacemaker pointed out. "Your choice what kind."

The one called Furley glared at him. "What does that mean?"

"It means if them guns ain't on the ground before I blink my eyes, ever' one of y'all is dead and just don't know it yet."

Four hand guns and a stub rifle clattered to the ground.

"Now that's right thinkin'," the young man said. "My name is Bobby Lee Smith, and all five hundred of these Busted S cows are mine."

"And mine," the range-bull type on the rise added.

"That's Shad Ames yonder," Bobby Lee said. "Ol' Shad, he hates herd-cutters worse'n he hates dip vats. Pappy Jameson yonder, he favors gut-shootin' over hangin', and the grinnin' gent is Willie Sutter. Willie, what do you favor?"

"Bob-wire long johns," Willie shrugged.

"This here is Joe Dell McGuire," Bobby Lee indicated slit-eye, and the looks on the rustlers' faces told him he didn't need to add anything to that. Lot of folks had heard about Joe Dell McGuire.

"And that there is Mouse Moore," Bobby Lee finished.

Furley frowned at the man beside him. "I thought

122

that feller was a friend of yours, Linc."

"I thought he was a friend of *yours*" Linc snapped.

"That's how Mouse is," Pappy Jameson said, easing his mount closer. "Everybody generally thinks he's somebody, and most times he ain't. It's a God-given talent, I believe. We aim to bury these jaspers, Bobby Lee, or leave their carcasses for the buzzards."

"Ought to give 'em cutters' spreads," Joe Dell suggested. "We can let 'em dig their own, I reckon."

"Pop their damn necks, and let's get back to the herd," Shad Ames said.

"Y'all see how it is," Bobby Lee told the rustlers.

"Now hold on . . . !" Furley started.

"I got me a notion, though," Bobby Lee cut him off. "I expect you gents know your way around this here No Man's Land?"

"Good as anybody," Linc allowed.

"Well, then, this is your lucky day, because we only just got here, and it wouldn't be right for us to pass on through without folks knowin' the facts of life about us. So I reckon we'll rely on you boys to spread the word."

"What word?" Furley gulped.

"Y'all spread the word that Bobby Lee Smith is here, pushin' five hundred legal Busted S cows up to the Chicago, Rock Island and Pacific railhead. Tell 'em I'm havin' me a streak of luck this spring, and it sure would be a shame if anybody run afoul of just plain luck. An' the worst kind of bad luck I can think of is what will happen to anybody that comes within hollerin' distance of even just one Busted S cow. Think y'all can spread the word about that?"

"Sure can," Linc assured him, turning toward the horses.

"Have to do it afoot, though," Bobby Lee swung in to cut him off. 'Y'all just lost your horses, along with your hardware."

123

"You can't take our horses!" Furley blurted. "It ain't . . ."

"Ain't what? Legal? Why, mister, this here is No Man's Land. There ain't any law here." With a flick of his thumb he drew the hammer on the Peacemaker and pointed it at one and then another of the wide-eyed cow-stealers. "Y'all have had a good look at us," he said, quietly. "Now just get along, an' tell ever'body you know all about us. You'll be doin' 'em a favor. Oh, an' by the way, the six of us you see here are the puny ones. There's another dozen where we came from, an' those other ol' boys can get downright mean."

XIV

In shortgrass country, above caprock and barring your occasional gully, folks don't generally have to have roads to go from one place to another. Places up yonder in the high plains, a man can see twenty miles on a good day, and if he looks twice he can see forty. And anything you can see, you can generally go to. You just set off and go. And if you keep on going, and don't get snakebit, gored, stomped, drygulched, short-looped, dragged or otherwise inconvenienced along the way, then eventually where you are is where you were aiming for back yonder when you set out.

It's how high plains caprock country is.

But roads are a valued artifact of civilization, and civilized folks have a tendency to go along with the road where there's a road. In that spring of 1890, there was one road that led south from Liberal, Kansas. In town, its name was Main Street—even when they changed the name to Kansas Avenue several years later in a fit of good Kansas pretentiousness, it would still be called Main Street. Main Street started at the north end of town where the road from Springfield and the Cimarron crossing came in, and it crossed Third Street, Second Street and First Street, then Front Street and the rail yards, and headed right on south toward the

Neutral Strip, three miles away.

Main Street was the scenic route through Liberal. Driving along it, as Annie Sue and Milicent did on a bright spring morning—in an ancient but repaired rockaway with a placid Morgan cross between the shafts—you could see all there was to see of Liberal. It didn't take long. Forty-seven houses, a half dozen barns, scattering of commercial buildings, a freshly painted railroad depot and a vacant lot with a sign proclaiming *Future Location: Seward County Courthouse*—a block over on Washington Avenue—were about all there was to see in the way of architecture. The county seat, in fact, was at Springfield, across the Cimarron. But folks in Liberal didn't intend for it to stay there any longer than it took to steal it.

What Liberal lacked in visual grandeur, though, the place made up for with the two great scenic advantages of all bald-prairie towns. There wasn't a hill, break or tree within twenty miles to block the view, and there wasn't another blamed thing to look at, to cause distraction. Although it was brand new as towns go, Liberal was just naturally the primest example of western Kansas visual interest that a man could ever find.

"I certainly hope this isn't an example of what the Cimarron Proposal looks like," Annie Sue said as she flipped the Morgan cross's reins, and the rockaway bounced across the foot-high gravel grade crossing of the Chicago, Rock Island and Pacific Railroad. Shading her eyes, she gazed beyond the attractions of the little town, at the prairie beyond. "It is rather bleak."

"But there certainly is a lot of it," Milicent pointed out.

Past the tracks a large man with a leather coat stepped out of a shed and strode to the roadway, raising an arm to hail them. The ladies had met Iron

126

Tom Logan only the day before, but they considered him a gentleman and a friend. Without his help, they might not have been able to purchase the carriage rig they needed for their trip to Beaver City. They had tried both wagon yards in Liberal, and all three feed barns, without finding a willing seller . . . until Iron Tom Logan stepped in.

He had seemed to fill the doorway of the livery office, and had stood there for a moment, just listening, as a man named Proctor said for the third time, "Ma'am, there ain't any way in the world that I'm goin' to sell a perfectly good rockaway carriage to two hare-brained females, this time of year."

The man in the doorway had taken a good look at Milicent, and a longer look at Annie Sue, then pulled off his hat and stepped inside. "Is that any way to talk to ladies, Proctor?" he demanded.

Proctor glanced around, and his eyes went wide. "Oh, Mr. Logan," he said. "Mornin', sir. I was just tellin' these charming ladies that I don't have a carriage I can spare right now . . ."

"Do you have a railroad contract you can spare, Proctor?" Logan's eyes never left the ladies, but his words were low and plain.

"Sir?" Proctor goggled at him.

"The ladies want to buy a carriage. Sell them one."

Proctor hardly hesitated. "Yes, sir."

Logan hung around while the sale was transacted, and he personally inspected the carriage. It was old, but in good repair. He even selected their horse for them, from the livery stock. And when it was done, he ordered Proctor to buy them both lunch at the Seward Hotel.

Such a nice gentleman, Mr. Logan, they agreed. Obviously smitten with Annie Sue, but then what man wasn't? It wasn't clear why he was called by the odd name of Iron Tom, but when they asked Proctor, all he

127

said was, "You done seen the reason, ladies." Logan, it seemed, was in charge of the C.R.I. & P. railroad's construction and supply operations, and he could swing a supply contract the way most men might swing a hammer. Logan was a newcomer in Liberal. But then, who wasn't?

It had been pleasant, encountering in these arid climes a gentleman who would go out of his way to be of assistance to ladies. But now, hailing them on South Main Street, Iron Tom Logan looked less gentlemanly than he had the day before. He looked, in fact, angry. Annie Sue eased back on the oiled leather reins with little gloved hands, and the Morgan cross eased to a stop. "Good morning, Mr. Logan," she said.

He strode to the rockaway, lifted a side curtain and frowned at the luggage and packages inside. "So they're right," he said. "And southbound, too." He stepped beside the driver's seat, glared at the women and demanded, "Where in hell do you two think you're going?"

"Mr. Logan, please!" Annie Sue's eyes went wide. "Mind your language."

Now, there isn't a healthy man west of Baltimore who can sustain a thunderous frown more than a second or two when confronted by big, startled blue eyes in an angel's face—maybe not even in Baltimore— and Iron Tom was no exception. The frown went sort of limp, but the determination behind it didn't. "I couldn't believe my ears when I heard," he sputtered. "Two women, setting out on their own . . . for No Man's Land? I won't stand for it, do you understand?"

"You won't stand for what?" Milicent tightened her grip on her handbag, and her own Irish eyes went cold.

Logan stepped back a little. Nobody knew what Milicent Moriarty kept in that handbag of hers, but a

128

tipsy hostler had learned the hard way—just the past evening—that it could make a sizeable bump on the headbone. The story had got around.

"I can't see that where we go is any of your concern, Mr. Logan," Annie Sue pointed out.

"I wish it wasn't," he assured her. "But I helped you get yourself this rig, so I feel responsible. And I can't have you going off to No Man's Land, don't you see? Sooner or later I'd probably hear what happened to you over there, and my conscience wouldn't ever give me a minute's peace, for it being all my fault."

"Happened to us? What do you think will happen to us?"

"Well, I can think of a dozen . . ." he started, then blushed and started again. "Ma'am, that strip yonder, there's no law there. Not any at all. And the men in that strip are the worst sort of villains you can imagine. They'll do anything. They'll rob, murder, burn, pillage, steal railroad property . . ."

"What does pillage mean?" Milicent wondered.

"Well, I'm not rightly sure, but it's real bad. And there's men out there that'll do it and never think twice about it. And two attractive ladies, traveling alone! I just hate to think what might . . ."

"Oh, nonsense!" Annie Sue shook her head in disbelief. "Mr. Logan, surely you don't think we would set off on a journey without some advance planning with regard to self-defense?" She reached into a straw basket sitting on the floor board, rummaged around and drew forth a large Smith and Wesson revolver, waving it under his nose. "We are quite prepared to . . ."

"Watch it! That thing's . . ." Iron Tom dodged aside, tripped and fell as the gun roared in Annie Sue's hand, and a slug ricocheted off the flag arm of a drop-post across the street. ". . . cocked," Iron Tom's voice came from somewhere below the coach.

"Mercy," Milicent said.

"It seems to have been cocked," Annie Sue looked at the gun, fondly, then handed it to Milicent. "Here, you put it back. And don't cock its hammer." Leaning out from the rockaway, she asked, "Are you all right, Mr. Logan?"

Shaken and disheveled, the railroad man got to his feet and dusted himself off. "God have mercy," he muttered.

"Anyway," Annie Sue assured him, "you can see that your fears were groundless, sir. Milicent and I are in no danger. Good day, Mr. Logan." She snapped the reins and drove on, leaving him standing there with his mouth open.

"In no danger," he muttered. "Maybe not. Maybe it's No Man's Land that ought to watch out."

The shot had drawn some spectators, and one of them was a large man mounted on a big horse with saddlebags and traveling gear strapped in place. This one leaned from the saddle to look down at the railroad boss. "You all right, Mr. Logan?"

Logan glanced up at him. "Hello, Marshal. No harm done, I guess. Accident." He looked again. "Doing some traveling, Marshal? Where's your star?"

"Not 'Marshal' any more," Ben Wiggins said. "Thought I might bounty-hunt for a while, what with Springfield gettin' smaller by the day. You still railroadin', I reckon?"

"What I do," Logan nodded. "Run track and tend crews."

"Yeah, an' feed 'em on uptrail beef. I heard you'd cut a deal with that sidewinder Scrannon to buy beef from him. Sorry I heard that, Iron Tom."

"It's business. I need beef, and Scrannon offers it for half what Kansas beef'll cost me."

"George Scrannon never owned a legal cow in his life," Wiggins frowned. "He's a chiseler and a thief, and

130

you know that as well as I do."

"I got investors to worry about, Ben." Logan scuffed the ground with his boot. "And across that line there, 'legal' doesn't mean squat. I have to buy what I can for the best price I can get."

"Your worry, I reckon," Wiggins shrugged. "I'm sort of looking for a stagecoach. A Concord coach, that came through here from the north couple days back. You see it?"

"Yeah. Fellers were in a hurry. They dropped off a couple of passengers, made a team swap with old man Channing and headed right on south. They wanted for something?"

"Most likely," Wiggins nodded. "You said they dropped off passengers. Happen to know where they are?"

Logan pointed at the rockaway carriage diminishing down the road. "That's them, there. Blamedest thing I ever heard of, too. Two women. A big, handsome one and a pretty little thing with yellow hair, just all by themselves, heading off into No Man's Land. They haven't got the vaguest idea what's over there, Ben. Hell, they'll be lucky if they get past Beer City with their lives, much less their virtues."

"Little one with yellow hair, huh? Face like an angel?"

"That's her."

"Yeah, I thought so. Fellow up at Springfield had that same hound-dog look on his face after he saw her. Just like you do, now." Ben Wiggins thumbed his hatbrim. "Don't worry too much about those two, Tom. I'll kind of tag along, for a ways at least."

"Obliged," Logan said. "But watch yourself, Ben. That little one's downright dangerous."

"Blamed if I see how we're goin' to deliver mail for

that postman," Sill said, glancing down from the duck-and-bow roof of the coach that—for the moment—was named *The Beaver City Exp*. "You know dang well if we cross the border they're gonna nail us."

"We'll think of somethin'," Bart Sherrell assured him. Bart was standing beside the offside door of the big coach, a paint can in one hand, a brush in the other. Now, thrusting his tongue from the corner of his mouth, he added a careful "r" to the lettering already in place. He stepped back, frowned at the letters, then nodded. "Lookin' pretty good so far," he allowed. "Mike, what do you think?"

From beneath the coach, Mike O'Riley's voice growled, "I'll look at it when it's done, Bart. I'm busy here, greasin' spindles. I don't aim to crawl out every time you add a letter and tell you how pretty it is."

"Well, it looks real good," Bart announced. He paused, thoughtfully. "How do you spell 'express'? Is there one 's' or two?"

"Sounds to me like there's three," Sill looked down, helpfully. "E . . . K . . . S . . . P . . . R . . . E . . . S . . . S. Need two 'S's at the end there, so it kind of hisses like a snake, you know."

"There ain't any 'K' in the word," Mike grunted, beneath the stage. "You don't do 'K-S' if a simple 'X' will do the job. Land, Sill, I thought you'd know that."

"Used an 'X'," Bart assured him. "I'll bet Sill's right about those two 'S's at the end, though. Express-s-s. It does sound kind of hissy." Concentrating, he applied brush to door to paint another letter . . . an 'e', followed by two 's's'. Then he stepped back grinning. "There, now! By golly! 'THE BEAVER CITY EXPRESS'."

"Good," Mike muttered, below. "When you start on the other side, try not to drip paint on me like you done before."

"What about the borders?" Sill asked.

"Oh, I reckon I can paint some frilly lines and curlicues around the words," Bart shrugged. "Wouldn't hurt anything."

"I mean those other borders! The Kansas border, the Texas border, the Territory border . . . if we aim to haul the U.S. mail, we got to cross borders. How long do you think it's goin' to take folks to figure out that this here stagecoach is fair game for the law if it goes where law is?"

"We won't haul across borders," Bart assured him. "That postmaster's problem is just how to get mail to and from the borders. Other folks can handle it from there. Don't worry about it."

"Well, I just get to thinkin' sometimes," Sill explained.

"Lord help us," Mike growled, beneath the coach.

"We'll make scheduled runs," Bart decided. "Beaver City to anyplace else that folks want to go, long as it's inside No Man's Land. Beaver City to Beer City to Haymeadow Flats to Tyrone Switch to Boise City, say, then back to Beaver City by way of Cow Spring an' Hardesty. Like that."

"With everybody an' his brother shootin' at us ever' mile of the way, just for the hell of it, most likely," Sill noted.

"Not more'n about once, they won't," Mike assured them, coming out from under the coach and adjusting his guns.

"Sir," Thomas Allen Fry wrote, "please understand the necessity for special designation in order to complete, or even to begin, an enumeration of residents in the area known as the Neutral Strip. I have been here, in the place called Beaver City, for only two days, and already my luggage has been stolen, I have lost my hat and I have been shot at by a total stranger for no better reason than that he objected to the color of my vest. This is by way of making it clear to you what conditions exist in an area that has no official designation and that, in many minds, does not even exist . . . an area of approximately 5,000 square miles in size, containing at least 2,000 de facto residents and where the only semblance of law and order are a 'vigilance committee' of outlaws and known rowdies and a postmaster.

"It is, to say the least, a challenge. My pre-census analysis is hereby submitted, based primarily upon drawings prepared for me by the local postmaster and several other gentlemen. There being no legal ownerships here, and thus no deeds, deed records or even area surveys, these drawings must serve as plats for they are all that are available.

"In the meantime, I request an emergency order designating the Neutral Strip as something—a county, a territory, a state, *anything,* so long as it is *something*—for census purposes. Further, I request authority to empower and designate the enumerators assigned here as census marshals, with powers equivalent to the authority of territorial marshals in areas that have territorial status.

"Believe me, sir, these steps are necessary, if there is to be a census in this area referred to as the Neutral Strip.

"Your friend and servant,

"Thomas Allen Fry, Regional Coordinator."

Fry read through his letter and its accompanying documents, then folded the package and sealed it. Both he and the package would go north on the Beaver City Express, leaving shortly. But while he traveled as a passenger, the package would travel as United States mail. Somehow, he felt that it might be safer that way.

He was still shaken from the experience of hiding

134

under a bed while two men staged a running gunfight in his hotel room, the previous night. It would have been bad enough, he felt, if the men were afoot. But the spectacle of two mounted drunks wheeling their horses around and around in a tiny room while they emptied their guns at each other was more than he could cope with at the moment.

XV

"I have never seen so many drunks in one place in all my life," Annie Sue said, turning to look back at the ramshackle little town diminishing behind them. Beer City, the place was called, and it hadn't taken her and Milicent Moriarty more than one quick look around to decide that their best course of action was to drive right on through and not stop for anyone. Even so, it had been a harrowing experience.

"I hope I didn't hurt that man," Milicent said.

"Which one?"

"The one that ran alongside and tried to climb into the carriage with us. I had to hit him several times to make him turn loose of the railing."

"I hope you did hurt him," Annie Sue disagreed. "I hope he's laid up for a week. You heard what he was suggesting."

"Of course I heard. And it was shocking. But you know, there are ladies who make their living that way."

"Women," Annie Sue snapped. "But not ladies. And any man who can't tell the difference deserves what he gets. I thought you meant that other one—the one you fired my pistol at."

"Oh, him," Milicent shook her head. "No. I wasn't aiming to hit him, so I didn't."

"He fell down."

"He ducked and stumbled."

"Well, I may have run over some part of him. We hit *something* back there."

"That bump? Was that what that was?" Milicent looked back. "Oh, well, this is a fairly light carriage." She squinted, shading her eyes. "Most of them have stopped following us. They're going back into town. There is a man on horseback, who seems to be chasing some of them."

"I am not in the slightest interested in any of those people back there. Beer City is a disgusting place, and I suggest that we say no more about it."

"I couldn't agree more," Milicent decided.

Annie drove along for a time, in silence, looking with disapproval at the bleak, featureless countryside around them. The land had become slightly rolling, with little hills here and there, but there were few signs of civilization. In the distance ahead, though, were hints of greenery and just the vaguest suggestion that the land yonder might have a feature or two if a body wanted to look for them.

"I can't imagine why a house of ill repute would call itself a railroad," Annie Sue said.

Milicent looked around at her, confused. "What?"

"Back there in that awful town, we passed a building that was obviously nothing more than a . . . a bawdy house. But the sign on it said, 'Chicago, Rock Island and Pacific Railroad.' I was just wondering why."

"I thought we had decided not to talk about that place anymore."

"You're right. We did. I suppose all those people have stopped trying to follow us by now."

Milicent looked back, squinting. "All but one," she said. "There is a gentleman on horseback who is either following us or just happens to be going the same direction that we are."

"Is it anyone we know?"

"I don't think so," Milicent decided. She turned to

137

look forward again, and pointed. "Is that a town ahead there?"

"Where?" Annie Sue peered into the distance. "Oh. Yes, it seems to be. Do you have the map that Colonel Booth-Sykes drew for us?"

Milicent got out the map and studied it thoughtfully. "The next town, according to this, is Beaver City, but I don't think it's that close." She squinted, trying to get a better view of the little town dancing in the hazes ahead, then gasped when the entire town rose slowly into the air, an island of indistinct structure floating above distant landscape.

"It isn't all that close," Annie Sue said. "That is a mirage."

"Mercy," Milicent muttered, looking at the map again. By her estimate, it was still at least fifteen miles to Beaver City. "This is very strange country," she noted.

By the time the sun was overhead and they found a shady spot beside a little stream to stop and rest the horse, the mounted man behind them was much closer. He was a large, middle-aged man with a full mustache. He was riding a big packed horse and carrying what seemed to be an unusual number of guns, both on his saddle and on his person.

Several times in the past hour, Milicent had turned to look back at him, suspiciously. Each time, he tipped his hat and kept on coming.

The little stream was nothing more than a rivulet flowing between grassy banks at the bottom of a sloped gully, but there were a few trees along it that provided shade, and Annie Sue pulled over and stopped beneath one of them. They stepped down, walked around for a moment to relieve the stiffness of a long morning's ride in a bumpy rockaway, then Milicent spread a blanket on the grass while Annie Sue got out the food basket they had packed that morning at the hotel in Liberal. While she spread their picnic lunch, Milicent freed the horse from harness, led it out of the carriage shafts and hobbled two of its feet with a sheepskin strap.

Annie Sue brought water from the creek in a kettle, and built a small fire which abruptly became a large fire as the prairie grass around it began to blaze. They spent the next few minutes putting out grass fires, and rescuing their picnic. "Mercy," Milicent breathed when everything was under control again. They respread their picnic, put water on for tea and looked up, to find the stranger a few yards away, sitting tall on his big horse and gazing down at them admiringly.

"Howdy, ladies," he said in a voice that sounded like it was coming out of a barrel. He pulled off his hat and managed a friendly grin—a strained expression on a face that looked like it had been hammered out of caprock stone—and said, "Wiggins is the name. Ben Wiggins. Thought you ladies might need a hand with your fire, but it looks like you've got everything under control here."

"We certainly do," Milicent assured him. "Have you been following us, Mr. Wiggins?"

"Seems like," he admitted. "But after seein' how you taken care of yourselves back yonder at Beer City, I'd say it wasn't necessary. Iron Tom Logan underestimated you ladies, seems to me."

"You came from Mr. Logan?" Annie Sue blinked at him.

"No, ma'am. I was comin' this way anyhow. But he did say I might look out for you, in a manner of speakin'."

"Well, that is kind of you," Annie Sue said. "Though we are quite able to look out for ourselves." She glanced around at the picnic lunch, then back at the man. "My name is Annabel Finch, Mr. Wiggins, and my friend is Milicent Moriarty. We are on our way to Beaver City, to take possession of some land I have bought there. Would you care to join us for lunch? We have plenty of fried chicken."

139

"Yes, ma'am, I'd like that." Wiggins stepped down from his horse and swatted its rump. It headed for the stream, where the carriage horse was drinking. With his back to the women, he muttered, "I surely can see why Sid got all foggy over the little one. Pretty as a picture, right enough. But Logan was right about the big one, too. That there is one right handsome hunk of woman."

"Did you say something, Mr. Wiggins?" Milicent asked, behind him.

"Talkin' to myself, ma'am," he turned and managed another grin, like reshaping caprock. "My, but that there fried chicken looks right tasty."

Milicent stooped to arrange the picnic service and Wiggins watched, admiringly. "Right handsome," he muttered again.

Annie Sue had a hand on the brim of her sun bonnet, holding it low to shade her eyes, peering southward. Beyond the little creek, where the prairie rose and receded, there was movement. In the distance, four riders crested a low ridge, paused, and turned their mounts, looking back the way they had come.

"Remarkable," Annie Sue allowed.

Wiggins had squatted beside the picnic blanket, reaching for the food basket. He turned. "Ma'am?"

"These mirages out here," she said, pointing. "Those men are probably miles away, but they seem so near."

Wiggins looked, and stood. "That's no mirage, ma'am. That's four hellions up there on that rise. Wonder what they're up to."

"Hellions?" Milicent asked.

"Yes, ma'am. This territory's full of the like. You see a passel of young bucks out here, and they ain't doin' something plain honest—like workin' or loafin'—you know they're hellions and probably up to no good."

The four had backed their mounts away from the rise, and were edging them into a stand of scrub oak. They were still looking the other way, toward the rise from which they had come.

"Up to no good, for sure," Wiggins said. He jammed a drumstick into his mouth, hitched up his belts and went to get his horse. He had just picked up its reins when a merry, rattling sound came on the breeze and a stagecoach appeared on the rise, a hundred yards to the west of the hidden hellions. Two men were seated up front, and another on top.

Just as it came into view, the four riders broke cover and raced toward it, guns drawn. The coach driver slapped his reins, and the coach bounded down the slope as its team stretched out to run. In a moment it was clattering down to and across the little creek.

"Mercy," Milicent said, "It's Mr. Sherrell, and Mr. O'Riley!" A gunbarrel poked from a window, pointing back, and a face appeared behind it. "And Mr. Sills," she added, waving.

The big man atop the coach fired then, a booming sound that echoed along the creek. Bart Sherrell saw them, then, and returned the wave. He nudged Mike O'Riley, beside him, and shouted something, O'Riley and the big man on top looked downstream at the picnic. There were two faces in the windows now, and five hats were raised in momentary greeting as the tall coach bounded up the north bank and veered away onto the faint trail northward.

"And Mr. Fry," Annie Sue noted. "I suppose he's finished his business at Beaver City. Look, Milicent, they've painted their coach."

The Concord coach had been red and yellow. Now it was green, with white letters on its side that proclaimed, *Beaver City Express*.

Bounding and rattling, the coach sped away up the north rise and disappeared over the crest there. The four riders behind it barely hesitated at the creek cut. Clinging to their horses, they sprinted into and out of the stream, spraying water. As they leveled out for the chase beyond, they all looked aside, prodding up their

141

hat brims with drawn guns as they saw the ladies there, then leaned to the run and headed on.

"Holdup!" Ben Wiggins shouted, swinging to his saddle. He drew a gun of his own and spurred his horse. A few seconds later, Milicent and Annie Sue were alone beside the creek, with only settling dust to testify that anyone else had passed that way.

They stood, staring where the coach and horsemen had gone. Milicent shook her head. "Mercy," she said. "They were abrupt, weren't they!"

"I have a feeling we should finish our lunch and be on our way," Annie Sue decided.

The sun was quartering in the west, and there had been no further sign of the stagecoach, the young riders or Mr. Wiggins, when the rockaway topped out on a hill decorated here and there by soapweed, sage and buffalo bones, and they saw Beaver City in the distance. It was no mirage now, but a real, ramshackle little town whose roofs—and a few cottonwood trees— rose above the swell of a sloping riverbank running along just to their right.

"I believe my land should be just over there, somewhere," Annie Sue pointed to the right, where treetops marked the hidden river valley.

Milicent squinted. "Are you sure? I don't see a house. A three-story house should be visible from here, if that's where it is."

"It may be hidden among the trees," Annie Sue pointed out. "We can get exact directions in town, I'm sure, but possibly we can have a closer look on our way." She pulled out the map, frowned at it, and peered again at the rolling terrain and the little river valley beyond. "I'm sure it is here somewhere. You see, over there where the far hills are? There is another stream coming down, toward the river. This must be where it is."

"I don't see any buildings at all," Milicent shook her head. "Are you sure about the house and improvements?"

"Colonel Booth-Sykes definitely said there was a house," Annie Sue insisted. "He said it is improved property. With a residence. I had the impression of three floors." Clicking her tongue, she turned the buggy horse to the right and headed for the crest for a better view. The land climbed ahead of them, then dropped away, and a rider appeared there, less than a hundred yards away. He was walking his horse, swinging a coiled rope, and looking back. He seemed to be talking to someone, but no one else came over the rise. Only a rangy-looking steer with wide horns.

As they approached, they could hear the man's voice. He sounded angry. "I don't know what's got into you today, Blue! Actin' like a weanin' calf, an' you the chosen leader of your herd! Land, but I'd thought you was trail broke by now. Come on, dang it! Show a little responsibility in what you're . . ."

The rockaway was almost to them when the brindle steer saw it coming. It stared at the carriage, its eyes went white-rimmed and it shook its head and bellowed a challenge . . . then swapped ends and took off at a high lope, back the way it had come.

"Blue!" the man shouted. "Dag nab, you miserable excuse for a bone-headed cow critter . . . !" He knee-reined his mount, and it skidded into a running turn, haunches down and aslant as it took out after the steer. "Come back here!" the man shouted.

"Fidget!" Annie Sue muttered. "I was hoping that gentleman might give us directions to my section of land." She slapped her reins and urged the buggy horse into a fast trot.

"I don't believe he ever saw us," Milicent noted, grabbing the side rail with one hand and her bonnet with the other. "He was so absorbed, talking to his cow . . ."

At a rapid clip, the rockaway went over the crest and down onto the slopes beyond, and suddenly there were cattle all around. Straight ahead, the brindle steer was

143

still running, seeming to slice through a long carpet of cattle as the man on horseback pursued it. Cattle veered away on both sides, lowing and skittering, many of them turning to follow, and abruptly the rockaway was surrounded by a sea of bovine frolic. Somewhere beyond, men's voices shouted, but it was all Annie Sue could do at the moment to control her reins, stay within the vanishing clear trail where the steer and rider had gone, and try to keep up as a mass of milling cattle closed in on both sides and behind, flowing with them toward the river at the bottom of the long slope.

XVI

If ever two people seemed meant for each other, Annie Sue Finch and Bobby Lee Smith weren't them. Oh, they made a handsome couple, all right—Bobby Lee being the strapping young six-footer that he was, his boots kicking up dust as he stomped around and swore every oath that could cut through the thunder on his brow, and Annie Sue about the prettiest little bit of absolute wrath that anybody ever saw, and each one of them so all-fired mad at the other that the air above the Beaver seemed to sizzle, and the river looked like it was about to boil.

The thing of it was, Busted S was scattered over a square mile of good graze on both sides of the river and up Jackson Creek, and the only place that there weren't any cows was right there on the riverbank where the ladies' rockaway sat aslant on three wheels and a broken hub.

"Five hundred cows!" Bobby Lee swore over and over again, kicking dirt and pounding his fists on the nearest cottonwood tree. "Five hundred legal cows, all the way up from Abilene an' not twenty miles from market! Rivers done crossed, rustlers buried an' jailed, an' what happens? Women! Dang fool women, with no better sense than to mosey right into a drove herd!"

A grizzled old cowboy on a lineback dun had paused to listen to the tirade, but now he took a look at the little blonde woman with her hands on her hips, and he saw the fire in those big blue eyes and said, "Now, Bobby Lee, what's done is done did. Maybe you just ought to . . ."

"Shut up, Pappy!" Bobby Lee snapped. "I'll handle this."

"That's right," the little blonde added. "You just stay out of this. This stomping oaf can dig his own grave without your help." She faced around to Bobby Lee, her eyes blazing. "I never saw the like in my whole life! A body just out driving along, minding her own business, and here comes some nitwit driving cattle on a public road! I have a mind to . . ."

"Public road?" Bobby Lee got a look on his face like from swallowing whole persimmons. *"Public road? Why you little . . ."*

Milicent Moriarty stepped toward him, threateningly. "See here, you! You mind your tongue!"

"Shut up, Milicent!" Annie Sue snapped. "I can deal with this lout."

"That's right, ma'am," Bobby Lee added. "You just stay out of this. It's between me an' this sawed-off snappin' turtle here. It was her a'driven' the rig." He spun back to glare at Annie Sue. "What do you mean, 'lout'?" Who's a lout?"

"You are, obviously," Annie Sue snapped.

Pappy stepped down from the lineback dun and led it over, thumbing up his hat, "Howdy, ma'am," he told Milicent. "Jameson's my name. I answer to 'Pappy'."

"Milicent Moriarty," Milicent nodded at him. "Maybe we should put a stop to this."

"I'm game to try if you got any idea how," Pappy agreed. "Looks to me like a body could get skun, though, steppin' betwixt them two."

Bobby Lee and Annie Sue whirled around to face them. "You two stay out of this!" they snapped, harmonic as a gospel chorus. "I don't need any help to deal with the likes of him/her!" Their stiff fingers pointed accusingly at each other.

"Mind who you point at!" Annie Sue hissed. "Lout!"

"You mind, yourself," Bobby Lee rumbled. "You . . . you little . . ."

"Little what?" Pappy wondered.

"Shut up! I'll think of somethin'!"

"Look what you did to my carriage!"

"Hang your carriage! Look what you did to my herd!"

"You ladies goin' far?" Pappy asked Milicent.

"We've been afar, but that town over there is our destination, if that is Beaver City."

"Believe it is," Pappy allowed. He strolled over to the broken-down rig and squatted to look at the hub. "Reckon this needs to be fixed," he said.

"So it would seem," Milicent agreed. "What would you suggest?"

"Well, ma'am, I suggest we get ol' Shorty Mars to have a look at it. He's a hand with rollin' stock!"

"I can't spare Shorty!" Bobby Lee hollered, still glaring at Annie Sue. "I need every man to round up our cows! Land, here we are in No Man's Land, with ever' yayhoo in miles taggin' after us to steal beef, last thing in this world we need is fixin' wagons for hare-brained females!"

"Have the men repair the carriage, Milicent," Annie Sue ordered, not taking her eyes off Bobby Lee. "I imagine this . . . this *imbecile* was dropped on his head as a baby, but I'd accept reparation by way of apology from the other gentlemen. It's the least they can do."

"Do nothin!" Bobby Lee rasped. "Y'all spilled my cows!"

"Your cows wrecked my carriage!" Annie Sue retorted.

In unison, Pappy and Milicent rounded on them. "You two! Both of you! Shut up!"

147

"The cows is bein' gathered, Bobby Lee," Pappy said. "Quit rantin' about it!"

"The carriage can be repaired, Annie Sue," Milicent said. "Don't carry on so!"

"That Bobby Lee is the stubbornest human bein' God ever saw fit to put ears on," Pappy explained to Milicent.

"Oh, you haven't seen stubborn until you've dealt with Annie Sue," Milicent assured him.

Willie Sutter was heading in from across the river, driving his lead steer, and some of the others were coming in with bunches of strayed Busted S cattle. Each man who wandered near was careful to tip his hat to the ladies, and several of them—mostly the younger ones—like to have fell off their saddles for gaping in wide-eyed adoration at Annie Sue. Bobby Lee and Annie Sue continued to square off like a pair of banties for a few minutes more, then couldn't think of anything more to say so Annie Sue stalked off to fume by the rockaway, and Bobby Lee stamped off to find his horse and count cows.

"There dang well better be five hundred head!" he grumped over his shoulder. "Five hundred, an' not one cow less."

"I expect my carriage to be as good as new!" Annie Sue shot back. "Or you'll hear from me!"

"Lord have mercy," Pappy shook his head.

"Mercy," Milicent echoed.

Bobby Lee's day horse was limping from a stone bruise, so he stripped off his gear and went for another mount, where the Burnett brothers had the remuda gathered. He might have made another choice, except that Tarnation saw him coming and met him at the rope, nuzzling him the way a puppy nuzzles its favorite folks. Mad as he was, it didn't make any difference to Bobby Lee what horse he forked, so he slapped his leather on Tarnation and swung aboard.

Five hundred cows! Scattered from here to yonder.

In the saddle, he looked around, breathing through his teeth, then shook his head. It wasn't such a bad spill, actually. Being right in the little valley like that, the cows had just sort of spread out and gone back to water, and his crew was all over the place, bunching them up and bringing them in. Bobby Lee got out his tally string and sighed. Maybe he hadn't lost any, he thought. It was true, there had been sightings for the past ten-fifteen miles, riders dogging the herd, but the strangers had kept their distance. It seemed likely the object lesson back yonder—when they explained the facts of life to those bunch-cutters—had taken good effect.

He headed Tarnation along the bank, picking out a good, clear area to bunch the herd for counting. There was a fair place up there, just beyond where the rockaway carriage sat akimbo at the water's edge. Approaching, he saw Shorty Mars on foot, hat in one hand and tool box in the other, fixing to fix the broken wheel. The rest of the boys were moving cows, keeping them clear of the bank, though it did seem they were going to a lot of trouble to get a good look at the ladies in passing.

That little one . . . mad as he was, Bobby Lee still had eyes in his head, and it occurred to him that he had probably never seen a prettier sight in his whole life—blonde hair stacked under a sunbonnet, little fists planted on shapely hips, and the breeze doing powerful suggestive things to her skirt like it just couldn't get over what fine underpinnings were hid there. She wasn't any bigger than a minute, he noticed for the first time. And her eyes were the most amazing shade of blue . . . he shut his head down on such thoughts, the way only a truly mule-headed stubborn man can.

A day and a half from prime market, and she had come rattling in with a funny-looking wagon and spilled his herd over half of God's country!

A few yards away from the wagon, he eased back on

149

the reins and pointed an angry finger at her. "One more thing!" he snapped.

She turned, her eyes beginning to blaze again. "Oh? And what might that . . . ?"

Tarnation had stood it just as long as he could. His ears went back, his head went down, he did a fast double crow-hop to shake Bobby Lee loose from his saddle, then bunched his hind quarters and launched the rider over his shoulders.

Bobby Lee bounced off the side of the rockaway, did a fancy dance trying to get his balance, and bowled into Annie Sue Finch like a Greek wrestler going for a pin. The two of them scooted off the bank and hit the water five feet out. The splash doused the rockaway and everybody within ten feet of it, and threw spray half-way across the Beaver.

Tarnation had been all set to spin and run, but he changed his mind. He just stood there, like everybody else, gawking at where Bobby Lee and Annie Sue had gone.

The water was about waist-deep out yonder, and Annie Sue was the first one to surface. She was spitting and hissing like a wet cat, raring for a fight. A second later, Bobby Lee came up beside her, and she glared lightning bolts at him, balled up her fists and turned a complete circle right there in the water, getting momentum into her swing. The fist that collided with Bobby Lee's head might not have been big, but its intentions were clear and a powerful lot of dedication was behind it.

Bobby Lee barely saw it coming, then he was doing a back-sprawl, throwing spray and disappearing into the stream again.

Annie Sue turned. "Milicent, find my gun! I intend to shoot this person, immediately!"

"Annie Sue, you just come out of there!" Milicent ordered.

"I will not tolerate such behavior! You saw what he

150

did. He did that on purpose!"

Bobby Lee made it to the surface again, blowing spray, and Annie Sue cocked her fists again, but this time he was too far away.

"Oh-h-h!" she fumed, and headed for shore.

There was just no end of willing cowboys waiting on the bank, to give her a hand to shore, but Milicent shooed them all away and brought a blanket to wrap around the wet calico that indicated more of Annie Sue than Milicent considered polite.

When Bobby Lee finally got himself out of the river, nursing a grudge and a bruised cheekbone, the ladies were secluded inside the rockaway and its curtains were drawn.

Bobby Lee growled like a wet bear, shook himself down and growled again. Then he stepped to Tarnation, swung aboard and clamped his knees. "Dadblame cayuse!" he swore. "You good-for-nothin' varmint! Let's see you try that again!"

Tarnation looked around at him with big, innocent eyes that deplored the fact that the rider on his back was dripping wet, but would forgive him under the circumstances. With all the dignity of a proud horse falsely accused, Tarnation nodded his big head, turned and ambled off toward the gather. Just like he knew that Bobby Lee aimed to count cows, and would carry him to do the job no matter how wet he was.

"I swear I never saw the like," Pappy Jameson pushed back his hat and scratched his head.

A curtain parted in the rockaway, and Milicent looked out. "What did he do to make that horse throw him at Annie Sue?"

"I reckon it was all the horses's notion," Pappy shook his head. "Tarnation just gets that way now and again."

It took Shorty Mars an hour and a half to rebuild the hub on the rockaway and get its rigging straightened out, but Bobby Lee Smith was still counting cows when the rig rolled away downstream toward Beaver City.

An hour later he put away his tally string and told Shad Ames, "Well, they're all here, no thanks to female intrusion. Five hundred head." He turned. "Willie! Get that lead steer up yonder! Shad, let's head 'em up an' move 'em out!" He looked all around. "Where's Mouse?"

"We ain't got but a few hours of daylight left, Bobby Lee," Shad Ames said. "How far you think we'll get before we bed them?"

"As far from here as we can," Bobby Lee frowned. "Hell, them women might take a notion to come back. Anybody seen Mouse lately?"

He was still steamy around the ears, but he had cooled off some during the count. Now, as the herd once again pointed out northward from the Beaver River, he looked around the little valley and his mouth dropped open. "This is it!" he muttered. "By dang, this is the very place."

And it was, just the way he had pictured it. Meadow, cottonwood trees, an easy slope down to a pretty little river, everything just the way he had imagined it. He had dreamed up the place he wanted to have, and all of a sudden here he was looking at it. Everything, just like he had imagined. And right over yonder, up on that rise, was where he would put his porch. He shaded his eyes, squinting, then looked again. There was *something* over there.

Without a glance back, he headed Tarnation up the quartering rise. The top of it was screened by bushes— a cutaway thicket of scrub oak—but within the thicket, almost hidden from the river, was a ramshackle roof. Bobby Lee pushed through the brush and gawked.

The building was no more than a slap-up cabin that some squatter had built on the high slope. It didn't even have a flat floor . . . just a series of shoveled-out shoulders like three separate floors a foot or two above and below one another. Not much of a cabin, at all, and

152

abandoned for some time by the looks of it. But it had a porch!

Just like Bobby Lee had seen in his imaginings, there was a shaded porch with an old, busted-down rocking chair, and it faced out toward the river.

"By dang," Bobby Lee breathed. "This *is* it."

He hadn't even heard Pappy Jameson ride up behind him, but now Pappy asked, "This is what, Bobby Lee?"

"It!" Bobby Lee turned, waving his hand toward the place. "This is my first section. It's just what I'm looking for."

"I swear," Pappy marveled.

"I got to find out who belongs to this, so I can buy it," Bobby Lee announced.

"Maybe not anybody," Pappy suggested. "This here's No Man's Land, remember?"

"Somebody does," Bobby Lee indicated the abandoned cabin. "This is improved land."

"Well, if you aim to buy it, we best get these cows to market so you'll have the money," Pappy pointed out. "If it can be had at all, it's likely gonna cost more than five dollars."

"You're right as rain about that," Bobby Lee admitted. He took a long look around, fixing in his mind the exact location of the place. There wasn't any doubt about landmarks. It was on the Beaver River, right across from where that creek entered it. "This is it," he said again, firmly. "Pappy, I am still on a lucky streak, an' this is the next piece of luck, just as soon as I get a price from the Chicago, Rock Island and Pacific Railroad Company for them five hundred legal cows. Let's get to movin'! We're burnin' daylight, by dang!"

Pappy watched him go, shaking his head as he remembered the young buck heading for the river with his arms full of irritated blonde angel. "I expect you're on a lucky streak, all right," he muttered to himself. "It's just a all-fired shame that you're too bull-headed to know how lucky you really are."

153

Pappy started to follow the boy, then turned back. The breeze through the scrub-oak had moved something, and it caught his eye. Edging the lineback dun around, he rode over to the forlorn, ramshackle little cabin and leaned down. A piece of paper had been nailed to a porch post, and it fluttered there. An old piece of heavy paper, discolored by the weather but still in place. He leaned out, grabbed it and pulled it loose.

There was no telling how long it had been there . . . maybe weeks or months, or more. But the scrawled words on it were still legible.

"Squatters," it said. "You have 24 hours to leave this place, or face the consequences."

It was signed, "The Beaver City Vigilance Committee."

XVII

When the Busted S veered left to steer clear of the little town in the valley, Mouse Moore decided to go and have a look at the place. He crossed the river at a ford below a frequent-seeming cemetery hill—judging by the patches of fresh dirt, the planting of people was a regular activity—headed his gray up the other bank and reined aside as an old buckboard splashed across the river behind him and overtook him. The wagon was empty, but the driver's hands weren't. The man had his reins in one hand, a revolver in the other and fire in his eyes.

Mouse moved over to let him pass, and the man glanced aside at him, then hauled back on the reins. "Don't I know you from someplace?" he demanded.

"Could be," Mouse said. "I been there."

"You a Scrannon man?"

"Don't believe so," Mouse allowed. "I'm Busted S."

"Sorry to hear that," the man sympathized. "But if you was a Scrannon man, it'd serve you right. You know where George Scrannon is?"

"Don't believe I know him," Mouse shook his head. "I just got here."

The man stared at him a moment longer, then snapped his reins and headed on into town.

Mouse shrugged and followed. Passing a house with

155

a sign that read: *Owen Lance Road Ranch,* he tipped his hat to a lady plucking a chicken on the porch and eased over to the fence. "Ma'am," he said.

She looked him over, doubtfully, and eased a shotgun onto her lap. "Howdy," she said.

"Is this here Beaver City?"

"That's what ever'body calls it, so I reckon it is. Don't I know you?" She frowned at him, then snapped her fingers. "I know who you are. You're Owen's cousin what's-'is-name, from Hardesty."

"No, ma'am, I'm . . ."

"I know who you are," she glared at him. "Well, Owen ain't here, an' even if he was, he wouldn't loan you any money."

"I wouldn't think of askin' him to," Mouse assured her. "I was just wonderin' where I could buy me some shells."

"Well, not here," she snapped. "Try the post office."

"Ma'am?"

"The post office! It's yonder. Sign says *Dobbs General Merchandise.* You can't miss it."

"Yes, ma'am." Mouse put his hat back on his head and went on into town. It wasn't much of a town, just some barns and sheds and slap-up little houses, and a main street about three times as long as it was wide. A few folks were out and about, and some of them looked at him like they were trying to figure out where they had seen him before, but Mouse was used to that.

The second building on the left on Main Street—not counting a couple of barns and an outhouse—had half a dozen fresh-painted signs out front that said it was the Scrannon Land and Cattle Company, that town lots could be had cheap, that it was the headquarters of the Beaver City Vigilance Committee, that it was the Provisional Capitol of the Cimarron Proposal, that unnecessary gunfire within the city limits was against the law, and that fresh-cut fence posts were available,

156

two for a nickel.

Mouse was impressed. The little building wasn't thirty feet on a side, but it seemed to serve a multitude of purposes. There were almost more signs than building.

The one about fence posts seemed to be accurate, because there was a big stack of freshly cut cedar posts out in front. The buckboard that had passed him was stopped there, and its driver was walking around the stack, gun in hand, frowning and muttering to himself. The man seemed to make up his mind about something, and looked across the street, then started that way. Mouse had to rein hard to keep from being walked right into.

Across the street and two doors along was a larger building with only one sign on it. It said: *Happy Times Saloon, Gov. Oliver Winshaw, Prop.* The man with the gun in his hand stalked toward it and stopped in the street outside. He raised his gun and fired a shot in the air, then yelled, "Scrannon! George Scrannon! Come out!"

When nothing happened, the man shouted again. "Scrannon! Blast your ornery hide, come out here! You stole my cedar posts, an' the evidence is right yonder. Get your thievin' butt out here an' settle accounts with me!"

The saloon door opened a crack, then wider, and a man stepped out. A slender, baggy-eyed individual in tailor-made clothes and polished boots. He stepped past the shade of the narrow awning and stopped. There was no expression on his face, but there was murder in his eyes. Mouse eased aside, out of the line of fire.

"Are you addressing me, sir?" the baggy-eyed slicker asked.

"You know who I'm addressin', Scrannon," the buckboard man snapped. "You stole my fence posts.

157

Now you're goin' to pay me for 'em, or put 'em back where you got 'em."

"Your accusing me of theft?" Scrannon hissed.

"Damn right I am. You're a thief and a sneak, George Scrannon, and everybody knows it!"

Scrannon's hand went to the open front of his coat, and the man leveled his pistol. "None of that!" he ordered. "You just haul that pistol out of there easy, and drop it on the ground."

"Why, of course," Scrannon said. "If you're that nervous. There is some sort of misunderstanding here, obviously."

"Haul it out! Easy!"

Carefully, Scrannon drew a revolver from under his coat, holding it by the butt with a thumb and two fingers.

"Now drop it," the man ordered.

"Certainly," Scrannon shrugged. With a casual motion, he tossed the gun so that it skidded to a stop at the man's feet.

"Now we're gonna talk posts," the man said. He stooped, reached for the fallen gun and shuddered as a bullet ripped into him. A second shot echoed the first, and the man pitched backward and sprawled in the dirt. A few feet away, George Scrannon lowered a small, large-bore Derringer and shook his head. "Stupid," he sneered.

Mouse was impressed. He had seen hideout guns before, but never one used just that way. It was a trick worth remembering.

Further up the street he found Dobbs General Merchandise, with its Post Office sign. He stepped down, looped his reins at the hitch-rail and glanced back down the street. There were a few people there, looking at the dead man, but nobody seemed particularly excited about it. It was as though things like that happened all the time.

158

Shaking his head, Mouse went inside, followed by a man in an apron who seemed to be both storekeeper and postmaster.

"Need a box of .44s," he said.

The postmaster shook his head. "Deplorable," he said, still looking toward the door. "Disgraceful."

"Sorry," Mouse said. "It's just what I shoot."

The man glanced at him. "What? What is?"

".44 caliber. It's what fits my iron."

"Oh," the postmaster rummaged on a shelf and handed over a box of shells. "Do I know you?"

"Not that I know of. Name's Moore. I'm just passin' through."

"Good way to be, around here. You saw what happens to folks that stay on."

"Yeah." Mouse shook his head. "I've seen folks shot over a poker hand, but never over fence posts. That all there was to it?"

"What else does it take? There's no law here. Will's mistake was trying to face down Scrannon. He should have just shot him."

"I'll keep that in mind," Mouse assured him. He bought his cartridges from the postmaster, then went back out and climbed onto his saddle.

There wasn't much to see in Beaver City, he decided, and he had seen enough. He headed northward, out of town, and angled to the west. A few miles away, a dust haze told him where Busted S was. A roofed carriage was coming toward him from upstream, and he squinted . . . blinked and squinted again . . . then reined the gray to a halt. He pulled off his hat and held it at his breast as the carriage passed, heading for Beaver City. When it was beyond him he looked after it for a time, then returned his hat to his head and whistled—a long, low whistle.

Mouse Moore had seen some good looking girls in his life, but never one to match the little honey at the

159

reins of that carriage. Maybe he ought to look around Beaver City a little more, he thought.

Milicent Moriarty turned to look back at the openmouthed, hat-crumpling cowboy sitting on a stopped horse, and a puzzled frown touched her brow.

"Is that someone we know?" she asked. "He looks familiar."

Haygood Dobbs stepped out to watch Scrannon's street-cleaners—as he considered the three hulking, brutish Jute brothers and their associates—clear away the evidence of George Scrannon's latest murder. Five of them had come from the Happy Times Saloon to pick up the remains of the cedarcutter, Will Sidey. Without ceremony, they hoisted the body, tossed it into Sidey's old buckboard and headed south toward Cemetery Hill.

"Another hole to dig and fill," Dobbs muttered.

Bert Mason had come across to stand beside the postmaster. "Another day in Beaver City," he nodded. "Another sad day. Nobody much to miss ol' Will, but he wasn't a bad sort. He never meant harm. Think anybody'll make complaint against Scrannon?"

"What good would it do?" Dobbs shrugged. "Complain to who? Beauregard Jenkins? The Vigilance Committee? Come to anything at all, 'Judge' Magruder would just rule self-defense, then send Jenkins and them to burn out the complainant." Casually, he gestured toward the scorched wall of his own store.

"You gonna send another letter to that district magistrate?"

"I expect so, just for the record," Dobbs said. "Though he can't do anything. He has no jurisdiction in the Strip. Nobody does. Will Sidey's murder will just get lost, like all the rest. Just like he never counted."

"Nobody counts in No Man's Land," Mason agreed.

Up the street, a vehicle rattled on rough ground, and both of them looked around. Coming from the north was a rockaway carriage containing two women. The carriage pulled to a stop in front of the post office, and both men goggled at its occupants—a big, sturdy-looking woman with fine features and red hair, and a little blonde with the face of an angel.

Mason pulled off his hat, and Dobbs touched his eyeshade. "Ladies," they said.

"Good afternoon," the big woman said. "Can you tell me where one records a deed?"

"Do what?" Mason asked.

"Record a deed," the little blonde said. "I have purchased property in this area, and I wish to locate it and record it."

"Purchased?" Dobbs squinted at them. "Property? Real estate property?"

"Exactly. I own a section of land just west of here, purchased from Colonel Booth-Sykes."

Dobbs shook his head. "My name is Haygood Dobbs," he said. "I believe you ladies ought to come inside for a little talk."

It didn't take long for a crowd to gather in Dobbs' store, what with Bert Mason spreading the word about the ladies. Polly Wentworth wandered in, and Ike and Sally Bundy, Bert Mason came back with Fred Silverstein, and others dropped by to gawk and listen. It wasn't the first time folks had showed up at Beaver City thinking they owned property. There had been a lot of that lately. But generally the swindled parties weren't ladies. The cowboy who had stopped in earlier to buy shells was back, too, and seemed to fit right in, though nobody was quite sure who he was.

"You poor thing," Polly Wentworth exclaimed over and over again as Haygood Dobbs explained the

161

nature of No Man's Land to Annie Sue.

No one owned property in the Neutral Strip. The Cimarron Proposal was a fiction promoted by George Scrannon. Any deed issued by anyone for any piece of property in No Man's Land was fraudulent and worthless. Scrannon and his bunch were liars, thieves and murderers, land sharks and no-account bilkers, and anyone who laid out good money for anything they claimed to have for sale was the victim of a swindle.

Milicent's eyes became wider by the moment as Dobbs recounted stories of Scrannon's swindles, but Annie Sue's eyes reacted differently. They narrowed, and their shade of blue slowly changed from sky to steel.

From a desk in the post office, Dobbs retrieved a large stack of wanted posters—there being no law in the area, the postmaster had no one to deliver circulars to, so he collected them. He leafed through them, and handed one to Annie Sue. "That fellow you say sold you your property . . . was this him?"

Annie Sue studied it for a moment, then nodded. "It does resemble him. But his name was Col. Chadwick Booth-Sykes. This poster says 'Chad Sykes, alias Slicker Booth'."

"Aliases," Dobbs said, "That fellow has a dozen different names, and all of them bad. He's wanted in . . ."

"Somebody comin', Haywood," Ike Bundy announced from the front door. "Stranger, I believe."

Some of them went to look out the shuttered window. In the street beyond, a big man had reined a tired horse in alongside Annie Sue's rockaway, and stepped down. Hitching his mount, he headed for the door and stepped inside. Eyes that seemed to see everything swept around the room, paused at Mouse Moore, then went on to look at Milicent and Annie Sue. "Ladies," he said. "Sorry I left you so abruptly,

162

back there."

"Quite all right, Mr. Wiggins," Milicent said. "Did you catch those people you were chasing?"

"Sorry to say, I didn't," he frowned. "They had a fresh team, and I had a tired horse. Had me a chat with some rowdies, though, the ones that thought they'd do a holdup. I don't expect they'll try it again. Those coachers shot 'em up some."

"Wiggins?" Dobbs peered at the newcomer. "Ben Wiggins? The lawman?"

"Not at the moment," Wiggins admitted. "I'm on private business."

"Mr. Dobbs has been telling me that I've been swindled," Annie Sue said. "He says the land I bought isn't really mine."

"I'm afraid he's right," Wiggins nodded. "I'd have told you before, but . . ."

"That's nonsense," Annie Sue said, firmly. "I bought it. It's mine. See, it's here on this map, and described on this deed."

Bert Mason looked at the map. "Few miles west," he noted. "On the river, at Jackson Creek. I know the place. The Palmers were squattin' there 'til the Vigilance Committee ran 'em out."

"Is it in the valley, where the creek comes down on the other side?"

"Yes, ma'am. That's about the middle of it. The Palmers settled on this side, on a few acres. This here map looks like a section."

"That is what I bought. A section. With a house."

"George Scrannon isn't going to let you have that place," Ike Bundy said. "I heard he figures on startin' a cow operation there. Though he might be shy of cows. Some of the boys been spreadin' the word about a bunch of tough drovers that it don't pay to mess with."

"Cow operation? Not on my land, he won't," Annie Sue said.

Ben Wiggins had thumbed through the post office wanted posters. Now he stepped to the door and went out, to look glumly up and down the street. "This place don't make any sense," he muttered. "Not any at all."

Inside, Annie Sue sat in thought for a few minutes, then made up her mind. "Where can I find Mr. Scrannon?"

Ike Bundy stared at her. "Ma'am, you don't want to go tanglin' with George Scrannon! Why, he's as like to shoot a body as not." He cleared his throat, blushing. "Even a body like, uh . . ."

"Put your eyes back in your head, Ike," Sally Bundy snapped. "And mind lest the devil get into your head again. Least 'til we get home."

"He's right, though," Polly Wentworth said. "Mr. Scrannon is not one to be dealt with."

Others took up the protest, but Milicent shook her head. "No sense arguing with Annie Sue Finch," she told them. "Just tell us where we can find Mr. Scrannon."

"Likely at the Happy Times Saloon," Bert Mason shrugged. "Where he generally is."

"Thank you." Annie Sue adjusted her bonnet, pulled on her gloves and collected her papers. "Are you coming, Milicent?"

Ben Wiggins stood beside the hitchrail, watching people come out of the post office to head down the street. "Shame," he said to himself. "Pure shame what a skunk can do to decent folks."

At his side, someone said, "Amen."

Wiggins glanced around, studying the man. "Do I know you from somewhere?"

"Danged if I know," the waddy said. "My name's Mouse Moore. Howdy."

"Howdy. You live around here, do you?"

164

"Up from Texas. I'm Busted S."

"Oh." Wiggins' stone-ledge face managed a look of sympathy. "Well, you hide it right well." He glanced at Moore again, then remembered. Busted S was what those yayhoos up the road had said . . . Busted S, a cow outfit it didn't pay to fool with.

Intuition told him that if Iron Tom Logan bought cows in No Man's Land, he'd more likely buy them from Busted S than from George Scrannon.

"Nice to make your acquaintance," he told Mouse Moore.

XVIII

Some folks said that George Scrannon came to No Man's Land from Ohio, some said from Pennsylvania and some said straight from hell. Some said he got out of Cincinnati a step ahead of that fine city's last recorded lynch mob. Some said he was wanted for murder and fraud in Philadelphia, and some said he just popped up out of the ground when the devil wouldn't have him. For that matter, they might all have been right.

For a place where the outlaws would have outnumbered the inlaws had there been any law to be in or out of, the Neutral Strip was relatively peaceful for several years before George Scrannon showed up. Oh, there was some thieving now and again, and some debates got settled by bullets, and there was a mite of drunken hell-raising from time to time up at Beer City, but considering that nobody in the whole strip—for whatever reason—was there legally, folks had generally done themselves right proud. There was no law, of course, but for a while there was a kind of order some places.

Like around Beaver City, where the citizens had formed a vigilance committee to keep the peace. There was no law that said they could have a vigilance committee, but there was no law that said they couldn't, either, and with no law they reckoned they had to do something. So they banded together and kept the peace.

Just good, common-sense vigilante justice. There were certain activities that most everybody agreed hadn't ought to be indulged in, like stealing other folks' cows and chickens, barn burning, horse theft, shooting unarmed men, molesting women, robbery, using vulgar language in the presence of ladies, town burning, fence cutting, ambush and other sorts of general misbehavior. There was a time there in the Neutral Strip when that kind of tomfoolery would get a man a visit from the vigilance committee, and punishment ranging from a dressing down in no uncertain terms to a rope around the neck.

It was that vigilance committee—the first one—that started the graveyard up on the hill south of Beaver City. And the first ones planted there were folks that would have been planted even had there been territorial law.

But then along came George Scrannon. Since that day, things just hadn't been the same. Scrannon was slick, and he was ruthless, and he thoroughly believed that anything he happened to want just ought by rights to be his. He stole cattle, and he stole sheep, and he stole horses, and he got some old boys around him to back him up. Then he got the idea to go into land-sharking, and the first thing anybody knew Beaver City was Scrannon Headquarters, and the vigilance committee had itself a new roster and was no better than a bunch of night-riders bullying the squatters for George Scrannon's benefit.

In the past couple of years, George Scrannon had stomped high and wide in No Man's Land. Not everybody liked it, and not everybody tolerated his behavior, but still things generally went the way he took a mind for them to go.

Now and then things back-switched on him. Like the

167

time the Olafssen family caught some of the vigilance committee stealing chickens, and fed them all the chicken they could eat—raw, at gunpoint. And like the postmaster standing up to him where the U.S. mail was concerned. Owen Lance and Ike Bundy and some others flat out refused to do any business with the Scrannon faction, and somebody kept hauling Judge Magruder out of his house when he was drunk, and hoisting him up a pole to hang by his heels in judicial ridicule. That had happened three times so far.

Now there was talk that Scrannon's cattle venture was the shortest-lived cow enterprise in history because the rustlers he sent out never came back, and a tough bunch from Texas was pushing a herd up to railhead and didn't give two hoots what George Scrannon or anybody else thought about it.

Some folks would stand their ground, but not very many ever backed him down. It was Scrannon's boast that—one way or another—nobody was man enough to face him squarely and get the best of him. Of course, that was before he made the acquaintance of Annie Sue Finch.

Late sunlight cast long shadows across Main Street as Annie Sue walked down the street and approached the Happy Times Saloon, with Bert Mason showing her the way. Behind them, Milicent was coming along with the rockaway, and a few others had tagged along to see what happened.

"Yonder's the place," Mason pointed. "Happy Times Saloon. Oliver Winshaw runs it. Him and Scrannon decided for him to be governor of the Neutral Strip when they commenced that Cimarron Proposal business, so that's what he calls himself. *Governor* Winshaw. Same way with Beauregard Jenkins. He runs the Vigilance Committee for Scrannon, an' calls hisself Territorial Secretary, though he can't hardly even write. They got theirselves a territorial judge, too, named Sylvester Magruder. Say

168

he was a lawyer once, but all he is now is a drunk."

"What is that over there?" Annie Sue was looking across the street, at the building with all the signs.

"That's Scrannon's place," Bert told her.

"One of those signs says 'Provisional Capitol'," she noted. "Does that mean government business is done there?"

"If there was a gover'ment," Bert shrugged.

"Then that is where I shall conduct my business," Annie Sue decided. "Please summon Mr. Scrannon for me."

"Summon?" Bert blinked. "Scrannon?"

"Yes, please. This building looks to be a low saloon. If Mr. Scrannon is on the premises, I'd like for him to step outside."

Bert blinked again, and looked around. In the crowd behind him, someone said, "You heard the lady, Bert. Go call him out."

Shaking his head, Bert Mason went to the door, opened it and told the gloom inside, "Mr. Scrannon is requested to step outside." Having said that, he backed away and flattened himself against the wall.

For a minute or two, nothing happened. Then a big, square-headed man with a bowler hat looked out and said, "What's goin' on out here?"

"I want to see Mr. Scrannon," Annie Sue told the man. "Please ask him to step outside."

The man looked her up and down and kind of licked his lips. "Mr. Scrannon is busy, darlin'. Won't I do, instead?"

"I don't know," she said, "Can you record a deed?"

"Do what?"

Bert Mason eased away from the wall. "Lady has bought herself some property, Governor. She wants to record it." To Annie Sue, he said, "This here is *Governor* Oliver Winshaw, ma'am. He owns this establishment."

"I don't record no deeds," Winshaw said.

"Then I need someone else," she decided. "Where is Mr. Scrannon?"

"He's inside," Winshaw shrugged. "Havin' a drink with the judge."

"Oh, good," Annie Sue nodded. "I'll see them both, immediately, please, over at the . . . ah . . . the Capitol."

She turned away and started across the street. Behind her, Oliver Winshaw ducked back into his saloon and beckoned. "Mr. Scrannon? Maybe you best come see about this. I don't know what's goin' on."

At the back table, Scrannon scowled and got to his feet. "I heard," he said. "Come on, Judge. Let's take care of this."

Judge Sylvester Magruder got to his feet unsteadily, belched, straightened his old frock coat and tagged after him. They stepped outside, in time to see Milicent Moriarty stepping down from the rockaway in front of Scrannon's building. Beyond her, Annie Sue had tried the door, found it locked, and retrieved a pry-bar from the carriage box. Calmly and efficiently, she pried loose the lock and stepped inside.

"What the hell . . . !" Scrannon hissed. He hit the ground at a run and headed across, with the judge weaving along in his wake.

Milicent hurried to the broken-lock door, open-mouthed with amazement. "Annie Sue! I never!"

Inside, Annie Sue was looking around. The interior of the building was cluttered and dusty, looking more like a storage shed than a place of business, except for the big oak desk and chairs in the center. With a frown of distaste, Annie Sue brushed clouds of dust off the desk and one chair, sat at the desk and began opening drawers. "This place is disgraceful!" she pointed out.

A baggy-eyed man skidded to a halt in the open door, looked inside, then looked at the door like he couldn't believe his eyes. "You broke my lock!" he rasped.

Annie Sue looked up from what she was doing. "A public building shouldn't be locked," she said. "This is a public building, isn't it?"

"This is my office! What are you doing at my desk?"

"Looking for paper and a pen, and for a public seal. Are you Mr. Scrannon?"

"I am George Scrannon." He stepped in, glaring at her.

"Then you must be the man who records deeds here," Annie Sue decided. "Ah." From a lower drawer, she pulled several blank sheets of paper, an inkwell and steel pens. "Here we are," she said. "Here, you come around and sit here. I'll need a receipt for registry, or whatever it's called here."

"Get out of my office!" Scrannon demanded. "You must be crazy!"

Annie Sue looked up at him with big, innocent blue eyes. "The sign in front says this is the Provisional Capitol of the Cimarron Proposal," she said. "Is it?"

"It's whatever I say it is!"

"Is that sign yours?"

"You damned . . ."

"Watch your mouth, sir," Milicent cautioned him, picking up Annie Sue's pry-bar.

"It's my sign," Scrannon amended. "Everything here is mine."

"Well, then, it must be you who said this is the Provisional Capitol of the Cimarron Proposal." Annie Sue moved away from the chair. "Here. Sit and write."

"Write what?"

"A receipt, stating that you have recorded my deed to the section of real property described on the deed—which, by the way, was presented to me by a representative of yours. If you don't know how to write a receipt for registry, I'll write it for you, Mr. Scrannon."

Scrannon's eyes narrowed with fury. "Get out of my

171

office!" he snapped. "Get out of here before I . . ."

Judge Sylvester Magruder had wandered in, followed by others. Now Magruder looked blearily at the drawing in Annie Sue's hand. "This here's the Jackson Creek place, Mr. Scrannon," he squinted. "I thought you aimed to put cows there. You had them squatters run out so's you could . . ."

"Shut up, Sylvester! You're drunk!" Scrannon glared at Annie Sue. "You little bitch, I'll . . ."

The gloved hand that whacked him across the face—a resounding slap that jolted him—seemed to come from nowhere. It wasn't a large hand, but there was strength behind it, and anger in Annie Sue's eyes.

"Told you you ought to mind your mouth," Milicent reminded him.

"I've had enough of this!" Scrannon's hand snaked toward the open front of his coat.

"I don't think so, Scrannon," a deep voice rumbled. The sound of a hammer being drawn was loud in the room. "Just pull the gun out, easy-like, an' drop it," Ben Wiggins ordered.

"They haven't got any right . . ."

"'Pears to me they got as much right to property here as you have, Scrannon. More, since it was your shark that sold it to 'em. You heard me, ease that gun out of there."

Gritting his teeth, Scrannon eased out the revolver and tossed it at Wiggin's feet. The old lawman glanced down at it, Scrannon's hand snaked to his hip and another hammer went back as cold steel was pressed against the side of his head.

Holding the land-shark frozen at gunpoint, Mouse Moore reached around and pulled out Scrannon's little derringer. "Man's right," he said. "The lady wants a receipt for her deed. You ought to give her that."

"I'll be damned," Wiggins breathed. "A hideout gun."

"Slickest I ever seen," Mouse nodded. Not gently, he

172

plunked Scrannon down in the chair. "Do what th' pretty little lady says."

Without a choice in the matter, Scrannon scrawled a 'document of record,' verifying Annie Sue's deed. When he looked up, there was murder in his eyes. "This doesn't mean a thing, you know. I don't know what you think you've gained."

"Of course it does," Annie Sue accepted the paper. "Mr. Scrannon, I believe you to be a cheat, a fraud and a swindler, but you've just given me your personal guarantee that the land I bought is mine."

"So what?"

"So, should anyone try to force me off my land, you will be held personally accountable. There may be no law here, Mr. Scrannon, but an agreement is an agreement. Good evening." Without a backward glance, she strode from the building, past what had become a gaping crowd.

Behind her, Milicent said, "I told you about Annie Sue. I believe she is the stubbornest one person I ever met."

"Like to see that little darlin' go up ag'in Bobby Lee Smith in that department," Mouse muttered. He emptied the derringer and handed it to Scrannon. "Admire how you use this hideout, mister. Sneakiest thing I ever seen."

As the rockaway headed west again by evening light, Milicent Moriarty had some troubling thoughts of retribution and mayhem, of night-riders and other plagues, but she put these aside for the moment. It seemed to her that Mr. Wiggins had been having a good time there in Beaver City, pointing his gun at Mr. Scrannon and all, and intuition told her that—though she didn't see him anywhere around—he might not be too far away, at least for a few days. It was a comforting thought. Mr. Scrannon was not a man to stand for humiliation, and he would be scheming some sort of revenge, of course. But he didn't strike Milicent as the

173

sort to step boldly forward and have his way at all costs.

Likely, he would be a problem, but not right away. She turned her thoughts to more pressing concerns. "Is is the same place, then, Annie Sue? The place where we met all those charming cowboys?"

"Charming?" Annie Sue's blue eyes looked thunders at her. "Some of them, perhaps. But that one! Oh! If ever I see that one again . . ."

"Mr. Smith, you mean?"

"That one. He would be well advised to stay a long way from me and my property, or he certainly will wish he had."

"He was just upset about his cattle," Milicent offered.

"He was rude! Rude and uncouth and . . . and . . . and he *attacked* me!"

"Well, never mind. We shall be home soon."

"Home," Annie Sue said, thoughtfully. "Yes. Milicent, did you have a good look around when we were there, at the river?"

"Things were a bit busy."

"Well, I don't recall seeing a house there. I suppose we might have missed it, but . . . well, how would a person not notice a three-story house?"

"You're absolutely sure the gentleman said three stories?"

"He said three floors. It means the same thing."

"Then it must be there, somewhere," Milicent conceded. Annie Sue had made up her mind that there was a three-story house on her property, and Milicent knew very well that, once Annie Sue had her mind made up about something, that was just how it was going to be.

XIX

The way that word can get around, in places like No Man's Land where a body wouldn't expect general communication to be a signal accomplishment, is nothing short of marvelous to folks from other kinds of places. It often is a source of puzzlement to folks from back East, for instance. They tend to believe that grapevines grow best where folks are most pressed.

But the fact is that news travels faster across prairies than it does along streets. It has been established beyond scholarly doubt, by no less an authority than Isaac Newton Clements, that a chance remark— especially a choice chance remark—can travel from DeWitt County, Texas, to Baxter County, Kansas, in the time it takes a change in odds on a horse race to travel from Newman's Cigar Store in Brooklyn to Harry McGuire's Smokehouse in Queens.

Isaac Newton Clements became the world's leading authority on gossip and the carrying of tales, by virtue of having lived in Brooklyn before he and his wife Mabel packed off to Baxter County, Kansas, about the same time as three of Mabel's sisters, and their husbands, moved to DeWitt County, Texas. In subsequent scholarly studies, Isaac Newton Clements clearly established that distance is no detriment in the dishing out of dirt.

175

What happens is, out in the big lonelies, folks get themselves a notion to talk to folks, which in places like Brooklyn it is generally best to take a notion not to. So, out in God's country, every time anybody meets up with somebody, everybody tells everybody everything that anybody has told them, with nobody holding anything back. Happens all the time. Riders passing through, folks on the grubline, drummers—everybody hears everything from somebody and tells anybody he sees next.

Most parts, you can't have even a bank robbery without all the robbers and robbees exchanging views on Mrs. Wagsworth's latest recipes and who lost stock in the blizzard. So in just no time at all, everybody knows everything that anybody knows and somebody is off in all directions passing it all along to everybody else like stone-ripples on a stock tank.

So, it was just plainly natural that by the time Busted S rounded up and pointed out on the last day of the great "Luck of Bobby Lee Smith" drive, most everybody in No Man's Land and the abutting parts of Kansas and Texas knew that George Scrannon had sent Pete Thayer and Slap Jackson to rustle that herd so Scrannon could sell the cows to Iron Tom Logan at the Chicago, Rock Island and Pacific railhead at Tyrone Switch. And everybody knew that Pete Thayer and Slap Jackson wouldn't be coming back from Texas, and that Busted S was headed for Tyrone Switch under its own steam, and that George Scrannon didn't have any cows—or anyplace to put them even if he did, because somebody had faced him down at Beaver City and made him sign over some land that he'd never owned in the first place, but had sold anyway.

On top of that, everybody and his uncle knew about the Beaver City Express's mail contract, and about Ben Wiggins being out on his own in the Neutral Strip, and about the new load of timbers that had just arrived at

176

Beer City, and about this little yellow-haired angel that was down yonder someplace driving a rockaway that Iron Tom Logan made somebody in Liberal sell to her before he figured out what she meant to do with it.

In gossip language, that all made sense—or most of it, anyway, and even the parts that didn't were public knowledge.

So before Busted S ever showed up on the horizon, Iron Tom Logan had fence crews and gun guards out at Tyrone Switch, mending pens and fixing to dicker. Thomas Allen Fry had been delivered by stagecoach to Tyrone Switch—which was as near the Kansas Line as the Beaver City Express wanted to go—and had made his way on up to Liberal by hand-cart with a load of tie-setters. He had spent some time sending telegraph messages back and forth to United States Census Office people and United States District Court officers and United States Marshals, and federal surveyors and the Corps of Engineers of the United States Army, then had gone back out to Tyrone Switch to talk to Iron Tom Logan.

"They're stealing me blind!" Logan told him, looking gloomily at the holding pens being tightened for the expected trail herd from Texas. "You see those holes in the ground over there?"

Thomas Allen Fry shaded his eyes and nodded. There was a long line of postholes leading out from a newly-constructed loading chute.

"Two days ago, those were uprights for a counting pen," Logan said. "Today they're holes. I swear, I don't know how they do it. Do you know where those timbers are by now?"

"I haven't the vaguest idea," Fry assured him.

"By now they're in Beer City, probably being nailed into place this very minute for some new whorehouse or gambling hall. By damn, it's high time this place got some law!"

"That's what I came to talk about," Fry said. "I need

177

your help."

"To do what?"

"Count the population of No Man's Land."

"You're crazy," Logan decided. "Hell, in this place even set timbers don't hold still long enough to be counted."

"It has to be done, though," Fry shrugged. "The census office intends for people to be counted, so people are going to be counted."

"I don't see what that has to do with me," Logan said. "I don't count people. I'm trying to operate a railroad. Look at that!"

He pointed, and Fry looked. "What?"

"Right there, by that shed. Yesterday there was a half a wagon-load of sacked feed there. Now it's gone."

"You need some law," Fry announced.

"That's what I just told you."

"Then help me count people."

"Why?"

"Before there can be law, there has to be a legal jurisdiction," Fry explained. "And before there can be a legal jurisdiction there has to be representative government, and to have representative government you have to know who's represented. That is what the census is for, you know."

"It is?"

"It certainly is."

"What do you want me to do?" Iron Tom stared at him suspiciously.

"Be a county census supervisor."

"Where?"

"For the Neutral Strip."

"This isn't a county."

"Well, for census purposes, we're going to call it one. The United States Census Office recognizes cities, towns, settlements, hamlets, villages, rural agricultural districts, delineated tracts . . . and counties. You'll be the census supervisor for Beaver County."

178

"Which doesn't exist," Logan squinted, trying to get it all clear in his head.

"No, not legally," Fry admitted.

"So you want me to drop my railroad job and conduct an illegal census?"

"Oh, no! Not at all. Census supervisors aren't fulltime. You can do it in your spare time. All it amounts to is selecting your enumerators, swearing them in and supervising their work. And it isn't illegal. The word 'county' is like 'hamlet' and 'delineated tract.' For census purposes, it means whatever the United States Census Office says it means."

"Yeah," Logan nodded. "Like 'secondary rights-of-way' in railroad terms. Means whatever the railroad wants it to mean."

"I knew you would understand," Fry grinned.

"And these . . . ah . . . enumerators I'm supposed to select? Who are they?"

"You decide that. Anybody you think can go out and count noses in a census tract. I'll provide you with a tract map and defined tract lines. We're a little short on surveyed data in the Neutral Strip, but the postmaster at Beaver City has given us a fair representation, and we have some Army surveys that will help. I'll designate tracts so there is no question of where the lines are. They will be physical boundaries—things an enumerator can bump into, trip over or drown in."

"For anybody dumb enough to count noses in No Man's Land, that's probably good planning. You realize, I'm sure, that there are just a whole lot of people down here who will object strenuously to being counted?"

"I've gotten some rulings on that," Fry assured him. "Since there is no court jurisdiction to provide marshals, we are authorized to empower each enumerator as a census marshal. That means he can defend himself, and exercise whatever force is necessary for the proper completion of his assignment."

179

"Gun-toting head-counters," Logan mused, intrigued by the idea although he still wasn't convinced. "What kind of qualifications do these 'enumerators' have to have . . . aside from being crazy as loons?"

"Basically, they just have to be able to read and write. It's a thankless job even in the best of places, so a streak of stubbornness is helpful. Oh, and it is preferable that they reside in the county where they will be assigned."

"But that's No Man's Land," Logan shook his head. "Nobody legal *resides* in No Man's Land."

"That should make it easier," Fry shrugged. "In a place that has no residence, the word 'reside' can mean anything you want it to mean."

Logan stared at the portly man. "Are you sure you're with the government?" he asked. "*Our* government?" He shook his head again. "Do I get paid for this?"

"You will receive a fee, just like any other coordinator. And supervisor's wages."

"And my 'enumerators?' Do they get paid?"

"They do. It's all spelled out in the census office manual. I'll give you a copy."

"I must be crazy as those people you want me to hire," Iron Tom decided. "All right, I'll do it. But tell me one thing. When some of those 'residents' who don't legally live in this county that doesn't legally exist start shooting at my 'marshals' who aren't legally marshals, and they shoot back, which they likely will . . . ."

"Unfortunate," Fry muttered.

"Yeah. Well, when all that happens, then what do the 'enumerators' do? Do they have to change their numbers?"

"I have a ruling on that, too," Fry assured him. "No, they don't have to change anything. Technically, they will have counted them before they killed them, because they begin counting on the official Census Day, and proceed from there. So the numbers will stand."

"Fine," Logan said, gloomily. "Maybe we should put up posters. 'Please feel free to shoot at your census taker. He will shoot back, but if he kills you, you still count.'"

Busted S watered on Goff Creek, giving the critters plenty of time to graze on the lush winter hay that grew along the little stream, then made the final five miles to Tyrone Switch in a day and a half. That was a day longer than five miles should have required. What happened was, those five hundred head of legal Texas cows had become right fond of Goff Creek. Cows don't think real fast, but when they do make up their minds about a matter, it puts cowboys to the ultimate test of their qualifications. That is, a cowboy had to be more determined than the cows he is pushing. There have been some truly epic tests of that quality in the history of cattle trails, and the "Busted S Reversal" as folks in the Neutral Strip came to call it, was one of the finest.

Part of it was because Willie Sutter's chosen lead steer had developed a talent by the time they got that far. Old Blue wasn't a milling cow nor a stampeding cow. He had a trick all his own, that he had tried out several times and found that it always seemed to work. Blue had split the herd the first day out of Abilene, and had done it again at the Beaver River, and when Busted S came up out of the Goff Creek lows and saw Tyrone Switch off in the high distance, Blue made up his mind.

Goff Creek, with its sweet water and sweet hay, had been cow paradise compared to that irritating vision of upright timbers, loading chutes, pens, fences, sheds and railroad gear that he saw yonder, floating on the mirages. So Blue did again what he had already done before. He turned around, loped directly into the herd following him, and just kept going.

At mid-morning of that day, Busted S had been on Goff Creek. At mid-afternoon, it had been within sight

181

of Tyrone Switch. Come sundown, though, Busted S was back on Goff Creek, and everybody was happy about that except the ones with hats.

It didn't take any time at all for word to spread that there were cattle wandering all over the Goff Creek haymeadows, and people came from Shade's Well, Beer City, Hardesty and Wolftrap to see the sight and—possibly—pick up a few strays.

Iron Tom Logan had seen the herd come up onto the prairie, and he had seen it disappear again. With a few of his shotgun guards, he headed out to see what was going on, and when the Busted S crew recognized him as the cattle buyer for the railroad, they directed him to Bobby Lee Smith and Shad Ames.

They howdied from horseback, and Logan asked. "What happened here?"

Shad Ames looked at the railroad man like maybe he was blind, then explained. "We spilled the damned herd, is what."

"I can see that," Logan admitted. "How many did you have?"

"Five hundred head of legal cows," Bobby Lee told him. "You got pens ready yonder?"

"I have pens," Logan said, "and I'm buying, but probably not that many because you'll lose some overnight. Hell, there isn't anything these yayhoos around here won't steel."

"You in the market for five hundred head?" Bobby Lee asked.

"I can use them, at the right price, but I just told you . . ."

"Then get them pens ready," Bobby Lee got one of those looks on his face, like a badger with a boot in sight, "because that is how many we're bringin' in. Five hundred head of legal cows, an' not a cow less."

Logan stood in his stirrups, shading his eyes from the setting sun. Miles of spring grassland rolled away east and west, a broad, shallow valley bounded by low caprock, with stands of wind-bent cottonwood here and there, clumps of sage like little islands rising from the flowing grasses, and the little ribbon of Goff Creek meandering through the landscape. There were cattle everywhere, spread out and grazing, while mounted cowboys spread and circled to begin the task of re-forming a herd.

And beyond, just at the limits of sight, furtive among the distant confusions of brush, caprock and outcrops, were other people. No-Man's-Landers, he thought sourly. Looking for something to steal.

Five hundred head of cattle, the young Texan said. Five hundred head to be delivered for sale.

"I'll believe that when I see it," Iron Tom Logan muttered.

XX

Annie Sue Finch and Milicent Moriarty finally located the "three-floor house" that Colonel Booth-Sykes had described in such glowing—albeit ambiguous—terms. They found it, sure enough, and Annie Sue was fit to be tied.

"This is a shack!" she shrilled. "Is this it? It's nothing but a hovel!"

Half-hidden by a thicket above the Beaver, the structure did in fact have three levels of floors—one in each room—as well as a porch. It also had two fireplaces—a wide-hearth creekstone log-burner in the front room and a slate-lined mud structure in the back. There was a serviceable roof and fixable walls, two hinged doors and four shuttered windows . . . and the porch. A series of occupants had given little thought to adding niceties to the place, except that somebody had put some care into that porch.

"The porch isn't bad," Milicent pointed out as Annie Sue paced furiously around and through the house. "It's a nice touch."

"The porch?" Annie Sue looked at her friend in disbelief, then stalked across the low-slung front room to look out. "The porch," she repeated. "Very well, the porch is all right. But it's the only thing that is. Oooh! I could strangle that man!"

"Which one?"

"That colonel. Booth-Sykes, or whatever alias he uses now. He led me to believe this was a fine home. Oooh! I've seen pigsties with more charm. How are we expected to live here?"

"I don't know," Milicent shrugged. "Do you want to go back to Kansas City and live with your brother Jason?"

"Absolutely not!" Annie Sue snapped. "This place isn't so bad. It will take work, but we can fix it up."

"My thought, exactly." Milicent looked away to hide her grin.

"Well, at least there is plenty of land," Annie Sue reasoned. "And it is a nice-looking view of the river . . . or it will be when we get it cleared so that we can see the river."

"Life is full of challenges," Milicent observed, opening the shutters to look out a side window. Beyond the screening brush, up the slope, she saw movement. Squinting, she followed it. A man on a horse . . . she recognized him, then, and smiled. It was Ben Wiggins. Like a big, dark angel on a big, dark horse, he was scouting the area. Taking care of the ladies.

Still smiling, Milicent went to find some firewood. She would start a fire in the hearth, put on a pot of coffee, sweep out a bit, then call the man in. If he had been out there all night, looking out for them, he probably would relish some hot coffee.

Annie Sue continued her tour of inspection, grim and determined to make the best of what she had bought. It has been just one thing after another, she thought. On the other hand, what else could possibly happen to complicate her life. Offhand, she couldn't think of anything.

The way things turned out, between Bobby Lee Smith and Mouse Moore, they thought of something, but of course Annie Sue didn't know about that. Not just yet.

The Busted S hands had their hands full that night on Goff Creek. Eighteen Texans like to wore out better than thirty horses in the hour and a half between sundown and dark, getting those cows compacted so Bobby Lee and Shad could count them while there was still light enough to see.

Then when Bobby Lee counted them, they came up thirteen short. Well, that didn't set at all with Bobby Lee, so he left Shad and a dozen gun-quick nighthawks on the herd, and the rest of them lit out to do some dark-hours riding. They came up with the first four drifts pretty quick. Fifteen or twenty drunks from Beer City had found these four strays, and were hazing them back toward Beer City. They weren't making very good time, because they were drunk, and it was getting dark and half of them were on foot, anyway.

The Busted S riders saw them, rode down on them like night vengeance, and within minutes those Beer Citians were all afoot except for the ones that were flat on their backs out yonder on the prairie. Bobby Lee sent Shorty Mars to take the four strays and nine recently-accumulated saddle mounts back to the herd, and he and the rest went on, scouting a big circle around the whole valley. Folks said later that it took those Beer Citians all night and most of the next day to get back where they came from, some walking and some being toted.

Of course, by then even the drunkest ones weren't drunk anymore, and had had plenty of time to reflect upon the troubles that corn liquor can bring on a man. Running afoul of that Texas bunch out yonder had been a sobering experience, for a fact. Word was, most of them pledged on the spot to mend their ways and tread the paths of righteousness. They were so serious about that, they all had a drink on it.

It was Mouse Moore who found the other nine

cattle. Some old boys from over in the Cimarron Breaks had them down in a little box canyon, and they had a fire going and cinch rings heating.

Now Mouse, he always was a one to want a close look, so he just ground-tethered his horse up on the caprock and walked down and joined them. When some of them caught sight of him and peered into the dusk to see who it was, he waved and said, "Howdy," and kept coming. They looked him over, decided he must belong there because he looked so familiar, and went back to what they were doing.

Mouse looked around a little, then walked over to where a big, whiskered gent was calling the shots. "Howdy," he said. "How many did we get?"

"Not but nine," the man glanced at him. "What'd you do, get lost?"

"Yeah. I do that ever' now and again." Mouse looked at the fire. "Where's the running irons?"

The man glanced at him again. "How long you been lost? We don't carry runnin' irons. Damn fools carry runnin' irons. Cinch rings is better." The man grinned. "Specially on some damn fool brand like that there C-back-C or whatever."

"Busted S," Mouse told him.

"I be danged," the man agreed, looking more closely at the haunch of a stolen cow. "That's what it is, all right. It's a busted S. You've read some brands, ain't you?"

"Some." Mouse shrugged. "This'n's easy, huh?"

"Sure is," the man said. "Just brand over the gap there, an' Viola! It . . ."

"What was that word you said?"

"Oh. Viola. That's French or somethin'. It means, 'hey, lookee there.' Anyhow, brand over the gap an' Viola! It ain't Busted S any more. It's a Lazy S."

"Sure enough," Mouse nodded. "That's right smart."

"Easy as fallin' off a log," the man said. "Why, I know a dozen ways to . . ." he glanced around. "Where

187

you goin'?"

"Gotta find my horse," Mouse called back. "He's still lost."

By the time Mouse led the other Texans back to the box canyon, five of the nine Busted S cows had fresh scorches, making Lazy S out of their brands. But they put a stop to that. Some of those Cimarron Breaks boys maybe hadn't heard that it's unhealthy to slap leather against Willie Sutter, and maybe they didn't have the vaguest notion who Bobby Lee Smith and Pappy Jameson were, but it seemed like they'd all have known about Joe Dell McGuire. Most everybody did.

At any rate, there were some unwise decisions and downright miscalculations made there in that box canyon that evening, and for a minute or two it sounded like it was fixing to rain.

"Dang fools," Pappy Jameson muttered, reloading his hogleg, "somebody should have explained the error of their ways to them."

"Little late now," Willie Sutter allowed. "There ain't any of 'em left to explain to."

". . . Nine." Bobby Lee finished counting. "All right, they're all here. But what's this mark on these five?"

"Lazy S," Mouse told him. "Easy to do, with a hot cinch ring, changin' Busted S to Lazy S."

"Cinch rings," Bobby Lee rumbled. "I'll tell you, I don't aim to stand for folks usin' cinch rings on my cows."

"That's plain to see," Pappy agreed, gazing around at the dead rustlers. "What now, Bobby Lee?"

"We got our cows back. Let's get back to the herd. I got dickerin' to do with that railroad man tomorrow. Willie, can you control that blue brindle steer, do you think?"

Willie just gazed at him and drawled, "Can you control your personal horse?"

"Just keep that steer in line in the mornin', Willie. I don't need any more interruptions in my lucky streak."

188

"I'll put a short stock on ol' Blue an' lead him home myself," Willie assured him. "What you gonna ask for these cows, Bobby Lee?"

"Eight dollars a head."

"You won't get it," Pappy Jameson assured him.

"'Course not. What I'll get is six-fifty." Bobby Lee swung into the saddle of his night horse and said, "Come on. Somebody gather up those loose horses, too. These folks got no further use for 'em."

Behind him, Pappy and Willie exchanged a look. "Six or less," Pappy said.

"Six-fifty on the nose," Willie grinned.

"Five dollars on it?"

"Sure."

At first light of morning Busted S came up from Goff Creek again, up onto the shortgrass prairie with Tyrone Switch in sight. And this time there wasn't any stopping them. Willie Sutter was out front with a double short-dog on old Blue's horns, so that the only option the lead steer had—short of getting right familiar with the kicking end of a cowpony—was to come along all peaceable and exercise the kind of leadership that the selected president of a cattle herd is supposed to provide.

The critters were full of hay, well-watered and rested up from their extended vacation on Goff Creek, and the boys moved them right along. It wasn't noon yet when the first of them entered the counting chute.

Bobby Lee Smith and Shad Ames swatted a couple of drifters into the wings, then tied off their horses and climbed up on the top rail with Iron Tom Logan and a railroad clerk named Hagerstrom. Bobby Lee had his tally string, and Hagerstrom had a little brass thing that looked like a pocket watch with thorns, and they went to counting cows.

"How many do you think you made it with?" Iron

Tom asked as they counted.

Bobby Lee didn't even look around. "Five Hundred," he said.

The job took an hour. It would have gone faster, except for some blame fool setting off a steam whistle at noon. When that happened, they had to uncount, re-sort and recount the critters that had turned tail right square in the chute. Texas cows never did cotton to steam whistles.

But finally the last one went through, and Hagerstrom clicked his thorn watch and nodded at Iron Tom. "Five hundred," he said. "On the button."

"Five hundred," Bobby Lee agreed, folding his tally string.

"I'll be damned," Iron Tom muttered. "All present and accounted for." He pointed at the packed-in critters. "I see a few with a different brand," he said.

"That's Busted S," Shad Ames assured him. "Take a close look, you'll see it's just been scorched over. Some jaspers tried to make us short-counted last night."

Iron Tom squinted at the critters milling around in the near pen, and got a better look. "I see," he said. "They used a running iron."

"No, they used a cinch ring. Kind of a Lazy-S way of rustling cows."

"But you fellows got them all back."

"'Course we did," Bobby Lee explained. "Them and some extra horses and spare cinch rings. I'm on a lucky streak."

"I swear. Well, let's get down to brass tacks." Iron Tom got a look on his face like a friendly tax-collector intent upon being helpful. "Generally I wouldn't do it, but since these are good-looking animals, and I'm on a tight schedule . . ."

"Legal, too," Shad Ames said.

"What?"

"These are all legal cows."

"Oh. Well, considering that, too, I'm real impressed

190

with what you fellows have done, and I'm willing to go as high a five dollars a head for the lot."

"Right decent of you," Bobby Lee said, getting one of those looks on his face, like a tame bear raised on sweet milk and panther juice. "Seein' as how you've gone to all this trouble to accommodate us here, an' all, I'm willin' to let 'em go for as low as eight dollars a head."

Pappy Jameson and Willie Sutter had moved in close, to listen.

"I see," Logan said. He got a look on his face like a man inflicting mortal pain upon himself for the betterment of his fellow beings. "Don't know how I'll justify this back home, Mister Smith, but since they're all right here in the pens and ready to load, I expect I can squeeze it up to six dollars."

"Sounds pretty fair to me," Shad Ames told Bobby Lee.

Behind and below, Pappy Jameson whispered, "Shad's right, I reckon. That's a good price."

"Shut up, Pappy," Willie Sutter hissed. "Bobby Lee's doin' the dickerin', not Mr. Ames."

Bobby Lee looked right thoughtful, then got a look on his face like a stage-play hero mortally wounded in the cause of righteousness. "I surely would hate to have to take 'em back where we come from, considerin' what I'd stand to lose, but . . ."

"You stand to lose four dollars and ninety-five cents," Shad Ames rasped into his ear. "It's my money that's at stake here, damn it!"

Bobby Lee ignored him. ". . . but it just wouldn't be fair to you, Mr. Logan, to let you have these cows for less than seven dollars a head. I don't believe I could live with myself if I did that."

Iron Tom looked at him in disbelief. "What do you mean, 'not fair'?"

"Why, a bargain like that can ruin a man for life. Gives him a whole false notion of what things is worth, an' he likely won't ever have another happy day on account of it. Seven dollars is my final offer."

"That's the damnedest corkscrewed logic I ever heard," Iron Tom allowed. "All right! Six-fifty!"

"Done," Bobby Lee said, just like there hadn't ever been any question about it at all. "Mr. Ames here is my ramrod. You can tally up with him." He swung down from the top rail and went for his horse.

"You owe me five dollars," Willie Sutter told Pappy Jameson. "Let's go find us a place to spend it."

On the top rail, Iron Tom Logan and Shad Ames looked after Bobby Lee, both of them shaking their heads. "What's that about a lucky streak?" Logan asked.

"He keeps sayin' that," Ames said. "made up his mind he was goin' to have a lucky streak, an' there just ain't any two ways about it. Stubborn streak, is what it is. I believe that there Bobby Lee Smith is the plain mule-headed, stubbornest young'un I ever seen. He sets out to do a thing, there just ain't any by-God way he won't do it."

"Interesting," Logan muttered. He pulled a pad of paper out of his coat, found a blank sheet and scribbled on it.

Candidates for enumerator, he wrote. And under it, the name, Bobby Lee Smith.

XXI

They all rode a work-train up to Liberal, out in front
of a steam locomotive, with four stock cars and a flat
car carrying everything that was left of the Busted S
outfit. That amounted to sixty-nine horses—which was
fifteen more than they had started out with, plus that
much extra saddlery that various bunch-cutters in No
Man's Land didn't own anymore—one chuck rig duly
blessed by Wesley Watkins, and a bank draft from the
Chicago, Rock Island and Pacific Railroad to the tune
of three thousand, two hundred and fifty dollars.

In the little town of Liberal, where a man couldn't
hardly turn his back but a new building of some kind
would spring up behind him, Bobby Lee and Shad
Ames sold their surplus horses to a trader, went to the
bank, then met the boys over at the General Sheridan
and squared accounts.

As ramrod, Shad Ames paid off the drovers and
cook, and reimbursed himself for his expenses, then
Bobby Lee and Shad split the rest down the middle,
after which Bobby Lee paid Shad Ames what he still
owed him for his share of the herd—which was all of it
except for four dollars and ninety-five cents.

That left one thing still to do. The entire crew—all
except Mouse Moore, who had gone off somewhere
like he generally did—put down a few mugs of Iron

Tom Logan's private beer, then walked out to the edge of town, lined up facing downwind and relieved themselves on the sandy soil of Kansas.

When that was done, Shad Ames went down the line, solemnly shaking hands with each man, then looked around him with a wolfish grin. He felt vindicated. It never had set well with him, how Kansas had greeted him with carbolic acid dip that time. Now he had returned the favor.

The paying off and breaking up of a trail crew is generally a solemn occasion, and that commemorative piss just sort of topped things off. There was hardly a dry eye among them as they wandered off their separate ways—which turned out to be not all that separate.

Several of the bunch saddled up to ride south three miles and have themselves a look at Beer City. Aside from a few private stocks like Iron Tom's, nobody would admit to there being any alcoholic beverages in Kansas, and with Beer City so close it didn't matter much to anybody in Liberal that might want a drink. Sitting on the sin side of the No Man's Land line like it did, Beer City would serve as Liberal's recreational center until the Methodist Church figured out what to do about it.

The rest watched them go, then had themselves a look at Liberal and went to find a meal at the General Sheridan.

And that was where they found Mouse Moore, thick as thieves with a conference of important-looking gentlemen at a back table.

The Texans had no more than got themselves seated and ordered their beefsteaks when Mouse came over and squatted down beside Bobby Lee. "You recollect that place down on the Beaver River that y'all saw, Bobby Lee?" he asked. "The place you been talkin' about ever' since?"

"I sure do, Mouse," Bobby Lee told him. "Right

194

there where that little creek runs into the river. There's a house there with a porch, but nobody livin' there. Why?"

"You still think you'd like to buy that place?" Mouse was grinning like a coyote with its own herd of sheep.

"What I got in mind," Bobby Lee nodded.

"Then I got a gent over here that you need to meet, Bobby Lee." He pointed toward the back table. "You see the jasper yonder with the slick hair and the two gold teeth? That there is none other than Col. Chadwick Booth-Skyes . . . least that's the name he favors today . . . an' he's the certified agent for the Scrannon Land and Cattle Company down at Beaver City."

"Good for him," Bobby Lee shrugged. "What about him?"

"Well, if you want to buy yourself that place on the Beaver River like you said, then he's the one to see, 'cause he's the one that's sellin' it."

"Well, I swear," Bobby Lee said, standing up. "Ain't it a small world when you're on a lucky streak! Mouse, I believe I'd like for you to introduce me to that gentleman."

As they walked toward the back, Willie Sutter glanced at Pappy Jameson. "Mouse is up to somethin'," he said. "I can always tell when Mouse is up to somethin' because he looks more like everybody when he is than when he ain't. He ought to go into politics. He'd be a natural."

"Expect you're right about that," Pappy agreed. "You think that gent he says is sellin' that land ain't sellin' it?"

"Oh, I expect he is, all right. Mouse don't lie. He just sometimes confuses. But I reckon that slick gent has that land to offer, all right. Five dollars says Bobby Lee buys it on the spot."

"That's no bet," Pappy frowned at him. "I believe he will, too. A whole section, just like he said he would."

"Well, then, five dollars says he buys the whole section for less than a dollar an acre."

"That's a whole different matter entirely," Pappy brightened. "Only a damn fool or a crooked dealer would sell land like that for under a dollar. You got a bet."

They were still shaking on it when Mouse Moore popped up beside them, looking over his shoulder. "Bettin' still open here?" he asked.

"We're bettin' on how much Bobby Lee will have to give for that land he wants," Pappy advised.

"Oh, I already know that," Mouse told him. "Feller was right anxious to sell. Bobby Lee paid eighty-five cents an acre for the section. They're over yonder drawin' up papers right now."

Willie Sutter stuck out his hand toward Pappy Jameson. "Five dollars," he grinned. "Pay up."

Pappy looked at him balefully. "I swear, Willie. You'd never of won that'n if it was anybody but Bobby Lee dickerin' with that slicker. That Bobby Lee Smith is the downright stubbornest young'un that God ever put ears on the sides of."

"That's what I want to bet about," Mouse Moore told them. "I don't believe Bobby Lee Smith is the stubbornest livin' human bein', an' I'll lay ten dollars on it."

"What's that?"

"Ten dollars says there's somebody stubborner than Bobby Lee Smith, and that he'll admit to it before first frost."

Everybody at the table looked at him like they couldn't believe their ears. "What kind of bet is that?" Shorty Mars snorted. "Who's gonna wait around for months to see if there's somebody stubborner than Bobby Lee Smith?"

"Dunno," Pappy scratched his chin, thoughtfully. "I might. Y'all got anything better to do?"

"I can think of lots of things better to do than hang

196

around No Man's Land all summer," Willie Sutter allowed, sprawling back in his chair. "An' now that Bobby Lee is a landowner down yonder, that's sure enough where he'll be."

"I can't just wait around," Clinton Sears said. "I got to earn me some wages. This cow money won't last forever."

"Do like me," Mouse suggested. "Now that Bobby Lee's got hisself a spread, he's gonna need hands. I figure to hire on."

"Might be he could use a few of us," Pappy nodded.

Iron Tom Logan had walked into the General Sheridan in time to hear most of that, and he stepped over and pulled up a chair. "So Mr. Smith is buying property in the Neutral Strip?"

"Well, that boot-slick feller calls it the Cimarron Proposal," Mouse said, "but I reckon it's the same place."

"Well, that comes as real good news. I'm in the market for some stubborn gents to do a job of work down there this summer, and from what I've seen there isn't anybody any more stubborn than that young fellow."

"You got that right, Mr. Logan," Willie said. "It's common knowledge that Robert E. Lee Smith is the absolute most bull-headed stubborn critter that ever walked on hind legs."

"No, he ain't," Mouse shook his head. "I used to think he was, too, but now I got ten dollars that says he ain't."

"You get a bet, Mouse," Pappy said. "And I'll be happy to take your money on it. Maybe make up for some of what I lost to ol' Willie on account of Bobby Lee bein' so all-fired stubborn."

"Might use some of the rest of you boys, too," Logan said. "If anybody's interested."

"Might be," Joe Dell shrugged. "What is this job of work you got to do?"

197

"Government work," Iron Tom told them. "For the census."

"Doin' what?"

"Counting people in the Neutral Strip. Job starts in June."

They all looked at him. "I don't reckon there's just a lot of folks yonder real enthusiastic about gettin' counted," Pappy drawled.

"Looked to me like there were some that didn't want the Busted S herd to get through, either," Iron Tom said. "But it did. So it didn't matter very much whether they wanted it to or not, then, did it?"

"Not much," Willie agreed.

"So if your government was to pay you boys to count some folks, and they objected, would that matter?"

"Not much," Joe Dell said. "Case like that, I reckon they'd get counted anyhow."

"I'll talk to Mr. Smith about it," Logan said. "Anybody else that's interested, just let me know."

"Gover'ment work," Pappy said thoughtfully. "Never done any gover'ment work. Might be right rousin'. Pay good?"

"Better than pushing cows," Logan said.

That evening, Iron Tom Logan looked up Thomas Allen Fry. "I guess I'll take you up on that census supervisor business," he told him. "Looks like I might have just the kind of enumerators No Man's Land needs."

"Good," Fry said. "What kind is that?"

"Bunch of tough-ass Texans with a stubborn streak and a lot of guns."

The Beaver City Express carried a package from Thomas Allen Fry when it got back to Beaver City, and Bart Sherrell delivered it to Haygood Dobbs along with the mail sack, while Sill changed out the teams and Mike O'Riley and Calvin Gable stood guard.

The package was printed handbills, fresh off the press at Hays, Kansas, announcing that as of the first day of June, 1890, the United States Census Office would be commencing the eleventh Census of Population and Social Statistics, and all persons residing within the states, territories, and holdings of the United States of America were to be so advised.

When Haygood Dobbs had the mail stowed for slotting, and Calvin Gable nesting on it, they watched the Beaver City Express head off westward, then Haygood took off his apron and headed out with a hammer, a stack of posters and a pocket full of tacks. Beaver City not being any bigger than it was, it didn't take him an hour to plaster every pole, post and stump with copies of the census announcement. He took special pleasure in hammering notice tacks into George Scrannon's repaired door at the "Provisional Capital of the Cimarron Proposal."

Scrannon and a couple of his vigilantes came out to see what the ruckus was about, and Haygood, grinning like a badger, handed him a fresh poster.

Scrannon read the notice, scowled and looked up. "What does this mean?"

"Means just what it says," Dobbs told him. "There's going to be a census, and the Neutral Strip is included."

"A head-count?" Scrannon sneered. "All right, if the government wants a head-count, I'll provide it for 'em."

"Won't work," Dobbs assured him happily. "This is gonna be a real, honest-to-Pete census, not some scam run by land sharks. They won't take your numbers for it, Scrannon. It's going to be official."

"Official?" Scrannon sneered again. "Whatever I report will be certified by Governor Oliver Winshaw and Judge Sylvester Magruder. Who else is there here that's official?"

"Those two are about as official as this 'Provisional Capitol' here is, Scrannon, and you know it. You might

199

as well just back off this time, because the United States Census Office will do the counting this time."

Scrannon's eyes went cold and his hand went to his coat, and Dobbs shook his head. "Uh-uh, Scrannon. Remember, United States mail? Federal marshals?"

"Get off my property," Scrannon growled, turning away to tear down the poster on his door.

Dobbs shrugged and started away, then turned to call over his shoulder, "Mail's in, Scrannon. There's somethin' for you from that land-shark salesman of yours, Booth-Sykes or whatever he calls himself today. Five cents' postage due."

Scrannon glared at the postmaster. "You came all the way down here, why didn't you bring it along and deliver it?"

"I told you. It's got postage due. If you want it, you can come to the post office and get it. Mind your manners, though. Calvin's trigger finger has developed a fearsome twitch lately."

Scrannon watched him go, then started into his office and almost collided with Beauregard Jenkins at the door. Jenkins was rubbing sleep out of his eyes and yawning.

"Wake up, you nitwit," Scrannon grumbled. "We have a problem."

Jenkins looked past him, at the retreating figure of the postmaster. "Him? I told you, boss, if you want him . . . uh, eliminated, you better do it yourself. None of the boys want to tangle with federals."

"Not him," Scrannon said. "Not right now, anyway. It's this!" He held a poster up for a moment, then remembered that the chairman of the Vigilance Committee could barely read. "They're planning a federal head-count here. We've got to put a stop to that."

"Why?"

"Why? Because . . ." Scrannon stopped. There was no way in the world that Beauregard Jenkins would

200

ever understand the ramifications of an official census. That once counted, the people in No Man's Land would be recognized as actually being there. That once recognized, they would be tabulated for representation under the Constitution of the United States. That the tabulation would lay open the fact that they *had no* representation, which would lead to an immediate investigation of the Neutral Strip and everything in it—and eventually to the creation of some kind of a local government.

A government that Scrannon wasn't ready for yet, that he wouldn't be ready for until the Cimarron Proposal became the Cimarron Territory, by the definition he himself had engineered. A definition that gave him absolute control over the disposal of lands and the structure of government.

All of which Beauregard Jenkins lacked the brains to even begin to understand.

". . . Because it means a bunch of do-gooders running around meddling with the peace and prosperity of this area," he finished. "We surely don't need that kind of meddling around here."

"No," Jenkins agreed somberly, "We sure don't."

"I'll want the Vigilance Committee to take care of this matter," Scrannon said, heading for his desk.

Jenkins followed him in and closed the door. "You say the word, Boss, we'll get it done."

"I count on it," Scrannon opened his drawer, looking for paper, then glanced up. "Have you run those women squatters off my cattle land yet, Jenkins?"

"Uh . . . not just yet, Boss." Jenkins looked embarrassed, "Some of the boys have been keepin' an eye on the place, but we haven't been able to get close so far. There's always folks around."

"Folks? What folks?"

"Oh, land, everybody, seems like. Freight wagons, drummers, folks stoppin' by to visit. An' that old lawman, Wiggins . . ."

"Is he still around here?"

"He comes and goes, but it's like he's always hangin' around out yonder. He's a spooky one, Boss. Nobody wants to tangle with him."

"Why is he still around?"

"Word is, he's layin' for that Beaver City Express stagecoach. Wants to take it back north someplace for a reward."

"Well, he's had time enough to catch it, hasn't he?"

"Dunno, Boss. It's like him and them got some kind of a standoff goin'. I don't know what it is. Then there's some as thinks he's soft on one or t'other of them women. Nobody wants to tangle with him."

"Find a way to get them off that place!" Scrannon snapped. "I don't want them there."

XXII

When Busted S finally did bust up, they went headed off in two general directions, both of them south. Old Shad Ames, though he hadn't ever stopped grumbling about the way Bobby Lee Smith had hornswoggled him into the whole trail herd deal, was nevertheless right proud of how it had all turned out. He could hardly wait to get back to Abilene to set up drinks at the Shades of Paradise and brag about his success.

Clinton Sears and Sam Nabors decided to head on back, too, and they all stopped off at Beer City to pick up some of the others.

The place was quite a sight when they got there. Beer City never did look quite the same two days in a row anyway—or so said those familiar with it—but it was generally a riotous little hell-hole, catering to the amusement of both tight-lipped Kansans who left their standards at the line when they went on a tear, as well as the wild bunch of misfits drifting up through the Neutral Strip because it was the healthiest place for them to be. But since all the old cattle trails were further east, and the dip-law had sort of nailed down the Kansas border, and since Iron Tom Logan's railhead had only just arrived in No Man's Land, turned out the Busted S was the first Texas trail crew that had come to join the festivities at Beer City. And

203

those seven old boys from Abilene did it the Texas way.

They had the place treed when Shad and them got there. Half the town was locked up tight as a fort, and the rest of it was at the mercy of those Texans. Wesley Watkins was holed up in the Chicago, Rock Island and Pacific Whorehouse, holding several dozen citizens and visitors hostage at gunpoint while he recited poetry at them. Bo Sayers and Christy Walker had taken over a gaming emporium and were setting their own house odds.

Rock Bottoms was well along on a plan he had to carry out the commandment of Genesis. There were maybe two-three dozen prairie angels working Beer City right then, and the strong majority of them had been given every opportunity to go forth and multiply, courtesy of Rock Bottoms.

John Jay Hastings was patrolling the town with a bottle in one hand, a big iron in the other and a quart jar lid pinned on his shirt, and there were few men more capable of keeping the peace than John Jay Hastings was, if that was what he took a notion to do.

The Burnetts were sleeping it off on a railroad-tie porch, and it was probably the quietest that Beer City had been in years. Nobody around Beer City wanted to wake up the Burnett Brothers. They had all seen them awake.

Well, Shad and Clinton and Sam, they rode in and gathered up their strays, and they say there were songs written about the relief the Beer Citians felt when they saw the backs of that bunch, heading back to Texas.

As to Bobby Lee Smith—well, he was within sight of the Beaver River when he reined in Tarnation and hauled around to face those who were behind him. He looked them over thoughtfully, then tipped back his hat and said, "Do you fellers mind if I ask you a question?"

"Ask away, Bobby Lee," Pappy Jameson told him.

"All right. How come y'all are followin' me like this?"

Mouse Moore was kind of off to one side, and he walked his pony forward. "I come along to show you the way, Bobby Lee," he said.

"Well, that's thoughty of you, Mouse, but I know the way, my own self. My land is right yonder a few miles."

"I mean the way to get your deed recorded," Mouse corrected him. "You got to go over to Beaver City to do that, an' it ain't exactly the way they record property other places. But I been there, an' seen it done, so I figured I'd help you out."

"Oh," Bobby Lee said. "Well, all right. Let's go to Beaver City, then." He glanced at the rest again. "Y'all want to come along, too?"

"Thought you'd never ask," Willie Sutter said. Jimbo Riley and Shorty Mars kind of glanced at each other, then fell in behind Joe Dell McGuire as they headed on, veering east toward the town.

Mouse hauled up alongside of Bobby Lee. "Feller you need to talk to is a gent name of Scrannon," he said. "He's the local land shark, and can't be trusted any farther than a shed-blind rattler can, but there's a proven procedure for gettin' your deed recorded. I seen it before."

"I'll do it, then," Bobby Lee agreed. "Want everything fit an' legal."

"If the feller calls you a bitch, you slap the salt out of him, is what you do," Mouse divulged.

"If he does *what?*"

"Likely he won't," Mouse assured him. "But if he does, that's what you do. An' if you feel like you want to take his gun away from him, an' he drops it on the ground, don't try to pick it up. He's got the slickest little hideout gun I ever seen, an' he'll shoot you dead if you take your eyes off of him."

Bobby Lee stared at Mouse, fascinated. "What kind of place is this, anyway?"

205

"No Man's Land," Mouse shrugged. "You need to meet the postmaster. He can give you the lay of the land."

After a while, they could see the rooftops of Beaver City. "Yonder's the place," Mouse pointed. "Some right nice folks thereabouts. I know a bunch of 'em."

"Hell, Mouse," Willie snorted, "everywhere you go, you know everybody."

"No, I don't," Mouse said seriously. "Not right off. But they generally know me. Wonder how come that is?"

They splashed across the river and came into town from the grove, then turned up the only regular street the place had. Mouse was giving them a guided tour, rattling on like a native. "See the hill yonder, just south of town?" he pointed. "All that fresh-dug ground is graves. There's no law hereabouts, so folks tend to plant one another when they have differences. There is a vigilance committee, but it ain't law. It's just a bunch that answers to that feller Scrannon. His place is yonder on the right-hand side, where all the signs are.

"Now this place here, where it says Dobbs General Merchandise, this is the post office. Postmaster's name is Dobbs. He's a law an' order man. Yonder's Wade Meeker's barn, where L. C. Stone provides teams for the Beaver City Express." Mouse tipped his hat to a woman carrying a shotgun and a basket of eggs. "Howdy, Miz Lance. Right nice day." He replaced his hat and told his companions, "That there is Miz Lance. Her husband has a road ranch yonder, an' she believes I'm his cousin from Hardesty. These handbills all over is somethin' new. They wasn't here before."

"Census notices," Pappy squinted. "That's what that feller Logan was talkin' about. You aimin' to hire on for that job, Bobby Lee?"

"I got to look at my land first," Bobby Lee said. "Told him I'd think on it. You boys interested in that, too?"

"Might be," Pappy allowed.

They pulled up in front of the Scrannon Land and Cattle Company, and Mouse swung down. "Watch," he said. "I'll show you how this is done." Rein-looping his gray, he walked across the street to stand in front of the Happy Times Saloon, took a deep breath and shouted, "Scrannon! George Scrannon! Get your thievin' butt out here!"

A man came to the door. "Who's calling for Mr. Scrannon?"

"I am," Mouse told him. "Tell him to get out here. I got a customer for him, across the street."

That done, Mouse strolled back across the street, fished around in his saddlebag for a fence tool, then walked to the door of Scrannon's building and methodically broke off the lock.

Noticing that the others were staring at him with their mouths open, Mouse explained, "That's how it's done. I told ya'll things are different here."

Across the street a shout of anger was raised, and men came running. "The baggy-eyed gent yonder is Scrannon," Mouse told his pards. "If y'all take a notion to shoot him, hold off 'til he gets done recordin' Bobby Lee's deed, because I don't know who else can." He opened the door and went in. The others followed, fanning out inside as several townsmen skidded to a halt at the door and peered inside. George Scrannon was staring at his battered door like he couldn't believe his eyes. "Who broke my God-damned door again?" he hissed.

From inside, Mouse said, "I did that, Mr. Scrannon. I was just showin' the boys how it's done. Come on in, Mr. Scrannon. Feller here has business with you."

Scrannon peeked inside, then started to back away. "I'll be damned if I'll . . ."

A strong hand shot out, grabbed his tailored lapel and lifted him through the door.

"Put him in his chair, yonder, Willie," Mouse Moore

said. "That's where he sits to write."

Willie plunked the land-shark into his chair and backed away. Scrannon's hand snaked to the front of his coat, then stopped when several hammers clicked back. At the front door, Joe Dell McGuire stood languidly, grinning at the men outside. "My name's McGuire," he said. "Joe Dell McGuire. Y'all wasn't thinkin' about drawin' any of them guns, was you?"

Mouse looked past him, then crooked a finger at "Judge" Sylvester Magruder, who at the moment was white-faced and reasonably sober. "Need your services, too, Judge," he said.

When the judge hesitated, Jimbo Riley stepped out, caught him by collar and britches, and carried him inside. "Need any more from out here?" he asked.

"Reckon that's all," Mouse said. Riley and McGuire stepped in and closed the door behind them.

"What is the meaning of this?" Scrannon was snarling, trying to get up from his chair. Hands kept shoving him back down into it.

"I understand you have to record the deed to property I bought in this area," Bobby Lee Smith said. He brought out his papers and spread them on the desk. "I bought this here described section of land, cash on the barrelhead, from your representative, Colonel somebody-or-other . . . uh, Booth-Sykes. It's mine, I own it and I want you to record the deed."

"I'll do no such thing!" Scrannon snapped. "This is my territory, and I say what's what here. You can just . . ." he glanced at the deed and description, and his eyes went wide. "It's the same damn place! The Jackson Creek place!" In a fury, he shoved the papers away. "I don't know what you're trying to pull, Mister . . ."

"Smith," Bobby Lee told him. "Robert E. Lee Smith. Just hush up and record my deed, Mr. Scrannon. I ain't got all day."

"You don't want Bobby Lee to pitch a fit here, Mr.

Scrannon," Mouse Moore said gently. "Just do it."

"By God, the son of a bitch can pitch . . . !"

Bobby Lee's gloved hand came out of nowhere, and Scrannon cartwheeled backward, chair and all.

"You didn't need to do that, Bobby Lee," Mouse Moore said.

"I'm just doin' like you told me, Mouse. You said to."

"He didn't exactly call you a 'bitch,' Bobby Lee. He said 'pitch.'"

"Well, I took offense at what he did call me."

Several of the Texans were helping a dazed George Scrannon to his feet, brushing him off and righting his chair. "Sorry about that, Mr. Scrannon," Bobby Lee said. "Now you just behave yourself and do like Mr. Moore tells you."

Scrannon glared at him with eyes like hellfire. "You son of a . . ."

Again he went cartwheeling backward, and Bobby Lee shook his head. "Maybe you didn't understand, Scrannon," Bobby Lee rasped. "I take exception to bein' called by that kind of language."

From outside the building, there were sounds of a ruckus, and Pappy Jameson stepped to a window, looked out and chuckled. The sounds went on.

Mouse Moore helped a pale, shaking George Scrannon get out his paper and inkwell, and stood over him as he wrote and signed a voucher of registry just like Mouse had seen him do before. After he signed it, they made the judge sign it, and Bobby Lee leaned across the desk to shake Scrannon's hand. "Nice doing business with you," he said.

He turned away, and there were sounds of swift movement behind him. He glanced around. Scrannon was staring at him with murder in his eyes and his hand inside his coat, where he seemed to be scratching his belly.

"I got your guns right here, Mr. Scrannon," Mouse

Moore said, emptying first the revolver and then the derringer. "You can have 'em back, now. I just didn't want to see you do somethin' foolish 'til Bobby Lee had his paperwork all done. 'Bye, now."

Outside, the crowd had backed away, and Tarnation stood in mid-street, looking down at a bruised and bleeding man who lay there flat on his back. Mouse walked over, peered down at the man, tipped his hat and said, "Well, howdy there, Governor." He turned. "This here is Governor Oliver Winshaw. That's his saloon yonder."

Pappy Jameson was still laughing, just like he had been while he looked out the window. "Seems like a governor would have better sense," he observed, wiping at his eyes. "Of all the horses in the world for a man to try and steal . . . !"

Bobby Lee swung into his saddle. "If we're all done here, boys, let's go see my new spread." Beneath him, he felt Tarnation gathering for a pitch, and he whacked him with his heels. "You done had your fun for one day, horse," he muttered. "Now behave yourself."

As the Texans rode up the street, there were various eyes upon them. In front of his office, George Scrannon wiped a smear of blood from his cheek and glared at the strangers. "Get me Jenkins," he told someone near at hand. "Go find him and tell him I want to see him, right now."

In front of the post office, Haygood Dobbs frowned at the passing cowboys, and turned as Wade Meeker hurried toward him. "Haygood, you ought to have been yonder," Meeker puffed. "Way I hear it, that feller there—the one ridin' next to Mr. Moore—he just went and made Scrannon register his deed for a piece of land. Done it the same exact way Miss Annie Sue done with hers. Scrannon's killin' mad, too."

"High time that snake got some decency taught to him," Dobbs said. "Who is the new landowner?"

"Name's Smith. But here's the thing, Haygood—the

land he registered on, it's the same identical section that Miss Annie Sue registered on. You suppose she sold out already?"

Dobbs shook his head, confused. "I don't know, Wade. I sure didn't have the notion that she planned to sell and move on. That little woman struck me as fixing to plant herself on that place so solid it would take an Act of Congress to budge her."

As they cleared the last traces of Beaver City and headed west, Mouse Moore told Bobby Lee, "Might have a slight problem, Bobby Lee. I got me a notion there's somebody livin' on your new place."

"Squatters?" Bobby Lee's eyes went narrow. "Wasn't anybody there before, when we come by."

"Well, there might be now," Mouse said. "Just figgered you ought to know."

"No problem," Bobby Lee shrugged. "Squatters is squatters. If they're there, I'll just run 'em off."

XXIII

There was somebody on Bobby Lee's land, all right, just like Mouse said there would be. But even Mouse didn't know the half of it.

Two miles out from Beaver City, they saw riders coming the other way. Half a dozen riders, just coming hell-for-leather and looking back over their shoulders like the Old Scratch himself was hard on their hindsides. They were close before any of them even noticed the Texans coming toward them, and when they did the one in the lead raised his hat and hollered, "Back off! That old man's yonder an' he's . . ."

Then, like they suddenly realized the riders they saw weren't anybody they expected to see, they hauled rein, stared at them for a minute and scattered every which way.

"Now that was peculiar," Willie Sutter drawled.

"Vigilantes," Mouse said. "I seen some of 'em around town."

They hadn't gone another mile when a spring wagon showed just ahead, coming up out of a draw. A wagon full of people, men and women both, all dressed up like they had been to a Sunday social. The wagon began to sprout guns as they approached, but when the Texans tipped their hats the folks howdied back and they passed at a respectful distance and paused in hollering range. "You boys come to work on the place?" a man called.

"I expect we'll be doin' a sight of that," Bobby Lee called back.

"You'll have to start off with rough-cut lumber," the man said. "An' nails an' tar, like you need. I have to check on the split shingles, but the rest is in stock. It'll be out directly. Obliged if you'd watch for it an' help guard it in. Folks the way they are, you can't be too careful." The man waved. "Howdy, Mr. Moore. Nice day."

"Howdy," Mouse called back.

"We'll be watchin'," Bobby Lee assured the man.

"Mighty good service in these parts," Pappy allowed. "You ain't hardly even got there yet, an' already they're shippin' out materials to you. What do you aim to do with rough-cut lumber, Bobby Lee?"

"I haven't got the slightest notion," Bobby Lee admitted. "I didn't know it was comin'. Mouse, did you order out buildin' materials?"

"Not me," Mouse shrugged. "But if Bert Mason says there's things comin', then there's things comin'. That's who that was, was Bert Mason. Him and the rest of them, they're from town. Good folks."

"Must be part of my lucky streak," Bobby Lee decided, a little puzzled. "I reckon I ought to build a barn, though. Place needs a barn." He glanced around at all of them, thoughtfully. "Y'all are still taggin' along, looks to me like."

"Seems like it," Shorty Mars agreed.

"Y'all by any chance lookin' for work?"

"Thought you'd never ask," Willie Sutter said.

They rode on, and Bobby Lee was looking at his boundary map. Within easy sight of the cottonwood tops that marked the river place, he hesitated, read his map again and looked around, judging distances. "Right . . . about . . . here," he announced.

"What is?" Pappy asked.

213

"Where my section starts. Boys, I'd say right here is where we come officially to the east property line of my new spread." He reined in, and the others did likewise. "Seems like an event that needs commemoratin', don't it?"

"I reckon," Pappy shrugged. "Ol' Shad's way's good as any." He swung down from his horse and started unbuttoning his britches. The rest followed suit, and Bobby Lee frowned for a second, then stepped down to join them. "Good a way as any," he decided.

"I reckon," Willie Sutter agreed. "Though by that test, ol' Shad has done staked claim to the state of Kansas."

"Doubt he wants it," Pappy noted. They lined up, facing downwind, and Pappy glanced at Bobby Lee. "What is it we're christenin' here?"

"My land, is what."

"Yeah, but what's its name? You got to name a name to have a christenin', you know. Otherwise it ain't official."

"Well, Busted S is my brand, so I reckon this here place is Busted S."

"Sounds right proper," Pappy agreed. "Let 'er rip, boys. Here's to the Busted S. May it never run dry."

"Amen," Jimbo Riley added.

Solemnly and ceremonially they baptised a bit of No Man's Land as the Busted S, and they were just running dry when a deep voice behind them said, "Just hold real still, there, fellers, an' don't even think about haulin' out anything you ain't already hauled."

Nobody ever said Ben Wiggins wasn't a fine lawman, when he was being a lawman, and nobody would ever have doubted him as a bounty man when that was what he took a notion to do. Folks just naturally fought shy of bracing Ben Wiggins, and he had gotten used to that. The problem was, in the years since Kansas had gone high-falutin' about dipping trail herds, Ben Wiggins

214

had sort of lost the natural habits that a man needs if he aims to deal with Texas drovers. That was why his mouth just kept hanging there, wide open, after those words got out.

It was because he just couldn't believe his eyes. Quicker than a codger can spit, those boys that had been lined up there with their backs to him were spread, crouched and facing him, and he was looking down the muzzles of six big revolvers.

Under other circumstances, it would have been an amusing sight. Kansans, being good Methodists by and large, would have taken the time to put away their draining gear and maybe button their britches before they spun around and drew iron on a man. He had just plain forgotten how sudden a bunch of bushy-tail Baptist drovers from Texas can be.

For a minute, they all just stared at one another, then Mouse Moore grinned and let his pistol droop. "Why, Mr. Wiggins," he said. "It's you."

Wiggins blinked and got his mouth to working again, though his own pistol didn't waver. "Howdy, Mr. Moore," he said. "I didn't know it was you. I thought I'd got me some vigilantes." He seemed to realize about his gun being in his hand, then, and he let it droop a little, his eyes taking in the others one by one. Next to Mouse Moore, a sturdy, broad-shouldered young buck with a stubborn chin glared back at him. Then there was a gray-haired old ranny with hard eyes, a lanky, rawhide-looking jasper who held his big gun like it was part of his hand, and . . . he stopped at the next one. "I know you," he said. "You're Joe Dell McGuire."

"As ever was," Joe Dell admitted. "And you're Marshal Ben Wiggins."

Next to McGuire, a waddy that wouldn't have come to the withers of a horse but was shaped like a logging maul raised an eyebrow and kept his gun steady. And beyond him was a sandy-haired sprout who might have been somebody's bumpkin cousin, except that his eyes said he wasn't exactly the way he looked.

And all of them just standing there, facing him, with their guns in their hands and their privates hung out . . . Wiggins made a sound like a belch, then did it again, and his rock-carved face just plain split wide open. "I can see I threw down on the wrong men," he laughed. Still rumbling and belly-chuckling, he put his gun away. "You boys are somewhat over-exposed," he pointed out. "Go on and get yourselves put together. You ain't the ones I was after."

"Glad to hear that," Joe Dell allowed, his gun disappearing into its holster. "Don't believe I'd have relished shootin' you."

Mouse was buttoning his britches. "This here is Ben Wiggins," he told anybody who hadn't already figured that out. "Met him in Beaver City last time through. He'd be law, 'cept there ain't any law here to be. Mr. Wiggins, this here is Bobby Lee Smith, new owner of the Busted S spread. That's Pappy Jameson yonder . . ."

"Howdy," Pappy said, working with his buttons.

". . . and Willie Sutter, an' you already know Joe Dell McGuire . . ."

"I reckon," Wiggins nodded.

". . . an' them others is Shorty Mars an' Jimbo Riley. We're out to have a look at Bobby Lee's new spread."

Wiggins leaned on his saddlehorn. "Nice to meet you boys. Busted S, you said? Where is that?"

"We're standin' on it," Bobby Lee told him. "I own this whole section. Legal an' recorded."

"You own . . . ?" Wiggins straightened, looking around. "You mean *this?*"

"Right as rain," Bobby Lee said. "One section. Got me a porch yonder, down by the river, that I'm gonna sit on after we get the barn built."

"This place?" Wiggins asked again. "You sayin' *you* own this place here?"

"Sure do. Who was that you said you thought we were?"

"Vigilantes," Wiggins said. "Bunch of toughs out of Beaver City, that come out here to make trouble for the . . . for the owner of this place. I been kinda keepin' an eye out."

"Well, that's thoughty of you, Marshal," Bobby Lee told him. "Right friendly. Like those folks that's sendin' out rough-cut lumber for my barn."

"For your . . . but that lumber is for . . ."

"Mr. Wiggins?" Mouse eased up alongside. "Wonder if I could have a word with you, *private*, while these boys finishes gettin' presentable."

Without waiting for an answer, Mouse got a grip on Wiggins' horse's bit-ring and led him off to the side. "We got kind of a situation, here," he explained. "Now you an' me, we know about the ladies yonder, an' how Miss Annie Sue has bought this place and got it recorded. The thing is, so has Bobby Lee. Bought from the same sidewinder, got his deed certified by the same shark, an' owns this here place just as much as that little darlin' does."

Wiggins stared down at him, wide-eyed.

"So what I'm thinkin' is," Mouse suggested, "the best thing a man can do is just sort of stay out of it an' let the two owners sort it all out their own selves."

"That's prepos . . . absur . . . ridic . . . that's crazy," Wiggins managed. "He can't own this land. It's hers!"

"I expect she'll look on it that way, sure enough," Mouse agreed. "But Bobby Lee, he's got just as much right as she has, seein' he bought it in good faith just like she did . . ."

"Were you there?"

"Sure was."

"Then why in God's name didn't you *tell* him?"

"Tell him what?"

"That this land wasn't for sale."

"Feller that sold it to him said it was," Mouse

217

shrugged. "Besides, just take a look yonder. That Bobby Lee Smith, now ain't he about as fine a lookin' young feller as you ever seen? Big, strappin' boy like that, an' good-lookin' to boot—not to mention bein' just all-fired stubborn. Why, I don't know how I'd live with myself if I was to circumlocute his best opportunity to get to resolve an interestin' business situation with Miss Annie Sue, who is just about the most adorable lookin' little thing a man ever saw—not to mention bein' all-fired stubborn her own self . . . you see?"

"No."

"Well, let me put it this way. You see Bobby Lee yonder . . ."

"I see him, all right. Reminds me of somebody, too."

"Some says he's the spittin' image of his daddy. You know Doc Holt?"

Wiggins' eyes widened again. "Doc Holt? You telling me that's Doc Holt's boy? You said his name was Smith."

"Well, that's for Nanny's sake, you see. That good woman's interests is best served by seein' Bobby Lee as a foundlin'. But he's Doc's boy, right enough. Anybody can see that."

"I reckon you're right," Wiggins admitted. "I'll be danged! Doc Holt's boy."

"Yep. An' just like his daddy, 'cept for one thing. Bobby Lee is a whole lot stubborner."

"Nobody on God's green earth is as stubborn as Doc Holt," Wiggins said, flatly. "I know that for a fact."

"Well, Bobby Lee is. Fact is, folks down home figger if it come to a stubborn contest between Bobby Lee Smith an' the devil, the devil'd back down."

"So what's that got to do with this land thing?"

"Well, I seen that little Miss Annie Sue take charge of that snake Scrannon, just like you did. So, what do you think?"

"About what?"

"Who do you believe is stubborner? Her or Bobby Lee? The boys an' me, we got money ridin' on that."

Wiggins stared at him like he couldn't believe his ears. "You got money . . . you got a bet on whether Doc's boy is stubborner than that little dumplin'?"

"'Bout the size of it. 'Course, the boys, they don't know about Miss Annie Sue . . . I mean about her bein' here, an' the land question an' all."

"But you do." Wiggins' gaze became admiring. "Mr. Moore, you might ought to consider goin' into politics."

"Whatever," Mouse shrugged. "Anyhow, I reckon we'll find out before long. My bet is, Bobby Lee Smith is fixin' to meet his mistress."

"His what?"

"Well, she can't hardly be anybody's *master,* can she? Not shaped like she is. But I believe that little gal will out-stubborn him."

"Just one thing," Wiggins said. "I'll tell you right now, if that Bobby Lee or anybody else here offers harm to those ladies, I'll shoot the man that does. Then I'll shoot you for startin' it."

Mouse looked pained. "Mr. Wiggins, we're all from Texas."

Willie Sutter hailed them and pointed. There were wagons coming from the direction of Beaver City, and in the distance to the north, a stagecoach had come into sight.

"Gettin' mighty busy around here," Wiggins muttered.

"You still out to collect bounty on that there stagecoach?" Mouse asked.

"Not right now," Wiggins shook his head. "I talked to those boys an' we kind of struck a deal. I let them alone to run their business, an' they give me everybody that tries to rob 'em."

"Around here, that could be quite a haul."

"It is," Wiggins admitted. "I've done delivered three

219

jaspers to the Kansas law and two to Texas. Bounty on 'em comes to about twice what the reward is for that missin' Concord coach."

It was a mystified Bobby Lee Smith who rode down the caprock slopes into the valley of the Beaver River. The closer he came to the old shack in the scrubs, the more folks he saw. There were dozens of them—women and children roaming around, gathering firewood and stringing clotheslines, men setting up a prissy-looking picket fence while some others whitewashed the outhouse, some boys up on the shed roof setting shingles, some fellows with scythes and axes clearing away underbrush—and there was smoke coming from a chimney and the smell of fried chicken on the wind.

Bobby Lee had his tally string out, thumbing knots. "Who are all these people?" he kept asking, over and over again. "Twenty-one . . . twenty-two . . . what are these people doin' on Busted S?"

The incoming stagecoach rolled past, stopped in front of the house and disgorged passengers and bundles, and the two wagons were closer now—merchant wagons loaded with goods and supplies.

"What in the name of Grover Cleveland is goin' on here?" Bobby Lee snorted, standing in his stirrups to get a better look. "What is this here? A spread-warmin' bee?"

They stepped their mounts down the slope, gawking around, and Willie Sutter pointed. "Lookee yonder! That there's the same rockaway carriage that we fixed up when we come through before!"

Bobby Lee peered, his brow settling into an ominous frown. "It surely is. By jing, I believe them women is . . ."

A gunshot rang through the grove, and a bullet clipped wind over Bobby Lee's head. Right behind it came high-pitched voices. "Annie Sue! You put that thing away! Mercy!" And, "It's him! I can't believe my eyes, Milicent. There he is, back again! The same one. And he's on my land!"

Bobby Lee heard the echoes of the voices as he dived out of Tarnation's saddle and rolled for cover. He didn't know what it was all about, but it did seem like the right thing to do.

XXIV

When coincidences come to downright collision, things can get almighty coincidental. And for a while that's how it was there on the banks of the Beaver River—folks scurrying everywhere, everybody trying to see who was doing what to which ones, half of them raring to shoot somebody if they knew who to shoot at and the other half disappearing into cover in case anybody took a notion to shoot at them.

Later on, Pappy Jameson would recall those moments fondly as "A Grand Confabulation of Concurrent Confusions." Of course, Pappy would never have used words like those sober, but sober wasn't always a permanent condition with him.

What it was, though, was pandemonium—for about a minute and a half. Then Ben Wiggins charged down into the middle of it all, roaring like a chute-hung bull, and brought order to the occasion.

After that, folks all just stood around gawking at one another while Bobby Lee Smith came out of the brush and assured himself that Annie Sue Finch didn't have a gun in her hand anymore. Satisfied on that score—Milicent had relieved the little thing of her hardware—Bobby Lee grabbed up Tarnation's reins and strode down into the middle of the clearing. It being his land and all, he felt like it was up to him to take charge, so he looked around at all the folks there and said, "My name is Robert E. Lee Smith, and I own this place!"

Several of the gents standing around touched their hats and said, "Howdy," and a couple of them said, "No, you don't. She does."

He looked where they were pointing, and went kind of tongue-tied when Annie Sue stepped forward. It wasn't rightly his fault that he did. Any healthy young fellow would have to be dead twice over not to go tongue-tied with Annie Sue's big blue eyes looking at him.

But it gave Annie Sue time to speak her piece, which she did. "My name is Annabel Susanna Finch," she declared, "and the only owner this place has is me. I bought it, and I recorded it, and I want you off my property, you . . . you . . ."

Well, that sprung Bobby Lee's tongue loose like a wagon-jack popping a jammed gate. "*I* bought this place," he announced, "an' *I* recorded it, an' I'm hereby takin' possession. It's mine."

"The devil it is," Annie Sue snapped. "Fairmeadow belongs to me!"

"Then go to Fairmeadow! Busted S is mine!"

"Your condition is your own problem," Annie Sue snapped. "Get off Fairmeadow."

"I ain't on any Fairmeadow! I'm right in the middle of Busted S!"

"I don't care where you think you are! This place is Fairmeadow, and I'm ordering you off!"

"This is Busted S, and you can't order me off my own property!"

"It isn't your property! Not an inch of it! It's mine!"

"Mine!"

By that time, what with her standing on her tiptoes and him hanging over her like a thundercloud, the two of them were nose to nose and yelling at the top of their lungs, and Bobby Lee's personal horse probably felt kind of left out. Horses do, sometimes. Anyhow,

223

Tarnation picked that moment to lower his head and butt Bobby Lee, then backed off when Bobby Lee and Annie Sue went head over heels together into a scrub thicket.

Into it, and out the other side like a hound dog tangled with a badger. It looked for all the world like Annie Sue had sprouted a dozen extra fists and some extra feet and knees, and Bobby Lee couldn't cover one spot fast enough to keep from getting hit in six others. And all the time, Annie Sue's outraged voice was hollering, "I knew it! You're nothing but a low fiend! Just like before!"

Bobby Lee had let out several ouches and was doing his best to get some space between them, but that little dumpling wasn't done yet. She pummeled him around the head and shoulders and belly and anywhere else she could get a fast punch to, and when he ducked and bobbed his head, she bit him on the ear. He yowled like a wounded bear and tripped over a root and rolled, and she was right on top of him. Then there were strong hands pulling them apart. Milicent and some of the ladies held onto Annie Sue the way folks might hang onto a wild cat, and dragged her back, and Ben Wiggins and Jimbo Riley had Bobby Lee, one on each side, rescuing him.

"Mercy!" Milicent declared. "That's enough, Annie Sue. You don't want to hurt the man."

"Yes, I do! You saw what he did! He did it again!"

"His horse bumped him, Annie Sue. He couldn't help it."

"His horse? What does that horse do, set that oaf up to assault ladies? I want that man off my land!"

"It ain't your land!" Bobby Lee yelled from the safety of restraint. "This here is my land!"

"This needs to be talked over," Ben Wiggins suggested. "Y'see, miss, this feller *does* have a deed to this place, just like yours, and it's recorded just like yours is."

"Let's all go in the house and discuss this," Milicent suggested. "I'll make tea."

Annie Sue was glaring at Bobby Lee and trying to get loose to start in on him again. "That is my house! I won't have that . . . that person inside my house!"

"What house?" Bobby Lee glanced around. It was the first time he had really noticed the house there, but there it was, connected to his porch. "You stay off of my porch!" he demanded. "That porch belongs to me!"

"I'd burn that porch before I'd let you claim it!"

"You so much as touch that porch, I'll burn your . . . I mean, *my* shack!"

"Milicent, let me loose and give me back my gun!"

"Ya'll turn loose of me! I'm fixin' to paddle the tar out of that woman!"

"If you touch me one more time, you . . . you *molester,* I'll see you in jail!"

All the time, folks had been dragging them farther apart, until now they were shouting at each other across the clearing. Meantime, Mouse Moore had been going around, introducing folks to other folks. The other Texans hadn't met any of the Beaver City folks, or the other settlers round about, and just a lot of them had turned out that day to welcome their new neighbors—whoever that turned out to be.

Of course, everybody knew Mouse. Or thought they did. It was just how Mouse was. So all the time Annie Sue and Bobby Lee were shouting dire things at each other, most everybody else that wasn't busy restraining the two of them was howdying and tipping hats and shaking hands, and there were some ladies setting out a spread of fried chicken and bisquits and gravy on plank tables under the cottonwoods.

Mouse was right in the big middle of it all, enjoying the sociability no end. But then Ben Wiggins happened to comment, "That Mr. Moore, he made a real mistake not telling you about Miss Annie Sue already buying this place, Mr. Smith. I don't believe any good can

225

come of all this."

Bobby Lee cut off in mid-shout and looked around at him. "Moore? Mouse Moore? He knew about this?"

"He was right there when she recorded her deed with George Scrannon," Wiggins admitted. "So was I. That little lady like to slapped that snake Scrannon silly, for what he said, too. Mighty nice job of recording a title, to my way of thinkin'."

"Mouse? Mouse knew about..." Bobby Lee clouded up like a summer storm. He heaved and shook loose from the ones that had hold of him. "Mouse! Where are you, you..." he turned full circle, just glaring thunders. "Ya'll! Where's Mouse?"

Some of the others looked around, but Mouse wasn't anywhere in sight. He had got everybody introduced all proper, then had gone off somewhere. Mouse always was like that.

The supply wagons from town rolled in about then, and the driver of the first team hollered, "Where does this stuff go?"

"Over there," Annie Sue answered, pointing at the house.

"I didn't order supplies," Bobby Lee said. "But haul up yonder by that grove an' I'll see what we need."

The man looked at them, first one and then the other. "I was told to deliver this stuff to the new owner. Who's the owner here?"

"I am."

"I am!"

"Lordy," Ben Wiggins rumbled. "Here it goes again."

"Mercy," Milicent allowed.

"Supper's on!" a lady shouted. "Come an' get it!"

"Let go of me!" Bobby Lee roared.

"Turn me loose!" Annie Sue demanded.

"You gonna behave yourself an' stop rasslin' with the little lady?" Ben asked.

"I wouldn't touch her with a ten-foot pole!" Bobby

226

Lee shook loose again, looking pained.

"Annie Sue, you behave yourself," Milicent urged.

Annie Sue pulled loose. "I wouldn't go near that . . . that *lout*," she declared. With a swish of skirts and a switch of hips, she stalked off toward the house, and every man in the crowd watched her go. Some even pulled off their hats in admiration.

"I believe Bobby Lee's got the wrong name for this place," Wiggins told Pappy. "'Stead of Busted S, it ought to be Waggin' S, with her on it."

"Puts me in mind of that French paintin' in Alf Tide's place," Pappy admitted.

"Anything female puts you in mind of that paintin', Pappy. Always did."

"Well . . . ," Pappy shook his head. "If I was thirty years younger . . ."

Bobby Lee stalked off to take a look at the supplies in the two wagons. "I reckon we do need stores," he decided. "Y'all can unload over yonder on my porch."

"The yard goods and things ought to go into the house, Mr. Smith." Milicent Moriarty was looking over his shoulder.

Bobby Lee took another look, frowning. "I ain't got any use for yard goods."

"Well, Annie Sue does. Besides, these are all her things. She ordered them."

"Where does she get off takin' delivery of goods on my property?"

"It's her property," Milicent said. "She bought it, and she bought these supplies."

"Then I'll buy 'em," Bobby Lee got one of those looks of his, like a cotton mule come balk time. "Anything on my place is goin' to belong to me." He looked around. "I reckon she ordered out some rough-cut lumber, too?"

"She certainly did. She plans to build a proper house."

"I'll buy that, too," he decided. "I need to build a barn."

"She won't want a barn built with her house lumber."

"It's my place, and I'll say what's built and what isn't."

"It's her place, by rights," Milicent insisted.

"No, it ain't."

"Mercy," Milicent declared.

Most all the visitors by that time were having their supper at the plank tables, and most of the Busted S bunch had joined them, and what with everything that was going on, nobody noticed the blue brindle steer that came wandering in from the north, sauntering right through the clearing. It was eighteen miles from that place on the Beaver River to Tyrone Switch, where Iron Tom Logan had bought Bobby Lee's herd. And it had taken old Blue that long to bust loose from the pens up there and head south.

Anyway, while Milicent was talking to Bobby Lee, Ben Wiggins was trying to talk to Annie Sue, in the house.

"He's not such a bad young'un," Ben insisted. "Bullheaded stubborn, but he's a gentleman underneath all that. I've knowed his daddy for years, though I didn't know this'n was his boy. Thing is, he's got a claim here, just like you do, an' beatin' on his headbone won't resolve anything. You an' him, you just ought to sit down peaceful an' work things out."

"There's nothing to work out," Annie Sue said, getting a look on her pretty face like a mule can get when it's set to balk. She was at the table, shuffling papers. "I have proper claim, preceding his claim, and that makes his claim worthless and I want him . . . oh, blast!"

"Ma'am?"

"Nothing!" She started stacking the papers, but Wiggins reached past her and spread them out again. "Oh," he said. "I see."

"It isn't dated," she admitted. "That swindler in

228

town, that Scrotum . . ."

"Scrannon," Wiggins corrected.

"Scrannon. Yes. He didn't enter the date of record. But it doesn't make any difference. I have witnesses."

"So does Mr. Smith," Wiggins noted. "I really think the two of you are going to have to talk this over."

"I'd rather talk to a thistle."

"Lordy," Wiggins muttered.

Well, what with the picnic under the cottonwoods, and Bobby Lee and Annie Sue temporarily separated, and everybody else just getting to know each other, things had quieted down considerably at Busted S . . . or Fairmeadow, or wherever. Then all hell sort of broke loose again.

There was a screech from the house, and the sounds of Annie Sue and Ben Wiggins hollering, and everybody looked around just in time to see a blue brindle steer come traipsing out of the shack, across Bobby Lee's porch, with a sometimes Kansas marshal right behind it, shooing it out.

Willie Sutter stared like he couldn't believe his eyes. "Blue?" he said. "Pappy, ain't that my lead steer yonder?"

"B'lieve it is, for a fact," Pappy Jameson allowed. "How come that critter is here?"

Willie got up and started for a better look, and the steer turned and saw him and started for him. Willie backpedaled and folks and fried chicken went every which way, and Bobby Lee hollered, "Watch it, Willie! That's a range critter!"

Blue wasn't exactly head-down charging at Willie. He was just trotting toward him like he was happy to see him. But with cows, a man's a fool to take a chance. Willie headed for the nearest tree, and Bobby Lee headed for his horse and swung into the saddle, reaching for his catch-rope. "Stay low!" he said. "I'll get . . . oh, sweet Jesus!"

The last part of that was said about four feet—and

maybe an octave—higher than the first part. Tarnation had been standing ground-reined ever since they came in, and he was full of vinegar. Bobby Lee no sooner slapped rump to saddle than Tarnation slapped hooves to hard ground and went into a bucking fit that did even him proud. He cartwheeled, crow-hopped, stiff-legged and switched ends, then when he had Bobby Lee shook good and loose he crouched, humped and high-bucked, and dodged away before Bobby Lee could come back down on him.

Bobby Lee hit with a thump, flat on his back in tall weeds, and just lay there stunned for a minute. There were folks running around all over the place, making for trees and whatever, a range steer chasing around this way and that, and Tarnation still stomping and bucking, his stirrups flapping like pigeon wings. And that was when Annie Sue came boiling out of her house with an iron skillet in her hand and headed for Blue. "I won't have cows in my house!" she yelled. "Get off my property! Git!"

Blue saw her coming, and decided he had met his match. He turned tail, and Tarnation took a notion that the cow had the right notion, and took out with him, and Bobby Lee picked himself up out of the weeds just in time for Annie Sue to run square into him. They went head over heels and the skillet went flying, and Ben Wiggins and Milicent came running and Willie Sutter came out from behind his tree to stare. Pappy Jameson appeared beside him and said, "Y'know, I believe them young'uns is just made for one another."

Willie looked at him. "I believe they're tryin' to kill one another," he said.

Pappy shrugged. "Sometimes it's a lot the same."

XXV

About the time all that preliminary negotiation and friendly socializing was going on out at the Beaver River spread, things were popping over at Beaver City. The Beaver City Express had just come in, on its eastbound run, with Mike O'Riley and Calvin Gable riding shotgun, and delivered the mail pouches from Liberal and Hays—which they picked up at Tyrone Switch, naturally.

Haygood Dobbs ran up his "in-came mail" flag, and the customers who were there to see it lined up for their deliveries.

There was quite a stack of correspondence for the Scrannon faction, and Dobbs handed it all over to "Judge" Sylvester Magruder, who carried it off to the Happy Times Saloon for George Scrannon to see. Scrannon took a table by the back window and went through it, getting madder and more murderous by the minute.

There was a letter to "Governor" Oliver Winshaw from the Office of the Secretary of the Interior in Washington, D.C., denying any and all claims for payment of federal appointees in the Neutral Strip, on the grounds that there were no federal officials resident in the Neutral Strip because there wasn't anybody at all in the Neutral Strip—and as far as the Cimarron

231

Proposal was concerned, there wasn't any such thing. Scrannon read that letter through and slapped it down on the table. He had fully expected to collect more than a thousand dollars in federal fees.

Then there was a letter of resignation from Col. Chadwick Booth-Sykes. The colonel had run out of Scrannon Land deeds to sell to folks, and upon giving the matter full consideration, had decided to go into some other line of work. There was no mention of the money he had received for the sold deeds, and no remittance enclosed for Scrannon.

Scrannon thought seriously about hiring bounty-hunters to track down and kill Booth-Sykes. The only problem was, where would the sharper be . . . and *who* would he be, wherever he was?

But the one that cut the cake was a letter from the federal district judge at Fort Smith, addressed to the "Provisional Government of the Area Known As the Cimarron Proposal." It advised that a petition had been received from citizens of the so-named region, requesting that the region be attached to a neighboring state or territory for purposes of insuring constitutional government under federal supervision. The letter advised those presently acting in any and all administrative capacities in the afore-mentioned region that they were to give full cooperation in the conduct of a United States Census count of population there, and that the petition of the citizens would be favorably reviewed should the census indicate that there were in fact citizens residing there.

Scrannon's brow sat right down on the top of his nose, and his baggy-looking eyes peered out through the crack like little glints of hell fire. "What petition?" he demanded, pounding on the table so that glasses and bottles rolled around. "What idiot had the gall to circulate a petition in my territory?"

There were a dozen other men in the place, and they all just stared at him.

"This has got to be stopped!" Scrannon roared.

"What has, Boss?" Governor Winshaw asked from the plank bar.

"All of this!" Scrannon waved the letter at them. "Somebody sent a petition to the courts, and they're gonna meddle in my territory!"

Judge Magruder blinked bleary eyes and looked like he had just remembered something. "I wonder . . . ?"

"You wonder what?"

"Well, seems to me some of the squatters was sendin' around a paper for folks to sign. That postmaster was one of 'em. He said it was a request to the court, but I ain't seen it."

"That was it," Scrannon hissed. "And it wasn't for your court, you idiot, it was for a real court! Now all hell is going to break loose . . . unless we put a stop to it."

"You want some of the boys to shoot the postmaster?" Beauregard Jenkins suggested. "I expect next time Calvin Gable is out ridin' that stagecoach, we could . . ."

"It's too late for that," Scrannon shook his head. "There's only one thing to do. We've got to stop the census."

Jenkins looked doubtful. He wasn't sure what a census was, but he'd never heard of anybody stopping one.

Scrannon got to his feet, picking up the mail. "I want this whole thing stopped!" he said.

Now, George Scrannon was already worked up, even before that mail delivery. He was plotting about three kinds of murder against Bobby Lee Smith on general principles, and he had some notions of how to make things downright unpleasant for Annie Sue Finch, too. And for Haygood Dobbs, for that matter, and for Mouse Moore if he could figure out who—or what—Mouse Moore was. But what with that old marshal hanging around, and the post office business,

233

Scrannon had sort of dragged his feet.

This cut it, though. It was time to put the lid on things around Beaver City, once and for all. Things hadn't been going George Scrannon's way lately, and he was fed up with that situation.

And, just in case he wasn't already mad enough to start a war when he stepped out of the Happy Times Saloon and headed across to his own place, there was one final insult waiting for him there. He stopped in the middle of the street and just stared, like he couldn't believe his eyes.

In front of his place, where the fence posts he had stolen from that cedar cutter were stacked, there wasn't a fence post in sight. Somebody had come along and stolen his stolen posts.

Meantime, up the street, the Beaver City Express had a fresh team and was heading out again. But Bart Sherrell was fixing to alter his outbound route a little. There was mail to be delivered to the Jackson Creek Place—to several folks yonder—and he had volunteered to drop it off. Anything Bart Sherrell could do to lend a neighborly hand to that little blonde darling out at that place, he sure aimed to do it up brown. He was so looking forward to it that for the first time since he had started his runs, he left Mike O'Riley in town to work out team-and-turnaround details with L. C. Stone.

Calvin Gable was standing guard over at the post office, so this time when the Beaver City Express lit out, the only ones riding it were Bart and Sill.

Now, George Scrannon had a fellow in his employ by the name of Wayne Stuckey. Wayne and his three brothers and two sisters had all been in the stagecoach robbing business in the past, out in New Mexico and over into Arizona. But the business had gone sour on them. One of the brothers had stretched hemp outside of Tres Ignacios, and one of the sisters was in the women's facility at Fort Leavenworth. The other sister wound up married to a judge in Arkansas, so Wayne and his brothers Stig and Zeno had come to No Man's Land. They had a little two-by-four place on the south side of the Beaver, that George Scrannon had sold them cheap after they ran off the previous buyers, and all three of them were active members of Beauregard Jenkins' Vigilance Committee when they weren't raiding over into Texas or stealing chickens or the like.

But those boys had never got highway robbery out of their blood, so when George Scrannon had said he wanted the Beaver City Express shut down, the Stuckeys decided they were the men for the job.

They had been prowling around, just waiting for that big Concord coach to roll out without its main guns, and sure enough, the time had done come when it did. And Stig was there to see it.

By the time he had galloped home and got Wayne and Zeno, the Beaver City Express was halfway to Jackson Creek, but they had a head start on it and they were waiting where the trail crossed Coyote Gulch.

Bart and Sill didn't even know they had company until Wayne Stuckey's first bullet plowed a furrough in Bart's brake leg, but they sure enough knew it then. Bart yelled, whipped up that fresh team and lit out across the flats, while Sill swung up from below, got belly-down on the stretched-canvas roof of the coach, and opened up with a Winchester.

It must have seemed like old times to Wayne Stuckey, him and the boys in hot pursuit of a live stage-coach like that. Nobody ever knew for sure what it seemed like, though, because Sill knew how to use that Winchester, and his third shot took Wayne right out of his saddle.

Stig and Zeno didn't see that happen. They had flanked the coach right at the outset, and were edging in, one on each side, to board, when they came up over a long rise and overtook a buckboard full of fence posts. They came up on it so fast that Stig veered off one way, and the coach veered the other, and old Zeno found himself with one foot through a coach window and the other sliding across his saddle as his horse took off for other places. He tried to grab the coach and missed, tried to shift back to his saddle and missed, and like the Good Book says, the very earth came up and smote him.

Mouse Moore was just sort of ambling along at the reins of the buckboard, with his mount rein-led behind, when a green stagecoach went thundering past on one side of him and a wild-eyed rider on the other side.

"Here, now!" Mouse allowed, then ducked when the fellow on the saddle-horse leveled a shot in his direction.

Stig Stuckey shouldn't have shot at Mouse Moore. Old Mouse was always one of the pleasantest folks a body would want to know—and of course there wasn't a soul that didn't know him—but he never was fond of being shot at. And being a natural Texan like he was, when a thing like that happened, he just plain shot back.

Stig Stuckey's horse kept running a ways, but Stig wasn't on it any more, and Mouse drove up, figuring he'd find out eventually what all that was about.

The Beaver City Express went on another hundred yards before Bart Sherrell got it stopped, and Sill was just helping Bart down when Mouse hauled up alongside.

"Howdy," Mouse said. "Have some trouble?"

"No, thanks," Sill told him. "We already had some. Fellers back yonder offered to rob this stage."

Mouse stood to look back. "Well, they didn't get it done. How many was there?"

"Three," Bart said, tying a cloth around his bleeding leg.

"Two," Sill corrected. "I got one."

"One, then," Mouse allowed. "I put one down a little ways back 'cause he shot at me."

"Obliged," Bart said.

"Think nothin' of it. Y'all goin' on?"

"Depends," Sill said. "Them boys might be worth somethin' to the marshal."

When the Beaver City Express rolled into the Jackson Creek spread, it had a busted Stuckey and two with holes in them inside, three saddle horses tied on behind, and a load of cedar posts following it.

The mail kind of got overlooked for a while, what with all the other commotion that was taking place at the time. But after folks got splints and wraps on Zeno Stuckey, got the hole in Stig's shoulder plugged up so he didn't leak quite so bad, and pulled a quilt over Wayne Stuckey who had gone to meet his maker, and after Ben Wiggins accepted the three of them as rent on the continued freedom of the Beaver City Express, then Bart Sherrell limped over to the house and handed a stack of mail to Miss Annie Sue.

"Special delivery," he said, kind of glazing over at the sight of her blue eyes and everything that went with them.

"Thank you," she said.

"Don't just stand there bleeding," Milicent told him. "Here, sit down on the porch, and I'll bring some lemonade."

Bobby Lee was wandering around with his tally string in his hand, counting uninvited folks on his property, and glared at Bart Sherrell, who was still looking moonbeams at Annie Sue. "You!" he snapped. "Do you have business with me?"

"He's here to see me," Annie Sue said, frostily. "He brought out the mail."

"Well, if this jasper is here to see you, then what's he doing on my porch?"

"It's my house! I'll welcome anybody I choose to welcome at my house!"

"Then welcome him in the house! This here porch is mine!" He glanced at the stack of mail. "My, but you

237

must be popular someplace. Why aren't you there?"

"Mind your tongue!" she snapped. Then she glanced down. "This isn't all for me. It's . . . Lord have mercy! Here's one addressed to you, Mr. Smith. I must say you have gall, having your mail sent to my place."

"It's my place! What's for me?"

"This first letter. The thick one."

"Then give it here."

"I'll thank you to say, 'please.'"

"I'll say what I please, thank you. Give me my mail!"

Bart Sherrell had listened to as much as he could stand, and he stood up, wincing, and stepped between them. He shot a glare at Bobby Lee. "That ain't any way to talk to a lady, mister."

Bobby Lee stepped around him, hardly giving him a glance. "You stay out of this," he snapped. He gave Annie Sue one of his best frowns. "Give me my mail!"

Sherrell tried to get between them again. "I told you, that ain't any . . ."

Annie Sue edged him aside. "You stay out of this," she told Sherrell. Then, with a frown that would have frost-bit a prairie fire on any other face but hers, she thrust out the thick package at Bobby Lee. "Here!" she demanded. "Take your mail!"

Bobby Lee stepped forward to reach for his mail just as Milicent Moriarty came through the door behind Annie Sue, which was where Bart Sherrell had wound up standing. And just at that instant old Blue came wandering around the corner, looking for Willie Sutter who was out yonder looking at the load of fence posts that Mouse Moore had brought in.

When Milicent, who had both hands full of lemonade and fixings, bumped the door open, the door bumped Bart Sherrell, who wasn't standing any too firm because of his sore leg. And when Bart went off balance he sort of fell all over Annie Sue. Old Blue had caught sight of Willie Sutter about then, and that steer bellowed with joy and took off, so that Bobby Lee had

238

to do a fast whirl and back-away to keep from getting hooked.

Had Alf Tide been there with his fiddle right then, and put the whole thing to music, it might have spelled the end of country dancing as we know it. There they were, all over Bobby Lee's porch and out front, too, Bart Sherrell dancing with Annie Sue, Milicent Moriarty dancing with the lemonade, Ben Wiggins high-stepping over busted Stuckeys trying to get to Milicent to cut in, Annie Sue showing Bart Sherrell a couple of break-away steps he probably never wanted to know and running square into Bobby Lee Smith in the process, then Ben Wiggins dancing with the lemonade, Milicent dancing with Bart Sherrell, Willie Sutter doing a sort of fox trot around the post wagon ahead of Blue, and Bobby Lee and Annie Sue spinning off across the yard with mail flying everyplace.

Now, those two had enough momentum that they were still going strong when most everybody else got untangled enough to stare after them in amazement.

"What . . . what are they doin'?" Bart Sherrell pointed, as Annie Sue and Bobby Lee disappeared into a salt-cedar thicket.

Milicent retrieved the lemonade from Ben Wiggins and smiled. "I don't know," she admitted, "but it seems like they do it every time they get together."

Ben picked up Bobby Lee's mail package, which had been scuffled around and come unsealed. It had an official look to it, so he opened it up. "Well, lookee here!" he said. "This is from the United States Census Office. Commissions for Mr. Robert E. Lee Smith et al as Enumerators and Census Marshals."

Pappy Jameson looked over his shoulder, as they say, though considering the size of Ben Wiggins, Pappy more looked around than over it. "Et what?"

"Et al. That's Latin. Means an' all. Means him and anybody else that wants to sign up, 'pears to me. Pays five dollars a head, accordin' to this. Half to the supervisor an' half to the enumerators."

"Five dollars a head? For what?"

"For countin' folks."

"Land," Pappy allowed. "Just to count 'em? Y'don't even have to round 'em up an' drive 'em to market?"

"Just count 'em, is all. But they *all* have to be counted." He looked at some of the other spilled mail, and his eyes widened. "Here's a letter to me." He opened it, read it and raised a thoughtful eyebrow. It was from Iron Tom Logan.

The Chicago, Rock Island and Pacific Railroad, it said, had been authorized by a federal court to appoint peacekeepers to defend its right-of-way in any area where existing counties were unequipped to do so. Secondly, according to one Thomas Allen Fry, the Neutral Strip had been designated a county for census purposes. It would be referred to as Beaver County. And being a county for census purposes made it a county, even though it wasn't rightly a county any other way. Thirdly, the C.R.I.& P., in cooperation with the United States Census Office, was hereby designating the entirety of the aforementioned Beaver County as temporary railroad right of way on the basis of the railroad having an installation at Tyrone Switch, and on the basis that the Neutral Strip wasn't anything else, so it might as well be right-of-way.

The C.R.I.& P. therefore requested Ben Wiggins to serve as special marshal to defend the railroad's interests in the Neutral Strip—temporarily known as Beaver County—until such time as proper civil authority could be established, based upon the 1890 United States Census of Population and Social Statistics, as well as to all pursuant interests.

And, since the temporary right-of-way was designated temporarily as a county, his authority would be equivalent to that of a county sheriff.

"I'll be danged," Wiggins muttered. "County law. Well, I got a badge in my gear. I guess it can be a sheriff badge . . . temporarily."

"A *county?*" Pappy scratched his whiskers. "No Man's Land a county? Ain't that a stomper! If there's gonna be a sheriff, though, don't there have to be a judge? An' I never seen a county that didn't have a courthouse."

"You got a point, there," Wiggins said.

"Where'd those two whirlin' dervishes get off to?" Bart Sherrell wondered. He had aimed to try his hand at courting Miss Annie Sue, but now for some reason he felt like he'd been out-courted without ever getting a courting chance.

"At the rate they were going, they're probably in the river by now," Milicent noted. "Would you gentlemen care for lemonade?"

Over by the post wagon, Willie Sutter was up on top of the load, looking down at Blue, who was looking up at him.

"I don't think he wants to stomp you, Willie," Mouse Moore said. "I think he loves you."

"I know what we better do with these here posts," Willie growled. "I've had a change of heart about open range. I believe cattle ought to be fenced."

"Busted S hasn't got but one cow, right now," Mouse pointed out.

"That's the very one I got in mind," Willie assured him.

XXVI

In evening shadows, Bobby Lee Smith fished himself out of the shallows of the Beaver River, and lent a hand to Annie Sue Finch to fish her out, too. He had sort of forgotten, in the time since their last encounter, how truly fetching the little blonde creature looked when she was soaked to the skin and madder than a wet hen.

But the latest plunge into the river had cooled them both off a little, and now when they squared off on the bank, their stubborn glares at each other turned a tad thoughtful.

"We really aren't accomplishing anything this way," Annie Sue suggested. "I mean, a shouting match is all well and good, but it doesn't solve problems."

"I reckon," Bobby Lee agreed. "Here we are, two growed-up people, an' this kind of carryin' on . . . well, it's silly."

"I'm glad we see eye-to-eye on that, at least," she said. "Now, how shall we address the problem?"

"What problem?"

"How to get you once and for all off my land."

"*Your* land? This here is *my* land!"

"It is not! It's mine! I bought it!"

"Well, so did I! Busted S is mine!"

"*Mine! And it isn't Busted Whatever!*"

Bobby Lee got a look on his face like a tabby cat with

feathery whiskers. "I thought you aimed to stop shoutin' about it."

"*I do!* I mean, I do. There must be some way we could reason this out. What will you take for your claim?"

"It ain't for sale. What do you want for yours?"

"Mine isn't for sale, either. I suppose we could go to court about it."

"What court? This here is No Man's Land."

"It's the Cimarron Proposal," she corrected.

"No such thing! This is No Man's Land."

"My deed says it's the Cimarron Proposal."

"So does mine, but there ain't any such a thing. That's just a bamboozle that Scrannon jasper dreamed up. This here is the Neutral Strip."

"I thought you said it was No Man's Land."

"It is. It's the same thing. But there's no law, so there's no courts, so think of somethin' else." Bobby Lee was having a hard time thinking about much of anything, right then. In the evening light, Annie Sue's eyes looked as big and dark as stock tanks on a starry night.

"I'm trying to," she snapped. Fact was, Annie Sue was having a hard time thinking about much of anything because Bobby Lee's dark hair was beginning to dry from their dip in the river, and when the breeze caught it, he had a distinct cowlick. He looked, she realized, for all the world like an impish little boy—a very large, wide-shouldered and stubborn little boy, but a little boy, nonetheless.

He snapped his fingers. "Property improvement!" he said. "That's the way to decide whose land this ought to be. Who's most likely to improve the place?"

"Possibly," she tipped her head, ringing out some of the prettiest light-gold hair Bobby Lee had ever gone tongue-tied over. "Just say this were your place, what would you do with it?"

"Run cows," he said proudly.

"I mean to improve the property! What would you build?"

"Oh," he said. "Well, let's see. A barn, first. And fences, an' chutes and a tackle-shed, an' a good bunkhouse for the hands."

"Is that all?"

"Well, I got some plans for fixin' up my porch."

She looked up at him the way a circling hawk looks down at a ground squirrel. "Then I believe this property is rightfully mine, because you haven't named a thousand dollars' worth of improvements. I plan to build a grand, three-story house with formal gardens, several barns and paddocks, and . . . and whatever else it takes to operate a successful horse ranch."

"Oh, you do, huh? An' just how much money do *you* intend to spend on improvements?"

"Maybe six or seven thousand dollars."

Bobby Lee looked stunned. "You have that much to spend?"

"If necessary," she said, smugly. "And you?"

"Seems to me like we ought to figger out a good way to settle this," he sighed. "Matchin' property improvements is a real dumb idea."

"I suppose a section could be divided," she said, shivering slightly in the evening breeze. "But only if I were willing to divide my section, which I am not."

"I ain't splitting my section," he agreed. "I paid for a section of land, an' I won't settle for less." He looked down at her with concern, then stepped close and reached to put an arm around her.

"Me, neither," she said. "What do you think you're doing?"

"Negotiating?"

"Why are you trying to put your arm around me?"

"Oh. That. Well, you're shiverin' like you're cold."

"I am cold. Cold and wet. Mind your hand, mister."

"Sorry. I tell you what, maybe we ought to get out of these wet clothes."

"Mind your mouth, too."

"Could be we ought to have two sections of land," Bobby Lee suggested. "That way you could have one, too."

"I already have a section. This one. You take the other one."

"Not on your life! This here section is the one I want."

"This is the one I want, too. That house is my house."

"What house? That's a shack."

"Well, there *will* be a house there when I get done. Right where that shack is, now."

"You aim to build your house attached to my porch? I won't stand for that . . . here, if you'd ease off a little I could get my other arm around you. No sense catchin' your death for the sake of argument."

"You're right about that, I suppose." She pressed against him. "Is this better?"

"Lot better. You know, this bein' No Man's Land, I don't expect there's anything sacred about land boundaries, long as they run generally square. Maybe we could add a half section on the north an' a half section on the south. Then we'd have two sections we could split down the middle. Survey it any way we want to, come to that."

"I suppose, as long as the house is on my property."

"And the porch on mine."

"And I'll thank you to keep your cattle off my property."

"You keep your horses off mine."

Up the bank, Milicent and Ben Wiggins came out of the brush, stopped and stared. "Would you look at that?" Ben pointed.

"Well, at least they aren't fighting," Milicent noted. "My, but that's downright romantic, isn't it? Mr. Wiggins, why don't you go fetch a blanket to put over them, before they catch their death. Maybe you should bring two blankets."

245

"Two? You really think we could pry them two apart for separate blankets?"

"No. The other one is for us to sit on. I believe it's time those two had some chaperoning."

"Ain't nature a wonder," Ben Wiggins muttered, heading for the clearing.

Meanwhile, the negotiations were proceeding beside a chuckling river where the ripples caught the rays of the rising moon.

"We could just claim the adjoining properties, I suppose," Annie Sue said, "but I don't consider that honest."

"I wouldn't do that," Bobby Lee agreed. "I ain't a squatter. Land ain't a body's land 'less it's bought an' paid for, is how I see it."

"So, we shall buy two half sections," she snuggled closer against him, vaguely aware that they seemed to have a blanket draped over them—a nice, warm blanket that hadn't been there before. "I'll buy one and you buy one."

"For how much money?"

"For what we paid per acre for what we already bought?"

"That's fair, I reckon. 'Cept I don't have that much money. But I'll get it."

"How will you get it?"

"I don't know. I could . . . I wonder how much they pay for census work, like that feller was talkin' about."

"Five dollars a head," a deep voice nearby said.

"Fine! That's what I'll do, then. I . . . where did we get this blanket?" Blinking, he raised his head and looked around. Just above them on the riverbank, shadows in the moonlight, Ben Wiggins and Milicent Moriarty sat side by side on a blanket. Beyond them, lining the crest above, were dozens of people—Texas cowboys, Neutral Strip settlers, people from Beaver City . . . everybody, it seemed, had come out to sit a spell and look at Bobby Lee and Annie Sue negotiating

246

by the river.

Annie Sue came back to reality then, too, and gaped at the crowd gawking at them. "Well, I never . . . ! Milicent? What is this all about?"

"Don't y'all have anything better to do?" Bobby Lee snapped. "We're tryin' to talk business here!"

Well, George Scrannon had himself a plan, right enough. He wasn't rightly partial to it, as a plan, but there wasn't time to be choosy. Scrannon had never drawn the line at scheming and conniving, at taking money from settlers and then driving them out as squatters, and promising anything, delivering nothing and walking off with everything. It suited him just fine to lie, cheat and steal, and he wasn't above committing murder on a regular basis as long as he could do it from concealment, or with his hideout gun. But it plain went against his better judgment to force a showdown. Direct confrontation was something he had never found much profit in.

As to the Jackson Creek place, and the scores he had to settle with Annie Sue and Bobby Lee, those were like the score he needed to settle with the postmaster. In George Scrannon's experience, time and pressure were the best of all persuaders. Pressure, like nightriders shooting through the walls of a cabin, like barn-burners and fence-busters and slaughtering whatever livestock he couldn't steal—these things would wear down the most determined squatter, to the point that even if he didn't leave, sooner or later he'd let down his guard. He'd go riding out alone. Or he'd go to his fields and forget to take his gun. Or he'd slip up and let a few vigilantes get between him and his defenses.

Given time, Scrannon had learned, that would happen as sure as the sun comes up. Then it was simple. Shoot the scutter and nobody the wiser. He'd had this in mind for Haygood Dobbs—there would be a time when the postmaster didn't have Calvin Gable watching his hind-side, and no witnesses around. Then Scrannon would kill him. He sort of had the same kind of thing in mind for Bobby Lee Smith, for humiliating him, and something of the kind also for Annie Sue Finch, with a few embellishments tossed in.

But all this business about a United States Census had changed all that. Sure as horseflies bite, a legal head-count in No Man's Land would lead to civilization—not the kind of signpost civilization that served Scrannon's purpose, with nobody but him in charge, but real, court-enforced legal civilization.

In other words . . . Law!

There wasn't time to do things the easy way now. It was time for all-or-nothing play. Scrannon marched into the Happy Times Saloon, went to his favorite table and sat down. There were a dozen or so men in the place, and he peered around, picking out the ones he needed. "Beauregard!" he called.

The leader of the Vigilance Committee turned and straightened. "Yeah, Boss?"

"Come sit down," Scrannon beckoned. "You, too, Judge," he ordered Sylvester Magruder, who was staggering in place at the bar. "My God, can't you ever be sober when I need you? Give him a hand, Sylvester!" Imperiously, he waved at Oliver Winshaw. "I need you, too, Governor. Run all the rest of these gents out and lock up. We have business to do."

It took a few minutes for Winshaw to clear out his customers, because some of them didn't want to go. But Jenkins pitched in, and finally they had the place to themselves. They joined Scrannon at his table.

"You still have that special list I told you to make?" Scrannon asked Judge Magruder.

The "judge" gaped at him, sobering up a little. "You mean, *that* list?"

"That list," Scrannon nodded. "Get it."

"I thought we . . . we weren't goin' to need that kind

248

of help," Magruder stammered.

"Just get the list! And bring paper and a pen."

"Y-yes, sir," Magruder sighed. He stood, not staggering so much now, and headed for his room in the back.

Scrannon turned to Beauregard Jenkins. "How many men do you have now, in the Vigilance Committee?"

Jenkins scratched his head, trying to concentrate. "Uh . . . about twenty, twenty-five."

"Have them stand by," Scrannon said. "There'll be work to do shortly."

"Yeah, Boss. What kind of work?"

"The kind they hired on for. Are there any of them I can trust to run an errand for me?"

"One or two, I reckon. Like what?"

"I want to know who is going to be taking this census count. Somebody knows who'll be counting, and I want the names. Send somebody up to Liberal, to look for a man named Thomas Allen Fry. He's in charge of it. And get somebody up to Tyrone Switch to see Iron Tom Logan. I know he's mixed up in it, too."

"Will they tell us?"

"One way or another, I imagine."

"Okay, Boss. Anything else?"

"Yeah. When we have those names, I want your Vigilance Committee to . . ."

Judge Magruder was back. He handed a folded paper to Scrannon, and set down paper and ink.

"Write," Scrannon told him. "The same letter to every man on this list. "Say, ah . . . ," he pursed his lips, looking into distances. "Say, 'Dear Mr. so and so, I have need of your services. Come immediately to Beaver City, the Neutral Strip. I will pay the sum of five hundred dollars, gold.' Write that to each one on that list, and sign it."

Magruder went pale. "Mr. Scrannon, there's better'n twenty names on this list! That's . . . why, you're promisin' better than ten thousand dollars in gold!"

"Do it!" Scrannon hissed. "Don't worry about it, there won't be anybody coming to collect."

"Yes, sir," the judge shrugged and began writing. Oliver Winshaw glanced at the list, and his eyes went wide. It was a list of names and addresses: Dwight Bingham at Wichita, Billy Tate at Tascosa, Earl Taylor Greer at Dodge City . . . it went on and on, and his eyes got wider and wider. Every top-rank hired gun he had ever heard of was on that list, and some that he hadn't—every bounty-hunter, bush-whacker, hired assassin and fast-draw artist in this part of the world.

The "Governor of the Cimarron Proposal" started to say something, then decided not to. George Scrannon generally didn't require adverse opinions.

When Magruder had finished all the letters—with a shaking hand—he folded and sealed them, and put on the addresses. Then he handed them over to Scrannon. "I hope you know what you're doing, Mr. Scrannon," he said.

"I know exactly what I'm doing," Scrannon snapped. With the letters in hand, he stood and put on his hat. "Wait for me," he told them. "I'll be right back."

When he was outside, the other three hurried to the window. "He's headin' for the post office," Jenkins muttered.

"He's not actually going to mail those, is he?" Magruder wondered.

"Looks like it," Winshaw noted.

Scrannon walked up the street to Dobbs' Emporium, sneered at Haygood Dobbs, bought postage and handed the letters across the post office counter. "For the next mail," he said.

That done, he went back to his office and rejoined his cronies. "Get those census-taker names," he told Jenkins. "Then get the Vigilance Committee in their saddles. I want them to track down every man who will be taking census in the Cimarron Proposal. Then I

250

want those people found and lost."

"Found an' . . . ?" Jenkins gaped at him.

"Find them," Scrannon said, slowly. "Find them, and make sure that nobody else ever finds them again after you do. Is that clear enough?"

"You want us to find those jaspers an' gun 'em down," Jenkins frowned.

"That's the idea," Scrannon nodded. "And bury them. Make them just disappear. Your boys know how to do that."

"Sure," Jenkins said. "Ah . . . I don't reckon census takers would be very dangerous, would they?"

"Not like the people we just wrote to," Magruder put in. "What do you want with that many hired guns, Mr. Scrannon? And where does the money come from?"

Scrannon glanced at the "judge," sneering. "You don't think those letters are ever going out, do you? That's why I mailed them personally. That postmaster is the biggest busybody in this territory. Those letters won't go anyplace. But some of the *righteous citizens* around here might. I wouldn't be surprised if a lot of them are packed up and gone by this time tomorrow. That's what those letters are for. And even if there are any left to count, the Vigilance Committee will see to it that there isn't anybody to count them."

"I guess census takers is a bunch of jaspers runnin' around with papers and pencils," Jenkins muttered. "That doesn't sound hard." Then he frowned, "But how 'bout that old marshal that keeps hangin' around? He's got a lot of the boys spooked."

"Leave Ben Wiggins to me," Scrannon sneered. "I'll handle him myself."

"Right," Jenkins nodded, remembering a few other men who had been in Scrannon's way in the past. They had a way of getting shot, usually in the back or from cover, and of course nobody ever knew who did it. "Right, Boss."

Scrannon looked at Winshaw. "Does Ben Wiggins

still ride out to meet the stage when it passes the cedars?"

"Still doin' that," Winshaw nodded. "He's got some kind of a deal with the stage bunch."

"Get somebody over to Hardesty," Scrannon said. "I want to know when that stage heads this way," he stood again, picked up his hat and flashed a look at Jenkins. "I'm counting on you."

"Sure, Boss. Don't worry. We'll take care of the census takers."

Scrannon headed across the street, and the three again went to the window to watch him go.

"Hope he's right about that postmaster," Winshaw said. "Hate to think of them summonses goin' out to that bunch. An' money owed to 'em? Lord! You best breathe shallow 'til this is over, Judge. You're the one that signed the letters."

"Me?" Magruder blinked. "Not me. Mr. Scrannon just said sign 'em. He didn't say what name. So I signed his."

XXVII

On the first day of June, 1890, Iron Tom Logan and Thomas Allen Fry drove down to Beaver City to swear in the census marshals for what would be called—for census purposes—Beaver County. Not Beaver County, Texas, or Beaver County, Kansas, or Beaver County of some state or other, like every other God-fearing county in the United States of America was. Just Beaver County.

Creative Countying, Thomas Allen Fry called it. But it was good enough. The Congress of the United States had decreed that there must be a census, and if No Man's Land wasn't exactly part of the United States, it was definitely in it, and even though nobody lived there, legally, all those folks who didn't live there were fixing to get counted, whether they wanted to or not.

For the purposes of the ceremony, Ben Wiggins invited everybody to George Scrannon's building. It did, after all, claim to be the capitol of whatever place this was, and Wiggins took it upon himself to declare it the Beaver County Courthouse—for census purposes, of course.

George Scrannon wasn't around to object. He had ridden out early that morning, with his buffalo rifle lashed behind his saddle, so it was generally agreed that he had gone hunting. The governor of the Cimarron

Proposal and "Judge" Magruder might have had something to say about it, but they were over at the Happy Times, with several citizens pointing guns at them. And Beauregard Jenkins was nowhere to be found, anymore than any of the Vigilance Committee were.

All in all, it was a mighty peaceful day in Beaver City, and a fine day for a solemn occasion.

"Raise your right hands," Thomas Allen Fry told those assembled before him. Eight hands went up—seven ex-Texas drovers from Busted S, and Calvin Gable from the post office.

"Repeat after me," Fry said. "I . . ."

"I . . . ," they said.

"State your name."

They all stated their own personal names, from Bobby Lee Smith and Pappy Jameson right on through to Shorty Mars and Mouse Moore.

". . . hereby swear to perform the duties of United States census marshal for the census district herein known as Beaver County . . . ,"

They said that, the best any of them could recollect it.

". . . in accordance with the policies and regulations of the United States Census Office, and to the fullest of my ability . . . ,"

They mostly got that said.

". . . to produce a full and complete enumeration of persons resident in this district as of this hour of this day. . . ."

They all hung right in there with him so far.

". . . without oversight, neglect or fail . . . ,"

They repeated that and Jimbo Riley whispered, "What does that mean?"

"It means count ever'body an' don't miss anybody," Pappy Jameson explained.

". . . and to proceed undeterred and in timely manner to exercise the authority of the United States

254

government for purposes of this census . . . ," Fry continued.

"That means don't let any jasper keep you from gettin' it done," Pappy whispered, when they had repeated the words.

". . . so help me God," Fry said.

"So help me God," they repeated.

"An' gunpowder as needed," Pappy added.

Then Fry broke out a crate of printed forms, all padded with glue edging and cardboard backs, and instructed them in what they had just agreed to do.

Each dwelling-house in the "county" was to be visited, and anything folks lived in was to be considered a dwelling-house. If persons not otherwise enumerated were encountered in any location other than a dwelling-house, the census marshal had the authority to count them where they stood.

If, for any reason, any citizen refused to be counted or to give the required answers to the questions on the forms, the census marshal had the duty and authority to take whatever steps were necessary to obtain the information.

"There's folks in No Man's Land that'll shoot first an' talk later," Joe Dell McGuire pointed out.

"You have the right to defend yourselves," Fry said.

"Generally, when Joe Dell is called on to defend hisself," Pappy explained, "there ain't anybody 'cept him standin' there when the defendin' is done. So how 'bout them that doesn't survive the introductory remarks?"

"They still count," Fry sighed. "That's been ruled on."

"You mean if a jasper is alive when I spot him, he don't have to be alive for me to count him?" Willie Sutter wondered.

"Something like that," Fry said. "Actually, what you're counting is how many people live here right now . . . this hour of this day. Today is Census Day.

But I guess it comes out the same."

"I reckon," Willie agreed.

Bobby Lee was reading over the questionnaire. "Lookee here," he said. "We're gonna get downright nosy, ain't we? It says we need to find out everybody's whole entire name, and how old they are, an' whether they been married in the past year, an' where they was born an' which side of the War Between the States they favored if they was there . . ."

"I don't know as I feel right, pryin' into folks' private affairs like that," Pappy frowned.

"You done swore you would, though," Willie pointed out.

"Still don't seem right."

"Five dollars a head," Bobby Lee reminded him.

"Seems some better," Pappy allowed.

"What's this about sex?" Shorty asked, turning kind of red as he ran a finger down the questions. "Does this mean I got to go around askin' folks to kindly tell me what sex they happen to be? Hell, in Texas they hang folks for less than . . ."

"You don't have to ask," Fry assured him. "Not unless you just can't tell by looking."

"I don't care too much for this twenty-third thing," Jimbo Riley piped up. "I mean, I can prob'ly tell by lookin' if a body is crippled or deformed, but this here about 'whether defective in mind,' I don't know about that. If I ask a jasper if he's crazy, an' he is, likely he'll say he ain't. An' if he ain't, how do I know he's tellin' the truth?"

"The one that bothers me is number nine," Pappy grinned. "Some men might take offense at bein' asked how many children they're the mother of."

"You just ask women that," Iron Tom said.

Thomas Allen Fry shook his head and put away his servicing papers. "You gentlemen have the general idea," he told them. "Now get out there and do your best."

"We'll divide up," Bobby Lee decided. "Mr. Gable, you can count folks here in Beaver City, since you live here. You prob'ly know most of 'em, anyway. The rest of us will go by sections, workin' out from here in different directions. An' we need somebody to go over an' count Hardesty, an' somebody up to Beer City.

"I'll take Beer City," several of them said, all at once.

"Y'all can draw straws," Bobby Lee shrugged. "Mouse, get me some . . ." he looked around. "Where's Mouse?"

"He done took off for Beer City," Pappy Jameson said.

"That settles that, then," Bobby Lee shook his head. "Well, boys, let's get started."

"Fine!" Pappy pulled out a pencil and faced Bobby Lee. "What's your Christian name in full, and middle initial?"

"You dang well know my name, Pappy."

"Answer the questions," Pappy scowled at him. "I'm startin' with you."

"Shorty!" Willie Sutter grinned, bracing Shorty Mars. "Are you white, black, mulatto, quadroon, octaroon, Chinese, Japanese or Indian?"

"How'd you like a mouth full of fist?" Shorty bristled.

"Just answer the questions," Willie prodded. "How many children are you the mother of?"

Fry and Logan headed out. "They'll do fine," Iron Tom allowed. "By the way, some gent came by to ask me for the names of all the census takers. Is that anybody's business?"

"It's public information, I suppose," Fry said.

Logan climbed up on his rig and lifted Fry's valise aboard. "All right. If he asks again, I'll tell him."

Ben Wiggins stepped out of the requisitioned courthouse and retrieved his black's reins from the hitchrail. "Y'all headin' north?"

Logan raised an eyebrow. "When did you start

257

talking like a Texan?"

"When I got involved with census takers. Are you gents heading north?"

"I have a census to conduct in Kansas," Fry said. He stepped onto the footrail of Logan's rig and swung aboard. Logan handed him a shotgun.

"And I have a railroad to run," Iron Tom said. "Word is, there are more cattle headed up from Texas for Tyrone Switch. Want to ride along?"

Wiggins swung into his saddle. "I got other business," he said. "Need to check on that stagecoach, then see a lady about a baked ham."

"Oh?" Logan grinned. "Which lady, Ben? The big one or the little one?"

"The big one, if it's any of your business. That's one fine woman, there." He touched heels to the big black. "You gents be . . . *y'all* be careful now, y'hear? Keep your eyes peeled for bushwhackers. Land, who knows how many undesirables there are in this here strip!"

"We shall know exactly how many, before long," the census office man noted.

Iron Tom flicked his reins, and they followed Wiggins out of town. At the fork, they headed north toward Tyrone Switch and Liberal. Wiggins rode a ways with them, to discuss some ideas he had about the natural progression of law and order—which are a lot like chickens and eggs, as he saw it, since you can't have either one unless the other one's already there. So they rode, and talked, then Ben tipped his hat and headed back toward the fork. From there he headed for The Cedars to wait for the Beaver City Express, coming east.

By the time Bobby Lee and the other census marshals got done counting one another, they all had a right good handle on how it was done, and they spread

258

out to commence counting other folks. Some of them went across to the Happy Times, where they gave the governor of the Cimarron Proposal and Scrannon's pet judge the honor of being the first regular citizens on the tabulation. When that was done, they counted the citizens who were pointing their guns at the governor and Hizzoner, then turned the rest of the town's count over to Calvin Gable.

The census office had provided tract maps to Haygood Dobbs. These were block-printed plats divided into a sort of patchwork quilt of census tracts, with a sector line running across a few miles west of Hardesty, about where Coldwater Creek hit the Beaver. The east sector was the first task at hand.

The Texans had taken one of Haygood Dobbs' maps and drawn more lines on it—a line running east and west through the middle of Beaver City, one running north and south through the middle of Beaver City, and one cutting across the whole strip at Palo Duro Creek. That divided the whole east sector into eight parts—five big rectangles of Neutral Strip and three main towns, counting Beer City as a town.

Since Mouse Moore had already headed for Beer City to commence counting drunks and other citizens yonder, and Calvin Gable had Beaver City, that left the town of Hardesty and the Palo Duro tract, and the four tracts quartering on Beaver City.

Now, they all knew that the worst nests of outlaws—the ones that were trying to hide out in No Man's Land—were over in the west sector. Out in the Cimarron Breaks and around Black Mesa, folks said, was where most of those gents were who didn't cotton at all to folks finding them. And the Hardesty tract was nearest to there.

So, naturally, Joe Dell McGuire and Willie Sutter inherited that area.

They worked it out between themselves. "You cover my hind-side while I count Hardesty," Willie said.

"Then I'll ride spotter for you while you count the countryside."

Shorty Mars would do the tallying southeast of Beaver City, Jimbo Riley northeast, Pappy Jameson got the northwest sector and Bobby Lee claimed southwest for himself. He wasn't about to let anybody except himself pull tally on Annie Sue Finch. There was just no telling how the official records might come out reading if that little honey got the chance to horn-swoggle some unsuspecting soul. She wouldn't hesitate for a minute, Bobby Lee was sure, to list herself as sole owner of Busted S—and she probably wouldn't even call it by its name.

So the census marshals of Beaver County, State of No State, spread out to count noses.

"Meet back here in a week," Bobby Lee told them. "We'll see where the tally stands, then." Tucking his own questionnaire pads into his coat, he stepped into the saddle. "Y'all have a nice tally, now, y'hear?"

Maybe Tarnation had been left out in the sun too long, or maybe that cayuse just couldn't stand being civilized for longer than a day or two at a time. Whatever the reason, the big horse looked around at his rider, slanted his ears back and bunched his haunches.

"Now, dang it, Tarnation!" Bobby Lee swore, "this ain't any time for . . . oh, for God's sake . . . !"

Tarnation was probably the one most creative bucking horse ever to come up out of Texas. He hadn't let loose for a spell, but it seemed like he had spent the entire time ciphering out new ways to part company with a rider, and now there wasn't anything else for it but he just had to test his theories.

He planted his front feet on the street of Beaver City, like braced corner poles, put his head down and hit the dirt with rear hooves so hard the whole town shook. Then he did the fanciest tail-over that anybody ever saw, recovered from that into a tight spin and crow-hopped sideways, just to get the ball begun. With

Bobby Lee Smith fluttering and slapping like loose packs on a stargazer mule, that horse got down to business. He was all over the place—jumping this way, stiff-legging that way, rearing and sky-rolling, doing Denver twists and carousel stomps so fast that it looked like three separate horses under one white-faced rider—and abruptly he came out of a slick-down three-step and swapped ends and headed for far places.

It was a plain miracle that Bobby Lee was still on top of that horse, and the others all pulled off their hats in solemn appreciation of what they had just been privileged to see.

"Five dollars says Bobby Lee don't make it back here in a week," Pappy Jameson intoned, like he was reciting psalms.

"You're covered, Pappy," Willie said.

"Rate he's goin' now, he'll be done an' back tomorrow," Jimbo Riley reckoned. " 'Cept he's sure gonna have to count fast."

"Danged if I understand why he keeps ridin' that horse," Joe Dell muttered. "Dang thing's tryin' to kill him 'bout half the time."

"It's his horse," Pappy explained. "You know how Bobby Lee is. Ridin' that horse is his notion of luck."

"Land, if he gets any luckier, he'll wind up marryin' that little darlin' out yonder," Joe Dell shook his head.

"Prob'ly be about the same thing," Pappy nodded.

"I'll thank you for my five dollars when we get back, Pappy," Willie grinned, reining around. "Come on, Joe Dell, let's go tally the badlands!"

XXVIII

The sign on the place said, "Chicago, Rock Island and Pacific Railroad," but there wasn't any railroad about it. It was a sporting house, sure as rain makes mud. And Mouse Moore reckoned it was just the place to start, since it was as near to the middle of Beer City as anything was. The ground floor had a plank bar lined with gents communing with the spirits, a roulette wheel, a dozen poker tables and a staircase that led to the second floor. The second floor had a long hall and short curtains screening little cubbyholes full of undressed ladies and visiting Kansans.

Mouse looked around a little, then decided to do his counting in a systematic fashion. He went to the bar, tipped his hat to the nearest bartender and said, "Howdy."

"Howdy," the man squinted at him. "Know you, don't I?"

" 'Course you do," Mouse assured him. "Most ever'-body does."

"So what can I do for you?"

"Just stand aside for a minute," Mouse gave him a friendly grin, then climbed up on the bar and cupped his hands. "Drinks on the house!" he shouted.

"The hell they are!" the barman blurted, but hardly anybody heard him in the rush as everybody in the room came running.

"Make mine whiskey!" someone bellowed. "Bring out the good stuff, Amos!" another shouted. "Give me two!" somebody else put in. "I got a pard sleepin' outside!"

The barman picked up a bung starter and glared at them all. "There ain't any . . . !"

"Come on, now, Amos! Drinks is on the house. I heard that just as clear as . . ."

"Not from me, you didn't! I . . ."

"Shut up an' start pourin'!"

If Amos even had a chance to look around for Mouse Moore, he didn't see him because Mouse was upstairs by that time. He pushed aside a curtain, stepped through and sat on the foot of the little bunk bed beyond, pulling out his pencil. "Howdy," he told the people gaping at him. "I'm your census taker."

Shorty Mars hadn't gone a half mile from Beaver City when he saw a slap-up little place down in a hollow alongside Dry Run. There were people there, so he commenced to tally. A red-haired woman in a sunbonnet, with a half-dozen children clustered around her, set down her hoe when she saw him coming, and picked up a shotgun.

Shorty rode to where the gate would have been if there had been a gate, and hauled off his hat. "Howdy, ma'am!" he called.

"That's near enough!" she snapped. "State your business!"

"I'm a U.S. census marshal, ma'am. Name's Mars. I'm countin' folks."

"Why?"

"Well, because I got it to do," he explained. "I have to ask y'all a few questions. Can I talk to the head of the household?"

"No," she said. "You can't."

263

"Why not?"

"Because he's dead, is why. Taken by the Lord not six months ago, an' left me an' these here children to fend for ourselves."

"I'm truly sorry, ma'am. Uh, how did your man die?"

"I shot him with this here gun," the woman glared from the hollow of her bonnet, "for bein' no-account."

"I reckon I'd best ask you, then."

"Ask me what?"

Shorty pulled out his pad and pencil, squinted at the printing, and asked, "What's the Christian name in full and middle initial?"

"His or mine?"

"Well, yours, I reckon. You're still among the livin'."

"An' aim to stay that way, too! Name's Hazel May."

"Hazel," Shorty muttered, writing it down. "Initial, M. Surname?"

"I told you, it's *my* name!"

"I mean, what's your last name, ma'am?"

"Toliver," she said. "That's like in the Tennessee Tolivers, you know."

"Yes, ma'am. Relationship to head of family?"

"I'm it," she told him.

She's it, Shorty wrote. He looked at the next question, started to ask it and decided to settle for observation. *She's white,* he wrote. Having dealt with that delicate matter, he breathed a sigh of relief, glanced at the next question and asked, "Sex?"

"Well, not lately," the woman raised the shotgun. "An' I don't reckon . . ."

Shorty turned bright red. "Sorry about that, ma'am. I'll tend to that, myself."

The shotgun wavered. "You'll tend to *what,* mister?"

"I mean, I . . ." turning even darker red, Shorty gulped and jotted down the obvious answer. "Uh . . . oh, Lordy! Ma'am, I have to ask how old you are."

"Oh, that's all right." The shotgun lowered again. "I'm twenty-nine. How 'bout you, Mr. Mars?"

"Twenty-eight," he said, then turned red again, taking in the six children around her. All of them had the same red hair that peeped from beneath her bonnet. "I hate these questions," he muttered. "Ma'am, were you married durin' the past year, between June the first of '89 an' May the thirty-first of '90?"

"Are you sure you're all right, settin' out in the sun like you are?" She seemed concerned. "Maybe you best get down an' step into the shade."

"Thankee, ma'am." Shorty stepped down and followed her to the shade of a cottonwood tree. "Uh . . . about bein' married, ma'am?"

"Durn right I was. Right up to the ninth of December. That was the day I shot Harry."

"God rest his soul," Shorty observed.

"God prob'ly never got his hands on it," Hazel May allowed. "Never thought I'd miss that skunk. But I do, sometimes. Are you a married man, Mr. Mars?"

"No, ma'am. I'm mostly just a drover." He concentrated on the pad. "Mother of how many children, ma'am?"

"Me? Why, these six an' two others that the Lord taken."

Shorty wrote it down.

"These are good young'uns," Hazel May said. "They do need the steadyin' influence of a man, sometimes, though."

"Yes, ma'am. Place of birth? Yours, I mean . . . I think."

"Bullard County, Tennessee. You still got a lot more questions, there? Why don't we sit down an' be comfortable while we talk."

It was nearly dark when Shorty mounted up and went on. He knew most everything there was to know about Hazel May Toliver, and suspected that she knew even more about him. He had repaired a sagging roof, weeded half a greens-garden, carried water to fill a trough, had a fine meal of fried chicken and biscuits,

265

and given his solemn pledge that he would come and visit again.

They all waved at him as he rode away, and Shorty muttered to himself, "If this keeps up, I ain't gonna get my part did in any week."

Joe Dell McGuire and Willie Sutter were a few miles up the Beaver when four men with drawn guns stepped out of the brush and faced them. "We'll have them horses," the leader snapped. "Just step down and unbuckle your . . ."

He didn't say anymore. Joe Dell's first bullet took him through the brisket, his second dropped the gent behind him and his third went through the hat of the gunman on the left—down about the hatband, where the jasper's head was.

Willie Sutter's big iron said amen to the matter, putting down the one on the right.

Still in their saddles, the Texans put their guns away and glanced at each other. "Shall we count 'em?" Joe Dell wondered. "They ain't in our precinct."

"Let's count 'em anyhow," Willie decided. "Nobody else is goin' to."

"How 'bout all these questions we're supposed to ask?"

"Go ahead on an' ask, if you're of a mind to," Willie grinned. "We'll put down, 'refused to answer on th' grounds of bein' deceased.'"

Jimbo Riley got himself a right good start on counting, not a quarter mile northeast of Beaver City. He was just coming up out of the lower valley when he found himself surrounded by armed men on horseback. He counted seven of them as they came out of cover, closing on him, and a smoke just ahead said there probably were more.

266

The riders ringed him, blocking his way, but none of them had slapped iron or anything else impolite, so he just thumbed his hat, looked around at them and said, "Howdy. You boys from around here?"

"Who wants to know?" one of them asked.

"Name's Riley," he said. "Folks call me Jimbo." He pointed up the trail. "That where you boys come from, yonder?"

"What if it is?" the same one wanted to know.

"Well, y'see, I got to establish residence if I'm gonna count y'all." He looked around at them. "I see seven of y'all. Is there any more, yonder?"

"Dang right there is. You lookin' for somebody in particular?"

"Everybody I can find. I got to count folks."

"Why?"

"Th' gover'ment wants to know who's where," he shrugged. "Let's go over yonder, an' I can count y'all, all at once." With that decided, he heeled his horse and pushed past the ones in front of him.

Behind him, someone said, "You gonna just let him ride in like that, Charlie? We don't even know who he is."

Jimbo turned to look back. "I done told y'all that," he said. "I'm Jimbo Riley an' I'm doin' a United States gover'ment census tally. Y'all come on, now. This won't take very long."

Because they didn't know what else to do, the seven riders flanked him and followed.

Jimbo had been a drover long enough to know a rustler camp when he saw one, and that was what he saw now when he rode in. The place was two Baker tents and a rope corral, kind of hidden down in a cove. At a glance, he saw how they meant to bring in cows, where they would hold them—in a brushy little draw— and where the fires would be to heat their running irons. The whole operation was plain, but it wasn't in use at the moment because there weren't any cows.

There were ten rustlers, altogether, and the one who stepped out of a Baker tent to squint at him when he rode up was the leader. Jimbo hauled rein, stepped down and looped his leathers on a stump. "Howdy," he told the man. "Name's Riley. I come to count y'all. I'll start with you." He pulled out his pad. "Mind tellin' me your Christian name an' the initial of your middle name?"

The man stared at him, then looked beyond him. "What's this all about, Charlie? Who is this jasper?"

"You know as much as we do," Charlie shrugged. "Says he's a census taker."

"Here?" The leader stared at Jimbo blankly for a minute, then shook his head. "Mister, you must be crazy! Now you get back on that there horse an' hightail out of here. We ain't got time for you."

"I'm right sorry," Jimbo said, standing his ground, "but y'see, I got these questions to ask, an' y'all got 'em to answer. You have to."

"Why do we have to?"

"Law says so," he shrugged, making a note on his pad. He reckoned that a rustler camp could be considered as a dwelling place, since everybody lived someplace and this was where these bunch-cutters had slept last. "Now, your Christian name is . . . ?"

"Kiowa Bill," the man snapped.

Jimbo looked up at him. "Your folks named you *Kiowa Bill?*"

"Hell, no, they didn't! But that's my handle. Look here, mister . . . !"

"I have to have your Christian name," Jimbo pursued. "It says so, right here. You don't want you an' me to break the law, do you?"

The man scuffed his foot and got kind of red in the face. Head down, he muttered something that Jimbo couldn't make out.

"What?"

"Shirley," the man repeated in a low voice, glancing

around at his pards, hoping they hadn't heard. "Shirley, initial W."

The others had heard him, though, and they exchanged astonished glances. Not a one of them had ever known that Kiowa Bill Slade's real name was Shirley. A couple of them grinned, some others stifled laughter and Charlie, still on his horse, glared at them. "That ain't so bad! My cousin Bear's given name is Evelyn!"

Jimbo stayed out of it, just writing down the name. "Your surname?"

"Slade!" Slade hissed. "Get on with it."

"Right. Were you a soldier, sailor or marine during the Civil War?"

"Hell, no!"

"Fine," Jimbo noted. "What's your relationship to the head of the family?"

"What family?"

"The one residin' here in this camp."

"I'm the boss."

"I reckon that'll do." He wrote "head of family," then added "white" and "male." "Your age at your nearest birthday?"

The tally went easy after counting Kiowa Bill. All the rest of the rustlers just sort of lined up and cooperated, and within an hour Jimbo had ten fresh noses in his pad. He didn't ask any of them Question 16. He just wrote down "cattle rustler" on each one where it asked about profession, trade or occupation. He drank a cup of their coffee, then got his horse. "I'll head on out, now, gents," he said, mounting up. "Know y'all got business to 'tend to."

He started to rein away, then hesitated. "Y'all mind some advice?"

"What advice?" Kiowa Bill squinted at him.

"Well, it ain't any of my business, but if I was in your line of work I'd set up yonder, past them hills. You boys try over-brandin' here, this close to a town, the law's gonna be on you before you get an iron smokin'."

"What law? There ain't any law here."

"There might be, now. The census office done decided this here is a county."

He left them to think about that and headed out, looking for other folks to count.

Pappy Jameson's first count was at a little sod-and-pole place a mile northwest of town. He saw the little squatter spread from a rise, noted the few animals in the corral and the cleared field where a crop of corn was growing in the sun. He also noticed that nobody was in sight, and that there were gun barrels poking out of the shutters.

So he studied it a little more, and saw furtive movements in a gully fifty yards from the shack. "Best do this the easy way," he muttered. Leaving his horse in cover, he took a coil of rope, slipped into the brush and headed for the gully.

About ten minutes later, he sat on the bank of the gully, pad in hand, interviewing three land-grabbers tied hand and foot. When he had them committed to form, he stepped out in sight of the cabin and waved. "In th' house!" he called. "It's all over out here! These fellers changed their minds 'bout drivin' y'all out!"

"Who are you?" a voice called back.

"Me? Why, I'm your census taker! Got some questions for y'all to answer!"

About the time all that was happening, George Scrannon was belly-down in a rocky draw, swatting flies and wiping sweat, cradling his rifle and watching the back road just below. It was where Ben Wiggins generally met the incoming stage.

The Cedars was just that—a little knob hill above the Beaver Valley, covered and surrounded by scrub cedars, except right on top where it was bald, eroded stone. It was just north of the Jackson Creek place, and the two-rut road from Hardesty ran around the toe of it. It was an ideal spot for an ambush, and Scrannon had used it more than once. His surrey waited over on the other side, out of sight, and from where he lay hidden he had a good view of the road below and of the trail that forked off southward toward the river. By raising himself at arm's length, he could see the road in the distance, going west, and a piece of it to the east where it wound around a cut above the river.

Any time now, the Beaver City Express would come along the road, coming from the west, and Ben Wiggins would come up the trail to meet it.

Scrannon wasn't certain what kind of deal the ex-lawman had worked out with the stagecoach entrepreneurs, except that whatever it was, they all seemed to be making money on it. And he wasn't getting a cut of the pie. But that would end soon enough, when he got Ben Wiggins in his sights. The old lawman was a nuisance that Scrannon intended to put down once and for all.

He raised himself carefully, shading his eyes to look westward. Beyond the nearby ripples of the prairie, a little plume of dust was rising. That, he assumed, would be the stagecoach. He peered at the river trail, saw nothing there, and glanced eastward. There, a half mile or more away, a rider on a running horse had just rounded the bend, coming toward him. He squinted, but could not see who it was. Whoever it was, though, seemed to be barely in control of his horse. The animal was running erratically, kicking up its heels and shying this way and that. Suddenly it set its legs and skidded to a head-down stop, and its rider parted company with it. The man flipped over the horse's head and tumbled on the ground, picked himself up and danced around furiously, waving his hands. The horse, relieved of its rider, merely stood patiently, watching. After a mo-

271

ment the man caught up its reins, swung into the saddle, and the horse went into a pitching fit, then veered northward and took off at a high run. Within seconds, the horse and rider were beyond Scrannon's sight.

He took off his hat, wiped out its inner band, put it on again and returned to his vigil. The stagecoach was on its way. He concentrated on the river trail, waiting for Ben Wiggins to come into view.

XXIX

Tarnation was truly feeling his oats that day. Four separate times, between Beaver City and the gully bend, he had tried to throw Bobby Lee. The fourth time, he got it done, and when Bobby Lee got through stomping and shouting and climbed back into the saddle, that horse took the bit in his teeth and headed off the trail to try again.

"Dag nab, horse!" Bobby Lee yelled into the wind. "Don't you ever just wear out?"

Ahead, the double-track road bent around the rise of The Cedars, leading to the track to Busted S. But he wasn't on the road now. Tarnation had taken a notion to go around the other way, and by the time Bobby Lee had his bit fought back to where it would do some good, they were just about north of the rise and there was something just ahead that seemed mighty curious to Bobby Lee. With Tarnation under some kind of control again, he went to see if it was what it looked like.

Sure enough, it was—a tan horse and a dusty surrey, just standing out there in the middle of No Man's Land like they didn't have any better place to be.

Bobby Lee hauled up alongside, looked the rig over and scratched his chin. "Runaway?" he wondered. He didn't know whether the rig was one he had seen before—to any Texas cowboy, every surrey looks just about like any other surrey—but the horse was one he recognized. A tan three-year-old with a left-half blaze and one short stocking, it had no brand, but then a lot of horses in the Neutral Strip were unmarked. Bobby Lee reckoned it was because horses changed hands so often in No Man's Land that it wasn't worth a man's time to put his pattern on them. He had seen this horse in town, though, sometime recently, and he guessed it might belong to somebody who had come out to work on Annie Sue's house—the house she *said* was hers, though it was attached to *his* porch.

He leaned from his saddle, slipped a lead on the animal and tugged. "Come on along," he said. "Somebody's prob'ly lookin' for you."

With Tarnation trotting along just like there hadn't ever been any question who would ride whom, and the tan with its surrey coming along behind, Bobby Lee tracked back around The Cedars and got to the road just as Ben Wiggins came in sight, coming from Beaver City. He held up to wait for him.

The old marshal looked him up and down, said, "Glad to see you're still ridin' that bronc an' not the other way around," and turned a thumb toward the surrey. "What's this?"

"A rig," Bobby Lee shrugged. "Prob'ly a runaway. Thought I'd take it home, see if anybody yonder belongs to it."

Wiggins' eyes were narrowed as he looked the rig over. "Where was it?"

"Around yonder, other side of this cedar bump. Nobody with it, though."

Wiggins circled entirely around the surrey, looking at it, then nodded. "Don't reckon there was," he said. "Mr. Smith, you go on an' take it in, but don't take the trail. Turn off right here, an' go in the hind way."

"How come?"

"'Cause I asked you to, politely."

"Oh. Well, I don't see why not. You comin' along?"

"Be there by an' by. You go ahead."

About half curious what the man was up to, but a lot more concerned about how to conduct the hardest part of the census—the enumeration of Annie Sue Finch—Bobby Lee did as he was told. Leading the found surrey, he crossed the road and headed off down the rough flank of the Beaver Valley.

Behind him, Ben Wiggins stood in his stirrups for a long look at the cedar knoll.

The Beaver City Express was running late on the first day of June, 1890, and Bart Sherrell wasn't just real happy about that. The reasons why the stagecoach was late were named Luke and Lanny Baxter, and their attempt to rob the stage had cost Sherrell a paying passenger, as well as a back-haul to Hardesty to leave the passenger with Doc Chilton, to be treated for a bullet crease. And all Sherrell and his partners had to show for it was Luke and Lanny Baxter, hog-tied and whimpering on the coach's bouncing roof.

"You fellers just hush up, back there," Sherrell snapped over his shoulder as he laid fresh leather on his team. "It's your own fault, you know. Didn't anybody ever tell you that robbin' stagecoaches ain't tolerable behavior?"

Mike O'Riley, riding shotgun, eyed the trail ahead and pointed. "Yonder's the cedar crest, Bart. Notice anything funny about it?"

Bart squinted. "No. What?"

"Well, usually Ben Wiggins is there, waitin' for us. But I don't see him this time."

"Oh. Well, if he wants these jaspers for bounty, he better be there to collect 'em. I'm tryin' to keep a schedule here."

"How come?"

"Because it's good business to run on schedule. If

folks can't depend on their stage company, they'll go to the competition."

"We ain't got any competition, Bart," Mike reminded him. "This is the only stagecoach in No Man's Land."

"Where folks make hay, others follow."

"What?"

Hooves pounding, gear rattling, the Beaver City Express closed on the cedar knoll, and still there was no sign of Ben Wiggins. At the head of the river trail, Bart reined in and looked around. "Well, he ain't here. Now what do we do with these jaspers?"

From up the rise behind them, a deep voice called, "Just sit tight, boys! I'll be there directly!"

George Scrannon had been watching the west road as the stage approached, and keeping an eye on the side trail beyond. All he needed was one clear shot at the old marshal. The stage came on, bounding along with its driver and shotgun in the box, and a couple of hog-tied gents up on top. It passed out of sight for a moment, then reappeared just below, at the head of the trail. The driver hauled his reins, and the tall vehicle rattled to a stop. The driver and guard looked around.

"Come on, Wiggins!" Scrannon muttered, pressing his cheek to the stock of his rifle.

Behind him a boot scuffed rock and a deep voice asked, "You lookin' for me, Mr. Scrannon?"

Scrannon jerked around. Directly above him on the slope, Ben Wiggins stood at ease, both of his hands full of six-shooters. "That's a plumb coincidence," Wiggins drawled, "because I've spent half the day lookin' for you, back yonder around town. Was you plannin' to shoot somebody just now, Mr. Scrannon? Or was you just out here restin' from your labors?"

Scrannon eased away from his rifle, getting to his knees. Wiggins glanced beyond him, down the slope, and called, "Just sit tight, boys! I'll be there directly!"

276

Then he lowered his gaze to Scrannon. "You can go ahead an' pull out your gun—and that hideout gun—but just with two fingers." When Scrannon hesitated, he said. "Do it!"

Scrannon got rid of his hideout gun and got to his feet. "What . . . what do you want with me, Wiggins?"

"Well, first of all. I want you to get out of the notion of shootin' at me, Mr. Scrannon. Notions like that ain't good for your general health." He put away his guns and picked up Scrannon's hardware. "Reason I was lookin' for you, though, was to tell you that your buildin' in town has been pressed into public service for the time bein', so you'll need to find yourself a place to sleep. Your place is now the Beaver County Courthouse."

Scrannon stared at him. "The what?"

"Courthouse. Counties need courthouses. Your buildin' is it."

"What county? This is no county!"

"For census purposes, it is. As of now—for census purposes—this here is Beaver County. An' bein' a county, it needs a courthouse. So I impounded it this mornin', for that public purpose."

"You? You . . . impounded my office? What right do you have . . . ?"

"Public domain," Wiggins said casually. "You see, for the time bein', for census purposes, I'm the acting sheriff of Beaver County. I'll serve pending a general election."

"You can't take my property!"

"Oh, it ain't like *takin',* Mr. Scrannon. It's a public domain seizure. You can apply for compensation. 'Course, that'll have to wait 'til there's a county government to apply to, which will come after the election, which hasn't been scheduled yet because there has to be a census first, but don't fret yourself, the census has already started."

Scrannon just stood there, gaping at the big man.

Wiggins shook his head and pointed with Scrannon's rifle. "Set yourself down on that rock right there, Mr. Scrannon, an' I'll see if I can explain to you how the cow ate the cabbage. Sit!"

Scrannon sat, and Wiggins sat on another slab, facing him. "You see, Mr. Scrannon," he said slowly, "it's like this. There just ain't any such thing as a place without law, if there's folks there. Where there's folks, there's law, of one kind or another. Just as natural as bugs goes to bait. You take a place an' put folks in it, there'll start bein' law there just as quick as the folks find out about one another bein' there.

"There's always a few folks whose notion of law is whoever's biggest gets what anybody else has got that he might want. You see them jaspers lashed up on top of that stagecoach yonder? I expect that's the kind of law they'd favor, except that somebody else bigger, or faster, or straighter shootin' came along. Then there's some that figures all it takes to make one another behave is a vigilance committee. Sometimes that works out, for a while, 'til some jasper like you comes along and takes over the vigilance committee, then things go to hell in a handbasket.

"The two worst things about laws are them that make 'em an' them that break 'em, but most folks aren't either one of those kinds. Most folks just want to feel secure that if they build a house nobody's gonna come along an' burn it down, an' if they feed up critters nobody's gonna come along an' steal 'em, an' that nobody's gonna go shootin' at them unless they shoot first.

"I reckon there'll be law in this strip pretty soon. That census is goin' to prove there's folks here, an' first thing you know there'll be more kinds of law than anybody but a lawyer can keep track of. But until that happens, we're goin' to have law anyway. Plain, simple law to keep the peace until the other kind sets in. Now, do you understand all that?"

Scrannon was glaring at him, plain murder glittering in those baggy eyes of his. "What do you want to get out of my way, Wiggins?"

The old lawman's stony face looked like it might crack a grin, if it knew how. "I want *your way* out of this strip, Scrannon. Simple as that."

"Why did you come down here and interfere? What's in it for you?"

Wiggins thought for a moment. "Well, I came down here to find a missing stagecoach. I hung around 'cause there's good bounty to be paid on bad folks, an' No Man's Land is just full of them. I'm interferin' because I feel like it, an' what's in it for me is just plain satisfaction, mostly. You see, Mr. Scrannon, I don't like you. I don't like you even a little bit."

With his piece said, Wiggins stood, tipped his hat, said, "Good afternoon, Mr. Scrannon," and strode off down the rise, toward the road where the stage waited. He took the land shark's guns with him.

At the road, Wiggins nodded to Bart and Mike, then climbed up to look at their prisoners. "Who we got here?" he asked, scowling at the hog-tied robbers. "Well, as I live an' breathe. Howdy, there, Luke. Howdy, Lanny. You boys been misbehavin' again?"

"They tried to hold us up just out of Hardesty," Bart said. "They worth anything to you?"

"Not too much," Wiggins climbed down. "Luke's got a dodger on him in Texas, maybe a hundred dollars. Doubt I'll get ten for Lanny. But I'll take 'em off your hands."

"We ought to get a cut this time," Mike put in. "They cost us a payin' fare."

"How much?"

"Ten dollars, plus time lost," Bart told him.

"Fare's fair," Wiggins decided. He pulled out ten dollars and handed it up. "Unload 'em, an' for heaven's sake let 'em down easy this time. That last owlhoot— the one you just booted off your roof—he did nothin'

279

but complain, all the way to Springfield."

They unloaded the Baxters while Wiggins went for his horse. When he returned, he told Bart, "I expect if you haul up yonder, past The Cedars, you'll find a payin' passenger into Beaver City."

"Who?"

"That Scrannon jasper. Right about now, he's figurin' out that he's afoot out here, because his horse an' rig has somehow come to wander away. Oh, an' by the way, from now on you can make deliveries to me in Beaver City, at the courthouse."

"What courthouse?"

"Go see the postmaster. He'll tell you all about it. While you're there, look up Calvin Gable an' get yourselves counted. Come election time, I'll be runnin' for sheriff or somethin', and I'll expect every count to vote."

XXX

"A person's home is where he sleeps!" Bobby Lee Smith had a look on his face like an apple gets after a summer on a window sill. He had considered tallying everybody else for miles around, putting off this task, but he had it to do and sheer stubbornness had set in. He shoved the sheaf of papers entitled *Instructions to Enumerators* under Annie Sue Finch's pretty nose and ran a large finger over the small print. "See? That's what it says. An' I sleep here!"

"You sleep on the porch," she snapped at him, pushing the papers away. "You do not sleep in the house. The house is mine!"

"But for census purposes it's all the same dwelling house," he snarled, pushing the papers under her nose again. "Look! Right here, it says, 'Dwelling places under one roof shall be considered as one dwelling place for census purposes,' and it says right down here that everybody living in a single dwelling place is supposed to be counted as one family. That makes me the head of the family."

"You are not the head of my family!" Annie Sue swatted the papers aside again. She had her own copies, and could read them just fine without Bobby Lee showing her the lines. "I am the head of my family. You are simply someone sleeping on the porch!"

"It's my porch!"

"Well, it's my house!"

"But there's only one front door," Bobby Lee pointed out. "It says here the only way a single building can be counted as different dwelling places is if it has different front doors. We only got one front door."

"But it's *my* front door! It's on my house!"

"It opens onto my porch!"

They sat at a plank table, under whispering cottonwoods beside the house, papers strewn between them and Bobby Lee gesturing with his pencil. There were people coming and going all around—workmen Annie Sue had hired to expand her house, stock tenders and fencers Bobby Lee had hired to spruce up Busted S, and several visiting ladies from Beaver City, taking charge of Annie Sue's furnishings.

"That doesn't mean anything!" Annie Sue snapped. "If you can't enumerate properly, then don't enumerate at all!"

"Does too mean something! It means there's only one dwelling place here, far's the United States Census Office is concerned, an' I'm the head of this household, and I'll be danged if I'll show it any other way. This is official United States gover'ment business here!"

"You're not the head of any household of mine!"

Milicent Moriarty had come from the house, carrying a load of linens. She paused, listening and shaking her head. Polly Wentworth and Alice Bundy came from the new, slap-up wash shed, and glanced aside at the debating table. "How they comin' along, Milicent?" Polly asked.

"Not very well," Milicent admitted. "They're still trying to decide the answer to Question Three."

"Mercy," Alice shook her head. "They been at it better'n a hour, an' still got twenty-seven questions to go?"

"I never seen two people more bone-head stubborn than those two," Polly said. "Land, I thought my

282

Orville was stubborn—rest his soul—but he couldn't hold a candle to them there pair."

"I reckon nobody could," Alice agreed, "but, my, ain't they such a lovely couple?"

The late sun filtered through cottonwood leaves, and a lazy breeze off the river lifted the sounds of workmen hammering and sawing beyond the house, and carried it away. Voices there were raised now, in greeting, and the ladies looked around. Ben Wiggins was riding in on his big black horse, with two hand-tied men trudging along ahead of him.

As he came around the house, he glanced at the debating table, then tipped his hat. "Miss Milicent," he said. "Ladies."

"Evenin', Marshal Wiggins," Milicent smiled. "More prisoners, I see."

"Yes, ma'am. Thought I'd borry the loan of that surrey that Mr. Smith found . . ." he looked around, spotted the surrey and pointed. "Take these two in for the bounty on 'em. After they get counted, that is." He edged his mount toward the table. "Mr. Smith?"

"All right!" Bobby Lee conceded, not looking up. "It's *your* front door, then! We'll say the porch entry is my front door! Lord a'mercy, woman! Let's get on with it!"

"And I am the head of my household," Annie Sue insisted. "Nobody else. Just me!"

"All right!" Bobby Lee glared at her for as long as he could hold a frown, gazing into those blue eyes, which was about two seconds. He lowered his head and wrote on his pad. "Fine! How about sex?"

"What?"

He turned red to the tops of his ears. "Never mind. I know the answer to that one."

"So do I! The answer is no!"

"The answer," he pointed out, glancing up smugly, "is, *female.* I thought you were keepin' up, here."

Annie Sue turned red to the tops of her little ears.

She tried to read what he was writing and found it difficult from across the table. She stood, went around to look over his shoulder, then sat down beside him. It was a far more comfortable arrangement for doing paperwork.

"Mr. Smith!" Wiggins demanded.

They looked up. "What?" they both asked.

"Do you want to count these here Baxters before I deliver 'em to justice?"

"Sure, but they'll have to wait their turns. What did they do?"

"Same as most of the others. Stagecoach robbery."

"We get a lot of that, don't we," Annie Sue noted. "I believe that makes nine stagecoach robbers you've caught, and there isn't but one stagecoach in the whole territory."

"Got a good price on 'em?" Bobby Lee asked.

"Not hardly worth the effort," Wiggins admitted. "They're not worth much on the dodgers." He stepped down from his horse, studying his two prisoners as though he had an idea. "Why don't you boys turn honest?" he asked them. "You haven't hurt anybody much yet, at least not in a legal jurisdiction. You ever think of changin' your ways?"

"Sure," the taller one nodded. "But a man's got to make a livin'."

"I have *never* been married!" Annie Sue's voice rose in irritation at Bobby Lee. "I don't care for the way you ask these questions, Mr. Smith!"

"It's part of the census," Bobby Lee shrugged. "Now, mother of how many children?"

"I resent the question!"

"Resent away. It's on the sheet. How many?"

"None!"

"None, *so far,*" he muttered, writing. He glanced up. "I don't think it would interfere with our official business if I held your hand, do you?"

The Baxter brothers gazed curiously at the pair at

the table. "What are they doin' there?" Lanny asked the lawman.

"He's enumeratin' her," Wiggins rumbled.

"He's doin' what?"

"Fillin' in her census."

"Some jaspers have all the luck," Luke said, looking kind of moon-eyed. "Maybe we ought to go into honest work, Lanny."

"Your mother was born in Norway?" Bobby Lee asked Annie Sue, almost getting lost in the subtle curvature of her rosy cheeks.

"My *grandmother* was," she corrected. "My mother was born in Rochester."

"That's nice," Bobby Lee gazed at her, forgetting all about the census for about the hundredth time in the past hour. "I bet you favor her."

"Do you reckon he's goin' to finish countin' her before dark?" Alice asked Milicent.

"Not if he's got a brain in his head," Wiggins offered. He turned to the Baxters. "Maybe I'll make an example of you two."

They went pale. "You gonna shoot us?" Luke wondered.

"I might hire you," Wiggins corrected. "I need some hands to stand guard on the courthouse in Beaver City while I'm out here . . . uh . . . while I'm tendin' to other things. You boys want to work off your bounty?"

Milicent tipped her head, looking curiously at the lawman. Could it be, she wondered, that he really intended to put his faith in a pair of outlaws?

"It ain't like you boys is exactly outlaws," Wiggins was pointing out to the Baxters. "I just don't think you ever had a chance to be *in*-laws. What you reckon you'd do if you had a chance like that?"

"Reckon we might give it our best lick," Luke decided. Lanny nodded.

"Well. I'm gonna take a chance on you," Wiggins said. "See that surrey there?" He pointed. "That's a

285

runaway rig, b'longs to somebody over in Beaver City. You boys take it on into town, get the postmaster to show you to the courthouse, an' go there. You tend to the courthouse for me. Whenever the owner of the rig shows up, you can charge him three dollars for handling and storage. You got all that?"

"Yes, sir." Luke nodded. "Ah, what authority we got for all that?"

"As of now, you are both acting deputy sheriffs of Beaver County."

They both gawked at him. "Deputy . . . sheriffs?" Lanny breathed.

"For census purposes," Wiggins nodded.

Milicent was listening in, fascinated. She blushed and smiled a quick smile when the big man glanced at her and winked.

Polly Wentworth noticed the exchange. "Well, I do declare," she said, under her breath. "It's catchin'."

The encampment was only a few weeks old, but it had a name. It was called Cartwheel, and nobody either side of the Kansas border knew quite what to do about it. In the first week of June, 1890, it was located more or less two miles east of Beer City, and more or less on the Kansas state line, though the way it shifted around, nobody knew exactly where it was at any given time. Cartwheel wasn't so much a place, as a situation.

Cartwheel was a migration, of sorts. Led by the Rev. Lyle Cartwright, Cartwheel was a motley collection of movers looking for a place to light. Some of them, including Reverend Lyle, hailed from Arkansas—a few families who had pulled up stakes during the Smith Point dispute. For a time, they had tried to settle in Indian Territory. When that didn't work out, they and a few others had moved over to the Oklahoma Territory until territorial marshals ran them out for being sooners. For a season, they had tried to build a settlement in the sand hills above the Cimarron, but drought and county law put an end to that.

Now they were bound for No Man's Land, in a last-ditch effort to find land to farm, and were stalled at the border by simple dread of what lay beyond. They had entered No Man's Land, been attacked by those already there, and retreated.

It would have worked itself out, right or wrong, the way those things generally do, but the United States Census brought it to a head.

The people of Cartwheel wouldn't be counted in Kansas, and they were afraid to go beyond, where there was no law.

So, at the moment, they sat out there on the short-grass prairie, waiting for a resolution to their problem while the Reverend Lyle conferred with authorities in Liberal.

It was Thomas Allen Fry who suggested a resolution, and Federal District Judge Omar S. Stenham who grudgingly gave it his blessing. Reverend Lyle went back to his people, and Thomas Allen Fry sent one of his Kansas census marshals across the line to Beer City to make arrangements with the census marshal there, one Theodore H. Moore, better known as Mouse.

The Cartwheel decision was, in its own way, an inspiration. It resolved the problem of Census Marshal Harry Quinlan of Seward County, Kansas, who couldn't establish Kansas residence for the Cartwheelers—on the first day of June, they might or might not have been north of the Kansas line, and most likely were some of both. And it resolved the problem of Mouse Moore about what to do with the seventy-one prisoners he had locked up in the Chicago, Rock Island & Pacific sporting house.

It was a good plan, and everyone agreed to it, readily.

So, on a bright morning, a haywagon rolled out of

Beer City, eastbound, and followed by a long line of walking men wearing boots, hats and underwear and nothing else. All the rest of their belongings were in the wagon, driven by one of them, while Mouse Moore rode guard on his gray cowpony to make sure nobody bolted across the line.

The men were Kansans—farmers, draymen, merchants and general upstanding citizens who had happened to be visiting Beer City at the time the census arrived there. They had refused to be enumerated in Beer City because they did not reside there and would probably never live it down if they were listed so, and who couldn't be enumerated in Kansas because their wives refused to answer questions when their husbands were away.

General opinion on the Kansas side had it that one Deacon Isaac Forbes had been around talking to the women, in hopes of stirring up a cause for repentance.

Mouse walked his long-handled flock to the Cartwheel encampment, and lined them up there. Census Marshal Harry Quinlan rode out to meet him between the lines. "How many do you have?" he asked.

"Seventy-one by tally, but not by role," Mouse assured him. "They're unenumerated, ever' last one of 'em."

"I have fifteen families and some unattached individuals," Quinlan said. "Comes to sixty-eight people, but Mr. Fry will compensate you for the difference. Is it a trade?"

"Sounds right to me," Mouse nodded. "If I was you, I wouldn't let these jaspers have their clothes until they're counted. That way you won't lose any."

"Good idea," Quinlan agreed. "You won't have any problem with the Cartwheelers. They just want to get someplace where they can hole up an' make a living. Where you gonna take them?"

"Beaver City," Mouse told him. "They'll be all right once they're there. Ben Wiggins is a sheriff or somethin' yonder."

"I heard about that," Quinlan said. "How'd he get to be law in a place with no law?"

"There's law for census purposes," Mouse pointed out.

They leaned from their saddles to shake hands, then touched their hatbrims and traded flocks.

At the wagon camp, Mouse reined in, and a man in a dark coat approached, squinting at him curiously. "Hello, there!" the man said, then hesitated. "I . . . ah, I *do* know you, don't I?"

"I reckon," Mouse nodded. "Name's Moore. I'm y'all's escort to Beaver City. We'll get ever'body tallied on the way."

"One man?" Reverend Lyle frowned. "There are vile outlaws ahead, sir."

"I'm from Abilene, Texas," Mouse reassured him, modestly. "Well, if y'all are ready to travel, let's get a move on. An' don't worry none about owlhoots along the way. I can count an' shoot at the same time."

XXXI

The very first soul that George Scrannon ran into when he got back to Beaver City was Calvin Gable . . . just bigger'n Dallas, as they say.

Bart Sherrell had made the land shark pay his fare in advance, for the ride back into town, which aggravated Scrannon's pre-existing irritation with the way things were going. Then when the Beaver City Express hauled up in front of Dobbs' Mercantile, Calvin Gable came out, shotgun in hand, to receive the mail.

George Scrannon pushed the coach door open, stepped down and bumped into something big and solid as a dray horse, but it wasn't a horse. It was Calvin Gable. Gable bent down to see who was under the hat that had bumped him, then got a look on his big face like a coyote would get if it tripped over a jackrabbit. "Aha!" he said, poking a large finger an inch from Scrannon's nose.

Scrannon backpedaled and bumped into the coach.

"You ain't counted yet!" Calvin Gable announced.

"I . . . what?"

"You ain't been counted. For the census. An' since you live in town, you're mine!" Gable took the mail bag in his shotgun hand, and Scrannon's arm in the free one, and marched into the post office. "Set," he ordered, aiming Scrannon at a bench. Scrannon sat, like anybody would if Calvin Gable told them to.

Gable deposited the mail pouch behind the post office counter, picked up his census pad and came back. "Christian name in full," he recited, "an' initial of middle name?"

"You know who I am!" Scrannon hissed. "I am George C. Scrannon."

"I know who you are, sure," Gable said, scribbling on his pad. "But you got to answer the questions. Everybody does. Let's see. Surname, Scrannon. Wait a minute, though. I got to put down where you live."

"You know where I live! In my office!"

"That's the courthouse, now," Gable advised him. "I don't believe you live there anymore. But I reckon you did before, so I'll put it down. 'Courthouse.' There . . ." he paused, and shuffled papers. "A courthouse don't qualify as a dwelling house, though. A courthouse is a . . . where is that? Oh. Here it is. *Institutions.* 'Whenever an institution is to be enumerated,'" he read, "'as, a hospital, asylum, almshouse, jail, or penitentiary . . .' yeah, I reckon that's good enough. An institution. Now, Mr. Scrannon, were you a soldier, sailor or marine during the Civil War, or are you the widow of such a person?"

Haygood Dobbs stepped in from the back, and paused. There was something about the sight of George Scrannon being counted that intrigued him. "Did the mail come in, Calvin?" he asked.

"Yes, sir. I put it under the counter yonder," Gable pointed.

"Fine," Dobbs nodded. "Evenin', Mr. Scrannon. Nice day for bein' enumerated. By the way, there was a fellow here while ago, lookin' for you."

"Who?"

"He didn't say his name, but I recognized him. It ain't every day a man sees a famous gunfighter in Beaver City. It was none other than Billy Tate, himself."

Scrannon's face went as pale as if somebody had just drained his arteries. "Billy . . . Tate?"

"The one and only. He said he'd be back. Somethin' about collectin' some money from you."

Dobbs turned away.

"What's your relationship to the head of your family, Mr. Scrannon?" Calvin Gable asked.

Scrannon jumped to his feet, ignoring the big man. "Dobbs!"

Dobbs turned. "Mr. Scrannon?"

"Those letters I mailed . . . you remember, I came in here and mailed better than twenty letters that day?"

"I remember," Dobbs assured him.

"What did you do with them?"

Dobbs blinked. "What I always do with postal material. I expedited their delivery to the best of my ability."

Scrannon stared at him, going even paler. "You . . . you *mailed* them?"

"No," Dobbs explained. "*You* mailed them. *I* saw to it they went out. That's what I do. I'm the postmaster."

"You weren't supposed to . . ."

"Can we get on with this?" Calvin Gable rumbled. "The question was, what relation are you to the head of the family?" With a large hand he eased Scrannon down onto the bench. "Just answer that, then we'll get on to the next one. There's thirty questions here, altogether."

Scrannon bounced right back up. "Dobbs, do you know what you've done to me? I can't . . ."

"I reckon you can stand up an' be counted," Gable conceded. "But I wish you'd pay attention."

Scrannon was paying attention, all right. He was paying attention to the idea of twenty or more of the most feared gunmen in the West, all looking for him, expecting to be paid hard coin upon arrival. "Oh, Lord," he muttered.

Gable shrugged, wrote 'Lord' on his pad and added,

292

by observation, 'white' and 'male'. "Now," he said, "I need to know your age at nearest birthday, an' if under one year, give age in months."

When George Scrannon got loose from Calvin Gable, he headed down the street of Beaver City like a man in a fog. Just in a day, it seemed, everything was changed. There seemed to be people everywhere—more than he had ever seen on the streets of the little town. A whole procession of immigrants had rolled in during the past hour, and their wagons were lined up in the street. Owen Lance and Bert Mason were there, talking to a group of the newcomers. ". . . 'bout three quarters of a mile out," Lance was pointing. "Used to be a rustler camp, but they moved out a few days ago. There's passable water, an' some graze. Be a good spot to settle in, I reckon. What did you call your bunch?"

"We've been called Cartwheelers," a dark-coated individual told him. "I suppose we shall call our community Cartwheel. We plan to build a church."

"How 'bout right here in Beaver City?" Bert Mason asked. "We never had us a church here. Might be a civilizin' influence."

Scrannon hurried past, then stopped, staring at his building just ahead. There were men working there. All of his signs had been taken down and stacked in the back lot, and a new sign was being hung. It read: *BEAVER COUNTY COURTHOUSE—Office of the Sheriff,* and under that, in smaller letters, *Census Headquarters.*

George Scrannon got pretty scarce after that. Some said he was holed up in the Happy Times Saloon, but hardly anybody really cared. Folks had better things to think about than whatever became of a washed-up land shark. It's how folks are, about people like Scrannon. Land sharks, fast dealers and the like, they can cause trouble for a while, and when they are in power it's like a long run of bad weather. But once a storm is past, folks don't dwell upon the storm. They tend to give their attention to how nice a day it is, now that it stopped fussin'.

From the minute he lost his grip on the Neutral Strip, George Scrannon really didn't matter anymore. All of his best laid plans lay in shreds at his feet, his "Official Capitol of the Cimarron Proposal" was now the Beaver County Courthouse, and the town—*his town*—was filling up with strangers who were doing business with everybody but him.

George Scrannon had declared war on the United States Census . . . and been done in by the postal service.

What did matter, though, was Beauregard Jenkins. The head of the Vigilance Committee never had been the smartest owlhoot to hit the strip. Matter of fact, most folks knew that Jenkins was dumb as a bucket of rocks. But he was single-minded, when he got started on something, and he was as mean as a snake when he was turned loose, and he didn't know that things had changed. He had his orders from Scrannon, and he hadn't seen Scrannon since the day he got them, and now he was out there somewhere, like a coffer dam that's been opened and never closed, fixing to do what he had said he would.

The Beaver City Vigilance Committee, when he got it together at the little shack in Rattler Canyon where it usually met, was down to about a dozen members, and nobody knew where the rest had gone. But they had a list of eight names—the names of census enumerators. And they had Scrannon's orders.

Their problem was, they hadn't the vaguest idea where to find most of them. Calvin Gable was on the list, but Calvin stuck close to town and they didn't know quite how to get to him. Most of the others—six of them, in fact, seemed to have disappeared. They might be most anywhere, but nobody on the Vigilance Committee knew where.

And that boiled it down to one. Bobby Lee Smith

was out at the Jackson Creek place.

"All right," Beauregard Jenkins told his men. "We'll all go after that one. Boss 'specially wants him dead, anyhow."

So, on a cloudy June evening in No Man's Land, a dozen armed men rode out of Rattler Canyon and headed for the Beaver—for the place where Jackson Creek came in from the south, and the boundary line between Fairmeadow and Busted S was a freshly-painted door between a house and a porch.

Kiowa Bill Slade and his bunch were plumb spooked, from having their censuses counted and from all that talk about law in Beaver City. It seemed like there wasn't hardly anyplace where a man could go any more, to do a little honest cow-stealing, without folks bringing in law. The future looked grimmer than it had since '87, when the federal marshals and the Texas Rangers began comparing notes along the camp supply trails.

There was some talk about throwing in the hand and taking up sod-busting, but Kiowa Bill just couldn't bring himself to give up the old ways without giving it just one more good lick, so they folded up their Baker tents and moved south a few miles, into the lonely breaks above Wolf Creek. From their lookout there, they could see Texas, and Kiowa Bill reckoned that if one Texas herd had come up through No Man's Land, likely there would be others to follow.

Some of the boys were nervous about that. They had heard what happened to Pete Thayer and Slap Jackson and that bunch when they tried to cut the Busted S herd down by the twin mesas. But Kiowa Bill shrugged that off as bad luck. "Them tough-asses with Busted S was an exception," he assured them. "Bunch of hard-nose rannies from Abilene, pushin' cows. But they've settled in now, up in the strip. It was just Thayer and Jackson's hard luck to run into a bunch like that. We'll be luckier. Lightnin' don't strike twice, you know."

That made pretty good sense, the way he said it, so they all allowed they'd give 'er one more shot.

And they didn't have long to wait. They hadn't been three days in their new camp, when Charlie Shine came in with news of a herd coming northward, right at them. Seven or eight hundred head of Texas cows, following the trail the Busted S had blazed, and they'd be into the breaks come morning.

So they built their rope pens in a brushed-off box canyon, and worked out the best way to fast-burn some running marks that would pass inspection at railhead, and they cleaned their guns and oiled their rigs and settled in to wait for a good day in the morning.

Things looked so cinched that Kiowa Bill didn't put out but two night guards.

Well, a full moon rose over the prairies, and the rustlers had their vittles and rolled in for a good night's rest, and had just started their chorus of snores when Kiowa Bill came awake and found people in his tent with him.

His two night guards were there, and somebody else, and there were others out in the open, past the open flaps.

"Kiowa Bill," one of the guards said, "it 'pears we made us a serious mistake."

"To say the least," the shadowy figure behind him said. "Now roll out of there and step outside, everybody!"

They ducked out, and Kiowa Bill followed them, and when he looked around he couldn't believe his eyes. All of his gang was there, standing around in their long johns with their empty hands in the air, and there were horsemen all around them with guns that just plain looked like they knew their business.

Somebody had thrown some fuel on the nearest fire, and as it blazed up there was light to see. Kiowa Bill looked up at the nearest horseman and his mouth hung open. It wasn't the first time he had seen John Jay Hastings—he had seen him once over in Missouri, walking out of a silent, smoke-filled saloon that nobody else came out of—but he had always hoped that last time would be the last.

"Cattle rustlin' ain't nice," Hastings rasped, and the big iron in his hand looked like the business end of a railroad tunnel.

Beyond Hastings were others, and among them was a square-built old gent with handlebars and the look of a range bull on the prod.

"Y'all ought to go into some other line of work," that one rumbled. "There ain't a man I know that's fixin' to tolerate cow thieves anymore."

"Who are you?" Kiowa Bill managed to ask. "You ain't that Busted S bunch all over again, are you?"

"Nope," the range bull said. "Busted S was just a Sunday school picnic. I'm Shad Ames an' this here is the Aces Over bunch, an' we ain't nearly as forgivin' as that last bunch was. Like I said, y'all had better go into some other kind of work . . . if you happen to live 'til mornin'. What we got here is a cow trail, an' we're fixin' to use it regular, an' we'll dig cutters' spreads all the way across No Man's Land if that's what it takes."

With that declaration, in the presence of Clinton Sears, Sam Nabors, Rock Bottoms, Christy Walker, John Jay Hastings and the Burnett brothers, the "Ames-Smith Trail" was on its way to being the most peaceable trail that a man ever pushed critters on.

XXXII

The "acting law" of Beaver County was simple and functional. There being no legitimate laws as yet, nor any legislative body to enact them or legal jurisdiction to enforce them, things hadn't had a chance to get complicated.

As acting sheriff, Ben Wiggins had two bases of authority—the Census Act of 1889, and the Railroad Lands Act of 1868. The first one enpowered him to keep the peace for census purposes, the second to keep the peace on railroad right-of-way, which—at least for census purposes—was whatever the railroad said it was, according to Iron Tom Logan.

With a few acting deputies and an acting county council—headed by the Hon. Owen Lance with the local postmaster as secretary and registrar—Wiggins made it plain what the interim rules would be in "Beaver County," pending the arrival or creation of some kind of legal authority:

—If it isn't yours, don't take it.
—If it isn't true, don't swear to it.
—If it isn't right, don't do it.

As of the first day of June, 1890, those commandments became the body of criminal law in the place called No Man's Land. Added to them was a point of civil law:

298

—If you think you have claim to it, file your claim at the "courthouse."

It didn't take long for word to get around about that one, and Beaver City became a right busy place within a matter of days. Wiggins figured it was about fifty-fifty, of those stating claim on property they believed was theirs, and those claiming what they knew was somebody else's by rights, so he invoked the "don't swear to it" law on each occasion. Being as it was Ben Wiggins demanding oaths, standing there big as a barn, bristling with hardware and reputation, and looking each swearer right in the eyeballs—that reduced the odds to about eighty-twenty on the side of the angels.

By Saturday, the seventh day of June, 1890, it seemed like there were folks just all over the place at Beaver City. Supplies were coming in, and migrant families by the dozen, and there were at least four new buildings going up. Bert Mason, Haygood Dobbs, Wade Meeker and others were doing a fine business, the Beaver City Express was running on schedule and the Rev. Lyle Cartwright was planning a prayer meeting Sunday morning at the Road Ranch crossing.

On top of everything else, there hadn't been a shooting in Beaver City for six days, and that in itself was worth considerable comment.

Out at Busted S and Fairmeadow, that Sunday dawned bright and fresh as a meadowlark's song. It was the first time since Annie Sue's arrival that there hadn't been a passel of folks around, hammering and painting, howdying and gossiping, clearing and building and passing the fried chicken. Matter of fact, there weren't but three folks and some critters on the whole spread when the red rooster somebody had brought over began to crow.

Annie Sue got up from her bunk, washed and dressed in her go-to-town clothes, and opened up the shutters to let the morning in. She fired the new iron stove, put coffee on to boil and went to shake Milicent out. She was on her way to the front door, to holler at Bobby Lee on the porch, when she saw him through the window. He was already up and around, working at the stacked lumber that he aimed to use for his barn.

He had saw horses set up, and was cutting lengths for a door frame, and she stood at the window for a moment, just watching. There was a nice rhythm to his work, the crosscut saw singing in his hand, the muscles of his forearms bulging past his rolled-back sleeves, and he was whistling a soft tune.

At her shoulder, Milicent Moriarty said, "Pretty, isn't he?"

"He's as hard-headed as a hickory stump," Annie Sue commented.

"Well, of course he is," Milicent chuckled. "Just like you are, Annie Sue. You know you'll never forgive yourself if you don't come to an understanding with that young man."

"What kind of understanding?" Annie Sue glanced around, frowning.

"How many kinds are there, where a man and a woman are concerned?"

"Well," Annie Sue conceded, "he really isn't the monster I thought he was at first."

"You see?" Milicent grinned. "Like I said, he's kind of pretty, isn't he?"

"Well . . . yes, I suppose so. Look! Someone's coming."

Up the trail, from the direction of the stage road, a carriage had come into view. Out in the clearing, Bobby Lee looked up from his sawing and waved. The driver of the carriage returned the wave and came on.

"Well, I declare," Milicent said. "It's Mr. Wiggins."

She looked so flustered suddenly, smoothing back her hair and fussing with her dress, that Annie Sue giggled. "You're a fine one to talk about understandings, Milicent."

Driving a rental rig and looking like a deacon in a

clean shirt and black coat, Ben Wiggins pulled up in the yard and stepped down. They went out the back door to meet him, and he pulled off his hat. "Ladies," he nodded.

"Good morning, Mr. Wiggins," Milicent said. "My, but don't you look just grand!"

"Yes'm," he admitted, "I do. That's because I come to request the honor of seeing you to Beaver City for Reverend Cartwright's meetin'. That is, if you'd do me the honor, ma'am."

Milicent went a sort of rosy pink and got flustered again. "Why, Mr. Wiggins, I . . ."

"Ben," he said. "I'll answer to Ben."

"Ben, then. Why, I'd be just delighted. It is such a lovely day for a drive, but . . ."

Wiggins glanced at Annie Sue. "Oh, that goes for the missy, too. Be pleased to have you ride along, miss."

Annie Sue was trying to stifle a grin that surely didn't aim to stay hid. "You two go ahead," she said. "I'm sure Mr. Smith will be going in for *his* meeting. The census takers are due back today. I shall bring the rockaway, and drive along with him." She turned toward Bobby Lee. "Is that all right with you?"

"Fine with me," he called from the woodpile, glancing up at the morning sky. "Be ready after a bit."

"He has decided to build a barn," Annie Sue explained to Wiggins. "On his side of the property, of course."

"Naturally," Wiggins said. Most everybody in No Man's Land by then knew about the Busted S and Fairmeadow—where the porch door was the boundary between two disputed spreads. To Milicent, he said, "I need to get started pretty quick, ma . . . uh, Milicent. Lot of folks around town today."

"Of course," she turned toward the house. "I can be ready in just a moment."

*   *   *

With Milicent stowed aboard, and Ben Wiggins—despite his stone face and gray hair—looking like a gawky kid on his first spooning run, they headed up the trail in the rented carriage and Annie Sue watched them go, grinning. "If that isn't something!" she murmured.

She returned to the house, did a few morning chores and got down a handled basket. Then she went out with a bucket and drew water from the rain cistern. She called, "Mr. Smith, I'll be ready to go in a few minutes! If you will harness my horse, I'll pack us something to eat on the way!"

He waved agreement, and paused to watch as she carried her bucket into the house. Annie Sue Finch could aggravate the blazes out of him, but there wasn't anything wrong with his eyes, or the rest of him, either. Just the sight of her there, blonde hair, bucket and behind swinging rhythmically as she walked, almost took his breath away. Not any bigger than a minute, he thought . . . but that sure is some minute. Whatever else she might be, Bobby Lee had to admit that Miss Annabel Susanna Finch was just about the prettiest sight he had ever seen.

If she just wasn't so all-fired set in her ways!

When she was out of sight, he went and got Tarnation and the Morgan cross and led them around for rigging. He looped the Morgan's catch-rope to the gate of Annie Sue's rockaway, then turned his attention to Tarnation. The big sorrel took his bridle and bit like he always did, just as smooth as peace cider, but there was a set to his ears that Bobby Lee recognized. "Is this gonna be one of those days?" he muttered.

With the big mount's head-gear in place, he picked up a saddle blanket and smoothed it out atop the broad, dark back. Under his fingers he felt the slight tremor of muscles fixing to bunch. "Tarnation," he said, "I'd just as soon not, today."

He picked up his saddle, tossed it aboard and glanced to his left. The horse was looking at him sideways out of one big, thoughtful eye. "Talkin' to you is like talkin' to a wall," Bobby Lee growled. "You just plain got it to do, ain't you."

He pulled the cinch straps under the big chest and tightened them. Tarnation offered no resistance, but there was a quiver in his flanks that Bobby Lee didn't miss. "All right, dang you," he muttered. "We'll do that dance again, but one of these days you're gonna realize that there's somebody here that's ornerier than you are, an' when you get that through your head-bone we'll both be better off."

With Tarnation saddled and ready, Bobby Lee turned toward the buggy and the Morgan, then paused, looking around. The birds had stopped their singing, and up on the slopes a covey of bobwhites flared out of cover and headed away, fast and low.

Bobby Lee's hand went to his hip, and he remembered that he had left his gun rig on the porch when he went out to saw uprights. His eyes searching the brushy rise of the trail, he picked up Tarnation's reins and started toward the house. Annie Sue was just coming out of the back door, carrying a picnic basket. "Miss Finch!" he called, waving her back. "Get back inside! There's somethin' wrong!"

She hesitated, looking like she was about to argue, and he shouted, "You heard me, dammit! Get indoors!"

Something like an angry bee buzzed past his ear, and there was a crash of gunfire—a shot, then several more that became a ragged volley. Gravel spumed a yard from his boot, and something else whined over his head. Beyond Annie Sue, splinters flew from a fresh bullet hole in the wall of the house. Gunfire crashed and echoed, and the morning air sang with the whine of lead. Bobby Lee felt something sting his arm as he dropped Tarnation's reins and ran for the porch. He

303

was almost there when his left leg went numb, and he pitched forward and rolled, coming up hard against the porch rail. The rattle of gunfire had grown to a thunder now, and there were horsemen coming into the clearing—a wide, half circle of them, coming down the slopes and firing as they came.

A bullet gouged wood beside him. Another dusted him with gravel and something tugged at his boot heel. He tried to stand, fell again, and grabbed a porch upright to swing himself up. A bullet scored the wall behind him as he dropped into the shallow cover of the railing skirt. He rolled, grabbed his belt rig and came to rest beside the front door with his peacemaker in hand and a horseman charging down on him. His shot pitched the man backward out of his saddle, and Bobby Lee glimpsed his face as he fell. It was Hag Tannen, one of Scrannon's vigilantes.

Men on horses seemed to be everywhere, yelling and firing. Bobby Lee triggered another shot, and a man slumped in his saddle, wheeling away. A lever-action Winchester clattered to the hard ground. For a moment, the riders milled in confusion, and Bobby Lee had a look at them. He recognized Beauregard Jenkins and snapped a shot at the vigilante leader, but the man's horse shied as he fired, and the shot missed.

One down and one hurt, Bobby Lee counted desperately. And at least ten left. Over by the lumber pile, three of them had grouped, and now they spurred toward him, leveling guns.

The door beside him banged open. Six fast shots crashed and echoed like chain lightning, and one of the three charging riders sprayed red mist from his throat. The others wheeled away, shouting, as that one slumped from his saddle to sprawl on the ground not ten yards out. His running horse pounded away around the house.

Bobby Lee noticed the horse, and then noticed another horse and his breath caught in his throat.

304

Tarnation hadn't moved. Through it all, the big sorrel stood perfectly still, right out there in the yard, just gazing around like a spectator as bullets whistled around him.

Small hands that were surprisingly strong had Bobby Lee by shoulder and short collar, dragging him back. "Will you move?" Annie Sue shrilled. "Get inside here where you belong."

"It's your house . . . ," he started, feeling dazed, then shook his head to clear it and scuttled past her, dragging her down as he went, pulling the door closed behind him. Bullets thumped into the walls and whistled through an open window.

"You're hurt," Annie Sue pointed out, on her knees beside him. "You're bleeding."

"Comes of bein' shot," he growled. He glanced around. She was fumbling with a double-action Smith & Wesson, reloading it awkwardly. He noticed vividly the high flush in her smooth, tapered cheeks, the anger and excitement in her lustrous eyes. "That was you shootin'," he realized.

"Of course it was. Stay down. How many are out there?"

"Nine left, by my count." He thumbed fresh loads into the Peacemaker and sent a bullet into a face that appeared at the window. "No, make that eight."

Abruptly, then, the thunder of guns subsided, and a stillness settled over the Beaver valley. Bobby Lee crawled to the window, raised himself carefully and looked out.

Behind him, Annie Sue asked, "Are they gone?"

"Nope," he admitted. "We got their attention, I reckon, but they're still out there. They'll be on foot, now, an' a little more careful."

As if to punctuate his statement, a bullet whanged through the wall above his head and shattered a pitcher on a shelf. "They mean business," he noted. "Now they're gettin' serious about it."

305

"How many shells do you have?"

"Plenty for most work," he said. "But not enough to stand off eight snipers."

"Then we'll have to try something else," she murmured. She was close beside him, her face against his as she took a quick look out the window.

She even smelled pretty, he noticed.

She backed away, hesitated a moment, then said, "Stay here." Before he could answer, the front door opened and slammed shut. Bobby Lee tried to whirl around, and his bad leg and bad arm dumped him on his face on the floor. He rolled over, struggled to the window again and looked out. Tarnation was still standing out in the yard, looking unperturbed, and Annie Sue was just stepping off the porch, crouching as she ran toward the horse. Beyond, heads were raised at the lumber stack, and the girl stopped, leveled her Smith & Wesson in both hands, and emptied it toward them. Splinters flew like snowflakes, and somebody yelled.

Dropping her empty pistol, she stooped, picked up the fallen Winchester and dodged as a bullet whisked past her ear.

"Son of a bitch!" Bobby Lee roared, in the window, and his Peacemaker roared its agreement. Beyond the lumber, a man screamed, stood bolt upright, and sprawled forward over the stacks.

Annie Sue wasn't waiting around. With three fast steps she was beside Tarnation, reaching up to grab the saddlehorn, somehow getting a dainty foot into the stirrup.

"Annie Sue!" Bobby Lee yelled. "You can't ride that horse! Get away from him!"

It was too late, though. Like a monkey climbing a buffalo, she was up, into the saddle and kicking the horse with her heels. "Go!" she yelled.

Tarnation blinked his amazement, bunched his haunches, arched his back . . . and a businesslike rifle

306

barrel whacked him between the ears. "You just cut that out!" Annie Sue yelled furiously. "Come on, now! Git!"

Tarnation changed his mind about bucking and took off at a belly-down run as guns barked around and behind him.

Bobby Lee's eyes were as big as dollars as he tore them away from the receding horse with its little blonde rider, and went to work with his .45.

XXXIII

There were two reasons why Beauregard Jenkins had been made head of the Vigilance Committee. One was that he didn't have the brains God gave a stump, and the other was that he had a natural-born mean streak. Maybe, though, that was only one reason, because generally folks with that second quality also have a good bit of the first. At any rate, George Scrannon had selected Jenkins because he was the right man for the job, and considering the job, he likely was right.

When Annie Sue Finch lit out on Bobby Lee's blaze sorrel, Jenkins emptied his gun at her and waved at a couple of his hands. "Lukey! Sky!" he shouted. "Get your horses an' go kill that woman!"

The two broke cover, headed for the horses and ran right into Bobby Lee's cover fire from the house. Sky never knew what hit him, and Lukey flopped back into cover with a shattered arm.

"Six, now," Bobby Lee muttered, pressing fresh loads into his hot iron. "Maybe five."

He raised up to fire again, and bullets ripped into the window frame. He scooted away, crawled across the floor into the next room, eased up to the window there and found himself a target—a shadow of movement past a gap in the stacked barn lumber. He leveled down, squeezed the trigger and a man shrieked outside. "Not more'n five," Bobby Lee told himself. Across the room, a shadow moved across the crack in the east shutter. He put a bullet through the planks there and heard scuffling footsteps beyond.

Minutes passed, then, without a shot. They didn't know where in that house he was, but they had learned their manners where his Peacemaker was concerned. There are folks who can't hit the hind side of a livery stable with a Colt Peacemaker, but Bobby Lee Smith wasn't one of them. Anything he lacked in natural skill with a six-gun, Doc Holt's instructions had made up for.

Silence hung on the air like drifting gunsmoke, and Bobby Lee changed position again. He noticed that he was leaving a trail of blood behind him every time he moved, making a mess of Annie Sue's floor, but it wasn't something he had time to worry about right then.

But those outside, they knew it, too. They had seen him fall, and they could see the blood on the porch.

"He's hit, Beau!" someone outside called. "Let's wait him out a while! Let him bleed!"

"Hold your fire!" somebody else called. "Spread out! Get a bead on that back door!"

"I'm here, Beau! I got it covered!"

"You in there!" the second voice called. "You ain't doin' yourself any good! Why not come out an' get this over with?"

Bobby Lee peered through a splintered crack in the front door, trying to see where the voices came from. But they were being careful now. Nobody moved, and he couldn't see . . . his eyes widened, and a wolfish grin tugged at his cheeks. Past the lumber stack was the slap-up shed the boys had set up for gear, and just beyond was the little pole corral that Willie Sutter had built from cedar posts. Its gate was held by a wooden bolt. Morning sun slanted across the clearing, and on the far side of the shed's shadow was a man-shaped extra shadow. One of them was there, behind the shed, between it and the corral gate.

Bobby Lee took off his hat, found a roll of carpenter's twine and tied an end to the bullet-holed crown. He eased over to the west window, clawed his way upright behind the hanging shutter and looped the twine over the top of it. Then he let himself down again and crawled back to the front door.

When he was in place, with the Peacemaker braced in the splinter crack, he pulled on the twine. Across the little room the shutter swung slowly back, and Bobby Lee's hat rose into view in the window opening. Guns roared outside, and the hat flew across the room, breaking its twine.

"I think I got him, Beau!" somebody yelled.

Beyond the shed, the shadow moved, and Bobby Lee took careful sight and fired twice. His second bullet smashed the bolt on the corral gate, and the gate swung open. Outside, somebody yelled, "Oh, Jesus!" and the man-shadow became a man, dancing backward out of cover with a blue brindle range steer aiming its long horns at his belt buckle.

Bobby Lee let the man back up three steps before he put a round into his chest.

"Maybe four, now?" he reckoned.

The loss of blood was beginning to tell on him, though. He suddenly felt shaky, and knew he had to do something, but he couldn't quite think what to do. As the silence outside dragged on, he found some fabric—frilly looking stuff with flowers and lace—and wrapped his shot leg in a tight bandage. That might at least cut down the bleeding, he thought. He was bleeding several other places, too, but they were minor. Using a bound-straw broom as a crutch, he tried standing up. He was shaky and light-headed, but he didn't fall.

The sun rose higher, and he ate a bit of the food from Annie Sue's picnic basket. There was water in a bucket, and he washed the food down with it and felt a little better.

Still, he had to admit he was about at the end of his rope. The remaining gunmen out there weren't giving him any more chances. They were staying low, now and then putting a random bullet through the walls but offering him no targets.

Four of them, still out there, he figured. They had only to wait their chance, and it wasn't likely that he could get them all before they got him.

An hour had passed, he guessed. At least it seemed like an hour. It might have been twice that, or only half that, but he had the feeling the vigilantes wouldn't wait much longer, and he knew what he would do if he were in their boots.

As though the man had read his mind, Jenkins' voice drifted through the open window. "I've had enough of this! Let's set fire to that shack an' burn him out!"

Bobby Lee shook his head, feeling suddenly lonely and sad. He could hear furtive movements outside, but he wouldn't have a shot at them. They would make their fires in shelter, and either sneak in low and covered, or fire the place from a distance. Either way, they would get it done. They would burn his porch, and they would burn Annie Sue's house before she even had a chance to make something of it like she wanted to do.

At least, she had got away. He had held his breath, expecting any second that a bullet would find her . . . that hot lead would rip into that adorable little body, would rip and sunder it. He couldn't have stood that, he realized. Just the thought of it was an agony to him, that brought hot moisture to his eyes.

I'll die here, he told himself. I'm at the end of my rope, and they've got me. They'll kill me today, out here on this spread, and they'll burn our place . . . *our* place to the ground.

Our place! His mind turned it over and over, realizing how right the notion was. It was like a new sun

311

had just come up on an old world, and showed him a landscape he could never have imagined.

They'll kill me, he told himself. They're fixing to, and they will, and I guess that's that. But they can't get Annie Sue now. She's clean away and out of their reach. They can kill me, but they can't break my heart because it isn't here now. It's where she is.

He smelled the smoke then, and heard the crackling of the flames as the old, dry wood of the shack caught and blazed.

"Hell!" he muttered, his jaw setting into that stubborn slant like so many times before. "Doc an' Nanny never raised no child for roastin'!"

He got up, propped the straw broom under his arm like a crutch, and staggered to the front door.

"Beauregard Jenkins!" he shouted. "I aim to take you with me!" With a deep breath in his lungs, he threw the front door open and stepped out, his Peacemaker in hand like a rattler fixing to strike.

Smoke roiled around him, billowing from the doorway behind him to obscure everything. A bullet whistled past his cheek and buried itself in a porch rail, and the peacemaker spat fire toward the sound of it. Another clipped the hair on his head and drew blood, and the roar of gunfire blended with the roar of flames to become a thunder that coalesced, crescendoed and drummed at his ears. Guns were blazing . . . too many guns. There were horsemen there, wheeling and pivoting, firing as they circled. Men were shouting, and someone screamed. A dim figure staggered through the smoke, faltered and started to turn, then went wide-eyed as he saw Bobby Lee and Bobby Lee saw him. It was Beauregard Jenkins, raising his gun.

Bobby Lee's bullet punched a neat hole in the vigilante's clavicle and blew his spine out the other side. He tried to send another bullet after it, but the Colt clicked on an empty chamber. He raised it, looked at it

312

curiously, and saw it fall from his fingers. He fell on top of it.

They took Bobby Lee into town, in the rockaway. He was leaking from some bullet holes and barely conscious because of a crease along his skull, but after a mile or two he commenced to come around. He stared around at them in bewilderment, like he just couldn't believe his eyes. There was Willie Sutter, and Joe Dell McGuire, riding alongside the buggy where he lay, making bets about his condition. There was Pappy Jameson, driving the buggy and swearing under his breath because somebody had shot his favorite horse. There was Jimbo Riley and Shorty Mars, and coming along behind was Mouse Moore, up on his gray and leading a blaze-face sorrel on rein. Bobby Lee saw that horse, and like to ruined himself trying to sit up. Somebody was holding him down, though, and he didn't have the strength to break free.

"Just ease off, there, boy," Pappy rasped at him from the driver's seat. "You ain't hurt all that bad, but you'd best just lay quiet for a while."

"That's . . ." he couldn't make his tongue work right, so he tried again. "That's Tarnation yonder!"

"Sure is," Pappy shrugged. "As ever was."

"What's he . . . how did y'all get . . ."

"You didn't make it to the census meetin'," Pappy drawled, "so the meetin' come to you, soon's we heard where you were."

"That's my horse!" Bobby Lee choked, still woozy but suddenly feeling a terrible dread.

"I'd say he ain't yours anymore," Pappy said. "Horse like that ought to belong to who can manage him. You never rightly could. Not stubborn enough, I reckon."

The memories were starting to come together by

then. "Annie Sue was on that horse!" He was getting downright agitated. "Where's Annie Sue?"

Pappy looked down curiously. The others, riding alongside, had edged closer, too.

"Son, what do you reckon that soft place is that your head is restin' on?" Pappy asked.

Bobby Lee rolled his eyes upward, and his mouth just sort of dropped open. Annie Sue was right there, with his head in her lap. It was her who had held him down.

"You rode Tarnation . . ." he stammered. "You rode that devil all the way to Beaver City . . . and brought help?"

"It was nothing much," she said, her eyes saying much more than her words. "Tarnation is a good horse, once he knows who's boss. We got along just fine."

Bobby Lee gazed into eyes that held more good luck for him than he had ever dreamed his lucky streak would bring him. "I swear," he said. "Annie Sue Finch, you are the stubbornest person I ever laid eyes on."

Behind the wagon, Mouse Moore grinned victoriously. "Pay me," he said.

EPILOGUE

Y'all might be proud to know—in case you hadn't heard it already—that No Man's Land didn't stay No Man's Land for much longer than it took to tell it, after those old boys did their tally of the Neutral Strip.

With Bobby Lee Smith laid up for a time like he was, and Willie Sutter and Pappy Jameson tending to the place for him, the counting of the county was caught short-handed. But Iron Tom Logan picked up a few more enumerators for Thomas Allen Fry to bless, and they set to it and counted every nose east of Hardesty, then sent a crew out west, past the Goff Creek hay-meadows and Bone Flat, right on out to Black Mesa and the Cimarron Breaks. Of course, folks out yonder being what they were at the time, that was a whole 'nother story. But even yonder where the ordinary world ends and New Mexico begins, there weren't many dumb enough to slap leather against the likes of Joe Dell McGuire and John Jay Hastings. And those that did, they got counted anyway.

Well, when it was all baled and shipped, they had tallied the better part of three thousand folks with established residence in that strip of territory where nobody officially was.

Then it was up to the government of the United States of America, back yonder at Washington, D.C., to recognize the obvious and say grace over it.

There is testimony to how well they did that, in the fact that when the state of Oklahoma was created a few years later, there was the old Neutral Strip, just bigger than Dallas as they say, sticking out of the west end of it like an accusing finger on a fist. Three counties of it—Beaver County, Texas County and Cimarron County—the three making up the Oklahoma Panhandle.

In the meantime, Beaver City became a right civilized place with the Scrannon faction gone. Under the guidance of Ben Wiggins, that town became a model of orderliness, though there were some who wished that Wiggins would pay more attention to the merits of his wife Milicent and a little less to who was selling corn liquor to whom.

Beer City, up on the Kansas border, ceased to exist one Sunday afternoon. A coalition of Methodists, maize farmers and miscellaneous citizenry went out from Liberal and descended upon Beer City like Pharaoh's Fifth Plague. They went with guns, plows and wagons. They ran everybody out, tore down all the buildings, carted off the usable materials and burned the rest. Then they scattered the ashes, and plowed the entire site under. They left not a trace that Beer City had ever been there, except that sometimes when it would rain—one of those frog-stranglers that occur in that arid country about as often as Democrats do—afterward the whole tract would be covered with corks . . . thousands of corks, resurrected by the purifying waters to cover the earth yonder like the mute, pining ghosts of good times gone.

Between Tyrone Switch loading Texas cattle for the Chicago, Rock Island and Pacific Railroad, and the starting of some good herds across the line in Kansas, the town of Liberal became a major beef cattle center. Later it expanded its enterprises into watermelon processing, politics and hard winter wheat.

But most of that came down the line a piece. Meanwhile, back on the banks of the Beaver River, by the time Bobby Lee Smith was healed up, he had come to understand that there is no future in arguing with angels. Bobby Lee and Annie Sue consolidated their interests on the twelfth day of August, 1890, with Reverend Cartwright officiating. From the union of Busted S and Fairmeadow came the spread of Fairmeadow, with Busted S as its working brand.

Somewhere along the line they changed the official name of the brand to Backtrack, but it was still Busted S and everybody knew it. They added a three-story house to Bobby Lee's porch, and filled it to the scuppers with the stubbornest brood of strapping, blue-eyed progeny the good Lord ever saw fit to bless with freckles. Anybody who ever saw that bunch remembered them, and no man ever laid eyes on their mother without realizing just what a lucky jasper Bobby Lee Smith was.

Like they say, it seemed to be catching. Shorty Mars was a married man by fall, and Willie Sutter not long after that, and Pappy Jameson was seen in the company of the widow Blake now and again.

Even that big blaze sorrel, Tarnation, sired a string of foals from some of the better mares around. Talk was that he had just plain been too contrary for productive collaboration before Annie Sue knocked some better notions into him with a rifle barrel.

The Beaver City Express became a three-stage line before its owners sold out and left the territory. There was a rumor that they had gone to New Orleans, stolen a steamboat and got into the river trade.

Thomas Allen Fry never went back East. He settled in Pratt, Kansas, and went into the warehouse business.

Mouse Moore stayed on in the Strip for a while, then moved back to Texas and went into politics. Word was, he never in his life lost an election that interested him.

Nobody could ever say for sure what became of

George Scrannon. With half the professional gun-hands in the southwest looking for him, he just disappeared. Some said he went to Philadelphia, some said to Colorado, and some said it would just tickle them half to death if the scoundrel had gone straight to hell.

Scrannon was gone, but not forgotten. A good many years would pass before the stories about him tapered off.

A man without conscience, they said. A man who found the perfect setting for a life without scruples. A man who came that close to building himself a little kingdom in No Man's Land.

A man who had everything going his way, until he came to his census.

AUTHOR'S NOTE

At the end of the nineteenth century, the entire area between Texas and Kansas—which are thirty-five miles apart—and between northern New Mexico and the Cherokee Strip in Oklahoma Territory—roughly one hundred and sixty-five miles—was known as the Neutral Strip. It was within the jurisdiction of no court, was neither a state nor a territory, and had no legal residents. Today, it is the Oklahoma Panhandle. But then, it was simply a 5,775-square mile rectangle in the heart of the Southwest Cattle Range, between the High Plains of western Kansas and the Llano Estacado or Staked Plains of northern Texas. Geographically, it existed. Officially, it did not.

To most people in the region, it was, simply, No Man's Land. A place without status . . . a place without law.

No Man's Land was included in the United States Decennial Census of Population and Social Statistics of 1890, under the surprising designation of "Beaver County." Surprising, because not being part of any state or territory, it had never been declared a county.

It was, and has since been, ruled by census officials that, in the event of a census marshal or enumerator causing the death of any resident of any area being enumerated for census purposes, the deceased should be counted as a living person as of the official date of that census. An explanation of this is that, since the deceased was alive before the census taker encountered and killed him, therefore the census taker counted him first and killed him afterward.

The Neutral Strip—No Man's Land, with no legal occupants—had an 1890 census population of 2,674 residents, all of them technically alive and so reported.

Further note: From 1790 through 1990, the population of the United States of America has been counted twenty-one times, by the United States Census Office and the subsequent Bureau of the Census of the Department of Commerce. Original documentation for twenty of these counts remains in archives. The missing one—the 1890 Census—was destroyed by fire.